The Magician as Cat

"Eminence!" he bellowed. "Courtak!"

Jarrod sauntered out into the sunlight. . . . he could tell that the man was embarrassed to be talking to a cat who was also a Mage. He could smell it.

"Well, they're gone . . . if you want to make your change, go ahead."

Jarrod sat back on his haunches and cleaned his whiskers for the last time. He felt a strange reluctance to abandon this body that was so much more supple than his own, so much quicker in reaction. Still, duty required. He tamped down his cat reactions and centered himself. He became oblivious of his surroundings, half-regretful of the need, and then he began the task of transformation.

The saga of Strand: a world of magic and wonder

Tor books by John Lee

The Unicorn Quest
The Unicorn Dilemma
The Unicorn Solution

THE UNICORN PEACE

JOHN LEE

TOR
fantasy

A TOM DOHERTY ASSOCIATES BOOK
NEW YORK

This is a work of fiction. All the characters and events portrayed in this book are fictitious, and any resemblance to real people or events is purely coincidental.

THE UNICORN PEACE

Copyright © 1992 by John Lee

Edited by David G. Hartwell

Cover art by Maren
Maps by Nancy Westheimer

A Tor Book
Published by Tom Doherty Associates, Inc.
175 Fifth Avenue
New York, N.Y. 10010

Tor ® is a registered trademark of Tom Doherty Associates, Inc.

ISBN: 0-812-51981-7

First edition: April 1993

Printed in the United States of America

0 9 8 7 6 5 4 3 2 1

To David Hartwell
For patience
For support
And for the occasional curve ball.

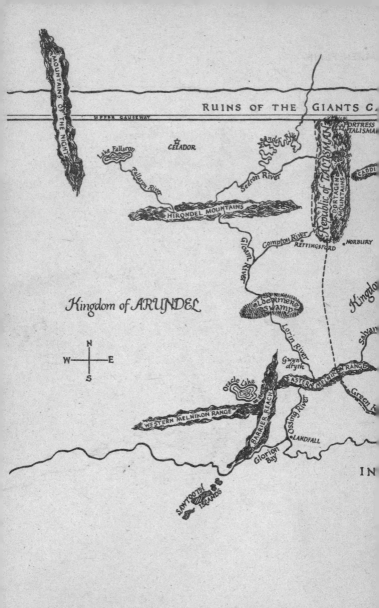

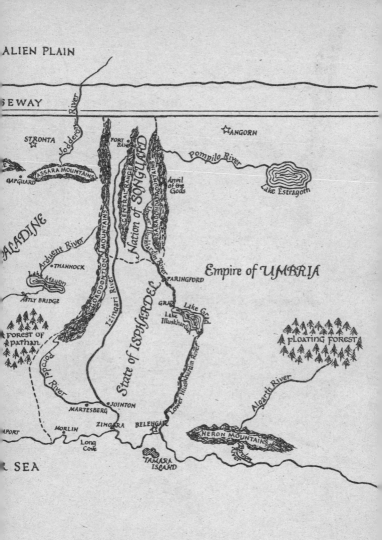

PROPOSAL for the DISPOSITION of CONQUERED OUTLAND TERRITORY

Kingdom of ARUNDEL

The
ARUNDEL

UPPER CAUSEWAY

Republic of
TALISMAN

TALISMAN

Kingdom
of
PALADINE

Alien
PALADINE

State
of
ISPHARDEL

SONGUARD

SONGUARD

ISPHARDEL

Empire
of
UMBRIA

Plain
UMBRIA

chapter 1

He was alone in darkness. Around him were the sounds of rustling and sighing. Not darkness, he realized; utter blackness. No nightmoon; not even a dusting of stars. He stood stock still; did not dare to move as the pricklings of alarm coursed up his spine. He reached out with his senses. The sounds seemed to come from everywhere at once, an omnipresent and suggestive sibilance. There was a strong odor of loam and growing things, but nothing more. Something brushed against his face and he shied violently, would have cried out, but no sound came. I'm dreaming, he thought. This is nothing but a dream. It didn't help. He was afraid.

He forced himself to reach out. His hand encountered stalks, or what he surmised were stalks. Moving up, he felt leaves and then something fuzzy. It was well above his head and he was a shade over eight feet tall. He took a deep breath; only a dream. It reminded him of the jungle area on the Island at the Center. Could the Guardian have pulled him back, all these years later, to punish him for his destruction of the Outlanders? The Guardian was capable of it, but he knew, instinctively, that he had not. With that came the realization of what this place must be. He was out on the Alien Plain. With the knowledge came light. Not centered, like a dawn, or spilling down, like the sudden unveiling of the nightmoon, but a seeping in from all quarters.

He was mewed up in grasses, tall and seemingly impenetrable. Good hunting country for wild warcats, he thought, and shivered. There was menace in the air, its source, in part, the feeling of being closed in. That, at least, he could do something about. He flailed around him, breaking the thick stalks, seeing the tops sag abruptly. The amorphous light grew stronger. He started forward, striking with his arms as if they were reversed sickles. He noticed that he was wearing his habitual blue robe. Could be worse, he thought with a flash of grim humor; I've been naked in some dreams.

He ploughed ahead, arms swinging unnaturally slowly and his sandals sticking to the ground. He glanced over his shoulder and the vague feeling of dread became concentrated in that direction. Worse, the grasses he had swept aside and trampled down had sprung up again. He pushed on, heart thumping painfully, breath whistling in and out. Logic dictated that he stop and take stock of the situation, but logic had no place in this dream. Fear drove him and the slug's pace, which was the best that he could do, added to the dread.

It went on forever and yet it was over in moments. He stood at the base of a mountain range that sloped gently at first and then soared up. He knew it instantly even though he had only seen it once before and then from above. This was the range that formed the northern border of the Alien Plain. Beyond it was a sea or an ocean. His glimpse of the coastline had been brief and he had been very tired.

The fear that had driven him was ebbing and he gazed at the slopes with something akin to relief. The spur of fear might be gone, but he was wary still. He turned slowly and looked at the way he had come. A towering wall of green crowded behind him. Upward then. As he turned back and glanced up, a building flickered into view and disappeared. That couldn't be. No man had ever set foot in these mountains. He took a deep breath and peered upslope. The building, large, turreted and shining, appeared and then vanished.

He stood, waiting for it to reappear, but nothing happened. He braced his shoulders. No sense waiting here while the gods knew what crept up behind him. He set off again. The slope was gentle at first, but soon became steeper. Massive boulders blocked his path, forcing him to detour. He stopped from time to time to look for the building. There was a glow, he was certain of that, and once he thought he saw a tower with a conical top. To reach it became a compulsion, but, hard as he climbed, he seemed to be getting no closer. The path turned treacherous with loose scree denying him puchase. He clung to the rocks, hauling himself up, desperate to reach the security of the insubstantial refuge. Then he lost his footing altogether and tumbled back, stomach dropping in sudden terror.

Jarrod Courtak woke with a start. His mouth was dry and his hands were clenched. His heart was pounding. He lay there for a while calming himself. The dream was still vivid in his mind and he tried to make sense of it. There were those, usually men or women in whom the Talent was weak, who made a living from the interpretation of dreams, but he had never been a believer. It was true that the Archmage had once seen the future, but that had been as a result of Magic, properly applied. He shrugged mentally and rolled out of bed. It would soon be time for the ritual of Making the Day.

He breakfasted in the Outpost's Hall with the rest of the Magicians and then returned to his rooms to prepare for the morning's meeting of the Commission for the Outland. The Commission, together with the research he had been doing for a history of Strand, had dominated his life for years now. He had been on the Commission since its founding thirteen years ago. Its deliberations had meandered on ever since. There had been no sense of urgency in the early days. Jarrod had been alone in his conviction that the soil was safe, free of whatever had caused mutations in the past, but the barren expanse had greened since then and become a vast, flat savanna. Pressure for colonization was growing.

He wondered if the past night's dream had any connection with the coming meeting. A vote on partition was a possibility. A draft of the proposal had been circulated. There was nothing in it for the Discipline. He had fought hard for territory in the beginning and had been told, politely but firmly, that the Discipline was not a sovereign state and thus had no role to play in matters territorial. He had persisted and a move had been made to oust him. He had appealed to the Archmage.

He smiled at the memory of what had come next. Archmage Ragnor had descended on Stronta like the specter of death, breathing anathema. In a speech before the Royal Council of Paladine, the Commissioners and the diplomatic corps, he had declared that the entire Outland belonged to the Discipline by right of conquest. The resulting furor dominated conversation in the capitals of Strand for many sennights. The printed broadsheets that had sprung up since the war had had a field day. Thereafter Jarrod had not pressed the Discipline's claim, but no one had challenged his right to sit on the Commission.

In the intervening years he had learned that there was little logic where matters of national interest were concerned and that his colleagues, intelligent, secure in their positions, often humorous in private, became rigid and inflexible when they got to the conference table. Only Otorin of Lissen, who represented Queen Arabella of Arundel (Queen now because she had married), retained his skeptical sense of humor. Everyone paid lip service to the idea of a new beginning, but they clung fiercely to the old order.

At one stage, Jarrod had suggested that the Outland be developed without boundaries, under international control, an idea he still felt offered the best solution. It had caused another uproar. The growing body of scholars and men of letters had endorsed it enthusiastically, but even the Isphardis, who of all people should have been international in outlook, had rejected the notion. Borr Sarad, the grizzled former Thane of Talisman, had been the only sympathetic ear.

Now, fifteen years after the war had ended, matters were coming to a head and none of the old problems had been solved. There was no agreed upon formula for the apportionment of land. Should it be based on the size of the individual countries? Their contribution to the war effort? How then to deal with Songuard, which had done nothing during the war, or Isphardel, which had never committed a single man but had provided a vast amount of money? What of Talisman, smallest of all the nations, whose cloudsteed wings and warcat battalions had fought so valiantly and suffered such losses?

There had been no formal agreement on any of these points, but Phalastra of Estragoth, the elderly Umbrian Elector who was President of the Commission, was pushing for a conclusion, motivated, in Jarrod' opinion, more by the growing civil unrest in the Empire that by conviction. For himself, he could not for the life of him see how they were to come to an equitable decision. He sighed. His own idea was still the only just solution, but, after all these years of argument, he could hold out no real hope for it.

He changed out of his blue robe and donned lay attire. With his height he could not pass for anything but a Magician, but he had found that it was more politic not to remind people of his status. He went down to the stables where his horse was saddled and waiting and took the long route to Stronta's western gate. He marveled anew as he rode at the difference the years had made.

The clean lines of the star fort were obscured by the wooden houses and shops that had sprung up outside the walls. The capital was almost surrounded now by a tangle of narrow streets replete with inns and bawdy houses. Only the well-founded fear of the Great Maze kept the area around Northgate clear. It now took far longer to get into the city than it had in the old days. With all the new mouths to feed, the roads were clogged with wagons and carts bringing produce to market. So much had changed since the war, he reflected as he kicked his mount into a trot. On this day, of all days, it would not do to be late for the meeting.

chapter 2

Connelan Malum, Lord Quern, sharpened his quills slowly and methodically. Taking notes at these sessions was rough. He had long since become accustomed to the various accents, but the Commission members talked fast when they were arguing, which was most of the time; they interrupted one another constantly. All the positions were so well known by now that members seldom got a chance to finish their set pieces. Once the session got going, there would be no time to sharpen a nib.

He sat at the scribes' table, his chair set somewhat apart from the others. He was an official member of the Umbrian delegation, but his patron, the Elector of Estragoth, wanted his own account of the proceedings, and it was Malum's job to provide it. He'd been doing it since he first came to Stronta at the age of eighteen. The job itself was fascinating for all it rigors. The Elector divided his time between Angorn and Stronta and was a key personage in both capitals. As the Elector's private secretary, Malum followed his master everywhere, and, because of his access to Phalastra, he was often courted by powerful men. While the pay was rather meager, he would never have been able to live at Court on the revenues from his estate, let alone travel to foreign lands.

Estragoth himself was a remarkable old bird. He had been well advanced in years when Malum was first taken into his household, and he must be pushing eighty now. That in itself was no mean feat, but the remarkable thing was that the old boy was still active. He no longer hunted and he was somewhat hard of hearing, but his mind was still sharp. He walked with the aid of a stout cane on those days when the gout or the rheumatism was bad, but Malum had seen him belabor a would-be Causeway bandit with it and drive the fellow off.

He put away his knife and lined the quills up in a row. He moved the inkwell closer to him. The water clock was approaching the tenth hour and the Commissioners would be coming in soon. They were an interesting lot, all except the Chamberlain who nominally represented Paladine. He was a fussy little man preoccupied with protocol and details, but everyone knew that the real decisions were taken by the Queen or her Arundelian paramour. There was noise from the anteroom and he looked up as the three regular scribes came in. Polite greetings were exchanged.

Borr Sarad, the former Thane of Talisman, was the first of the Commissioners to arrive. He was a compact man with an outdoor face and iron grey hair. He was always on time, usually early, and Malum could predict the opening words. Sure enough:

"Beat me to it again, eh Quern? One of these days . . . one of these days."

Malum stood and ducked his head. "May the best of the day be before us, Thane," he said, and smiled. Borr Sarad had been voted out of office by his people in the first election after the war, but everyone still used the old title.

"Selah to that, young man," Sarad replied as he advanced down the room to the desk. "Greetings, gentlemen," he said to the scribes as he passed them. "Well, what do you think will happen today?" he asked. "Think we'll be able to get this thing wrapped up? I certainly hope so. I've no wish to spend the summer here. It's too damned hot."

"At least it's dry heat here. You should try summer in the south, where I come from."

"I thank you, but no. I'll take my mountains any time of year. Seriously though, what's your opinion of how things stand?"

"Truth?" Malum asked.

Sarad grinned. "Of course not. Educated guess."

"Well then, the idea of the Outland as an international territory without boundaries doesn't stand a chance, no matter what kind of authority or combination of authorities govern it. The only thing that has kept it alive this long is the Mage's reputation."

"I have to agree," Sarad admitted. "If it had come to a vote any time in the first five years, it might have stood a chance, but not now." The Thane paused and looked at Malum speculatively.

"D'you have an opinion, one that you're prepared to divulge, about the draft proposal?"

"The partition would seem to address most of the problems," Malum said judiciously. "The Songeans are provided for, the Isphardis get an equitable share and, with all due respect, Talisman would do very well out of the settlement."

Sarad looked Malum squarely in the eyes for a long beat. A slow smile that threw every last wrinkle into relief crept up. "Stop being so damned diplomatic," he said. "You're an intelligent young man, you've been in on all the discussions and, unless I miss my guess, you can think for yourself. You must have some personal thoughts about the division. In fact I'll warrant you saw the finished map before I did."

Malum returned the smile. Smiling easily and convincingly was one of his talents. "You're right about that," he said. "The penmanship on the map is mine.

Personally, I don't think the Isphardis will be enchanted, but, given their geographical location, I don't think anything we did would be ideal for them."

"That's as may be. You mean to tell me that you can't see any other problems?"

The Umbrian shrugged. "Well, it's true that the portion of the Outland allotted to Talisman might be considered to infringe on Arundel's share, but then again, they can expand westward across the Unknown Lands and nobody knows how far that stretches."

"The same could be said of Umbria," Sarad commented dryly, "but I see that she is apportioned the full width of her present frontier. Do you feel that that's equitable?"

"I don't know about equitable, but it's certainly logical," Malum retorted.

Sarad's answering smile was tight and had little humor in it. "I'm afraid that your logic may not go far enough. There is too much room in this plan for future disputes."

Malum's ready smile flashed out again. "I'm not convinced, Thane, that the Commission's job is to ensure eternal peace. I very much doubt that that is possible. But don't you think that you're being a little pessimistic? After all, there is so much land out there."

"Oh, come now, Quern, spare me the wide-eyed approach. Nobody has taken geography into account. What happens if one nation's territory turns out to be barren and its neighbor's is fertile? How long do you think your agreement will hold up?"

"I am not a Magician, my lord," Malum said, raising his hands, fingers splayed. "I do not claim to be able to see the future. We can only go on the best information that we have—and a great deal of that comes from your friend Jarrod Courtak. He is, after all, the only man to have seen this mountain range that is supposed to border the territory to the north. Think how much more difficult the Commission's business would be if we did know how productive the various areas of the plain were, or where minerals lay. I think that is all for the best that the allocation is based on existing borders. There is less ground, forgive the pun, for dispute that way and any decision by the Commission is better than none."

Borr Sarad pursed his lips and shook his head. "You're wrong, Quern, quite wrong. You have an altogether too optimistic view of Strandkind." He shook his finger for emphasis. "We're used to war, though it isn't popular to say it these days. Mark my words, when it comes to it, any excuse will do."

"In that case, it doesn't really matter what the Commission decides, does it?" Malum said with another shrug.

Sarad gave a short laugh. "Cynic," he said.

Footsteps made both heads turn as Jarrod Courtak entered. The Mage strode across the room, hands extended with the palms turned out, to greet the Thane.

"Morning, Borr. You all set to vote?" He smiled and nodded to Malum of Quern.

"Well, if you propose your international idea, I'll vote for you on the first ballot. After that it'll be every country for itself."

"History will judge you, you know," Jarrod said lightly.

"Yes, and I understand that you're the one that'll be writing it," Sarad replied with a laugh. "I never had to bother about history when I was Thane and I'm too old to change my ways now. Besides, I know what my people want and what they have earned."

Jarrod shook his head. "It will lead to trouble," he said.

"Anything will lead to trouble," the Thane replied. "Ask Quern."

Malum and Courtak looked at each other. Jarrod's face was open, curious, the eyebrows raised in gentle question. The Umbrian's face was pleasantly unrevealing. He did not like the Mage. He had no overt reason for it. The man had always been polite, had treated him as an equal, which was more than could be said for some members of the Commission, but that hadn't affected Malum's emotional reaction to the Magician. Part of it was undoubtedly due to an innate distrust of Magic, some of it to the difference in height.

The Mage was a tall and imposing figure, while Malum was short and thin. The Paladinian moved with grace, while the Umbrian was all too conscious of his imperfections. When it came right down to it, though, those weren't the real wellsprings of his dislike. Those were factors that he had schooled himself to ignore. No, what irked him was the man's assumption of humility, of ordinariness. All this went through his mind in a flash; none of it showed on his countenance.

"I simply remarked," Malum said with a deprecating smile, "that there were so many unknowns on the map that anything decided now was bound to be challenged later. The Thane made the very valid point that some land will inevitably prove less productive. Any country that finds itself endowed with unprofitable land will become disgruntled, may even cast envious eyes on their neighbors."

"My point entirely," Jarrod agreed. "It would be so much better if people of all nations could move freely about the Outland, settling where they wish. It is clear, however, that apart from my friend here"—he smiled and placed a hand on Borr Sarad's shoulder—"my poor notion is a virtual orphan."

At that moment they were joined by Otorin of Lissen, now Holdmaster of Ostering.

"Well met, my lords," he said briskly. "You pontificating again, Jarrod?"

"I wouldn't quite put it that way," Jarrod remonstrated mildly.

"I admire your persistence, but I'm paid by Queen Arabella. We both know that."

"Yes indeed," Courtak acknowledged, "but I keep hoping that the thinking man trapped in the oath will emerge before it's too late." It was said with humor.

"You have an ability to weight phrases," Otorin returned amiably, "but they are more suited to the broadsheets. You must know that my instructions are to vote for partition."

Otorin of Lissen was a well-built man with a pleasant but unremarkable face and a dusting of grey in the hair. He didn't look particularly formidable, but Jarrod knew that he had considerable influence in both Arundel and Paladine.

"And if the Commission cannot agree?" he asked mildly.

"Let's face that jump if the hounds veer that way," Otorin said with finality. "Ah, I see the Elector of Estragoth. Give you good morning, my Lord Elector." His voice was loud and he moved off toward the Umbrian.

"Good morning, Lissen." The Elector was bird-thin and stooping. The voice was light and high. He waved in the direction of Jarrod and the Thane. "These stone floors are dreadfully cold. D'you suppose they have any mulled cider?"

It was a familiar complaint and request. Malum was prepared for it. He went to the hearth and got a leather jug. He poured a mug of cider, took it to the Elector and withdrew without a word. He was a part of the furniture again, observing the other Commission members as they came in. They all went to the Elector first. It was, of course, partly politeness. His master was the oldest person in the room and he was president of the Commission, but the Elector had always been a magnet.

He had watched the shifting patterns of popularity over the years. The Arundelian, Lissen, had been a nonentity at the beginning, but he had worked quietly and assiduously to build a constituency. The Mage, on the other hand, had been much courted in the early years but, once the glamour of his achievements had faded, had become increasingly isolated. The thought pleased Malum.

The last of the Commissioners, the Isphardi representative, entered the room in a blaze of saffron silk. The Elector took note and cleared his throat.

"My lords," Phalastra's thin voice floated out over the assembly. "Let us to the table. There is much to do today."

The old man took his accustomed seat at the head of the long refectory table. When he had been elected no one had thought that he would last this long. He had been old then and it had seemed a fitting gesture, but he had stubbornly refused to die. He had never offered to step down and no one was ill-mannered enough to suggest it.

"Madam Oligarch, my lords," Phalastra said once they were all settled, "we are here today to draw the boundaries for the new territories in the Outland."

He turned his head and nodded to Malum, who got up and distributed copies of the map on which he had spent so much time. The delegates had seen the draft, but it was the sort of detail that the Elector insisted upon.

"Now," Phalastra said, "if I have done my job aright, you are all going to be disappointed, so please do not all speak at once. I will be the first to admit that the allocations are not perfectly logical, but that is because our past and our geography have little to do with logic. Please try to look at the document from the viewpoint of the other Commissioners. We all know one another's positions well enough by now, so please spare us the obligatory national anthems." There was a touch of curtness in the voice.

There was silence, broken by an occasional cough and the squeak of a chair on the polished wood of the floor. Study it, Malum thought. There are years of notes and endless hours of arguments in that map. Given the current political climate, it was the most equitable division possible. Surely they could see that.

Phalastra of Estragoth looked down the table and caught Jarrod Courtak's eye. He gave the faintest of shrugs and nodded quickly and discreetly. The Mage would be the first to speak.

"Excellence," he said, "since the Discipline is the only party without a territorial stake in the proceeding, do you go first."

"My thanks to the President," Jarrod replied. "For the record, the Discipline has never formally rescinded a claim to territory and reserves the right to challenge any decision based on the map as it is presently drawn. My current question is, however, to the status of the Upper Causeway. You all know that I favor its dismantling, but, failing that, I feel most strongly that it should be an international thoroughfare, maintained by the countries through which it passes, but not subject to national control. I further suggest that uniform tolls be collected at each border and that the monies be used solely for the upkeep of the roadway. Trade throughout the world would benefit."

"Hear, hear," from the Oligarch Olivderval.

"A point to consider, Excellence," Phalastra said, and

wondered if there was a deal afoot between the Magicians and the Isphardis.

Otorin of Lissen looked up. "That would make a country's control of its own borders somewhat parlous, don't you think?" he asked lazily.

"Not necessarily," Jarrod said. "Individual countries can still control who enters their territory. Customs points are easily established at the foot of the wall."

Phalastra turned toward the Oligarch, expecting her to speak. She did not. She sat, small, plump and composed, hands folded in her lap, listening and waiting. "Any other comments?" he asked.

"My Lord President." The voice was deep and rumbling, the effect enhanced by the rolling r's typical of the Songean accent.

"By all means, my Lord Hodman."

Phalastra had anticipated questions from the Songean delegation. The Hodman of the Territi, who had joined the Commission on the death of Siegitander, seldom spoke, but, when he did, he had the knack of cutting to the heart of things. His grasp of international politics was nil, but his hold on common sense was formidable. Generally speaking, Estragoth considered all Songeans illiterate barbarians, but he had come to respect this one.

"The position of Fort Bandor, our capital, does not appear to be regularized on this map."

"We have left all place names off the map, my dear Forodan," the Elector said, using the man's given name. "You will also note that there are no geographical details, unless you care to count the Upper Causeway."

"Ah, Lord President," the Hodman replied genially, "you are making a joke no doubt. It is well known that Umbrian soldiers occupy the Fort. If it were upon this map it would be plain that it is far from the border.

There is no reason, after fifteen years of peace, for your men to be there."

Phalastra produced a smile and sat forward slightly. "As the Hodman knows," he said, with his voice lifting a little on "knows" to indicate a certain playfulness, "the Emperor is merely waiting for the implementation of the recommendations of this Commission before withdrawing his troops."

"So His Imperial Majesty has declared through your lips on numerous occasions, my Lord President, but I myself doubt it. Why is that, you ask?" A heavily jeweled forefinger rose and wagged. "Because the Emperor hopes to control the Causeway with his new cannon and because, by denying us our capital, he hopes to keep us from forming a true nation." The geniality was gone from the voice.

"Ah, Forodan"—Phalastra managed to put a world of injury into the two words—"you disappoint me. You know that His Imperial Majesty has no designs on Songuard, indeed would rejoice to see a stable country upon his border."

He lies so well, Malum thought admiringly as he sanded one sheet of paper and moved to the next. The last thing that the Emperor wanted was an organized and cohesive Songuard. The only problem was that the occupation of Bandor had become a rallying point for the clans.

"Whoever controls Fort Bandor controls the valley and that is of interest to us. The more so should the final partition conform to the lines drawn on this map."

The new voice was deep and musical. It could have come from any of the men around the table, but Malum knew from experience that it belonged to the Oligarch Olivderval.

"You sound unhappy, madam," Estragoth said with the faintest tinge of sarcasm.

"Don't try to play games with me, Estragoth," Olivderval returned with asperity. "You knew perfectly well that I would be unhappy with this." She gestured dismissively at the map before her. "I have been at pains during the past several years to explain our position with clarity and consistency. . . ."

"And the Framing Committee, dear lady, was well aware of that position. There is, however, the small matter of geography."

"Accompanied by a certain smallness of vision," Olivderval retorted.

"And I suppose that you have a better alternative to offer. Perhaps we should move all the inhabitants of Songuard north of the Upper Causeway and give Isphardel all their ancestral lands?" The sarcasm was patent now.

"By no means." Olivderval was urbane in response to Phalastra's veiled hostility. "Your Lordship cannot have failed to notice that we of Isphardel are a trading and seafaring nation. I would suggest, therefore, that Umbria cede its coastal region in exchange for the piece of the Outland currently allocated to us."

There was silence, an almost tangible withholding of sound. Malum felt a thrill run through him. Quern was on the south coast. The idea was absurd. Never, in all the years of discussion, had such a possibility been voiced. It was unthinkable that a nation would give up sovereign territory. He glanced quickly at the Elector to gauge his reaction and saw, to his surprise, that the man was smiling.

"An original conception, madam, and not without a certain logic. Politically, however, it is entirely unacceptable." He sounded a note of quiet regret.

"Stuff and nonsense," the Oligarch said briskly. "What you really mean is that Varodias is too dim to grasp the long-range advantages."

The statement was greeted with little hisses of indrawn breath. Eyes were wide and darting. There was no other movement. The only ones who seemed entirely at ease were the Oligarch and the Elector.

"That is unkind and unwarranted," Phalastra said in mild reproof. "You must be aware that any such move would be resisted by force of arms. Not the Imperial armies, you understand, but by the local people. Love of His Imperial Majesty and of the Empire of Umbria runs deep."

"As I said, you people think only in the short term." Olivderval was relaxed and unrepentant. She sat back in her chair and looked slowly around the table, taking her time.

"There is one other alternative," she said at last. "It's far more dangerous in the long term, but I can see no other solution."

Phalastra steepled his fingers and looked over them at the Oligarch. He seemed to be enjoying himself. "Perhaps if you explained we should be able to make that determination for ourselves," he suggested.

"We come back to geography. Isphardel must have permanent right of passage through Songuard, old and new. Roads will have to be built, the Causeway will have to be pierced. Without that we cannot administer the proposed territory."

"But that would disrupt the grazing and watering patterns of the summer herds," the Hodman objected.

"Precisely," the Oligarch replied. "And of course"—she turned back toward the head of the table—"under those circumstances the continued occupation of Fort Bandor would be equally unacceptable to my government."

Malum's pen hand hovered over the parchment and his eyes flicked toward the Elector. Estragoth had a spot of color on his cheek and his body was very still; neither of them were good signs.

"Strong words, Oligarch, strong words."

The Elector spoke calmly and even mustered the ghost of a smile, but Malum knew that the accord was in trouble and his master was angry. They had both known that it was possible; the Elector had even discussed it with him. In fact, in one of those brilliant flights of analysis that never failed to impress Malum, the Elector had outlined the consequences of the vote for decades to come. Olivderval had obviously come to those same conclusions and was moving now to thwart them.

Malum allowed his attention to wander for a brief time. The Oligarch made him intensely uncomfortable. She had cultivated him, that was the only word for it. She had sought him out at diplomatic gatherings and had quizzed him in a friendly way. She had been frank with her own opinions and had listened to his with respect. She was fun to debate with, despite his nagging suspicion that she had a better mind than he did. He rather enjoyed her company. He just wished that she would behave more like a lady.

"I have a reputation, my Lord President," Olivderval said, breaking into Malum's thoughts, "for being blunt, and I am. Not from any lack of sensibility, I assure you, but because time is precious." She pushed herself up in her chair and gazed around the table, compelling attention.

"We have all wasted far too much time on this matter. We have been dancing diplomatically for fifteen years and I have gone along with it. We do not have the luxury of time anymore. The Outland is ready for settlement and every sturdy beggar, every disgruntled younger son, every escaped criminal in the world, will be heading out there to make a life for themselves. If we do not set up controls there will be a lawless society. Now, I don't think that any of us want that."

She looked up and down the table again, but there were no comments. "Very well then," she resumed, "the time has come to talk truths—all the nasty, little sticking places that it has been 'bad form' to bring up. Consider that, according to this map, the Kingdom of Arundel appears to have ceded to Talisman an area about four times the area of Talisman itself. I assume that Queen Arabella has decided that when the lands beyond the Mountains of the Night are explored, Arundel will have more than enough territory. The Empire, on the other hand, with who knows how many leagues of Unknown Lands to exploit, hasn't given an inch, thereby forcing Isphardel, and only Isphardel, to settle for a territory separated by close to a thousand leagues from the homeland."

"Does anyone else have a 'sticking place' to bring to our attention?" Estragoth asked as Olivderval paused for breath.

"With the Lord President's permission," Jarrod said. He had not intended to make this proposal, but it suddenly seemed imperative.

"Yes, my Lord Mage?" Phalastra said politely.

"I have discussed the earlier draft of this document with the Archmage and he insists that the Discipline be afforded an autonomous base in the Outland.

"I do not think," Jarrod said, hurrying on before anyone could cut in, "that I have to remind the Council that, without the Discipline, we would not be discussing partition now. Besides, with the vast distances involved, the Discipline needs a center from which to organize and control the Weatherwarding." He had not in fact received any such instructions, but he felt sure that Ragnor would approve.

Phalastra sipped delicately at his cider. "Since the

control of weather is of interest only to the Magical Kingdoms, I should imagine that it is up to them to cede whatever territory is deemed necessary. Umbria has no objection."

"Nor Isphardel," Olivderval added.

"Songuard does not object," the Hodman rumbled.

"Very well then," Phalastra resumed. "I think we can safely leave the Discipline and the Magical Kingdoms to work out the details. Does anyone else have a problem that they would like to raise?" He looked around the table.

"Well, it would appear that Paladine has been somewhat shortchanged." The voice, soft and diffident, came from the Paladinian Chamberlain. "The portion marked is consistent with our northern border, but that is the narrowest part of the Kingdom."

There was a buzz of conversation that began to grow louder. Estragoth banged on the table in an effort to regain control of the meeting, but he was ignored. Finally he stood, pushing his chair back, and used his mug on the tabletop. Slowly the meeting came to order. When he spoke, he was calm, but the effort showed in his rigid stance.

"The Oligarch has given us much to think about," he said, "and it is clear that we shall make no headway today. I suggest that we adjourn for four days and reconvene here at the eleventh hour. If there are further problems with the proposed partition, I shall be most happy to meet individually with Commission members." He looked from side to side. "Are we agreed?"

Taking silence for assent, he stalked from the room. As soon as he was through the door the voices started up again. Malum began to pack up his things. The meeting had been a disaster. It was supposed to last the day and now his master had cut it off inside of an hour. The old man was going to be in a foul mood. Somehow they would have to devise a way of neutralizing the Isphardi suggestion that the Empire give up territory. Varodias would never stand for it and the Emperor, when angry, was an exceedingly dangerous man. He looked over at the Commissioners and found them clustered around the Oligarch. Damn that Olivderval!

chapteR 3

Jarrod Courtak looked up from his reading at the knock on his door.

"Oh, hello Tok," he said to the plump Magician who entered without waiting for permission. "What did you do, sneak past the Duty Boy?"

"Hardly," Tokamo said good-naturedly. "I'm not exactly built for sneaking. I passed the poor tyke on the stairs buried under a pile of your washing."

Jarrod smiled fondly at his oldest friend. Tokamo still made jokes about his girth, but he had in fact slimmed down considerably since his thirtieth birthday. He had become an important man in the Discipline of Paladine, taking on more and more administrative responsibility as Agar Thorden got older. He did most of the traveling these days, supervising the Weatherwards and the Village Magicians, collecting the Tithe and adjudicating disputes.

"I haven't seen you for a fortnight," Jarrod said. "You been off terrorizing the scullery maids at the post inns again?"

"No such luck. I've been stuck in the countinghouse going over the Tithe receipts. Master Thorden's got an attack of the ague again. Needless to say, Naxania's late with the Crown's share. So, how did the big meeting go? My spies tell me that you were back early."

"It was a disaster," Jarrod said with relish," but it

looks as if we're going to get something out of it after all."

"You sound as if you had a good time," Tokamo commented as he went to the sideboard and helped himself to a flagon of ale. He took a chair from the side of the room and brought it across.

"Oh, I wasn't the one who caused the trouble."

"I see. Who did you get to do the dirty work for you? Borr Sarad?"

"No. Olivderval and Estragoth had one of those classic, extremely polite, head-on clashes. Why the Elector thought that the Isphardis would accept a divided territory is beyond me. The basic problem is that the Umbrians despise the Isphardis."

"The Umbrians look down on everybody," Tokamo commented.

"True, but they have this attitude that commerce is beneath them. Mining and manufacturing support most of the Electors, but they maintain this fiction that actually selling the stuff is plebeian."

"More fool they; there's nothing wrong with money."

"It seems to me that, as far as the Empire is concerned, having it is one thing, but working for it is something else entirely."

"Surely this head-on clash wasn't about money."

"Territory, access and administration on the surface, power beneath it," Jarrod said succinctly.

"Power? Isphardel doesn't have an army and . . ." Tokamo was halted by a knock at the door.

"All right if I come in?" Darius of Gwyndryth inquired. "There was nobody to announce me."

"By all means, my lord. Be welcome," Jarrod said, rising. Tokamo followed suit.

"I hope I'm not interrupting anything," Darius said as he advanced.

"No, no. Tokamo and I were just discussing this morning's Commission meeting."

"Ah, just what I came to do."

Tokamo fetched another chair. "Wine or ale?" he asked.

"Wine, please."

"What have you heard about this morning's to-do?" Jarrod asked when they were all seated.

"That Isphardel was a burr under the saddle and that you made your own grab for land."

Jarrod smiled and leaned back. He contemplated the Holdmaster. The man had aged well. His hair had been white when Jarrod first met him some twenty years ago. He had seemed an old man then, recovering as he was from the terrible wounds he had suffered fighting for the Empire against the Outlanders. He looked better now than he had then. His age had caught up with the color of his hair, but, from Jarrod's vantage point in his mid-thirties, the Holdmaster no longer seemed all that old to him.

"I must admit," he said, "that I had not expected such precipitate opposition from the Oligarch, though I knew that Isphardel would never agree to the plan."

Darius smiled in his turn. "She's a formidable woman," he agreed. "And I must admit that I like and admire her. Mind you," he added with sly humor, "I am known to be partial to strong women. My old friend Phalastra, I hear, does not share my tastes."

"I think that her suggestion that Umbria cede its sea-coast upset him," Jarrod said judiciously.

"I know," Darius said, suppressing glee. "Otorin told me. I love the old boy dearly, but I wish I'd been there to see the look on his face."

"He would have disappointed you," Jarrod said. "He got a little red, but his demeanor was impeccable."

"He hasn't survived as Varodias' chief councillor all

these years without learning how to hide his feelings," Darius concurred. "He's a remarkable man. I only hope that I'm as spry and as lucid when I get to be his age. Still, he does what the Emperor tells him to and the consequences of this particular move could be grave." He nodded his head for emphasis and took a drink.

"The solution is simple," Jarrod said.

"Ah, yes. Your international territory. It's a magnificent concept, but I'm afraid it's quite unworkable. The Queen is willing to go along with your idea of an enclave for the Discipline but she's unalterably opposed to the international scheme. Varodias will never agree and Otorin assured me that Arabella has no interest in it. None of the other powers has the capability to enforce it, except perhaps the Discipline, but the Discipline, unfortunately, is perceived as being in decline these days." The words were said gently, but they caused both Magicians to sit up.

"Indeed, my lord?" Jarrod's tone was politely quizzical, but there was no mistaking the iron beneath it.

He's certainly grown up, Darius thought. He's a proper Mage of the Discipline and no mistake. "Simmer down, my friend," he said easily. "I'm not attacking the Discipline, I'm just reporting what is generally thought."

"Have people such a short memory that they have forgotten that it was the Discipline that freed them from the Outlanders?" Tokamo asked with a touch of belligerence.

Jarrod gestured with one hand to quiet him. "Are you sure that you are reporting accurately?" he asked in his turn.

"When was the last time someone tried to touch your robe?" Darius countered.

Jarrod froze and then relaxed. "I take your point,"

he said, "and Tokamo tells me that we are having problems collecting the Tithe."

"There you are then. The main problem remains, however. We must have an equitable partition and we must have it soon." Darius sat forward, intent on convincing. "We have had a goodly taste of peace and most of our citizens have prospered. Trade, the arts, architecture have all blossomed, but there is still a core of discontent. Young men feel that they lack a challenge, that the excitement has gone from life. Discontent can lead to rebellion and rebellion can lead to war. We cannot have that again."

"If you'll forgive my saying so," Tokamo interjected, "while I agree wholeheartedly with your sentiments, I find it somewhat strange to hear them coming from someone who has the reputation of being the greatest warrior of his age."

Darius turned to look at him. "Young man," he said, "old soldiers are the best ambassadors of peace. They have seen the horrors of war at first hand. My body will bear its scars to the grave. I would not see the same marks upon my grandson."

Tokamo retreated in his chair, abashed by the Holdmaster's sincerity.

"We are far from war, I think," Jarrod put in. "The Isphardi government's weapons are economic, not martial." He paused and cocked his head slightly. "But you know all this as well as I. I think you had another reason for seeking me out today."

Darius relaxed a trifle, produced a smile and then sipped at his wine. "Well, I certainly wanted to enlist your support for a partition, but I must confess that, for myself, I wanted to inquire after Joscelyn."

Jarrod laughed. "Short of the tides, there is no force on Strand to equal the love of a grandfather for his only grandson. Yours continues to do well. He'll be going to the Collegium in a month for the start of the summer term."

Darius shook his head. "I still haven't quite adjusted to having a Magician in the family. Oh, I know that Marianna talked with the unicorn, but then, on that one extraordinary occasion at Bandor, so did I. That's not the same somehow. Marianna was chosen to look for the unicorns precisely because she was Untalented. No one in the family has ever been Talented."

"Then it must come through the father," Tokamo said. "The boy is strongly gifted."

"The Trellawns have been our vassals for twelve generations and there was never a Magician among them," Darius said. "As for my former son-in-law, his major asset is his looks."

Tokamo was discreetly silent. Marianna of Gwyndryth's sudden marriage and swift divorce had been a much-discussed scandal in their time.

"The Talent crops up unexpectedly," Jarrod said soothingly. "My own family is a case in point. I must admit, though, that I was surprised when I heard that young Joscelyn had crossed the Great Maze."

He remembered Marianna bringing the boy to him seven years ago. He had been tall for his age, but not outstandingly so. He had his mother's red-gold hair and pale skin, but his eyes were as blue as hers were green. He was fourteen now and had grown considerably. He lacked the physical awkwardness of most boys that age, but his voice was in the process of breaking, much to his embarrassment. He blushed easily.

"Are you sure he's ready for the Collegium?" Darius asked anxiously. "Celador's such a long way away and there's no one to keep an eye on him."

Jarrod and Tokamo exchanged a look. "I can assure you that he's quite capable of looking after himself and may even benefit from not having a doting grandfather around to spoil him."

Darius smiled ruefully. "Frankly, it's what happens after the Collegium that bothers me," he said.

"How so?"

"Well, if his Talent's as strong as you seem to think it is, he's not likely to want to settle down to a life at Gwyndryth."

"You haven't," Jarrod pointed out. "Then again, I'm more than a little surprised that Marianna spends as much time there as she does."

"I know." Darius drank some more wine and wiped his mouth with his left hand. "I'd like to see more of her, but she and Naxania don't get along all that well. I'd also like to see her remarried," he added in a burst of candor. "If anything happened to young Joscelyn . . ." He let the sentence trail off.

"The boy's in robust health," Tokamo said, "and at least you don't have to worry about him being killed in the war."

"I wish I could be sure of that," Darius replied. "I don't like the sound of what happened this morning. You'll forgive my saying so, but I wish the Discipline had more clout."

"The people still rely on us," Jarrod said.

"Yes, but it's been fifteen years since the Discipline did anything dramatic. People become accustomed to having dependable weather and mill wheels that turn even when the rivers are low. They take you for granted." He paused. "What I'm really suggesting is that it is time for another grand gesture to reassert your authority."

"Do you have any suggestions?" Tokamo asked skeptically.

Darius gave a little shrug. "Perhaps Greylock would

like to flex his Magical muscles. After all, he's seldom seen these days."

"You must understand, my lord," Jarrod said quickly before Tokamo could intervene, "that the Mage is not as young as he used to be."

"Who among us is?" the Holdmaster said. He finished his wine, and it was apparent that he was going to take his leave. "On the other hand," he added, "he does have you two strapping lads to help him, doesn't he? Look, I'm not trying to tell you what to do, but I wish you'd think about what I've said. The Discipline's always been the binding force in the Magical Kingdoms and I have a nasty suspicion that we're going to need you now more than ever."

He got to his feet, bringing the other two with him, and parting courtesies were exchanged.

"Well, Jarrod, what do you make of all that?" Tokamo asked after the Holdmaster had been ushered out.

"I think that Queen Naxania has more problems than we are aware of. I've known the Holdmaster for a long time and he's never been adept at dissimulation."

"I think he was sincere," Tokamo objected.

"Oh, he was. I've no doubt about that. I just don't think that the visit was his idea. Naxania wants something from us and she doesn't want to face either Ragnor or Greylock directly. She used the Holdmaster instead."

"Speaking of that, it's time she married the man, don't you think? She isn't getting any younger either and she's the last of the line."

"He's a foreigner," Jarrod replied. "That's tolerable in a lover, but not in a consort. Besides, she's got time. Her Talent enables her to control her body in ways denied other women—as long as she doesn't perform really strong Magic."

"Well, what do you think we should do?"

"I think we should go and see Greylock."

"In that case I'll leave you to it," Tokamo said, finishing off his ale.

"Not so fast. Where d'you think you're going?"

"I still have a great deal of work to do in the countinghouse . . ." Tokamo began.

"You're still afraid of Greylock, aren't you?" Jarrod said, not altogether kindly.

Tokamo stiffened, and then his shoulders relaxed. "Who wouldn't be? The man's come back from the dead."

"He was never dead and you know it. Honestly, Tok, you're as bad as a village midwife."

"You should get out into the country a bit more," Tokamo retorted. "Midwives are among the wisest people I've met."

"That's as may be, but Greylock's quite normal and you know it."

"What about those times when he goes away? One moment he's talking to you and the next he's totally oblivious. I'll be in the middle of a report and suddenly his mind is somewhere else. I could stand on my head and he wouldn't notice."

"He's seen things that we haven't," Jarrod replied. "There are questions that he's trying to answer that you and I wouldn't know how to ask and, once in a while, they preoccupy him. He knows that the sand is running out for him. He's almost seventy and, for a Mage who has been as active as he, that's a remarkable span."

"Ragnor must be in his eighties," Tokamo pointed out.

"Granted, and that borders on the miraculous. I'm tempted to think that the unicorn horn that we ingested for that last spell has something to do with it."

"Is that why you look thirty rather than sixty?" Tokamo asked acidly.

"Could be," Jarrod said with a grin. "And now we're both going to see Greylock and discuss Lord Darius' suggestion."

"Is that an order, Excellence?" Tokamo asked with an edge on his voice as he returned his flagon to the sideboard.

Jarrod sighed to himself. Tokamo had always been touchy, even as a boy. "Of course not," he said lightly. "You've been out in the countryside and you're a good listener. You have a perspective that Greylock and I lack. I need you there."

"Gods but you've grown smooth-tongued," Tokamo said, but Jarrod could see that he was pleased.

"Let's go and see the old man," Jarrod said.

chapter 4

Greylock sat dreaming in front of the fire. These were pleasant moments, the musings benign, the occasional drifts into sleep unhaunted. Not like the nights when he woke screaming against the entrapment of the grey void. These periods of rosy drifting were a welcome respite, a restorative haven. He had resisted the lure of simples to achieve the same results. He had known too many Magicians over the years who had abused their knowledge. The only problem was that he would slip away into states like this when there were other people present, so where was the difference? He always pretended that he was contemplating questions beyond the mere mortal, but the truth was that he tired easily and most of their prattle bored him.

He would be Archmage one day, if Ragnor ever decided to die, and then he would need all his wits about him. It didn't seem terribly important at the moment, though. It was doubtful that he could do anything as Archmage that would eclipse his present notoriety—the Mage who came back from the dead. It wasn't a bad sobriquet. It would make a good title for a ballad. Or was that one he had heard already? He really couldn't remember.

His head came up off his chest, spurred by some noise. He focused and saw the Duty Boy in the doorway. "Saw" was a little strong; "perceived" was closer to it. The boy's outline was fuzzy. Greylock's eyes had been getting steadily worse.

"Yes, what is it?" he asked, aware of the querulous note in his voice.

"His Excellence the Mage Courtak and the Honorable Tokamo to see you, sir," the boy said.

"Show them in. Give them a glass. Try to make them feel welcome," he instructed, and watched the boy do his awkward best. The boys seemed to be getting stupider. He remembered when Courtak had been a Duty Boy: always falling over his feet trying to please. Still, he's turned out well, Greylock thought complacently, and he is the only one who doesn't treat me like a sacred relic. He screwed his eyes up and saw that the second shape was indeed Tokamo. Never did have much Talent, he thought. Still, Thorden swore by him; wrote good, clear reports, too.

"Come in, come in. Make yourselves comfortable," he said.

Strange how different the two of them were, he thought. They had been inseparable as boys, Courtak always in the lead. The pattern hadn't changed.

"What can I do for you lads?" he asked.

"Sorry to barge in on you like this, Mage," Jarrod answered, "But Tok and I have just come from a rather unusual meeting with the Holdmaster of Gwyndryth and he brought up a very interesting point that we felt we ought to discuss with you."

"I see," Greylock said, "and I daresay that the territorial settlement was the subject." He caught Tokamo's frozen stare. "It isn't that difficult," he added testily. "Given the circumstances, it's downright obvious." The boy had always been slow.

"You're right as usual, sir," Jarrod said, "but I bet you can't guess what the thrust of his suggestion was."

Greylock sat back and considered. He pursed his lips

and locked his fingers together. It was a familiar routine for both the younger men.

"That means," the Mage said, "that he wasn't pleading either Stronta's or Celador's case. Talisman, from the map you showed me, has no reason to complain and I can't see Darius supporting Isphardel. So, as the hero of Fort Bandor, he was espousing the cause of the Songeans." He sat back, pleased with himself.

"A very deft analysis, sir," Jarrod said, "but, alas, not the fact. No, the Holdmaster feels that Magic has lost the respect of the masses, no longer enjoys the authority it once possessed. In short, he believes that it is time that the Discipline reminded people of its power, performed some startling feat of Magic."

"Oh he does, does he?" The old Mage was fully alert. "Did he have any suggestions?"

"Aren't you going to challenge his assumption?" Tokamo asked.

"Of course not. The man's absolutely right. It's been years since we did anything dramatic. Did he suggest anything?"

"Nothing specific," Jarrod said.

"Typical of the laity," Greylock said dismissively. "Why now, I wonder?"

"Because there's another rebellion brewing and Naxania wants a distraction," Tokamo blurted.

"A rebellion, Tok? Are you sure?" Jarrod was startled.

"I caught hints of it on my last trip. I put it down to tavern talk at the time, but now I'm not so certain."

"I think you ought to tell us about this, young man," Greylock said.

Tokamo was clearly uncomfortable in the limelight, but he girded himself. "I can't be sure, sir, but people have been commenting on the number of armed retainers the Duke of Abercorn keeps. The general opinion is that he is aiming for the throne."

"But that's absurd," Jarrod remonstrated. "He sided with the Crown during the Lindisfarn rebellion and that turned the tide."

"Yes I know," Tokamo said apologetically. "I'm only reporting what I've heard. The talk is that there has always been bad blood between the House of Strongsword and the Dukes of Abercorn and that Duke Paramin wants the throne for himself. They say that he backed the Queen before because her troops were too strong. Well, that was just after the war and the Royal Army was a lot stronger than it is today. There are rumors of secret alliances between Abercorn and the Earls of Rostan and Southey."

"I have heard nothing of this," Greylock said, "and I have very reliable sources."

"With respect, Excellence," Tokamo replied, looking intensely uncomfortable, "your sources are all at Court. I've been all through the country in the past few years and, if I'm not wearing my gown, I look more like a fat, jolly trader than a Magician. People tend to talk freely in front of me, especially after a few pints of ale."

"I wish that you had confided in me before," Greylock said, "but you have done well, very well indeed. So, Naxania feels threatened and her paramour thinks that the Discipline should do something dramatic. Very interesting."

"With all due respect, sir, Lord Darius did make a very valid point. People are taking us for granted these days. In light of the present difficulties with the partition treaty, he felt it was time that the Discipline reasserted itself."

Greylock was silent for a long time and Jarrod was afraid that he had slipped away. Then he noticed that the right hand was drumming quietly against the arm of the chair. The Mage roused himself.

"I haven't performed any Magic since I returned from the Place of Power and neither has Ragnor, come to think of it. Gwyndryth is right, people forget. I think that we should remind them, don't you?"

Greylock's eyes were glinting, but Jarrod couldn't be sure if it was humor, enthusiasm or the firelight.

"I haven't performed any serious Magic for a long time," Jarrod said, excitement in his voice.

"No you don't," Greylock countered. "You've done quite enough as it is. There's no need to create more envy."

Jarrod winced inwardly at the implied criticism, but managed to keep a bland face. "Have you any suggestions, sir?" he asked.

"Something fairly spectacular and in the public interest," Greylock replied.

"A grand exhibition demonstrating our skills," Tokamo suggested.

"We could always do away with the Upper Causeway" came, with humor, from Jarrod.

The old Mage smiled. "You think big, laddie, I'll give you that, but I scarcely think that Strandkind would thank you for it. They're attached to the wall. It's represented safety to them for as long as they can remember. Besides, it's a source of revenue now."

Jarrod couldn't resist. It was a favorite hobbyhorse and he had ridden it often. "But the Upper Causeway will divide the old territories from the new," he said. "It will keep the new lands out as effectively as it did the Outlanders. It'll create new divisions."

"Good thing too," Greylock said shortly. "That'll give the new territories a chance to develop a character of their own, not to feel that they're a second-class offshoot."

"I hadn't thought about it in that way," Jarrod said.

"Of course you hadn't." Greylock sounded triumphant. "But it's true nevertheless. Still, that doesn't solve the question of what we should do. You, Tokamo, give me a thought."

He's reverting to the days when we were boys and he was teaching us, Jarrod thought. He was also delighted that Tokamo was being asked the question. If the past held true, though, he ought to be thinking of an answer.

Tokamo's tongue peeked briefly out between his lips. "Well," he said, "it ought to affect the whole of Strand and it has to be something that people can see. Ideally, it should have something to do with the Outland and it should be something that could only be achieved by Magic."

"You've stated the problem admirably, lad," Greylock said, "but I don't hear an answer."

Jarrod heard the words faintly. He was flying above Strand again in his memory. Affecting the whole of Strand. Weather and the Upper Causeway. What else? Then it came to him and it seemed so obvious.

"The Giants' Causeway," he said.

"I beg your pardon?" from Greylock.

The memory of the dream flickered in the back of Jarrod's mind. He brushed it aside. "The Giants' Causeway," he repeated. "It's unsightly, it serves no useful purpose and it stretches across most of Strand."

"What about it?" Greylock enquired.

"If we could get rid of it . . ." Jarrod left the idea hanging. The stone had always been used for building. This very tower incorporated stone from the Giants' Causeway. The images of the elusive building in the mountains came back. Should he mention it to Greylock? No, not yet.

Greylock sat back and contemplated. "Where would the rock go?" he asked.

"Out onto the Plain?" Jarrod suggested.

"Glib answer as usual, Courtak." Greylock reverted to his old pedagogical manner. "That's all very well for the moment, but we'll get colonization at some point. Can't have good farmland strewn with rocks. People wouldn't thank us for that."

Jarrod kept his own counsel.

"It's not a bad idea," Greylock said into the silence. "I think the two of you should go away and work out the details." He nodded several times and then waved his right hand in farewell and dismissal.

By the time the two younger men had reached the door, his chin had sunk back down to rest on his chest.

"See what a mess you've got us into?" Tokamo declared as they went down the stairs.

"Don't get in such a lather," Jarrod said. "This will have to be approved by Ragnor. The odds are that he'll kill the whole idea." He halted and put his arms out across the stairwell. He looked back up and grinned. "If I were you, though," he said, "I'd try to think up the logistics of such an operation."

"Why me?" Tokamo asked rhetorically. "I've enough to do collecting Tithes and trying to keep the accounts straight."

"Because you're good at that sort of thing," Jarrod said, resuming his descent, "because Ragnor will expect it and because I'm going to be tied up with negotiations on an enclave for the Discipline. That might even solve the problem of what to do with all the stone."

"Where are we going to get the labor force? You can't call out the Farod anymore."

"Wouldn't help if we could. This has to be done with Magic, remember?"

"Well, it isn't fair. You get to do all the glamorous stuff and I get stuck with the logistics."

"You're wrong there, Tok," Jarrod replied seriously.

"You get to travel all over Paladine, living like a normal man, drinking ale with ordinary people, and I get stuck here playing Mage, watching every word I say lest I offend some great lord or ambassador. There's no glamor in that." He paused and added maliciously, "Of course, if you'd prefer to confront the Archmage and explain to him that the Discipline is in a decline . . ."

"Would that I could," Tokamo returned, straight-faced, "but unfortunately Agar Thorden needs me."

They both laughed, secure in the familiarity that almost thirty years of friendship brings.

chapter 5

In the deep woods of Oxeter, pronounced "Oxter" by the locals and in Court circles but invariably mispronounced elsewhere, men mustered quietly. Two hundred of the Duke's retainers, fifty of them mounted, prepared to move against the neighboring estate of Sparsedale. Duke Paramin of Abercorn watched them in the waxing light with a feeling of satisfaction. They were well armed and moved with the automatic competence of two years of intensive drilling. His son, who would lead the expedition, sat his horse easily a few feet away. A decade of planning was about to be put to the test.

The Semicount of Sparsdale was a distant cousin of Queen Naxania and a fervently loyal vassal. His lickspittle loyalty had been rewarded by the loan of a company of the Royal Guard, fifty seasoned veterans of the Outland wars. The significance of their billeting had not been lost on Paramin. They were there to act as a warning and a check. An attack on Sparsedale was an assault on the Crown. There could be no going back after today. The men were not wearing his livery, but they carried it in their packs. As a result of his neutrality in the previous uprising, he must be seen to lead when the time came— at least if he wanted to wear the crown, and he did.

He had felt that the first uprising was ill timed. Naxania was the beneficiary of both her father's reputation and the general euphoria at the unexpected coming of peace. The cottars were sick of war, the merchants saw no advantage in civil strife and the Royal Forces, though weakened by the battle for Stronta Gate, were still formidable. Events had proved him right. The foreign upstart Gwyndryth had put down the rebels swiftly and efficiently. The gibbets at Stronta had stretched a goodly number of aristocratic necks and the Crown lands had swelled with the forfeitures.

Ten years had elapsed since then and the bloom was off the young Queen. She was now seen as remote and high-handed, predisposed to the northern counties and indifferent to the mid and southern regions. Taxes were still high. The cottars did not care that the roads had improved or that bridges had been rebuilt. Since the Farod had been dissolved, they traveled no farther than the nearest market. The great landowners may have profited from the peace, but the small farmer and the day-worker had seen little improvement in the condition of their daily lives. It amused the Lord Paramin to be thought of as the champion of the poor and the oppressed. It was they who had paid for the men who were riding out on this clear morning, but they were too stupid to realize it. Nevertheless, their passivity, their belief that their lord acted in their interests, would be the key to victory this time. The witch Queen had no offspring and the accursed House of Strongsword would be no more.

Paramin watched as his force moved out of the woodlands in orderly fashion. He had brief words of encouragement for his son, Bardolph, words that brooked no failure, and then he withdrew to his castle. If the assault failed, he intended to disavow it. His errant, glory-hunting son had acted on his own initiative in an attempt to set up a fiefdom for himself. Young men these days, deprived of the release and the discipline that war had provided, were prone to such things. If, and the gods forbid such an outcome, his men were driven off, Paramin would be contrite for his failure to recognize his son's ambitions and dissatisfactions. He would, of course, have to mount another, more sizable, attack at some other target fairly swiftly or lose his credibility as a leader. If the worst came to the worst, he would lose his son. It was an entirely acceptable risk. If all went well and the other disaffected vassals rose, he would be king. He was still capable of siring other sons. Indeed, on this morning the future seemed to stretch before him limitlessly. He turned his horse's head, clapped heels to flank and galloped back to the castle. He was hungry.

News of the fall of Castle Sparsedale and the annihilation of the Royal Guards reached Stronta four days after the event. Added to the shock were rumors that two of the southern provinces had declared against the throne and that the Earls of Rostan and Southey were coming out for the rebels. There was conflicting information about six of the thirteen counties, but it was obvious to Darius that a serious rebellion was under way. The summons to the Presence Chamber came as no surprise.

Queen Naxania sat upon the throne, pale as ever, black hair hanging straight past her shoulders. Ordinarily the sight of her exhilarated Darius, even after all these years. Today, however, the white face was set, the mouth was a grim line and the long-fingered hands gripped the arms of the throne tightly. Greylock, the Mage of Paladine, stood before her, and Darius was aware that his entrance had brought their conversation to a halt. His eyes flicked around the room as he advanced across the polished floor. No ladies-in-waiting, no courtiers, just the three of them. He came to a halt the required twelve paces from the throne and bowed.

"Give you good morrow, my lord," Naxania said,

using the Formal Mode. There was no warmth in the voice.

"May Your Majesty prosper," he returned, using the Formal Mode in turn. He had become adept at it during his years at Court, though he would never speak Pallic with the accent of a native.

"Whether we prosper or no depends on you," Naxania replied tartly. "We presume that you have had reports of the insurrection."

"I have, ma'am."

"And what, pray, do you intend to do about it?"

Darius glanced in Greylock's direction.

"Oh, the Mage is refusing to assist us, but we do not think him a traitor." It was angrily said. "You may speak freely."

"I have dispatched a company of archers, two hundred foot soldiers and about a hundred horse to recapture Sparsedale. Support units will follow. Unfortunately we have no siege engines; none have been needed until now."

"And think you that a mere three-hundred-odd men is a sufficient force?" Naxania's tone was sharp.

"I can only hope so, ma'am."

"Why are we not sending more men?"

"If Your Majesty will recall," Darius said patiently, "the Royal Forces have been reduced to three thousand men—two thousand foot, including archers, and one thousand cavalry. We have, in addition, two Cloudsteed Wings, but I believe that permission is needed from Talisman before they can be used in combat. If this dastardly seizure prompts a more general rising, we must have troops on hand to counter it."

Naxania rounded on Greylock. "You see, Excellence, why we need the assistance of the Discipline? How can you stand there and deny us?"

"Daughter"—Greylock used the Discipline's nomenclature deliberately—"you know, better than most, the answer to that."

"But you cannot stop us from using our art in the defense of our throne."

"Have a care, daughter. Do not challenge me," Greylock said evenly. "I both can and will deprive you of your power if needs be."

Darius turned to the Mage in surprise. He had not known that someone with the Talent could be deprived of it. The Mage's face was weary, but his expression left no doubt that he meant what he said. Darius faced the Queen again. Her back was straight, her eyes wide and her nostrils flared, but she said nothing. The threat hung in the air.

"If Your Majesty will permit," he said to break the tension.

Naxania's head turned slowly. Her gaze was far from grateful. "Proceed, my lord," she said coldly.

"I think that the remainder of the Royal Forces should move south without becoming engaged in the relief of Castle Sparsedale, and I think that it would be best to ask the former Thane of Talisman for permission to deploy the cloudsteeds."

Naxania took a deep breath. "Do what you think best, General."

Her attention returned to the Mage. "You have not heard the last of this, Excellence," she said, "and if you expect your Tithe, you may whistle for it." She drew herself up. "We need detain you no longer, my lord Mage, but we would have further speech with you, General."

Greylock gave a court bow and withdrew. Naxania watched him leave, her lips compressed into a line once more. When the door had closed she looked at Darius and, abandoning the Formal Mode, said, "That man tries my patience. He's so fixed in the traditions of the past. He doesn't seem to realize that the world has changed, and the same goes for the Archmage. They are both anachronisms. There ought to be some rule about retirement so that we could get some new blood into the upper ranks of the Discipline."

Darius made no reply, knowing that anything he said would be wrong. He had come to know her very well. Naxania got to her feet.

"We need to talk," she said. "Let us go and sit by the window. There's no point in your standing all the time and that throne isn't the most comfortable of seats."

She led the way to the embrasure that looked out over the garden and turned her chair so that she could see it. Darius followed suit.

"It's serious this time, isn't it?" she said.

"Rebellion is always serious, my love," Darius replied gently, "but you have overcome one challenge and you will survive this one. If you remember, you thought that doom was at the gates the last time."

She looked at him and smiled, then reached out and stroked his cheek. "What would I do without you. I was green then. In retrospect they were a disorganized rabble of petty lordlings. Besides, we had a lot more troops in those days. Whoever is behind this plot has had years in which to plan. They have all built up their private armies in defiance of my ordinances while my forces have dwindled. I shouldn't have listened to you. I should have raised taxes and kept my forces up to strength."

"And have a disaffected people all too willing to see you overthrown," Darius reminded her.

"Old arguments," she said with a sigh.

He realized how tired she really was, and the old instinct to console, cradle and protect her rose up as strongly as it had almost twenty years before. He leaned forward, took one of her hands in both of his and rubbed it gently. She allowed her shoulders to droop and turned her head to him with a soft little smile that caught at his heart. The impartial light from the window showed the stains beneath her eyes that powder had concealed.

. "This time," she said, "the Duke of Abercorn has committed himself and he has better than a thousand men under arms, or so my spies tell me."

"He hasn't exactly committed himself," Darius corrected. "My information is that his son attacked Sparsedale with a force of about two hundred men. If we retake the castle, and it'll be a tough nut to crack, I'll wager that the Duke will be full of chagrin and protestations of innocence."

"We'll have to scotch him one way or another. He isn't going to stop this time. He wants my throne and he is no longer a young man." She squeezed his fingers and looked into his eyes. "There's something I want you to do for me, my dear."

"Of course, my love."

"I want you to go and take charge yourself. After all, you are the man who retook Fort Bandor. Will you do it?"

Darius leaned back a little as if to see her more clearly. "Well," he said, "I had hoped that you were going to ask me to take you to bed."

Caught by surprise, she laughed, withdrawing her hand to cover her mouth. When the laughter had subsided she said, "You are an unregenerate, loin-driven old goat. But you will do it, won't you?"

"I'm getting too old for this," he said with resignation.

"If you're young enough to tumble me, you're young enough to retake an old castle."

"There's only one way to find out," he said, standing

up. He reached out, caught her hand and pulled her to her feet. "First we'll have to see if I'm young enough to tumble you."

"Well, Otorin," Darius said some hours later, "how about it? Will you join me? It'll be like old times."

"Not quite, I hope. I was playing the squire then, if you remember. I'm not going back to polishing your armor and currying your horse."

"I should hope not," Darius replied with gruff humor. "I've got a proper squire now, one who knows how to keep my armor greased and not just bright."

"Besides," Otorin continued, ignoring the jibe, "I have to get Arabella's permission to bear arms on behalf of another monarch."

"No real need for that," Darius replied. "I want your brain, not your swordarm."

"It's the technicalities that can ruin a man's career."

"Well then, do what I did at Angorn. Apply for permission and go ahead in the meantime. It didn't do me any harm."

"True," Otorin conceded, "but then again, I'm not one of the Queen's major vassals."

"No, you're more secure than that. You work for her. So we'll have no more argument."

Otorin sighed theatrically. "I don't know why I listen to you, let alone why I let you bully me. Besides, the Commission for the Outland is due to vote on partition."

"The Commission has waited for thirteen years, it can wait a mite longer. And, if you need a better reason, you're as bored of life at the palace as I am. It'll be good to be out in the field again; admit it."

"Oh, very well, but I'm not going into battle again and that's flat."

"Good enough. Now, as you undoubtedly know, I've

dispatched two hundred infantry, a hundred horse and about fifty bowmen. Brant is in charge of the foot. Olmsted the horse and Katon has overall command. Borr Sarad has taken the responsibility of releasing one Wing to me. I intend to send them south and take the rest of the Royal Forces with me."

"I would advise against that," Otorin said.

Darius looked up, surprised. "Why so?"

"Two reasons. Even if you leave the balance of the Royal Forces at Gapguard, there is always the possibility of a flanking move through the mountains and I think it would be unwise to leave the capital defenseless. Secondly, I don't think you want to retake Sparsedale right away."

"I concur on the first, but I don't understand the second," Darius said a shade defensively.

"Young Bardolph's nothing but a stalking horse. Paramin of Abercorn is the one you need to tame. He sits secure in Oxeter and lets others, in this case his son, do his dirty work. You'll have to draw him out and a nice, slow siege might just do it. If you keep Bardolph securely bottled up it should discourage others from joining the fray."

"Well, if there was any doubt about it," Darius responded, "you've just proved how much I need you."

Otorin smiled warmly. "You always were a good field commander." The smile died. "If you'll forgive my asking, how secure are you in the Queen's support?"

Darius' shoulders stiffened.

"I'm not trying to be impertinent, I'm just being practical," Otorin said, reading the signs.

Darius relaxed. "As secure as I'm ever likely to be," he said, remembering with pleasure the way the morning's audience had ended. "Mind you," he added, "I'm perfectly well aware that I shall always be 'the foreigner' and, in the last analysis, disposable, but so long as I can defeat her enemies and if I can hold on to her affections, I should be all right." His mouth twisted into a wry smile. "Neither of them is getting any easier. The men keep getting younger."

Like the Marquis of Bethel, Otorin thought. "You have one enormous advantage over them," he said briskly. "You have no ambition to sit on the throne. That may be less compelling in the bedchamber, but when it comes to the army, it's of paramount importance."

"Let's get back to the siege," Darius said. "What about Rostand and Southey?"

"What about them?"

"Don't tell me that you haven't heard of them."

"Both of them are earls, both have very large holdings on the coast. Both engage in trade, both are very wealthy."

"And both of them are in league with Abercorn," Darius finished.

Otorin smiled. "Their names have come up."

"Well, you don't expect them to sit around and do nothing, do you?"

"Oh, I rather imagine that they will allow the Duke the honor of rescuing his son, don't you? My information is that they would not be too upset if Abercorn were taken out of the game. All three have ambitions and there is only one throne."

"Let's hope that you're right."

"It's my job to be right about things like that and Arabella's gold has been judiciously spent to make sure that I am."

"We'll be riding out the day after tomorrow," Darius said. "Can you be ready by then?"

"I'll be ready just as soon as I send a bunglebird off to Celador. I have a squire of my own these days to do the packing."

"Fair enough. We'll be starting at first light."

Otorin groaned. "As the General commands." He gave a mocking half-bow.

"Any other suggestions?"

"I'd put the word around that you are requisitioning every wagon and draft horse. I'd give the Royal Armorer an order for half a dozen ballusters. Make sure that the troops here engage in some highly visible maneuvers outside the walls."

"I see. You want all this to get back to the Duke."

"And to the Earls."

"You're a devious man, Lissen."

"One of us has to be," Otorin said, and grinned. "Oh, and you might send a Royal Messenger to either Southey or Rostan, it doesn't matter which."

"Bearing what message?"

Otorin shrugged. "Something innocuous. An inquiry about crop rotation in the south, perhaps. It'll give the others something to worry about."

Darius shook his head and his lips curled up. "I'm glad you're on our side," he said.

chapter 6

Jarrod Courtak rode toward the mountains of Talisman, leaving the preparations for putting down the rebellion behind him. Tok had been right, he thought; there had been trouble brewing and now his own cousin had attacked Sparscdale. He had never met his relatives and had no feelings for them, but he was not pleased at being kin to traitors. Nor was he particularly pleased with this slow trip to Celador. He had been spoiled by the almost instantaneous trips through Interim on the back of a unicorn, but there were no unicorns on Strand at the moment. Pellia, his favorite, came back occasionally to introduce a new crop of foals. Her mother, Amarine, came more rarely still and then only to visit Marianna. Nastrus was the most constant of them, but he was off on one of his explorations. Jarrod's mind shied away from the thought of Beldun. He no longer had nightmares about killing Beldun, but the memory, though buried deep, was still there.

The quiet of the morning had been dispelled by the clopping of horses' hooves and the creak of cart wheels. Jarrod rode slightly ahead of the rest. Their presence, too, was an irritant. If he had had his own way he would have traveled alone, but these days his dignity demanded an entourage of servants and men-at-arms. It was almost enough to make him miss the overfaithful Sandroz. Sandroz had finally gone home, though. Times had changed.

The soldiers behind him on the raised road that ran through the leagues of rice paddies were testament to that. Since the war's end, bands of "sturdy beggars," as the broadsheets called them, roamed the countryside stealing from farmers and waylaying travelers. Most of them were former fighting men who had no taste for peacetime occupations. They were the scourge of every country, but, if the tales were to be believed, were particularly active in the Empire. Merchants now banded together in caravans and hired bravos of their own.

Off to the left, atop a gentle rise, was one of the new lantern houses that were all the rage. Monuments to their owners' egos, they appeared to be more glass than masonry. Not a shutter or a pail of damp clay to be found in them, no fortifications, commanding nothing but a view. They were impressive, especially at night when they could be seen from leagues away, that much Jarrod had to admit, but, if Darius of Gwyndryth was right and war came again, of what use would they be? He shook his head and urged his horse into a canter along the elevated roadway. The column adjusted its pace and the driver of the baggage cart swore and cracked his whip.

Celador, as they approached it from the east, seemed unchanged. There were no new dwellings outside the walls and the delicate spires still pointed ethereally at the sky. There were guards at the gates, but they were offered no challenge. No wardcorn blew a welcome or a warning. The courts, as the party clopped their way through them, were crowded and progress was slow. People took no notice of Jarrod. Celador was the unofficial center of the Discipline, and Magicians were a common sight. The welcome at the stables, where Jarrod was remembered for the unicorns, was warm. He hoped that it was a good omen for his coming meeting with the Archmage.

"His Excellence, the Mage Courtak," the Duty Boy announced in a stentorian voice worthy of a Court Chamberlain.

As Jarrod advanced into the well-remembered chamber, Ragnor roused himself and the sharp-faced cat that had been curled up on his lap jumped down and stretched. It had been a while since Jarrod had seen him and he hoped that the shock he felt did not show on his face. The long, white hair had dwindled to wispy strands that revealed the pink scalp. The face was lined, but then it always had been. Now it was blotched as well. There were little, vertical lines around the mouth that Jarrod didn't remember. The neck was scraggy and the skin loose. The mouth seemed too small, but when Ragnor smiled Jarrod realized that it was because there weren't too many teeth left.

"Come in, lad, come in," the Archmage said somewhat indistinctly, beckoning with a long, bony finger. "Pull up a chair." He waited while Jarrod complied and then rang a bell. "When the Duty Boy comes, ask for a bumper of sherris."

"Thank you, sir, but it's a bit early for me."

"It's not for you." Ragnor leaned forward conspiratorially. "My prison guard of a Wisewoman has forbidden me spirits. Says it affects my balance. Since I can't get around as well as I used to, I'd be obliged if you'd go along with this little deception. Pleasures are few and fleeting at my age."

"Now," he said when the Duty Boy had left and the thick glass was safely cradled in his hands, "what brings you to Celador? I thought the Commission was poised on the brink of decision."

"Not entirely," Jarrod replied and launched into an account of what had transpired.

"You did well," Ragnor said when he was finished, "though I do think you might have consulted me first."

"I'm sorry, sir. It was a spontaneous move on my part. I'd had an unusual dream the night before, and, during the session, a kind of compulsion came over me."

"Dream?" Ragnor said sharply. "What sort of dream?"

"I was out on the Alien Plain, all alone, shut in by grass. When I got clear of the grass I saw a large building of some kind up in the mountains. It kept appearing and disappearing, but it seemed to offer refuge. I tried to climb up to it, but things kept getting in the way. I finally lost my footing and fell. That's when I woke up." Described baldly like that, it seemed trivial, but the Archmage seemed to be taking it seriously.

"Can't say that I can see any particular meaning in it," he said after a couple of minutes of thought. "I certainly don't remember seeing anything like that in my glimpses into the future." He waved a hand. "But that future was changed by the unicorns. It might have something to do with this idea of territory and mountains are always good places for Weatherwards, but in the near term I think we need something a little closer to home, don't you?" He looked over at Jarrod before sipping at his sherris.

"Do you have any suggestions?" Jarrod asked diplomatically.

"Since the Collegium is here," the Archmage replied, "the new center ought to be in Paladine's territory. The only trouble with that is that Naxania will be far harder to deal with than Arabella. The wretched woman's bound to want something in return. Still, I suppose I should send a special envoy." He gave Jarrod a speculative look. "No," he said, "better if it wasn't you. Naxania's not too fond of you as I recall."

"I wasn't aware of that."

"Yes, she objected when I made you a Mage. Jealousy I imagine. She knows perfectly well that you can't have Mages sitting on the throne."

Jarrod decided to change the conversation. "Lord Darius came to see me," he said. "He seems to think that the Discipline is losing its clout. Thinks we should do something about it. Greylock agrees with him."

"Does he indeed? And what, pray, does he suggest we do?"

"Well, Greylock's idea is for us to clear away the rubble of the Giants' Causeway with Magic."

Ragnor sat back and stroked his thinning beard. "It's certainly ambitious enough, but I can't see how you're going to do it."

"Greylock is working on that. You know how he loves that sort of challenge."

Ragnor smiled. "Finding a 'scientific' answer," he said. The smile disappeared. "You better make sure he gets it right." The voice had a hard edge. "If anything went wrong it would make us a laughingstock and then we really would lose our clout."

"Yes sir," Jarrod said hastily.

"You keep me informed, understand?"

"Yes, sir." He may look frail, Jarrod thought, but I wouldn't care to cross him.

"Good." Ragnor sniffed and finished his drink. "I think you're ready for another glass and then you can bring me up to date on things in Paladine. Naxania's got a rebellion on her hands, I hear."

"D'you think that's entirely wise?" Jarrod asked, referring to the sherris.

Ragnor glared at him and rang the bell.

When Jarrod got back to Stronta, he found that the insurgency was the topic on everyone's lips. General Gwyndryth had gone south with a force whose numbers varied wildly depending on who one talked to. Despite the crisis, the diplomatic dance continued. The work of the various committees was supposedly over and Estragoth convened no formal meetings, but the politicking went on. Each of the Commissioners was wooed in one fashion or another by both Umbrians and Isphardis. The difference in style was instructive.

Estragoth stayed above the fray, leaving the footwork to Malum of Quern. The latter was punctiliously polite, sending a squire over to request an appointment, appearing at the exact hour agreed upon and being professionally pleasant on arrival. He spent ten minutes inquiring after Greylock's health, made a pretty admission of the awe in which he held Magicians in general and Jarrod in particular, presented Jarrod with the gift of an armclock and tendered an invitation to dine with the Elector. The man was entirely amiable and no overt pressure was applied; indeed, the matter of the partition was not mentioned.

The Oligarch, on the other hand, arrived with no prior warning, bustling in behind the Duty Boy.

"Don't bother to announce me," she said. "He knows who I am and I know that he's here." She grinned at the boy and tousled his hair. "Welcome back, by the way."

"To what do I owe this honor, Olivderval?" Jarrod asked, rising from his desk.

"Bribery and shameless arm twisting, of course," she replied cheerfully. "You going to offer an old woman a seat and a drink?" She turned back to the Duty Boy without waiting for an answer. "Something long, cold and innocuous," she declared, smiled, moved over to the fireplace and thumped down in an armchair.

"I'll have the same," Jarrod said. He turned to the Oligarch. "I take it that this is about the partition?" He crossed the floor and took the other chair.

"Of course it's about the partition. I love you dearly,

but I only heave my bulk up four flights of stairs if profit or the national interest are at stake."

Jarrod smiled at her directness. "I still believe that the Outland should be an international zone administered by the Discipline."

"Of course you do, but we both know that you can't muster enough votes to carry that," Olivderval said comfortably. "And partition's too important for you to waste your vote sitting on your dignity and abstaining. Besides, I backed your bid for land and you owe me. When it comes right down to it, you're no different from the rest of us."

They broke off as the Duty Boy returned with the drinks. Jarrod raised his glass to her and they sipped as the boy withdrew.

"I can't support your claim to the Umbrian seacoast," he said. "Besides, Varodias would never cede it even if every other nation voted for it."

"I'm well aware of that, but I had to say something to shake Estragoth out of his appalling superiority. And it worked, didn't it? I'll wager that Malum has been around to see you."

"He has."

She chuckled. "What did you get? The armclock or the miniature steam engine?"

"The armclock," Jarrod admitted.

The Oligarch shook her head. "Umbrians are so stupid. Don't they realize that Magicians detest machines? Mind you," she added disconcertingly, "I rather fancy young Malum. Why is it, d'you suppose, that large women like me have a weakness for small, slender men?" She looked up from her watered fruit juice and smiled broadly at him.

"I don't think I'm qualified to answer that," Jarrod replied cautiously.

"Really?" Olivderval said pleasantly. "I would have

thought that anyone who had bought a brothel in Belengar would be something of an expert on the subject of women."

Jarrod controlled himself with considerable effort. He sat back in his chair and sipped his drink. After the defeat of the Outworlders he had gone on a triumphal tour of Strand with Ragnor, and when they were in Belengar he had visited the brothel where Samanthina had worked, hoping to find her. She had moved on, but, on impulse, he had provided dowries for all the other girls. He had done it anonymously, however.

"If you know that," he said slowly, "you undoubtedly know that I did it to give the girls their freedom."

"As you did when you bought all those birds in the Exotic Bird Mart and released them."

There was a long moment of silence.

"You are very well informed," Jarrod said finally.

Olivderval smiled. "Information is the lifeblood of a merchant, my dear."

"I thought that I'd been clever," he said sadly. "I did everything through third parties and I paid them well to keep their mouths shut."

"Oh, you did very well for an outsider. The truth cost me far more than I was originally prepared to pay. It wasn't so much your money that did it as fear that if you found out, you'd cast some terrible spell."

"Youthful follies," Jarrod said with a shake of the head and a small smile. "Mind you, I don't regret it and I could well afford it." What he did regret was that he hadn't been able to find Samanthina. At least Olivderval didn't know that.

"No doubt." Olivderval's tone was smooth. "But it wouldn't look too good if it got out now."

"Ah, the arm twisting." Jarrod was back in control of himself again. He knew where she was heading. "A gamble on your part, of course. Disclosure can always work more than one way. Now, what about the bribery?" He raised his eyebrows.

"You're a cool customer, Jarrod. I somewhat underestimated you, though I still think that, if it came down to it, you would protect your reputation. The public doesn't like its heroes buying brothels."

"Oh, I don't know," he countered with a purse of the lips, "it might humanize me, don't you think?" It was his turn to smile.

"You're really very good." Olivderval allowed her eyelids to droop, producing a calculating look. "Nevertheless, you're a sensible man and I know that you see the merits of our position."

"I might if I knew what your position really was."

"Internationally guaranteed access through Songuard and the new Songean territory." Her lips tightened. "Administration and communication will still be enormous problems, but we're rather better at functioning a long way from home than is the rest of the world. The Umbrians will have to abandon Bandor, that goes without saying. That'll bring the Songeans to our side.

"On the other hand, Songuard isn't exactly a law-abiding place. It wouldn't take the mountain tribes long to figure out that there is more profit to be made by raiding Isphardi caravans than by herding their ronoronti. That means that we shall have to provide military escorts and that would mean building fortified guardposts on Songean soil. That in turn would mean friction with the government—if they get themselves a proper government by then."

"And how do you propose to finesse that?" Jarrod was beginning to enjoy himself, but he remained wary.

"The valleys would have to be patrolled by a force composed of Paladinians, Arundelians and Talismanis.

The Songeans will have to provide us with a base at or near Bandor." Olivderval paused and shot him a measuring look. "The cost to be borne by the Umbrians and ourselves."

"And you think that the Umbrians will agree to give up Fort Bandor and pay for your security." He allowed himself to sound skeptical.

"I don't see why they shouldn't," Olivderval replied offhandedly. "After all, we have been paying for their garrison at Bandor for a very long time."

"I see." Jarrod was noncommittal. "And what does the Discipline gain by supporting this plan?"

Olivderval shrugged. "The Discipline has no interest in major territory and this arrangement wouldn't cut into your Tithes."

Jarrod shifted in his chair and sipped his drink. "Not nearly good enough," he pronounced. "Had it not been for the Discipline, there would be no new territory. People have forgotten how close the Outlanders were to victory, but I am sure that your fellow Oligarchs are not unmindful of the effects of peace upon commerce."

"It has fostered competition is what it's done," she rejoined. "You did us no favors by obliterating the enemy. Most of the best and brightest men were engaged in the war; now they are bored and they have turned their skills to making money. Your friend Marianna of Gwyndryth is a case in point. She has invested in ships and is doing a thriving business exporting the produce of her region. She has factors at Seaport and at Belengar."

"She's never said anything about that and neither has her father."

"Of course not. They're an old aristocratic family and commerce is supposed to be beneath them. However," and an admiring note crept into Olivderval's voice, "that young woman has access to a very large amount of capital and she hasn't taken the usual route of buying up the neighboring estates, which is what I suspect Lord Darius would do."

She gave Jarrod a speculative look and followed it with an open smile. "I haven't been able to trace the source of her backing and that, I confess, intrigues me. I thought for a while that the Holdmaster was plundering the Paladinian treasury when Naxania wasn't looking, but there are two major problems with that supposition. The first is that there isn't a moment when Naxania isn't looking and, having made friends with Lord Darius, I cannot believe that he is capable of doing anything that devious." Her slightly hoarse chuckle came again. "It's disconcerting, if somewhat reassuring in a strange way, to come across a completely honorable man. Even fifteen years with Naxania hasn't corrupted him and that's saying a lot."

"This is all very interesting," Jarrod said, "but I don't see what it has to do with the Discipline."

Olivderval's humor vanished. "Do I have to remind you that the Discipline has but one vote and that Isphardel has considerable influence?"

It was Jarrod's turn to smile. "Ah, but you seem to be forgetting that the rulers of Paladine and Arundel are members of the High Council of Magic. You should not underestimate the power of the Archmage. If we were to campaign openly against you, where would you stand? Songuard might vote with you if you promised them the return of Bandor; the Empire will vote against, no matter what you do. Even if you got Talisman's vote, you would still lose by four to three."

"The Discipline has a long history of not intervening in political matters," Olivderval said sharply.

"But as you so aptly pointed out, my dear Oligarch, this is too important a matter for us to sit on our dignity."

"I see." Olivderval gave him a long weighing look. "And what would it take to gain the Discipline's support?"

Jarrod relaxed a little and raised his glass again. Let her wait, he thought as he drank. He let the silence lengthen and then he looked up.

"I think a Concordat between Isphardel and the Discipline would be appropriate," he said. "Mind you, I can only speak for myself. Ragnor is the one who could make that kind of decision and then in consultation with the High Council."

Olivderval sat back and he saw her body relax. She was confident in her abilities to haggle, and it showed in her posture. "I understand, of course, but it might be instructive to find out what you would feel comfortable recommending to the Archmage."

Jarrod pursed his lips as if considering, though he had, in fact, thought about this eventuality. "Isphardel might agree to pay the Tithe in return for the extension of weather control to its territories," he suggested.

Olivderval's muscled tensed, though her hands remained calm and her face showed nothing. "We are talking about a great deal of money," she said, "and about the establishment of Discipline outposts on Isphardi soil."

"And on Songean soil, too," Jarrod agreed. "But I should think that the guarantee of predictable winds for your shipping and an amelioration in your climate would be worth it."

"And in return, we should be assured of your support?"

"And in return, I will undertake that no pressure will be brought to bear on either Naxania or Arabella. They will be encouraged to make their decisions in accordance with their consciences and their national inter-

ests. My own vote will, of course, depend on the will of
the High Council."

Olivderval sat and looked at him. Then she devoted
some attention to her glass.

"I think you're bluffing," she said at last. "Besides,
that's not a decision that I can take on my own. We
both have councils to report to."

"I quite understand," Jarrod said politely. "This is a
difficult and complex matter." He put down his glass
and stood to indicate that the meeting was over.

"Here, take this," Olivderval said, holding out hers.
"I need both arms to get me out of a chair these days."

He obliged and she heaved herself erect. She collected
her cloak, and he escorted her to the door. She turned
at the threshold and looked up at him with an unexpected grin.

"Ragnor's taught you well," she said. "I used to
enjoy jousting with him when I was at Celador. I can't
be sure that the others will approve this Concordat,
but it's a very shrewed strike because it has a spurious
appearance of parity. I can't say that it has been a
pleasure doing business with you, but it's been stimu-
lating."

She turned to leave, thought better of it and turned
back. "Oh, by the way," she said, "I'm having a little
party three days from now and I shall expect you to
attend. My apartments, the nineteenth hour and don't
eat anything that day."

She smiled, reached out and patted his arm in a pro-
prietary way before taking her leave. Jarrod watched
her crab her way carefully down the stairs and surrendered to an intense feeling of relief and satisfaction. It
was no small thing to get the better of Olivderval. Her
jolly, outgoing personality masked one of the best minds
he had ever met. The Concordat had been his own idea
and, though Ragnor had embraced it enthusiastically

during their last meeting, he had doubted that he could sell it to the Isphardis. He still wasn't sure, but the Oligarch's apparent acceptance was a good sign. Well, thirteen years on the Commission had made a diplomat. He had made his mistakes and he had learned. Practice was giving him confidence.

chapter 7

The double walls of Sparsedale lofted grey and grim, defying the summer sunlight. The fortified manor was old, and there was no hint of the new style in its architecture. It was built on an artificial hill, the better to avoid the corrosive power of the now nonexistent Outland atmosphere. A space around the bottom of the hill was enclosed by blind walls with square towers at the corners. There were only two gates in the outer walls, one north, one south, their doors defended against fire by sheets of iron. The flat hilltop was surrounded by the inner walls, and these were pierced by arrow slits. The manor house itself was invisible from beyond the outer gates.

In happier times the demesne fields that lapped against the somber walls would have been a patchwork of greens, grain followed by peas and beans, fallow, then forage. There had been an extensive kitchen garden in the lee of the southern wall with an orchard beyond it. The men from Oxeter had felled the fruit trees and destroyed the garden. The fields had been trampled, first by the raiders and then by the Queen's troops. The besiegers' tents now rose where wheat would have been ripening.

There were three villages dependent on the manor—Upper Waltham, Middle Waltham and Nether Waltham—and in these the officers of the Royal Forces were billeted. Since bed and board were paid for, the more affluent of the freedmen and cottars who had space available were happy to be inconvenienced. All the locals were happy that the lord's boonwork was in abeyance. Indeed, there was an almost festive feeling in the villages. This feeling was, in no little part, due to Darius' strict regulations on dealings with the landsmen.

Upper Waltham boasted the only inn in the area and it was there that the General had established his headquarters. Of all the local folk Elfreg, son of Elgast, was probably the happiest. With the foreign General in residence, there wasn't a hint of trouble, despite the fact that the Stook and Plough had the only supplies of wines and spirits in the region. Ale, of course, was a different matter. That was brewed in almost every household, with varying results, but, if the siege lasted long enough, Elfreg confidently expected to make his fortune. True, he had lost the use of his back bar, taken over by the General as a strategy room, but it was a small price to pay.

The General was, in fact, sitting in that same room, legs thrust forward, hands linked over an incipient paunch, staring morosely at drawings of Sparsedale pinned to the paneling. There were side views of the outer fortifications, but most were of the interior, seen from above. The cloudsteedsmen had proved unexpectedly useful.

Though the drawings did not show as much, the main house, which occupied the central position, was built of stone and slate-roofed. Darius knew from reports gleaned from former servants that it was constructed over a ground-level undercroft, used for storage. A small chapel shared one wall. There were no indications that the Semicount was a Maternite, so Darius supposed that the chapel was dedicated to local deities.

The inner courtyard contained a number of separate buildings. There was a kitchen, a bakehouse, a smokehouse and a privy. The well stood close by the kitchen. The drawings were unrevealing, but the outbuildings were wood-framed with wattle-and-daub walls and thatched roofs. Two gates, one east, one west, gave onto broad stone stairs that descended to the lower courtyard. Given adequate amounts of food and the continued operation of the well, a small force could stand off a much larger one, even if the outer walls had fallen.

The bailey contained a wooden granary against one wall and a stone stable for horses, plough oxen, carts and harnesses. Workrooms for the saddler and the wheelright were against the north wall, together with a mews for hawks with weathering stones for the young birds outside it. There was a second well close to the stairway and a large communal privy in the southwest corner. All in all, a well-set, well-thought-out establishment. There were weaknesses, though. For one thing, the place hadn't been constructed with cloudsteeds in mind. Thatched roofs and timbered walls were easily fired from above. He had not resorted to that yet, but a trip to the privy had become a risky adventure.

He heard a rumbling of voices and his head came up. A moment later there was a rap on the door and Otorin came in.

"Well, welcome back," Darius said, sitting up and drawing his legs in.

Otorin deposited his saddlebag on a chair and grinned at his old chief. "I thought you'd be here so I took the liberty of ordering some ale. I've been riding for seven hours and the roads are damnably dusty."

Elfreg appeared as if summoned by the words, obsequious smile firmly in place. He put down a tray containing two tankards, some bread and a pot of meat paste. He bowed himself out and closed the door quietly.

"Would it be indiscreet to ask where you've been?" Darius asked.

Otorin put his tankard down and wiped his mouth with the back of his hand. "Of course it would be, especially"—he raised his voice—"because we both know that that miserable innkeeper is listening at the door." Then he added in a more normal tone, "What I have to tell you will make it obvious enough."

"Take your time," Darius said, knowing he had no choice.

"Where d'you want to begin, Stronta or Oxeter?"

"Oh, Oxeter by all means. I've had a stream of impractical suggestions from the Queen."

"Her Majesty finds herself deprived of wise counsel in your absence," Otorin said diplomatically, and then spoiled it with a wicked smile. "Oxeter it is, then," he added noting Darius' expression.

"The doughty Duke is lying low; keeps to his chamber most of the time, waiting for word from his son. Your siege would seem to be tighter than he expected."

"No one's got out and we've shot down five bunglebirds to date. They're tricky, but they're slow." Darius' voice rumbled with satisfaction.

"Yes. I don't think they expected cloudsteeds. Your experience at Bandor has come in handy."

"Can I expect more forces coming to raise the siege?" Darius asked.

"I think not," Otorin said judiciously, "at least not yet."

"Then perhaps we should add some fagots to the fire."

"How so?"

"By setting the granary and the other wooden buildings alight."

"And allowing a bunglebird to get through," Otorin added.

"Precisely."

Otorin smiled. "You learn fast, my friend."

Darius raised his tankard. "I have a good teacher."

"In that case, may I suggest an added stratagem?"

"By all means."

"Organize a company to sap the outer walls."

"Is that necessary?" Darius asked.

"Probably not." Otorin was imperturbable. "On the other hand, with the cloudsteedsmen keeping the enemy indoors, there's no danger. A company of experienced sappers would be invaluable to the Crown. Warfare has changed and I suspect that there will be a lot more sieges in the future."

"I take your point," Darius said, allowing admiration to surface. "I'll see to it. Think it'll draw old Paramin?"

"If he's drawable."

"Would you get sufficient warning if he does decide to move?"

Otorin got up and went over to the window before replying. "Probably, but if he does rise, he'll not do it alone. As far as I can tell, he hasn't contacted the southern group, but he's a devious bugger and I can't be sure."

"It sounds as if I should order the cloudsteeds to make regular reconnaissance flights."

"A good idea, but if we're going to keep them this busy, it might be sensible to bring down the second Wing."

"The Queen won't like it," Darius said. "Active duty costs more."

Otorin turned from the window and raised his eyebrows, but said nothing.

"Well," Darius said into the silence, "at least we'll be doing something."

"You are to be commended on your restraint," Otorin said, and Darius was not sure whether he was being ironic. "It isn't like you to sit and do nothing."

"I've been riding around talking to the locals," the General admitted.

"And?"

"The more I see the less I like this Semicount."

"Oh, really?"

Darius sighed and took another drink before replying. "When we first arrived the people around here sang his praises; understandable, of course. We'd ridden to his rescue and it was safer to say what they thought we wanted to hear. There's grumbling now though and what I see are hedges, lots of hedges, and sheep, most of 'em bearing the lord's brand. The common pasture's been enclosed."

"You should get out of Stronta more often," Otorin said, recrossing the room and taking his seat. "It's going on all over. Manors are being strengthened at the expense of the small tenant farmers. Boonwork is being commuted for money, and at a very rapid rate. What used to be the privilege of the freedman is becoming a burden on the cottar."

"Can't say as I like it," Darius remarked. "I'm old-fashioned, I'll admit, but the old customs and the old duties worked well. The lord consumed and controlled, but the villagers ran their own lives, made all the agricultural decisions when it came to their own holdings.

"That's another thing. This Semicount kept meager estate by all accounts, stints on feastdays, provides thin beer, serves oat bread instead of wheat at the Plough Supper." He snorted. "It's no way to treat one's people."

"Peasants always gripe about their lords," Otorin observed mildly.

"Oh, there's more to it than that," Darius replied. "The bailiff's nowhere to be found. It's said that he's in the castle with his master, but I have a feeling that he was murdered. And I can't find anybody who'll admit to being reeve."

"So there's no one to look out for the lord's interests," Otorin said.

"No tallage has been collected; though there have been deaths, no one has paid heriot or gersum. There hasn't been a Hallmoot since Greeningale."

"So Sparsedale hasn't collected any taxes or fines to tide him through the loss of the harvest."

"More to the point, justice hasn't been done," Darius returned. "Once order goes, a small society like this one crumbles." He stopped and cleared his throat. "I'm thinking of presiding at a special Hallmoot."

Otorin smiled. Typical, he thought. "Why not?" he said. "It'll give you something to do instead of sitting around and swilling ale."

"You take altogether too many liberties for a subordinate," Darius growled amiably. "Now that you're back, you might try and make yourself useful. Organizing that team of sappers might be a good place to start."

"That'll teach me to make suggestions," Otorin said wryly. "Seriously though, if you hold this Hallmoot, are you going to collect Tithe and taxes?"

Darius grinned. "Only where absolutely necessary. We depend on the goodwill of the local population. If the Semicount had been an exemplary lord, I might feel differently, but my gut tells me that he's an exploiter. He'll have no complaint about our treatment of his lands, unless it's unavoidable, and I'm having a tally kept of everything we eat that has his brand on it. He'll be paid for that."

"And who's going to pay for his tumbled walls?" Otorin asked teasingly.

"Oh, I should think his freedom ought to be worth something," Darius replied, deadpan.

"And if he doesn't survive, it won't bother him," Otorin added.

"True."

Otorin shook his head and smiled. "You're such a wonderful old relic," he observed. "Sparsedale's petty malfeasances have really riled you, haven't they? They offend the tenets of your class. I have a suspicion that if the manor house was occupied by a contingent of his tenants and cottars, you'd support them."

"Let's not go too far," Darius said. "The social order must be preserved. When you look closely at the way of things, a Holdmaster's tenure is a precarious thing. Rebellion and the resulting anarchy can never be condoned."

Otorin smiled lazily and finished his ale. "Gods but I hope your kind survives," he said lightly. "Honorable, old-fashioned, cleaving to tradition and giving it meaning." He put his tankard down on the tray. "The world's changing, old friend. Enclosure's but the beginning. There will be a mad dash to the new and the best of the old will be forgotten."

"Gloomseeker," Darius said good-naturedly. "The old ways will survive because they're good ways. My daughter runs Gwyndryth as I ran it. Our people would not have it otherwise."

"And your grandson will be a Magician," Otorin said, almost as an aside, as he got to his feet. "I'll take a bath, General, and then I'll get about organizing the sappers."

"You'll dine with me," Darius said sternly. "There's a deal more I need to know about your trip."

"As the General commands," Otorin replied, mocking smile back in place.

chapter 8

During the slow days of high summer, the Hall-moot was held within sight of the walls of Sparsedale. The villagers gathered to pass judgment on their peers. Fines were levied for the brewing of inferior ale; there were two cases of "lying together before the banns," five of slander, six of illegal entry into tenure stemming from the disappearance of some of the cottars. Decisions were arrived at for the harvest, simplified this year by the destruction of a large part of the crop, and for the autumn ploughing. By the end of the sennight a hundred petty details of everyday life were settled.

Otorin watched the proceedings with a nostalgia for an age-old practice that he had never shared. He was a new landholder and an absentee at that, but here, in the center of Paladine, the immemorial ritual unfolded with a solemn civility that pleased him deeply. Darius, as Otorin had expected, presided superbly. His Pallic was serviceable though far from elegant, but his quiet air of authority was undeniable. The villagers themselves increasingly turned to him for decisions despite the fact that he was a foreigner. Darius held firm for the lord in the matter of fees and fines, but over the thorny question of the evening impoundment of livestock he took the other tack.

By long tradition, all livestock were brought back from their daily grazing across fallow belonging to the lord and penned in areas adjacent to the outer walls.

This ensured that demesne lands remained well fertilized. Since the seizure of Sparsedale, the locals had kept their beasts on their own land, claiming, not without reason, that the lord's pounds and sheepcote were no longer safe places. The General concurred, knowing that this year's lean harvest would have to be remedied by a larger than usual winter wheat crop. This, the final judgment of the session, was met with approbation, and the villagers dispersed peaceably to their homes.

Darius was clearly pleased with his own performance. He bantered lazily with his officers at dinner that night. Though there was an air of celebration, Otorin noticed that the General drank very little. His officers, perforce, did likewise. The reason came clear at the end of the meal when he ordered a doubling of the guard and told the men to be on the lookout for a sortie attempt around dawn. After he had dismissed them, he and Otorin returned to the back room of the Stook and Plough for a nightcap.

"You really think they might try to break out?" Otorin asked, feeling slightly put out that Darius hadn't discussed the matter with him beforehand.

"Problem is, I don't know young Barthold, but it's what I'd do. That Hallmoot was a gauntlet thrown down. He must know that he'll get no help from that quarter. Combine that with the firing of his fodder supplies and there's not much choice. He may have supplies in the manor's undercroft, but most of the food for the horses would have been in the outbuildings. Without healthy horses he has no hope of fighting clear and getting away."

"Weren't you taking a bit of a risk holding the court within sight of the walls? Billeted troops are seldom popular, and if there had been a ruckus, it would have given considerable heart to our opponents."

"It was a small risk," Darius said complacently, accepting a glass of sack. "Our men have acted honorably and there is a general craving for order and tradition in the countryside. Mind you, I don't think the Semicount will be all that happy with some of the results."

"I don't see why not," Otorin demurred. "You upheld his suzerainty and preserved at least a portion of his revenues."

"That's as may be. He'll be irked that I let his rights of pasturage and penning lapse. I doubt he'll be able to get them back now that precedent has been broken. Another thing: I don't know if you were there when harvest duties were discussed, but there was no mention of the lord's boonwork."

"If he's halfway intelligent," Otorin remarked, "he'll commute it for money. There are no Farod levies to contend with so there's more than enough labor available."

"It's the principle of the thing," Darius growled.

Otorin smiled.

"Don't you mock me, young man," Darius said. "Wait till you're older and have become attached to your land and the ways of its folk."

"Let's change the subject," Otorin said amiably. "I got word this afternoon from a friend of mine at Oxeter. A messenger galloped out two days ago, heading southwest. I'd post a sharp watch for incoming bunglebirds if I were you."

Darius looked up sharply. "You think the Duke is preparing to move?"

Otorin swirled the amber liquid in his glass thoughtfully. "I'm not sure," he said. "It would be far more in keeping if he got his allies to attempt the relief. On the other hand, I doubt if they will be willing to move to the aid of his son without a greater commitment of troops on his part. In terms of a throw of the bones for a throne, this is a very small gesture. I think we can look for some sort of movement, though from which quarter I cannot be sure."

"The game's afoot then," Darius said with relish. "Damn, but this has been a good day!"

Otorin tightened his lips and a ghost of his smile appeared. "I'm glad you think so."

Darius' smile was broader. "You know me," he said, "I can't stand sitting around doing nothing."

The sortie took place just before dawn, as Darius had predicted. Flight, however, was not the objective. The housing erected to protect the sappers was, and the defenders were able to inflict considerable damage before they were beaten back inside the walls. The besiegers pressed them hard, trying to gain access to the lower court, but were, in turn, repelled. Six of Darius' men were killed, and ten from the manor. The only good thing to occur, from Darius' point of view, was that one of the bodies was found to be wearing a piece of the Duke's livery under his mail. The commanders endured a lacerating tongue-lashing from the General.

The following day, outriders from the cloudsteed squadron patrolling to the south reported a concentration of armed men approaching the market town of Aldersgrove, some twenty leagues to the south of Sparsedale. Estimates of numbers were sketchy, but the bulk of the men were on foot and shouldering pikes. Darius ordered the patrols to limit their range to fifteen leagues with occasional solo reconnaissance flights at maximum altitude. When Otorin found him in the back bar, he was poring over maps.

"What news?" Darius asked without looking up from the table.

"My friend reports that a force of two hundred mounted retainers remains at Oxeter," Otorin reported.

"What about footmen?"

"No footmen."

Darius looked up slowly. "Abercorn has more men than that. Naxania estimated that he had over a thousand retainers. What happened to the rest of them?"

"Well, first of all, I have questions about the accuracy of the Queen's figures, but that aside, I suspect that the rest have either gone to ground in an effort to confuse us, or are on their way south to join the main rebel band."

"Could they have done that without your friend being aware of it?"

"It's possible, though I should not like to think so. It is also possible that they were sent south some months ago to train with the other forces."

"I thought your informants were reliable," Darius said irritably.

"Well, they're not professionals, if that's what you mean," Otorin returned urbanely. "The government of Arundel has no reason to plant spies in the household of a Paladinian nobleman. The people I recruited are motivated by grievance and greed—a fairly reliable combination in my experience. Let us not forget, though, that Duke Paramin has been laying his plans for a very long time and that he is a very rich man. There is no law that says that a man's declared retainers have to be kept on his own estates."

"What I have to know to be able to formulate a strategy," Darius said with studied resonableness, "is if I must detach forces to protect against an attack from the south, or if I have to defend my back from Abercorn."

"If I were a wagering man, I would bet on the south."

"So would I, but I can't just lift the siege and march away."

"No, but you can appear to do it." Otorin drew up a chair and looked at the maps. "Bring down three hundred men from the garrison at Gapguard," he advised. "Keep them hidden in the woods north of Upper Waltham, assemble your men with panoply and march them away. If you're lucky, Bardolph will be tempted out and then your new rear guard can fall on him."

Darius nodded. "I'll send a cloudsteed to Gapguard with the orders. I think you should stay here and take charge of this end of the operation. That'll allow you to keep your lines of communication to Oxeter open. I'll leave you two squadrons of cloudsteeds."

"I rather doubt that Queen Arabella would approve of that," Otorin said.

Darius produced a rather wolfish grin. "I have no intention of telling her. Have you? Besides, for all your theoretical knowledge, you've never actually had a field command, have you?"

"You are an exploitive, old bastard, you know that?"

"Yes, I do," Darius said comfortably.

"I wish to go on record as officially protesting this high-handed action on the part of the General of the Paladinian Forces," Otorin said formally, and then smiled.

"Your protest is noted and overruled," Darius replied.

"In that case, I have no recourse but to accept. Now, I think you should leave the sappers here and you'll need a token force in front of both gates or he'll become suspicious."

"Stop trying to teach your grandmother how to candle eggs," Darius replied with high good humor. "The orders have already been given."

"You were that sure of me, were you?"

"Yes, I was," Darius replied smugly.

"I'm losing my touch," Otorin said in a mock grumble. "Have you picked a spot for the battle?"

Darius stabbed a finger at the main map. "They

probably crossed the Salvant at Astly Bridge. From the description of their arrival at Aldersgrove, they must have spread out to forage. Not too much coordination between the commanders, I suspect, and scant discipline among the men."

"The Duke's men are well trained, I'll vouch for that," Otorin commented.

"Same informant who missed their departure?" Darius asked.

Otorin shrugged. "Try to remember that I have to depend on Paladinians." The two Arundelians exchanged a smile. "So, when do you expect to engage them?"

"Can't tell. I'll want them to move north of Aldersgrove. There's a range of hills running south-southeast." His finger traced a line on the parchment. "If I could coax them out onto the plain with my troops waiting behind the hills, I could attack them from the flank." The finger flicked across the map.

"Nice plan," Otorin said approvingly. "Seems to me that I saw something like it in Umbria."

"Bite your tongue," Darius replied. "That engagement was a disaster."

"It's always best to learn from other people's mistakes," Otorin said sardonically.

A sennight later, Darius marched south, banners flying. Otorin watched them go. He had great faith in Darius' capabilities; he'd seen them put to the test outside Angorn, but that had been eighteen years ago. Other than the recapture of Fort Bandor, an altogether different kind of operation, and a couple of skirmishes early in Naxania's reign, he'd had no battle experience since. Skills, like suits of armor, rusted when they were not used. Otorin was fond of the General, more fond than he would readily admit, and Darius was no longer young. It worried him. He turned his horse and headed back toward Upper Waltham.

Now that he was on his own again, Otorin allowed his natural pessimism to surface. Not that he thought of it as pessimism; being realistic was a phrase more to his liking. It was true, however, that he normally expected the worst. If it happened, he was ready for it. If it didn't, he was grateful. In this present pass, he gave Darius no better than an even chance of winning. The recapture of Sparsedale, at this point, would be relatively simple, but the real fight would be won, or lost, by Darius. In either case, he himself would soon be free to continue his real calling.

He tossed his reins to a groom and strode into the inn. Darius had thought that he was doing him a favor by leaving him behind and putting him in charge of the siege. The man had, with his usual shrewdness, acknowledged the uses of information, a trait not commonly found in generals. The problem was that Darius had only been thinking of the present situation. Back in Stronta messages would be accumulating, always dangerous, and going unanswered, which was worse. Stronta, for the moment, was the center and he was away from it. Otorin of Lissen was a worried man.

chapter 9

The Paladinian capital basked somnolently in the summer sun. There was little sign of crisis, though the barracks wore a hollow air. Cats prowled languidly and dogs lay panting in the shade of buildings. The Court continued, cool behind the thickness of the ancient walls, but most of the courtiers, following a tradition that had grown up since the war and doubtless spurred by the political uncertainty, had returned to their estates and would remain there through the harvest. Sheep and kina now grazed the land between the Great Maze and the Upper Causeway. The Outpost drowsed peaceably.

Most of the members of the Commission for the Outland had returned home, pending developments, but the Elector of Estragoth, using his advanced age as an excuse, had remained at Stronta. Malum of Quern, his chief deputy, had returned home for a visit, but was expected back any day. There were Isphardi traders to be seen, as usual, but, commerce apart, the Umbrians were the only foreign presence in the city. It was a situation that pleased Estragoth.

He had been surprised and somewhat flattered when Varodias had chosen him as the Empire's representative to the Commission. The partition of the Outland was a major concern, and that took the sting out of the involuntary exile that went with the post. It was, he thought, a fitting conclusion to his service to the Crown.

He had helped to steer the Empire's course for more than forty years, always trying to look to the future with eyes unblinkered by factionalism. The partition was the future and the signing of the treaty would allow him to retire on a triumphant note. He had never dreamed that it would take this long. The wretched Isphardis . . .

He shifted in his padded chair and winced as the gout that plagued his joints twinged. He had been less happy when the Emperor had charged him with the task of developing a network of informers in the Magical Kingdoms. He had had his sources in Umbria, no politician could survive without them, but he had never considered himself a spymaster. Now he was and he had come to enjoy it.

The Paladinian landowners had but a rudimentary feel for intrigue, though their Queen saw plots everywhere. Even the Duke of Oxeter, by far the craftiest of his clients, had handled this uprising clumsily. It was doubtful now that the Umbrian treasury would recover its investment. Still, he had relished his dealings with Paramin and the entrée they had provided to the other disaffected nobles. He had a good grasp of what was going on in Paladine and a fair understanding of Arundel.

His major weakness, ironically, was that he no longer knew, with any certainty, what was going on back home. He was too old, he reflected, to protect his own interests at Angorn when he was out of the Emperor's sight. Varodias' support had always been his best defense, but the Emperor was notoriously fickle. The Emperor's constant suspicions of foreign intrigue were his safeguard, and he had taken pains to see that Varodias was kept well informed. It had cost a great deal of money, some of it his own, to obtain the information, and he wasn't entirely convinced of the veracity of some of it.

His instincts, so well honed at home, were unanchored here.

There was a rapping at the door and the head of his bodyservant appeared around it.

"The Lord Malum craves admittance, sir."

"Show him in and fetch us wine," the Elector commanded.

Malum, when he entered, was attired in fresh clothes, but his wet hair attested to the fact that he had changed quickly and had come directly to report to his master. The Elector sat up with difficulty.

"Come in, come in: fetch up a chair. I've ordered wine. When did you get in?"

"Barely an hour ago, my lord," Malum replied, smoothing down the sides of his head self-consciously.

"And how did you find Quern after two years of absence?"

"Better than I had feared and not quite as prosperous as I had hoped."

"Good seneschals are hard to find," Estragoth commiserated.

Conversation was suspended as the servant brought the wine in and poured it. Once the man had withdrawn the Elector said, "I know that you will present a written report, but I'd like to hear how things are at home in your own words. Don't worry if you digress, you never know what will turn out to be important."

Malum permitted himself a smile. "It's amazing how time spent abroad alters one's perspective," he said. "The comfort of rediscovered familiarity is overwhelming, but certain things show themselves in a new light."

"Go on," Estragoth said.

"Well, the trip back along the Causeway was uneventful, but it's getting more expensive to cross borders. It cost us three imperials to get into Songuard and twelve to get out again. Angorn itself was unchanged, quieter than usual because it's summer, but I was surprised by my reaction to the place. As you know, I came late to the capital, but when I went back this time I felt as if I was going home." Malum's face was softened by reminiscence.

"I'm sure that it was all very touching," Estragoth said dryly, "but how were things at Court? How was the Emperor?"

Malum collected himself. "The Emperor," he said briskly, "was well—as far as I could judge. I saw him at a distance at a morning robing."

"You did not have a personal audience?" Estragoth was sharp.

"No, sir. I requested one and explained that I had a message, a personal message, from you. I was told to make a report to the Chamberlain. I did so, but I took the liberty of omitting those parts that I deemed for the Emperor's eyes only. That part of the message I put in a letter and paid a gentleman-of-the-bedchamber to deliver it into His Majesty's hand."

"I see," the Elector said wearily. "And do you really think that it got to the Emperor unopened?"

"As a matter of fact I do," Malum replied complacently. "The transaction took place at the robing and I saw the packet delivered."

Estragoth smiled. "I underestimated you, young man. You are to be complimented. Nevertheless, it disturbs me that Varodias would not grant you an audience."

"I don't think that His Majesty was aware of my request. I believe that it was denied at a lower level. The Court seemed to be on edge. I mean more than usually so. There have been a number of, ah, differences of opinion between landowners. The Electors tend to side with their vassals and that has increased the friction between the Electorates."

Estragoth produced a paper-thin chuckle.

"Ondor and Beltran are virtually at war," Malum continued. "The Elector of Rodenlac has annexed estates belonging to Adelfras of Hodial; even the Church has not been immune from depredation. No one touches the Imperial holdings, but that, it seemed to me, had more to do with the strength of the Imperial Forces and the number of members of the major families who are His Majesty's 'guests' at Angorn than to any great reverence for the Crown."

"You paint a disturbing picture," the Elector remarked, and sipped cautiously at his wine.

"It gets worse," Malum said tersely. "From Angorn I headed south for Estragoth. People travel in armed groups these days. Bands of sturdy beggars are a constant threat. In fact, we came under attack nine times between Angorn and Estragoth."

"And does the Emperor do nothing about this lawlessness?" the Elector asked.

"Oh, aye," Malum said with bitter amusement. "He hires out soldiers to provide the escort."

The Elector shook his head and clicked his tongue in disapproval. "Surely the roads in Estragoth itself were safe?" he said.

"They were. Mind you, with the tolls your son is charging, they damned well ought to be." Malum knew the remark was impertinent, but it was an accurate reflexion of the outrage his traveling companions had felt.

The Elector sat up and winced anew. "Tolls?"

"Six vards per person every ten leagues," Malum said dryly, "with men-at-arms doing the collecting."

The Elector leaned back again, his mouth drawn down in displeasure. "Did you tell them that you were bearing messages from me?"

"Indeed I did. I even showed them your seal. They were most polite, but quite insistent."

Estragoth's brow furrowed and a flush appeared on

his cheeks. Malum, knowing the signs, hurried on. "The Margrave refunded my money as soon as I reached the castle."

"And how were things at home?" The question came out in a low growl.

"Your son, the Margrave, keeps proper estate. His wife is charming and the children are noisy and healthy. The Electorate seemed peaceful and it looks as if the harvest will be good this year. I was told that the coal trade was progressing smoothly, though profits are down because of the need to protect shipments." He paused and drank some wine. "Manufacturing is not doing so well because of disruptions in the supplies of raw materials from the other Electorates. This has caused some unrest in the towns, but not as much, I was told, as elsewhere in Umbria." He stopped again to see how the old man was taking his recital. The lined face was impassive once more.

"I wonder if I might have some more wine?" he asked. "Talking is thirsty business."

Estragoth gestured to the tray and Malum got to his feet. He took the opportunity to extract an oilskin-covered package from his belt pouch. It was closed with the seal of House Estragoth. "These are letters from your family," he said, laying it on the Elector's lap. "I'm sure that they will give you a much better picture of things than I can." He stooped and poured himself another glass of wine.

The Elector turned the package over a couple of times and then set it aside. "You did not mention Coppin," he said. "As I recall, my youngest was a friend of yours. You must have seen him at Angorn."

"No," Malum replied, taking his seat again, "but I saw him at Estragoth. There is a letter from him among the others."

"Not at Angorn?" The question came out on a rising note.

"No, my lord. He had returned home to attend a wedding." It was a partial truth. The wedding had taken place a month earlier and Coppin had stayed on for the hunting.

Estragoth relaxed. "It is never wise for a House to be unrepresented at Angorn," he remarked, "but family obligations must be honored." He nodded to himself. "How long were you at Estragoth?" he asked.

"A little over a sennight," Malum replied. He smiled. "I should have liked to stay longer. Your family was most hospitable and I got to do some hunting with Coppin, but it is a long way from Estragoth to Quern."

"And is the South as turbulent as the rest of the Empire?"

"Not really, but I think that's because it is basically agricultural. Most of the unrest seems to be in the towns. Although, even in my county, there has been some, er, consolidation of estates."

"Why all the trouble in the urban areas?" the Elector asked.

"It's the subject of considerable debate. Prices have gone up and wages have stayed low. There are more able-bodied men available for work since the war ended and now there are a lot of fifteen-year-olds starting to look for employment. Taxes are high, housing's becoming scarce, the last two harvests were bad and the price of bread is high." Malum shrugged. "Some say that the nation's sense of purpose has gone." He paused and sipped his wine. "And then there's Simlan the Hermit."

Estragoth waited a couple of beats. "And who is he?"

"He's an intinerant preacher," Malum replied. "I'm told he comes from Clovermede in the Electorate of Pathan. At first he wandered around the countryside preaching against the Church of the Mother. He considers the church too rich and too closely allied with the aristocracy. He contends that they do nothing for the poor. He attracted considerable crowds.

"He was arrested and brought to trial for sedition, but there was no proof that he had spoken against the Emperor." Malum produced a wintry smile. "There is, apparently no law against inciting peasants to seize church lands. So they let him go and he shifted his focus to the plight of the workers. He has a lot of people very upset."

"All in all, not a very reassuring prospect," Estragoth said gloomily. "It makes our job more vital still. If we had the Outland to settle, there would be ample land for all. It would give the Empire a new sense of purpose, a new challenge."

"Any news on that front, sir?" Malum asked.

"Alas no. Sarad and that witch Olivderval have gone home to consult their governments, Courtak is away again on some strange mission, Naxania is preoccupied with a rising of disaffected nobles, Otorin of Lissen is off trying to put down the rebellion. Only Forodan of Songuard is still here and he's busy playing the gentleman. It will be at least another month before the Commission reassembles."

The old man sighed and finished his wine. He looked across at Malum. "There are days when I doubt that I shall live to see the work completed. The infernal Isphardis undermine everything I do."

"There are ways of taking Olivderval out of play," Malum said quietly. "There is a price for everything in Belengar, even the life of an Oligarch."

Estragoth gave a wintry little smile. "I doubt if it would do any good. She speaks for the rest of them and a couple of the other Oligarchs would be even harder to deal with." He shook his head absently.

"Pay me no mind. It's late and I'm tired. Do you go

and get yourself something to eat. I'll stay up a while longer and read these." He reached out and touched the packet lightly.

Malum rose and took his leave. Surely, he thought as he made his way back to his room, there must be a way to get the treaty signed. They had worked too long and too hard to be cheated at this point. If it couldn't be achieved by fair means, then perhaps by foul. Nothing to be done about it for the moment, though. He'd get caught up tomorrow on what had been going on in Paladine while he had been away. This rebellion sounded interesting.

chapter 10

The Outland was much on the mind of Jarrod Courtak. The work on clearing the rubble of the Giants' Causeway was proceeding almost too well, thanks to the reappearance of the unicorn. The Magicians and cloudsteedsmen had been seconded and had evolved a smooth routine. Best of all, Nastrus wasn't bored as yet. Jarrod had no illusions about the unicorn's staying power. He would work hard until the novelty wore off, but, after that, he was liable to disappear on an unannounced holiday again. He would stay at it until they reached Celador, of that Jarrod was certain. He had promised Nastrus that he could demonstrate his prowess in front of the Queen, the Archmage and all the notables. He smiled to himself. After all these years he knew just how to appeal to the unicorn's vanity.

He himself was already at Celador, preparing for the display. It was here in the Arundelian capital that the Discipline's new service to the people of Strand would be officially unveiled. He had cleared the date with the Chamberlain, made arrangements with Dean Handrom for a new roster of Magicians to be trained in the art of cooperative levitation, and now it was time to pay his respects to the Archmage. He mounted the familiar stairs of the Archmage's Tower with trepidation. In the old days the feeling had been caused by fear; now it was caused by concern.

He was fond of the old Magician. He had come to

appreciate him during the tour of Strand that the two of them had made after the defeat of the Outlanders. The warmth that was usually concealed behind a scathing volley of words had come to the fore. The Archmage had seen to it that Jarrod's head had not been turned by the adulation that had surrounded them during that first euphoric year of peace and, in retrospect, Jarrod was grateful. No, he wasn't afraid of Ragnor's justly famous tongue. He was afraid that infirmity had dulled the sharp mind. There had been no sign of it a month ago, but, at his age, one never knew.

He followed the Duty Boy into the room and saw that Ragnor was seated in his favorite chair by the fireplace. Despite the warmth of the day, there was a lap robe over his knees. A pair of spectacles was perched on the beaky nose. A long, thin hand rose and a forefinger beckoned. Jarrod walked forward.

"I'd get up and hug you if I could," the reedy voice said, "but my rheumatics are bad today."

Jarrod smiled, advanced and embraced the old man. "How are you, sir?" he asked as he straightened up.

"The better for seeing you. Now, go and get yourself a chair and pour us both a cup of sack. I told the monster that I was entertaining important company today and it would look bad if I couldn't offer some decent refreshment." He chuckled creakily. "I have problems walking of late," he continued. "If it isn't my hips it's my knees, but there's nothing wrong with my wits or my digestion, the gods be thanked." He took the cup that Jarrod was holding out and drank deeply.

"Ah, that's better. That overprotective charlatan will kill me with her ministrations."

"She's undoubtedly thinking of your health," Jarrod said reasonably.

"Arrant insubordination!" Ragnor snapped, and Jarrod knew that his fears were groundless. The old man hadn't changed.

"So," the Archmage said with a complicitous smile, "you're here for the grand demonstration that will restore the luster of the Discipline, are you?" He drank again. "I never cease to be surprised at how short the memories of the Untalented are. It wasn't that long ago that we pulled off the impossible, you and I, and yet they tell me that the Discipline is in danger of being considered irrelevant."

"Well, it was fifteen years ago," Jarrod reminded him.

"That long? It seems five years at the most to me."

"It's not that we're irrelevant," Jarrod explained, saddened at the need to do so, "it's just that we are taken for granted these days. People expect the seasons to be regulated and the crop rain to fall at the appointed hour. The local Magicians who keep the mill wheels and the looms going when the wind is low tend to be thought of as workers rather than miracle workers. It's bad for morale."

"It's also bad for our influence in international affairs," Ragnor said shrewdly. "I assume that's why you and Greylock chose the Outland as the setting for this experiment."

Jarrod smiled. "It had crossed our minds." Had the old man forgotten their previous conversation? They had been over this ground on the last visit.

"Bad business this, ah, disagreement over the Outland." The old man sniffed and finished off his sack. He held his cup out for a refill. "It could undo everything we have tried to achieve in the way of relations between governments, although I do like this idea of a Concordat with Isphardel. What I don't like is the way Varodias is stirring the pot."

"The Emperor?" Jarrod said as he returned to his seat, trying not to sound relieved.

"Of course the Emperor," Ragnor said impatiently.

"Things are going badly in Umbria—there's a deal of civil unrest and the Electors are becoming increasingly independent of the Crown. Varodias is losing control and he's desperate for a way to reunite the country, or at least to reassert his own authority. What better way than to point the finger at the perfidious foreigner out to rob the Empire of its rightful due?"

"That wasn't the impression I got from Estragoth," Jarrod objected, marveling anew at the extent of the Archmage's knowledge.

"Course it wasn't. I'll wager he didn't tell you that he was setting up an intelligence system either, but he is. The Elector is a wily old fox and he's devoted to Varodias." He looked up and caught the look of surprise on Jarrod's face. Misinterpreting it, he added, "I don't just sit here dreaming, son. I've spent fifty years developing a network of informants in the Empire. People think of me as a doddering, old Magician." He raised a spotted hand. "Oh, don't bother to deny it. What they forget is that I ran this country for nigh on twenty years and I've kept my hand in ever since."

"If Varodias is looking for an excuse to damn all foreigners, won't the Concordat play into his hands?" Jarrod asked.

"Certainly. But the extension of our influence eastward is the best thing that could happen for us. Do us a lot more good in the long run than this rubble-clearing effort of yours. What you don't seem to understand is that if you give Varodias what he wants, all you're doing is forcing him to pick another fight."

"Are you saying that another war is inevitable?" Jarrod asked, unwilling to hear Holdmaster Gwyndryth's opinion confirmed.

Ragnor sipped on his sack and then pursed his lips as if to consider the question. "Nooo. We could have the bastard assassinated. He's killed off the only sons he had that showed a scrap of talent. The remaining boy is a weakling. The ensuing struggle for the throne would probably occupy the country for a good twenty years. It would, at the very least, provide a breathing space."

"But Varodias is a duly consecrated monarch," Jarrod said, eyes widening.

"Spare me," Ragnor said witheringly. "You sound like a Maternite. You can't be that naive. Consecration, as you call it, usually comes from blood on a sword."

Jarrod took a deep breath. "If the Concordat is ratified, we become one of his prime targets."

"Of course," the Archmage agreed, "but then we always have been. They loathe the Isphardis, but Umbrians think that we are unnatural. Magic violates the rules of what they consider to be science, and the Maternite Church considers us anathema. Without the mortar of a common enemy, conflict is bound to occur. Songuard and Isphardel are a natural buffer between us, and it would be the ultimate folly to allow the Empire to absorb them."

"I can't say that I care for your analysis, Archmage, but I can't fault it," Jarrod said placatingly, wondering as he did if Ragnor had wandered off the beam again.

"I shan't live to see it, the gods be thanked, but we shall have to face the Empire one of these days. Perhaps our presence in the east will delay it."

"Well, that's still up in the air," Jarrod said. "The Oligarchs haven't agreed and the new terms of the treaty haven't been voted on."

"Olivderval speaks for the Oligarchs," Ragnor said decisively. "As far as the treaty is concerned, Arundel and Talisman will follow our lead. It really doesn't matter which way Naxania decides to go, though it would be nice if the Magical Kingdoms could present a united front. It might be an additional deterrent."

"Do I construe that as an order?" Jarrod asked with as much lightness as he could muster.

"Oh, I think you might," Ragnor replied, matching him, and in that instant Jarrod knew that not only was the Archmage in control of all his faculties, but that he was aware of Jarrod's doubts. "Now let's discuss this demonstration," the old man continued. "I think it's important that Greylock play the leading role. It will enhance his reputation and he'll need that to assure his succession. I hate to say this, but he's been too quiet too long."

"Of course he'll play the leading role. After all, the whole thing was his idea," Jarrod said mendaciously. "That's what he's here for."

"Good. Exactly how do you, ah, does he intend to carry out the ceremony?"

Ragnor sat back and listened, sipping absently, while Jarrod laid out the details. When he had finished, the Archmage pushed his spectacles higher on his nose and said, "I'll have myself carried up to the Causeway in a sedan chair." He grinned, showing the few remaining teeth. "It's not as much work for them as it used to be; still, it'll make a nice change and I'll be able to wear something fancy." He looked over at Jarrod and his eyes twinkled behind the circles of glass.

"I don't suppose you brought anything decent to wear? No, I thought not. That plain blue gown has become quite an affectation with you. Never mind, it'll be quite like old times. You, me, the Gwyndryth girl and a unicorn."

"Marianna?" Jarrod said, surprised. "Is she at Celador?"

"Yes indeed. Came to see that boy of hers. Dropped by to pay her respects. She's grown into a deucedly handsome woman. You should have married her when you had the chance." He finished his wine and put the cup down. He settled himself and the head began to droop. "Odd that she should have produced a Magician," he said, the voice soft and muffled, "but you never know about that sort of thing. Errathuel's blood turns up in the unlikeliest places. . . ." The voice faded away and the chin sagged.

Jarrod got up quietly and put his chair back against the wall. He returned his cup to the sideboard and then went and removed the Archmage's spectacles and put them on the table beside him. As he went back down the stairs he was pleased with the thought that Marianna was visiting the capital. It had been five years, he realized, since he had seen her last. Ragnor was right, it was somehow fitting that they all be together for this occasion. He would have to see to it that she got a good seat.

He saw her at Hall that same night, as he had half expected to. Ragnor's eye for a pretty face was still undimmed. She was a beautiful woman. Slim still, though a mite less so than the portrait that memory held. The red-gold hair rippled past her shoulders. She wore a dark green gown, cut square across the bust. A very large emerald hung on a thick gold chain, emerald teardrops peeked out from under the hair and her waist was girdled by a hammered-gold belt that was studded with jewels. Jarrod was shy about wearing any of the things that he had brought back from the Island at the Center, but Marianna obviously had no such inhibitions. He waved to her and she smiled back.

They were both in the withdrawing room after the meal, where Arabella, Queen since her marriage, received the important guests, but again they could not talk, at least not right away. Greylock and Jarrod got the first ten minutes of the Queen's conversation. Though this was ritual, a ritual that she had repeated endlessly since she was thirteen, Arabella had the knack of making people feel that she was genuinely pleased to see them and valued the opportunity of hearing their opinion on whatever topic she chose to bring up. As a member of the High Council of Magic, she had no shortage of interests in common with the two Mages. That she also managed to make them laugh was a tribute to her skill. She then passed them smoothly on to her Consort.

Saxton Horbinger was tall for an Untalented, coming up to Jarrod's shoulder. He was broad-chested, narrow-waisted and had enviable calf muscles. Jarrod surmised that it was for that reason that long, white hose had become the fashion at Court. He was fair-haired like his wife, had well-set hazel eyes, a straight nose flanked by high cheekbones. The chin was firm and dimpled and the lips were a little too large for perfection, lending the face a sensual air. It was obvious to the people who saw him in person, or his likeness on broadsheets, why Arabella, after resisting the Council's prodding to produce an heir and secure the succession for so long, had chosen him. The people approved.

Saxton Horbinger was also Holdmaster of Thorp, with lands adjacent to the royal estates. He had fought in the battle against the invading Outlanders and, in the five years he had been married to Arabella, had fathered three sons. Jarrod had met him once before, at the wedding, and had dismissed him as an amiable lummox picked for his looks. He had heard since that Arabella discussed matters of state with him and that he had considerable influence with her. He made the required bow and prepared to observe. The Consort's opening remark to Greylock surprised him.

"It is good to see you again, my Lord Mage. It has been too long, for friendship's sake, of course, but also for you. Celador is the center of the Discipline and the next Archmage should not be such a stranger."

"Your Royal Highness does me too much honor," Greylock replied, the deep voice making the intonations of the formal mode sing. "I am but a Mage among others and Ragnor is far from ready to go."

Prince Saxton—the title had been conferred upon him when he married—smiled. It was an open, friendly smile. "Were I a wagering man, I should put my money on you," he said. "I still think that it is an excellent thing that you have honored Celador with this demonstration of the Discipline's prowess." He turned to Jarrod. "Will you be assisting the Mage of Paladine, Excellence?"

"Indeed, Your Royal Highness," Jarrod replied, "though I shall be doing nothing more than coordinating the efforts of the other Magicians."

The Consort's smile grew broader, and there was a disconcerting glint in the eyes. "Power cloaked in humility is an extremely effective combination, would you not agree?" He addressed the remark to Greylock.

"Only the naked truth is stronger, sir," Greylock responded. Their eyes held for a beat, and then the Consort turned again to Jarrod.

"We thank you for your last naming gift, Excellence," he said. "Young Harrald played with it for nigh on a month which, for a baby, even a royal baby, is a remarkable span."

Jarrod began to mumble something, but noticed that the Consort's eyes had slipped past him to the people in line behind. He bowed instead and Greylock and he moved on.

"What do you think of the Prince Consort?" he asked once they were clear.

"I think the Queen made a remarkably shrewd

choice," Greylock replied. "And now that we've done our duty, I intend to retire. Are you going to stay?"

."I'd like to have a word with Marianna," Jarrod said. "It's been a while since I've seen her."

"Very well, but try not to stay up too late. The demonstration's only two days off and I need you to be fresh. You heard what the Prince said. I'm going to have to prove myself and you and I know that I can't do it without you." Greylock's tone was soft, but urgent.

"The operation's been going very smoothly for three sennights," Jarrod said reassuringly. "They could do the whole thing without us."

"Don't take things for granted," Greylock retorted. "Mind me. Don't stay up talking till all hours."

"Yes, sir," Jarrod said, knowing that acquiescence was the best strategy.

"Good night then," Greylock said and headed for the door.

"Good night, sir," Jarrod called after him and swung around to find Marianna.

chapter 11

half a world away, Marianna's father had killing on his mind. He was camped some ten leagues north of Aldersgrove behind a line of hills that formed the western boundary of the broad plain that ended at the River Arduent. His scouts had told him that the rebel forces had provisioned themselves for a march by stripping the town and the surrounding countryside. Their departure, Darius thought, would probably be hastened by the animosity engendered by their depredations. So much the better. He checked the map for the umpteenth time.

They would have to take the road on the far side of the hills. It was the only thing that made sense, and, since they were counting on surprise themselves, they would not be looking for an enemy this far south of Sparsedale. If they continued to dally at Aldersgrove, he was prepared to confront them with a small force and draw the rebels north until the rest of his men could fall on them, but he hoped it would not come to that. He would inevitably lose men during the withdrawal and he would avoid that if he could. Getting old and sentimental, he thought as he rolled the map up.

To the best of his information, the enemy had mustered about fifteen hundred troops, most of them foot soldiers armed with pikes. The majority, according to reports, ill-disciplined, though there was a core of well-trained men. Probably the men missing from the Duke of Abercorn's estate at Oxeter. There was a well-equipped unit of cavalry consisting of about two hundred seasoned men with the addition of a rowdy group of young nobles that included both Rostan and Southey. It was a considerable force for these days, almost twice his own numbers.

The toughest problem would be the Duke's men, even though they were but a fraction of the total. If he was any judge of character, the two young Earls would insist on giving the orders, and they were more accustomed to the jousting field than the battlefield. It was also a good bet that they would be in the van during the ride north. If the gods were with him, they would lead a relatively small scouting party more intent on picking a pleasant campsite than in looking for enemies in the hills. If that was the case, he could let them pass by. He sighed and heaved himself out of his chair. He began to pace across the tent. At this point it was all a matter of guesswork. There was ample water and firewood in this place and plenty of grazing for the horses, but the food would start to run short in about a sennight.

"With the General's permission."

The Adjutant's gruff voice broke Darius' train of thought and stopped him in midstride.

"Enter."

The tent flap opened and the Adjutant ducked in, followed by a short, bowlegged man with dust-streaked clothing and face.

"Your pardon, General, but this man claims to have ridden up from Aldersgrove. He insists that he speak directly to you."

"Indeed? Have you searched him?"

"We have, sir. He was carrying a shortsword and a dagger. There is nothing concealed about his person."

"Very well, you may leave us."

The Adjutant saluted, spun on his heel and exited. Darius looked the man over.

"Sit down," he said, indicating a stool. "I imagine that you'd find talking easier after you've washed your throat with ale."

"That I would, General, and I thankee kindly." The man's Southern burr made his Common sound remarkably pleasant.

Darius filled a cup from a leather jug and handed it to him, then got himself into a chair and watched the ale disappear.

"Now," he said when the man was done, "what's your name and how did you know how to find us?"

"Name's Jehan Attemill, lately in the service of the Earl of Rostan, General sir. I received a message ten days gone from Lord Lissen to report to you as soon as I knew when the march on Sparsedale would start."

Darius concealed his surprise. Otorin had taken a damnable chance. "And did Lord Lissen tell you where to find me?" he asked quietly.

Something in his voice made the man look up. "Not he, General. I rode north and cut into the hills at a venture, since that's where I'd be if I was you."

Darius relaxed slightly. "Let us devoutly hope that our enemies do not think the same," he said dryly.

"Not much of a chance of that. They all think you're at Sparsedale."

"I'm happy to hear that. When do they intend to start?"

"Tomorrow firstlight. They reckon to do five leagues a day. I think they'll be lucky to do three." His opinion of the opposition was writ clear on his face.

"So we've two days by their count, three by yours. How far ahead will the advance party range?"

"Not going to be an advanced party, at least not yet awhiles. Mounted will be in the van, foot in the middle and baggage train in the rear. There's plenty of ponds and little lakes hereabouts, so picking a campsite's no problem."

"I see. Well, I thank you Jehan Attemill. I shall probably want to talk to you again, but for now you can go and have a wash and get something to eat."

Attemill got up stiffly and bowed his head in salute.

"Oh, one more thing," Darius said. "Won't the Earl of Rostan miss you?"

The little man's dirty face cracked into a grin that revealed missing teeth. "The Earl," he said contemptuously, "is only interested in his honor, young girls, wine and cards. He doesn't notice the likes of me."

"Surely someone will notice."

"The Master of Horse, like as not, since I've a good reputation as a groom, but I reckon he'll think I've finally gone off and got soused like the rest of them. I stole the horse from the Earl of Southey's lines, so I doubt they'll put two and two together."

"You've done well," Darius said, nodding his approbation, "and if you need employment after this is over, I'll find a place for you in my household."

"Thankee kindly, General sir, but unless I miss my mark, Lord Lissen will have work for me to do." He smiled his gappy smile. "A good groom's welcome most places and no questions asked." He did his quick little bow again and pushed his way out through the flap.

A feeling of calmness came over Darius. The thing was begun. In two or three days it would be decided, one way or another. He got up and poured himself a cup of ale. How long, he wondered, had Attemill been working for Otorin? And for how long had he been planted in Rostan's household? No matter; he was grateful for the man's intelligence, but it would be foolish to place too much reliance on it. He went over to the desk and made a list of orders for the Adjutant.

Metal to be muffled by rags, silence to be observed by the men, fires doused, lookouts to be posted and the cloudsteeds to be grounded until further orders. He made sure that they were carried out by touring the encampment and the sentry posts at regular intervals. If the men grumbled, they did not do so in his hearing, and his caution was rewarded on the morning of the second day when a cloud of dust was spotted to the south.

He scrambled up the slope and lay in a brake of hawberry bushes. He was annoyed to find that he was panting. He waited until his breathing was steady and then deployed the spyglass that Phalastra of Estragoth had given him back in the days when he was the Lord Observer. He adjusted the eyepiece and a troop of horse wavered into focus. Most of the riders were soberly dressed in brown and green, but conspicuous among them was a handful of knights in bright costume. None were wearing armor. Menassah, his Adjutant, slithered up beside him and Darius passed him the glass.

"What do you make of it?" he hissed as if the horsemen might hear him.

"Couple of hundred, I reckon. Too big for a scouting party. Can't be sure because of the dust, but it don't look like there's troops behind them."

Darius grunted and took the spyglass back. He readjusted the eyepiece. He chuckled suddenly. "By the gods, the stupid bastards got tired of riding at a pikeman's pace. We have 'em, Menassah, we have 'em."

"Fall on them as they pass?" the Adjutant asked, an anticipatory smile creasing the weathered face.

"No, we'll let them go by," Darius said with evident satisfaction and began to wriggle backward.

Menassah followed suit until both men could stand without being seen from the road. "I'll pass the word," he said, slapping leaves and earth off his tunic, "but can I ask why?"

"You may indeed." Darius was in high good humor. "Our archers are good, but a moving target is hard to hit, especially when there are so many of them. Those colored popinjays down there are treating this part of the journey as if it was a hunt picnic. By midafternoon they'll be looking for a pleasant place to make camp and after that the wine will come out. They're traveling light by the looks of it, but I'll wager that they'll be carrying wineskins. The Earls' men will do the hunting for supper and they'll get to drinking later. The men-at-arms will probably stay sober. They're in strange country, so they'll keep the campfires burning, but I doubt they'll post sentries.

"We'll stay back so that the hunters don't trip over us, but once they're asleep they'll be easy pickings. We don't have to catch up with them until dusk and they won't be difficult to find. I want a bowman riding behind every saddle. We'll give them an hour's start. Silence is to be maintained. Understood?"

"Understood, General."

Nightfall found Darius and his men on the western slopes two and a half leagues north of their base camp. The archers were crouched twenty feet below the hillcrest. Lower still, the cavalry stood beside their horses. On the plain, campfires blazed and men settled down to sleep. Their horses had been hobbled and turned loose to graze. Noise drifted up from the central fire, where a group was gathered in a circle. From time to time, shadowy figures moved, feeding the fires. A cheer, mingled with groans, floated up. Darius, lying on his stomach just inside a coppice, was muttering under his breath.

"Degenerate little buggers," Menassah heard him say, "stop gaming and go to sleep."

It took a while for the General's wish to be granted, but, two hours later, the group by the main fire had dispersed, relieved themselves, found a spot and slept. Darius took a deep breath and worked his way backward. Whispered orders passed and the archers moved to the crest. They set up in groups of six with ample space between for the horsemen to ride through. Arrows were notched and loosed at the dark shapes on the earth below. Four courses flew before the cavalry swept through the gaps and down the slope. Resistance was futile and escape, with the horses hobbled, impossible. The slaughter was total.

By dawn, when Darius, with Menassah at his side, picked his way through the bodies, the stream that had been the reason for the campsite was running clear again. Flies were already clustering on the drying pools of blood. The archers were methodically going around retrieving arrows. The leaders of the rebellion were easy to spot by their long hair and fine clothes. The two Earls were there, together with a dozen others that Darius did not recognize. Each time they came across one of them, Darius signaled for the body to be dragged off to the side. When they had completed the grisly tour, he turned to the Adjutant.

"Any idea which of these"—his hand indicated the sprawled corpses—"is the leader of Duke Paramin's men?"

"No, sir. They don't seem to be wearing any badges of rank."

"Did that Attemill fellow ride with us by any chance?"

Menassah gave a grim half-smile. "I insisted on it. I don't trust the man. He's betrayed one master, he can betray another."

"I'm going to get upwind of this stink. See if you can find him for me."

"At once, General." Menassah saluted and went off at the double.

Darius walked carefully out of the killing ground and sat down on a scruffy patch of grass. He didn't have long to wait.

"Adjutant said you wanted to see me, General." The little man was showing the strains of a sleepless night.

"Yes I do," Darius said, getting to his feet. He winced as his hip twinged, and he walked around a little to work off the pain.

"Know who commanded the Duke of Abercorn's horsemen?" he asked.

"Man called Walter of Huspeth."

"Know what he looks like?"

"Saw him once or twice," Attemill allowed.

"Good. See if you can identify him."

Darius was loath to follow the man back among the bodies, but he forced himself to it. It took about ten minutes before Attemill shoved a body with his foot.

"This 'un."

"Excellent," Darius said. "I'm obliged to you." He turned to Menassah, who had rejoined them. "Have this one taken over to where the others are. Then I want their heads cut off."

"General?" The Adjutant's voice rose in inquiry.

"Make sure the blades are sharp," Darius said dispassionately. "I want a neat job done. I've a use for those heads."

"Yes, General." Menassah had recovered his professional composure. "Should we bury the bodies, sir?"

"No, I think not." Darius' voice was cold. "Ground's baked too hard at this time of year. It would take too long. We need to get back." He looked up at the sky. "This area's uninhabited," he added, "and the kites are waiting. We'll take the heads back with us. Have their horses rounded up and see that their swords are collected. No sense wasting them. Report to me when we're ready to ride."

He turned on his heel and strode off up the hill, leaving the two men staring after him.

"Well if that don't beat all," Attemill said.

Once the party was back at base, the word of the victory spread quickly. Spirits were lifted and men who had been slouching around in boredom two days before walked with a spring to their step. There was one gruesome piece of work, however, that gave all who saw it pause. The General ordered a dozen stout saplings cut down and then firmly planted in a line across the enemy's route. Each sapling was crowned with a head. The following morning the archers and some of the foot soldiers were mounted on the captured horses and positioned among the trees along the hilltops to await the enemy.

By midafternoon, the van of the column was in view. The spyglass revealed a disciplined company of pikemen in the lead. More of the Duke of Abercorn's men, Darius thought. The rest of the force trailed back in an unwieldy straggle. There was no way of estimating numbers accurately in the cloud of dust that billowed around them. Darius lowered the glass and went to make his final arrangements.

An hour later, the pikeman reached the line of heads and pulled up in obvious consternation. They peered up at the hills, but Darius' men were silent and hidden. Those at the back of the lead company came up to see what was amiss, and the well-controlled ranks broke down into knots of arguing men. The rest of the column began to catch up and the area of pandemonium spread. The level of noise rose steadily until it was cut off by a blast of trumpets. As the men on the plain turned to look uphill, Darius rode out from the trees under a green flag of truce, a group of officers around him. As he moved down the slope, the horsemen came into view behind him, forming a solid line along the hilltops.

There was no resistance. Men without leaders do not fight for a cause that is not theirs. A good number of the rebels threw down their weapons and fled. The rest surrendered. Darius took their weapons and turned them loose. He had no stomach for further slaughter. The captured weapons were loaded onto the baggage train and sent north. The heads were collected again, put in a sack and flown to Sparsedale by cloudsteed with a letter to Otorin suggesting that they be dropped into the manor's inner court.

A fortnight later, Darius was in sight of Castle Sparsedale. His spyglass had already shown him that the royal standard was flying over it so that, when a small party of horsemen appeared riding toward him, he spurred forward without hesitation.

"Welcome back, General," Otorin of Lissen said as he reined in. "I understand that you are to be congratulated on yet another great victory."

"I see that Sparsedale is yours," Darius replied. "I trust you haven't drunk all the good wine in celebration. I could do with a flagon of that rascal Elfreg's best. Then I want a hot bath and a sennight's sleep."

Otorin smiled. "Not only have I made certain that there is a sufficiency of more than passable Assara—I took the precaution of sampling it to be sure—but I have, ah, persuaded our ever-genial host to donate it as a thank offering for the restoration of peace."

"He'll be the only one sorry to see us go," Darius remarked as Otorin turned his horse's head and they moved off in the direction of Upper Waltham.

"So what happened?" he asked, gesturing toward the blank, grey walls. "Did they try a sortie?"

"No such luck. They sat tight waiting for rescue. It

was the heads that did it. I had each of them put in separate bags with cotton wadding so they wouldn't be too badly damaged by the fall. After that it took them three hours to surrender."

"Did the Semicount survive his ordeal?" Darius asked.

"He survived"—Otorin's voice was hard—"but he probably wishes he hadn't. They raped his wife and his daughters and they made him watch. He had a ten-year-old son who was treated the same way. The boy killed himself."

A deep, angry sound issued from Darius' throat and he rode on in silence, his face set in a tight mask. "What of Bardolph?" he said finally.

"He's in chains in the inn's cellar awaiting your pleasure."

"Send him to Stronta under heavy guard with a letter to the Queen detailing his offenses. And don't let me see him. I don't trust myself around blackguards like that." Darius' voice was bleak and bitter and Otorin knew better than to say anything.

Darius kept his counsel until they were installed in the snuggery. Elfreg's effusions of welcome were stilled by a stone countenance and a basilisk's eye. He had needed no prompting to serve the Assara and he did so without words. The General tossed off the first bumper and held it out for a refill. Elfreg obliged and withdrew. Darius sat slumped in his chair, sipping now, rolling the wine around his mouth before swallowing. It seemed to restore his humor, bit by bit. Otorin waited patiently.

Darius sighed. "I'm sorry, old friend," he said, sitting up. "I've a daughter, and a grandson not much older than that unfortunate boy." He paused. "So, any word from Paramin of Abercorn?"

"Not a peep."

"Does he know?"

Otorin got up and refilled his cup before answering. "I can't be certain. As far as I know, no bunglebird or messenger left Sparsedale before or after the surrender. I have had reports that bunglebirds arrived at Oxeter's cote, but I have no sure knowledge of whence they came."

"What?" Darius tried for his old, teasing jocularity. "The cote keeper isn't your man?"

"He was," Otorin returned somberly. "The Duke hanged him three sennights ago."

"I'm sorry," Darius said, not knowing what else to say.

Otorin looked at him and nodded. "I rather imagine," he said, "that if the Duke has had news, it has come from Aldersgrove. The news of his colleagues' defeat has almost certainly reached him and he must realize that his son is doomed. He committed almost all his retainers here and with the two Earls. I don't know what he knows, but my sources tell me that he has shut himself away. He has not appeared at Hall of late."

"By the way," Darius said, "I must thank you for the services of Attemill. He gave us excellent warning."

Otorin smiled faintly. "Resourceful man."

"Has Abercorn got any more sons?" Darius asked.

"No sons, no daughters. The oldest boy died in a hunting accident, another in a tavern brawl and the daughter in birthing. This one's the last."

"Is there anyone to inherit?" Darius asked, looking up.

"Indeed there is and you'll never guess who." Otorin sounded amused.

"I haven't the slightest idea."

"Take a guess."

"I'm too tired for games, Otorin." Irritability surfaced.

"The Assistant Mage of Paladine," Otorin said smugly and watched Darius' eyes grow larger.

"Jarrod Courtak. Yes, I'd forgotten about that."

"The very same. He's old Paramin's nephew."

"Well, well, well." Darius sat back, eyes hooded. "That means that young Bardolph's headed for the execution block for sure."

"He'll join the other heads on Stronta's walls," Otorin agreed. "No doubt about it."

"Can't say I'm sorry, but someone ought to persuade Courtak to marry and have children. It would certainly neutralize a threat to the throne."

"It must be time for your bath and bed," Otorin said sardonically. "You're starting to think like me."

chapter 12

Jarrod finally caught Marianna's eye and was rewarded with a flashing smile. She excused herself from the group of men with whom she had been chatting and came toward him. He noticed that almost all the men in the room watched her. As she neared, she opened her arms, and, with a fractional hesitation, Jarrod moved forward and hugged her. She pushed back after a long moment, held him at arm's length and looked up into his face.

"You've been out in the open," she said. "It's given you some color and it suits you."

"And you get more beautiful by the year," he replied. "Every man in the room who isn't talking to the royals is looking at you and most of the women are trying not to."

She grinned. "My, ah, jewels," she said, glancing down at her cleavage, "seem to be much admired. Besides, they are also watching the reunion of 'the discoverers of the unicorns.' " Her voice gave the phrase the full weight of bombast, and they both laughed.

"Nobody at home bothers," Jarrod said. "Nastrus is such a familiar figure that even he is taken for granted."

"The same's true at Gwyndryth. Oh, people get excited when Amarine comes to visit, especially if she brings new foals with her, but the rest of it was a long time ago and people have short memories."

"True, but for me it seems like yesterday. Well, not

yesterday exactly, but certainly no more than a couple of years ago."

Marianna linked an arm through his and they moved to the side of the room. "I know what you mean," she said as they moved.

"D'you miss it?" he asked. "The action I mean, the being part of something important."

"Not really. I don't envy your still being in the public eye, if that's what you mean. That sort of ambition seems to have died. Running Gwyndryth is a full-time job. Sir Ombras is too old to do much of anything, poor darling. He fell asleep in the middle of the Moot last month. Still, I shan't replace him unless he asks me to. We owe him too much to shove him aside just because he's old."

"He was always very kind to me," Jarrod commented. "And how is Lady Obray doing?"

"Dead, the gods be thanked," Marianna said bluntly. "I never could abide that woman."

"I see," Jarrod said noncommittally. "Have you seen the boy?" he asked, changing the subject.

"Yes, that's why I'm here."

Jarrod's eyes widened at her tone of voice. "You don't seem too happy about it."

"I'm not." She glanced around. "But I don't feel like talking about it here. The Chamberlain has assigned me one of the royal apartments upstairs. Why don't we slip away and have a civilized drink and a chat?"

"Won't that compromise your reputation?" he asked teasingly.

Her head tipped back and her robust laugh rang out. "A divorced woman has no reputation at Court," she said, "surely you know that. But perhaps *your* reputation . . . After all, a Mage of the Discipline, alone, at night, with a divorced woman . . ." The laugh came again.

"I'm prepared to risk the scandal," he said with mock gravity, steering her toward the door. "How discreet are your servants?"

"If I can't bribe them, I'm sure that you can threaten to turn them into something interesting." She giggled.

"Now, what's the problem with young Joscelyn?" Jarrod asked once they were installed in her sitting room.

"He's been feeling his oats. Dean Handrom described him as 'a menace to the institution.' " She caught the Dean's pompous delivery perfectly.

"Strong words. What on Strand has he been doing?"

"He translated one of the magisters onto the roof of the simples house, he used the Spell of Invisibility to obtain the answers to a test and then sold them to his fellow Apprentices, he gets into fights; shall I go on?"

Jarrod sat back and made a soft whistling sound. "Stealing test results is grounds for immediate expulsion. I don't understand it," he said, puzzled. "He was never like that at the Outpost. He was high-spirited, but he never got into serious trouble. I wonder what's got into him?"

"He isn't very communicative on the subject," Marianna said. "He's at the age where mothers aren't popular. I think that part of it is that this is the first time that he has been on his own, so to speak. When he was small, he was under my control. He's been at Stronta since then, under the eyes of his grandfather, the General, Greylock, and his famous 'uncle,' the great Magician. I hope it's nothing more than his making up for lost time and that he'll grow out of it, but how can one be sure?" She leaned forward and touched his sleeve. "I'd appreciate it if you could have a word with the Dean."

Jarrod sighed. "I'll see what I can do," he said, "but I was never exactly his favorite pupil."

"Yes, well you're a Mage now," she replied. She stopped and took a small sip of her cordial. "D'you like Joscelyn?" she asked unexpectedly.

"Like him?"

"Yes; as a person."

"Well, I'm fond of him, of course, but I've always thought of him as a little boy. He's a disarming little rogue with a knack of appearing good as gold."

"Not so little," Marianna countered. "He'll be as tall as you are in a couple of years. He already reminds me of you when we first met. Not quite so awkward, of course."

"Oh, that's simply because he's young, tall and hand-some," Jarrod said, trying to bring some humor to the conversation.

Marianna gave him an obligatory smile and looked at him speculatively. "Have you ever thought of having children?" she asked.

He shrugged. "Once in a while, but there's the little question of a wife first."

She pursed her lips. "Not necessarily," she said.

She was looking directly at him, and the conversation, combined with that look, was making him feel nervous.

"All in good time," he said as lightly as he could.

"All very well for you, you're a man," she replied, "but I don't have that luxury. If I want another child, and I do, I only have a couple of years left."

This was not the kind of talk that Jarrod was used to. "And do you have a prospective father picked out?" he asked uneasily. As he said it, the suspicion hit him. He knew that his hands had clenched. He swallowed and tried for an appropriate smile.

"Oh yes." Her answering smiled looked feline to him.

"Surely you're not suggesting . . ." Jarrod began.

The smile broadened. "Modest as ever," Marianna

said, and took another sip of her cordial. "Sure you won't have one?"

"No thank you."

"You're right, of course," she said, and a fluttering feeling started inside Jarrod. "I need another child to safeguard the succession to the Holding. Joscelyn has a strong gift, one doesn't need to be Talented to see that. I very much doubt that he'll be interested in running the estate. He may never marry—so few of you seem to—and there's no guarantee that he won't die before his time. I can't risk having the line die out."

"But why marry me?" he asked, his voice sounding scratchy in his ears.

"Oh, I wouldn't marry you, my dear," Marianna said sweetly. "I wouldn't ask you to change your life. No one has to know that you're the father."

Jarrod pushed himself back in the chair. "You've done some crazy things in your time," he said, "but this is the strangest proposition you've ever come up with. Not that I'm not flattered," he added quickly.

She laughed. It was genuine and the tension fell away. "So you bloody well should be. Time was when I had to beat you off with a stick."

"I had a young boy's crush on you," he corrected good-naturedly.

"Ha!"

"I think I'll take that drink after all," Jarrod said, getting to his feet. He felt more in control standing. The fluttering feeling had subsided, but he wasn't entirely back to normal. He poured himself some wine and went and leaned on the mantelpiece. Marianna swiveled to face him.

"I am, as I said, enormously flattered, but if Joscelyn has turned out to be Talented, despite the fact that neither you, nor your former husband are, surely a child fathered by me would have an even greater chance of being Talented."

The feline smile returned. "Exactly the same chance," she said, "and I'm prepared to take that risk."

"Why not find some beautiful, young aristocrat and seduce him?" Jarrod asked. "You can have almost any man you want, you know you can."

"That's true." Marianna looked pleased with herself. "And I have given the matter a great deal of thought, but you see, I like my son." She emphasized the like. "I think he's bright, he's considerate, he's got a quick sense of humor, he's not afraid of hard work and he's going to be very handsome. I would be perfectly happy with another son or daughter just like him." She took another sip and watched him over the rim of her glass.

Jarrod mulled over what she had said, trying to find the thread of logic that linked it to him. A thought intruded, a memory of the Island at the Center. His mouth opened and he stared at her. "You didn't," he said accusingly.

"Oh but I did. Joscelyn is the proof."

"With my double? You wouldn't. I don't believe you." He pushed himself away from the mantelpiece and began to pace.

"You must have noticed the resemblance," she said reasonably.

"I certainly have not," he retorted. He was upset. His insides were churning and he wasn't entirely sure why. Jealousy? Disappointment? A streak of prudery he hadn't known he possessed?

"I must say that surprises me," she said as if she were having a perfectly ordinary discussion. "Even my father has made some halfhearted attempts to comment on the matter."

"And what did you tell him?"

She smiled, seemingly relaxed. "Oh, that was simple.

I said that it was only because Joscelyn was tall and, because you were his idol, he tried to walk like you, copy the way you use your hands. Daddy was only too happy to believe me."

Jarrod stopped pacing and went and sat down opposite her. He took a deep breath. "You're right, of course, now that I come to think about it. He's got your hair, but his eyes are blue. It never occurred to me." He looked across at her. "After all, I knew I wasn't the father."

He took a drink of wine. "Tell me," he said when he was sure that his voice wouldn't betray him, "when did this momentous event occur?"

"After you left the Island at the Center. You remember that I stayed behind to help your double adjust to getting all your memories. Well, it was a lot more work than I thought it would be." She smiled at him mischievously. "I know a great deal about you, Jarrod Courtak."

He didn't smile back at her.

"I had to put it all in context for him," she continued. "We have so many assumptions about the world around us that don't register as specific memories. Anyway, I had to spend a lot of time with him and, to make a long tale short, he fell in love."

"And one thing led to another," Jarrod concluded. He was calm again. Now that it was out in the open, the palpitations had stopped. He was a trifle disturbed to find that curiosity was the strongest component of what he was feeling.

"You make it sound so mundane," she said. "He couldn't help himself. I was the only girl he was ever going to meet and he was predisposed to it by your earlier, ah, infatuation." She cocked her head and pushed her hair back. "Besides, it was the only chance he'd ever get to have sex. Now, how could I deny him?"

Her eyes were wide and she conveyed an air of innocent seriousness.

Jarrod laughed. "You're impossible," he said. "I suppose you'll be telling me that the whole thing was a noble sacrifice on your part."

She grinned at him. "Very astute."

"What did you call him?"

"Jarrod. It was what he thought of himself as being."

"I see, and did your husband know about this when he married you?"

"Oh yes. Ruppy Trellawn and I have been friends for years—played together as children. The whole thing was arranged in advance, including the divorce. It suited both our purposes."

"Well, I can see what you got out of it," Jarrod said. "You got a legitimate heir for Gwyndryth, but I'm not sure that I see what he gained."

"He gained an impeccable reputation and the freedom not to have to marry again." She smiled at his bafflement. "Ruppy, you see," she explained, "prefers men, he always has. The local gentry are not so much straitlaced as they are insistent on decorum as they see it. By marrying me, he not only had a wife, but he could prove his manhood by appearing to have fathered a child. It's the appearance that counts in our part of the world. I agreed to be the one who asked for the divorce so that people could accept the notion that he was still in love with me and was therefore not interested in other women."

"And the divorce didn't hurt your reputation?"

The smile was rueful. "The Gwyndryths have been the chief family in the Marches for generations. We are permitted our eccentricities."

"Surely you must have had other offers of marriage?" Jarrod asked.

"Oh indeed," Marianna said with a sigh. "Gwyndryth is a very tempting fief and Daddy's influence at the Paladinian Court doesn't hurt." She looked wistful for a moment. "A couple of my suitors were very handsome and I was tempted, especially after I realized that Joscelyn was Talented." She spread her hands as if to soften the explanation. "The deciding factor was that I'd be damned if I'd let anybody take control of Gwyndryth away from me."

Jarrod crossed his legs and sipped. He was at ease again. "And this second baby," he said, "would your upright gentry accept that as an eccentricity?"

"Well, I suppose that I could ask Ruppy to marry me again, but that would mean that I would have to put up with him for the rest of my life and I don't think I'm up to that. I mean, he's a dear and he makes me laugh, but a fortnight's about all I can take." The rueful smile was back. "The truth of the matter is that I'm set in my ways. At this point in my life, I really don't think I could abide having a man underfoot all the time—and having to be pleasant to his hunting cronies who have about as much regard for the family furniture as, as . . ." Words failed her.

Jarrod smiled to himself. Even that short year couldn't have been easy for the hapless Sir Ruppy Trellawn.

"Just suppose," he said, "purely hypothetically, that you could find a husband whose business took him away a great deal of the time and who would be happy to give you free rein at Gwyndryth, would you still want me to father your child?"

"Do you have someone in mind?" she inquired, "or are you just fishing for compliments?"

"I seldom get compliments from women," he said, lips curving.

"Does that mean that you would consider it?" she said banteringly.

Would he? Well, the whole thing was rather intriguing, and though her beauty was different than it had been at twenty, she was a very desirable woman. "Compliments first," he teased.

"Oh, all right," she said. "I just hope Joscelyn hasn't inherited your vanity. Yes, I'd still like you to be the father. As I said, I like my son."

"If we had a daughter, it would be a shame if she took after me." He chuckled.

"So you are thinking about it."

"It has a certain perverse appeal," Jarrod said, still not willing to be entirely serious.

"In that case," Marianna said, raising to her feet in a single, fluid motion, "I think we should adjourn to the bedchamber and discuss it." She smiled at him wickedly. "I'm supposed to be leaving in three days."

She held out her hand. Jarrod put down his glass and got to his feet with considerably less grace. He took her hand.

They started gently, tentatively, exploring one another's bodies. They became more sure and more spontaneous and, to Jarrod, it began to feel like the most natural thing in the world. He had wanted to make love to her for a very long time. Passion mounted as they joined and, when it was over, they lay together, breathing and pulse returning slowly to normal. He bent his head and kissed her hair.

"Three days, did you say? I think it would be best to make absolutely sure, don't you?"

She turned and punched him lightly on the arm. "Animal," she said. "You men are all the same." She giggled softly. "Under the circumstances, that's more true than ever."

"Absolutely the same?" he asked, knowing that she would understand what he meant.

"Uhm." She seemed to be considering the matter. "There are only two significant differences."

"Really?"

She tipped her head back and looked up at him, eyes bright with mischief. She waited. Then, "The other Jarrod doesn't have scars on his back, and . . ."

"And," he prompted.

"He was a virgin and you most certainly are not."

He gave her a little shake and she chuckled softly.

"Contrary to popular opinion," she said drowsily, "it has been a long time since there was a man in my bed."

She yawned and then there was silence.

chapter 13

While Celador was preparing for a Magical display, Angorn, capital of the Umbrian Empire, was also caught up in excitement. First there had been the trial of Simlan the Hermit, then the rumor of a massacre in Baldania and now an official visit by the Mother Supreme. The Holy Church of the Mother was the official religion of the State and the head of the Church was, technically, the Emperor's equal. Arnulpha, the Mother Supreme, came as visiting royalty, but the truth was that she had been summoned by Varodias. The formalities were maintained, by the fact was otherwise.

The two met in the Private Stateroom. They sat opposite one another in ornate bezelwood chairs and presented a study in contrasts. The Emperor was thin, the face made longer by a receding hairline and a sharply pointed beard. He was elegantly but soberly dressed. The Mother Supreme was tall, stout and florid, her face made rounder by her wimple. She was dressed voluminously in gold. Tradition, hallowed by five hundred years of practice, decreed that, in the presence of the Mother Supreme, the Emperor should come down from the throne. This Emperor preferred to avoid that; hence the choice of the Private Stateroom. Though the two chairs appeared to be identical, detailmongers would have found significance in the fact that the legs of Varodias' chair were six inches taller than those of the chair to which the Mother Supreme had been assigned.

"We bid you welcome," Varodias said when the small flock of courtiers and attendants had been dismissed. The Emperor, as was his habit, used the Formal Mode even though they were alone.

"I am most pleased to visit the Chief Upholder of the Great Mother," she replied with equal ceremony, and accompanied the words with a totally artificial smile that had no echo in the small, grey eyes.

Varodias' lips arranged themselves into a professional curve. "Let us dispense with the pleasantries," he said, the high voice chilly but flexible. "You are here to discuss the disgraceful outcome at the cathedral. Two hundred and forty people killed and twice that number wounded. The news is spreading to every corner of the Empire and talk of revolution follows it. How could you have been so stupid?" The white-gloved hand that had been illustrating his words formed into a fist and pounded down onto the armrest.

"If Your Imperial Majesty will permit," Arnulpha said imperturbably. She adjusted the cloth-of-gold robe to emphasize the belly.

I remember when she needed padding to suggest pregnancy, Varodias thought. Too many years of good living. He tried to estimate the Mother's age. She had been elected thirty years ago so she must be at least sixty, but it was difficult to tell. The hair was covered as was the throat and the lines in her face had been erased by her gain in weight.

"The figures you quoted are exaggerated. A hundred and thirty-two people died and about a hundred had their wounds tended by the Sisters. That is still regrettable, but a mob was prepared to commit sacrilege against one of our holy places and that I could not allow."

"It was, of course, the merest accident that you had

four hundred armed retainers on call," Varodias said, the sarcasm evident.

Arnulpha flashed her non-smile again. "I am sure that my intelligence is no match for that of Your Imperial Majesty, but I did get sufficient warning."

"And you chose to hire mercenaries rather than appeal to us for assistance."

The Mother Supreme drew back her head and cocked it slightly to the left. The eyes, unwavering, weighed the Emperor. The lips moved slightly, suggesting that she had made up her mind about something. She leaned forward.

"We could, of course, have come to you, but I doubt that you would have reacted fast enough. Besides, there is a considerable body of opinion within the Church that blames you for the whole thing."

Varodias pushed himself back in his chair as if to gain height and distance. "Have a care, madam," he said.

"Well," she said, unabashed, "if you had condemned that infernal Simlan instead of letting him go, people would not have taken it into their heads that Church property can be attacked with impunity. At least now they will think twice before they try it again. Besides," she added in a more moderate tone, "it would have been very poor politics."

"Pray tell us more." The words were spaced, the high voice skeptical.

Arnulpha shrugged, and the quivers seemed to course down her body. "The Church and the Emperor are allied in the minds of the people. How would it have seemed if Imperial troops had dispersed the rabble and caused the casualties? You should be grateful that you can disown the action."

"Oh, sweet, very sweet," Varodias said, hands hovering at midchest. "All done for our good." The tone was almost caressing. He sat straight and the right fore-finger jabbed out. "You did not ask us for our assistance because you wished to establish an independence of us. That is the truth. Well, know this, woman, despite the fact that the Church and the Crown are intertwined in the popular mind, we do not countenance the slaughter of our subjects." The finger was jabbing again.

The Mother Supreme drew in her breath. "Your Imperial Majesty is in a great deal more trouble than the Church," she said evenly. "The mob, apprentices and journeymen for the most part, were inspired by the Hermit, but they were not really interested in the Church; the Church was simply thought to be an easy target. You are the one this Simlan is aiming at. He is a fanatic and, like most fanatics, he believes what he preaches. He would not be as effective as he is if he did not.

"It is true that, in the beginning, he took on the Holy Mother Church, but he no longer inveighs against us. He has money behind him now, and where do you suppose that money comes from? My opponents?" Her hands splayed out and her eyebrows rose. "Scarcely. The majority of the population is devoted to the Great Mother. That is not a tenet of belief. That is a fact. No, my friend, Simlan is a stalking horse for those who would supplant you. They begin by making it seem as if you cannot govern the Empire." She sat back slightly, weighing the effect of her speech. Varodias was a volatile and dangerous man who did not take kindly to criticism. Her aggressive performance was a deliberate gamble, and she was not at all sure that she was winning.

"It would be simple enough," the Emperor said lightly, "for us publicly to condemn the Church for the massacre and thus allow the people's anger to focus on you."

Arnulpha allowed herself an audible and derisory puff

of breath. "If you were going to do that, Majesty, you would have done it right away. It is too late now. Besides"—the smile was genuinely amused this time—"you made the mistake of receiving me in state. I am sure that the word has already gone out."

Varodias tipped back his head and appeared to study the ceiling. "You have been grossly deficient in your judgment, both in your actions and in your opinion of us." The voice floated out. People who did not know him, and almost no one did, would have assumed that the Emperor was in an amiable mood. The neatly tapered beard descended slowly until he was looking directly at the Mother Supreme. His hands were still. "While it is true that the Crown and the Church are supposedly inseparable, the same is not true of Emperors and individual Mothers Supreme." He smiled, but there was nothing amiable about it. "My condemnation would be of the misguided priestess, not of the organization, and it is by no means too late for that."

"Is Your Imperial Majesty trying to threaten me?" Arnulpha asked, striving to match his lightness.

Varodias' smile returned. "My Wisewoman tells me that obesity can put too great a strain upon the vital organs. Then again, a glutton may choke on a sweetmeat."

The laugh started low in the Mother Supreme and rose until she threw back her head and gave it free rein. It was a totally spontaneous release of tension and it disconcerted the Emperor. She wheezed; she wiped her eyes. The intrigues of men were so crude when compared to the machinations of women, she thought, and she had ruled more than two thousand women for longer than she cared to admit.

"Nicely done, Majesty," she said, controlling herself, "but I am not so easily replaced. The hierarchy is loyal to me and to my way of thinking. No complacent vessel of your choosing would be elected and the next Mother Supreme might well be even less to your liking."

She paused and looked at him levelly and, despite the disparity in the height of the chairs, it was an exchange between equals. It was Varodias who looked away first.

"What do you suggest?" he asked.

"Oooh"—it was a drawn out and soothing sound—"an alliance of necessity at the very least. There are forces abroad that need to be dealt with."

"Agreed, but how?" He stopped himself and held up a hand to stave off a reply. He tucked his lower lip between his teeth and bit down gently.

The gesture heartened the Mother Supreme. She had taken an enormous risk and the rapid beating of her pulse told her so. That the Emperor was showing signs of indecision was a relief. The worst was behind her, though she would have to play him carefully from here on in.

"There are a number of factors that would have to be brought to bear," she said cautiously, "most of them political."

Varodias nodded, reviewing the possibilities in his mind. He was aware of the general unrest in the realm, but none of his spies had reported a concentrated effort to get him off the throne. The Mother's argument did make some sense, however, and it was always best to anticipate trouble and strike first. His eyes darted toward her. He did not like this woman. She showed too little respect, for one thing, but she was intelligent and as much of a survivor as he was. He knew that, behind his back, people said that he ruled by personal whim. The fools did not realize that behind each seeming whim there was a calculated vigilance. When it came down to it, his fortunes and those of the Church were linked.

"We do not think," he said graciously, "that the Emperor and the Holy Church should be quarreling. Rather, we should be searching our minds and our hearts for the solution to the present dissatisfaction among the people, who are your congregants and our subjects." The head inclined slightly and then rose immediately.

The Mother Supreme exhaled gently and inclined her head in turn. It would not do to let him see how close to rattling her he had come. "I do agree, Your Imperial Majesty," she said. "There is, of course, one obvious way to distract the public mind, to deflect the energy into a more profitable channel, and that is to open the Outland." She gave a little shrug that stayed at the level of the shoulders. "As I said, a political decision."

"Would that it were that simple," Varodias replied, sadness in the cadence. "We have been trying to do that for years, but we have been thwarted by the Magical Kingdoms and by Isphardel. We promised our valiant soldiers at the close of the dreadful war that their loyal service would be rewarded by a grant of land in the captured territories"—his fingers began drumming on the arms of the chair—"and we have been prevented from keeping our sacred word."

Mostly because the land wasn't fit for settlement before now, Arnulpha thought, but she kept it to herself. "Infidels will never do anything to help us," she said. "They lack the moral framework from which the knowledge of right and wrong flows." She smiled and her hands made motions that suggested hesitation. "There are a couple of things that Your Imperial Majesty might consider. . . ."

Varodias' hands were calm again. "Would you care to elaborate?" he said smoothly.

"An ordinance against retainers, perhaps? If coupled

with an offer of land beyond the Causeways, it might make Electoral service less inviting. After all, if the Crown allotted tracts in the area directly fronting our current northern border, who could gainsay it? In your wisdom, you have waited this long to ensure that the perils of mutation are past. That is to be commended. The Church would, naturally, encourage settlement from the pulpit."

She paused and, hearing no denial, gathered herself to propound the plan she had long nurtured.

"The Church would, of course," she said as if it were a foregone conclusion, "expect to have a presence in the new territory. The people would need something to anchor them to the old life, some sense of belonging to the Empire even though they were forging new boundaries; a sense of kinship and continuity." She smiled openly at him. "It goes without saying that Imperial grants in perpetuity would preempt a broad range of problems."

Varodias laughed. It was an unnerving sound. "You are a piece of work," he said, not without appreciation, the gloved hands fountaining upward. "You will preach and we shall donate land to you." His head wagged from side to side. "Most droll; highly amusing."

The affectation of mirth died as quickly as it had been kindled. The eyes became slitted.

"No more independent defense force," he said. "From hence forth Imperial forces will be deployed to protect centers of worship." The professional smile appeared again. "You will of course implore us to do so. You will instruct your priestesses to preach the virtues of stability and to impress upon their congregations the evils of internal dissension. Emphasize the advantages of a strong, united state. Tell the people that our prosperity is being threatened by foreigners. The Isphardis bleed us, the Magical Kingdoms thwart us by holding up the division of the Outland." He was kindled anew and his dark eyes shone.

"To assert our own just sovereignty and prosperity, we must be united, regional differences must be subsumed. The Imperium is all. The nation will succeed. The Empire will triumph!" He stopped, mouth open as if surprised at what had come out of it.

The man's mad, Arnulpha thought, but Imperial protection is a sight cheaper than hiring men-at-arms and the rest of his ideas can fit nicely with what I want for the Church. Gently, now, gently.

"I am sure that the Church can play a vital role in Your Imperial Majesty's plans," she said placidly, "plans with which I entirely concur. I shall issue a plea for Imperial protection against the barbarians who threaten us before I leave the capital, and I can assure you that you will not be disappointed at the voices that will issue from our pulpits. We shall stress the need to spread the Imperium to the Outlands and, of course, the necessity of the the presence of the Great Mother on this new Imperial frontier."

She gripped the arms of her chair and heaved herself to her feet.

"And now, with Your Imperial Majesty's permission, I beg leave to retire. Your Majesty has given me much to think on."

Varodias rose easily from his seat. "When you have finished thinking, make sure that we are of a mind, madam," he said, returning to his cool and menacing mode. He made a small inclination of the head in her direction.

"I shall mention Your Imperial Majesty in my prayers," the Mother Supreme said enigmatically. She gathered up the front of her robe and swept to the doors. Her grand exit was hampered somewhat by the necessity of opening them for herself.

Varodias watched the departing expanse of gold with mixed emotions. The woman hadn't reacted at all in the way that he had expected. She did not appear in the least to have been intimidated. He thought, however, that he had got what he wanted out of her, but he wasn't certain and that irritated him. The woman was a trial, but, for the moment, he needed her. He looked forward to the time when he would not.

chapter 14

The Outpost was still sweltering as Jarrod prepared for a meeting of the reconvened Commission for the Outland. The breezes that the Weatherwards had provided afforded very little relief, a mere passing of warm air over hot ground. A day like this, he thought, might cause Olivderval to reconsider her offer. Still, despite the heat, it was good to be home again after so many sennights away. Except for the dreams. Since his return he had dreamed of the castle in the mountains almost every night. He had never been able to reach it, but the building itself was clearly visible and, while unreachable, at least stayed put. Something in him itched to make the dream real. He had, he realized, been working toward that end. Nastrus had been directed to send the stones from the Giants' Causeway to the foot of the mountains. The ostensible reason had been to get them out of the way of potential settlers, but, in retrospect, it was obvious to Jarrod that there had been another agenda behind that. In all truth, the would-be settlers could have done with some building materials on a woodless plain. Somehow, and he couldn't explain why, this seemed more important.

On a happier note, he had to admit that the demonstration had been a roaring success. The Queen, the Prince Consort and the Court had been seated on the Upper Causeway. A number of Arabella's major vassals had returned to Court from their estates, and they had brought their families. Ragnor had made a notable entrance, resplendent in ornate robe and biretta of office, carried up in a gilded sedan chair. There had been a festive, almost jubilant, air about the occasion. It was as if this were a return to the distant days of high purpose and great deeds.

Greylock, in the full regalia of the Mage of Paladine, diamond tiara blazing in the sun, stood on a special platform by the parapet. Nastrus, groomed to within an inch of his life, stood behind him. The unicorn's mane and tail gleamed with threads of gold, and his silver hooves shone. The mother-of-pearl spiral of his horn seemed to genrate a glow of its own, holding the sunlight at bay. The Mage had explained to the gathering what was going to occur and then turned slowly to face the Alien Plain. A silence descended, broken only by the wailing of a small child. Greylock raised his arms and began to intone a levitation spell.

As if summoned by his words, four cloudsteeds rose above the Causeway with a net dangling below them. Jarrod, standing inconspicuously to the side, began to provide power to match the chant. He was careful; enough to help the Magicians on the ground below without making them feel unnecessary. Blocks of stone rose and deposited themselves, one by one, in the net. The cloudsteeds beat their way higher, so that the viewers on the Causeway had to crane their necks to see, and then hovered, the net swinging gently.

Nastrus, ever the showman, tossed his head so that the mane flew dramatically, and, behold, the stones were gone. The crowd gasped. The cloudsteeds dropped back out of sight. There was applause and cheers rang out. The proceedure was repeated, but this time, just as Jarrod was about to join in, he noticed that the runes on Greylock's gown had begun to move. The hairs on the back of his neck began to prickle. The Mage was using his own power. Jarrod opened himself and, with infinite caution, fed a small amount of supporting energy to Greylock. The cloudsteeds appeared again and the heavy chunks of stone disappeared again. The third time Greylock had no need of Jarrod, and the younger man had a lump in his throat and felt the tears prick at his eyelids. His mentor was in total control once more.

The demonstration lasted about half of an hour and was followed by a lavish reception. The Magicians, Jarrod included, were made much of. The wine flowed and the whole thing had the feeling of a victory celebration. At one point Jarrod found himself face-to-face with Dean Handrom.

"Excellent show," the Dean said. The man was obviously in good humor and Jarrod resolved to ask him about Joscelyn.

"Your fellows performed wonderfully well," he said. "Indeed, they have been exemplary throughout this project. They are a credit to the Collegium and the Collegium has, as always, been a credit to the Discipline." He wondered, briefly, if he hadn't laid it on a little to thickly, but the Dean's satisfied smile had reassured him.

"While we have a minute," Jarrod said, "I understand that you are having a discipline problem with young Joscelyn of Gwyndryth. Since I was involved in his early training, I feel partially responsible."

"Yes, I can see that you would." Good humor or no, Handrom was incapable of keeping an ironic inflection out of the statement.

"His mother seems to think that he is in danger of being kicked out of the Collegium."

"That's what I intended for her to think," the Dean replied.

"And is he?"

"Not if I can help it. He's got too much potential and it's badly in need of molding and direction. You managed to get out without completing the course and you have attained high rank." There was no mistaking the disapproval. "That is extremely bad for the Collegium's morale and reputation. I have no intention of allowing it to become a trend."

"So I can tell Lady Gwyndryth that she has nothing to worry about," Jarrod said mildly.

"You will do no such thing," the Dean said sternly, the authoritarian tone of the schoolmaster surfacing. "The boy is headstrong, stubborn and disrespectful. One hopes that he will grow out of it, but he will need a firm hand, both here and at home." He paused. "I understand that there is no father in residence. All the more reason for that woman to exert her parental authority and help to instill some sense of obligation, discipline and manners in the boy. He has obviously been overindulged and that has to stop. You will oblige me by saying nothing to the mother."

Jarrod had his doubts, but he simply nodded and turned the conversation to the future supply of Magicians for the Causeway project.

When he saw Marianna after Hall, he told her that the Collegium hadn't given up on Joscelyn, but considered that he needed firm handling when he was home for the holidays.

"He obviously takes after your side of the family," she had retorted.

"Headstrong, stubborn and disrespectful were the words that Handrom used," Jarrod had countered. "Sounds just like his mother to me."

He had been joking, but things seemed to go downhill from there. He had expected to spend his last night with her, but Marianna had begged off, saying that she was leaving first thing in the morning and needed to get as much rest as possible.

"You'll let me know if . . ." he had said, not quite wanting to put it into words.

"I'll write to you when I'm sure," she'd said coolly. "Oh, and thank you."

She had smiled at him and pressed his hand briefly. Then she had turned away and left him. Jarrod was not comfortable with the memory. Part of him had wanted to go after her and part of him was oddly relieved. There was also an element of anger. She had got what she wanted, as usual, and now she would ignore him until he became useful once more. He was still confused by the encounter. He had no right to feel cheated, especially since he didn't know what he wanted.

He had tried to analyze his feelings toward both Marianna and Joscelyn, now that he knew who the real father was. His feelings for Joscelyn were easier. He had always been fond of the boy and he still was. It was a good thing, though, that the youngster had moved on to the Collegium. Adolescence was traditionally the time of rebellion against authority and he was relieved, cowardly though that might be, that Joscelyn would have another target for those roiling feelings.

Real paternity, on the other hand, was something else again and he was a sea of contradiction on that subject. He tried to dispel the crowding thoughts. Time enough to sort them out when and if Marianna became pregnant. Now was not the time to be distracted by this anyway, he told himself. The all-important vote was scheduled for the morrow and that would change the future in a way that no single child could do.

Ragnor had assured him that Otorin of Lissen would side with the Isphardis and that pressure would be applied to Queen Naxania to do likewise. The precise nature of that pressure was left deliberately vague. The Songeans had no love for the Empire, the eastern clans especially. Generations of their young men had been taken off to work in the Umbrian mines. If Ragnor was right, and there was no reason to think that he would not be, the Empire's proposal would be voted down. What bothered Jarrod was the Archmage's other predictions. Would it really mean war? If so, there ought to be some way to avoid it.

He got up and went around the room blowing out the lamps and snuffing the candles. Life had become extraordinarily complicated in the last month. He started to think about Marianna and the baby again. When it came right down to it, he hoped that there would be a baby.

Malum of Quern was at his place at the scribes' table again. The sandbox, inkhorn and quills were all neatly arranged. He felt the tinglings of anticipation. Today would be the day. The Isphardis would be put in their place, the partition would be ratified and a treaty drawn up. The Elector had spent an hour with Queen Naxania and had met with Lord Lissen. He had seemed happy with the outcome. The Songeans knew where their interests lay. Since it was a question of siding with one of two neighbors, who in their right minds would pick shiftless merchants over the power and tradition of Umbria? It really didn't matter how Talisman and the Discipline voted. It would be more satisfying if ratification was unanimous, but the final tally was what counted.

The Isphardis would be humbled and that was the necessary first step. With the Oligarchs discredited, and with no army or fortified places, the absorption of Songuard should be easy. The Imperial garrison in Fort Bandor, coupled with the conquest of Isphardel, would give them de facto control of Songuard, and the Empire's effective sway would be extended to the Gorodontiou Mountains. He smiled to himself. Perhaps they could change the name to something that fit more easily on an Umbrian tongue.

In any case, with the treaty signed, they would be returning to Angorn to bask in the Emperor's approbation. Not before time, either. His recent visit to the capital had shown him how little influence he had there. The Elector was old and his son the Margrave had no taste for Court life. He would need some time to build a power base or find himself a new patron. A triumph at Stronta would be a good beginning and a broad knowledge of foreign conditions ought to be an advantage. His contemplations of the future were interrupted by a noise. He glanced up and saw Borr Sarad coming through the door. Looking, thought Malum, fit and vital after the recess.

"Give you good morrow, my lord," Sarad said pleasantly.

"May the best of the day be before us, Thane," Malum replied. "If this day's session goes well, our little contest may be at an end."

"Leave us hope that the gods are listening to your words. I enjoy these visits to Stronta, of course, but this has been going on for far too long and I would as lief be at home on my farm watching my sons work while I take my ease."

Malum smiled at him. "Will Talisman allow you to retire?" he asked.

"Hah." It was a derisive snort. "They turned me out of office after twenty years. I only accepted this post because I wanted to travel and I thought that it would last no more than a couple of years."

"And how will your sons take to having their father watching them every day?" Malum said slyly.

Sarad cocked his head and gave the Umbrian a beady look. "Good question, young man. I can still swing a scythe when the haymow is due and they'll be grateful for that, but they and their wives have always treated me as a honored guest on those rare occasions when I have been able to take time away from Fortress Talisman." He paused and a slow smile raised the wrinkles round his eyes. "On the other hand," he said, "they always knew that I would be leaving before too long. I shall have to remember that both my sons are grown men and as set in their ways as I am in mine." The smile broadened. "Still, there are the little ones. I am about to become a great-great-grandfather and, if nothing else, I can be useful watching bairns until I become one again."

"Fortunate bairns," Malum said. "I never knew my grandparents."

Their colloquy was brought to an end by the approach of Darius of Gwyndryth. The two older men embraced warmly and Malum was forgotten for the moment.

"You old rascal," Sarad said, dropping into Common. "I've been hearing tall tales about your triumphs. In fact, the rather fragrant reminders of your success greeted me from the battlements as I rode in."

"Rebellion's a bad business," Darius said noncommittally.

"And how did the Duke of Abercorn take the execution of his son?"

"I hear that he has taken to his bed," Darius replied.

"And what brings you here this morning?" Sarad asked, changing the subject diplomatically.

"The Chamberlain is indisposed and the Queen has asked me to fill in for him."

"Not fair, Gwyndryth, not fair." The Thane chuckled. "The rest of us have been slaving at this for years and you trot in for what may be the final vote."

Darius' answering smile had an apologetic aspect. "I am sensible of the honor," he said, "and you may rest assured that I have been exhaustively briefed by Her Majesty."

Today's the day all right, Malum thought. She wouldn't have sent Gwyndryth unless she expected this to be the final session. The other two kept talking, but Malum's attention was diverted by the arrival of the other members of the Commission. The day, though young, was already warm and the men looked uncomfortable in their velvet and ruffs. The Oligarch, by contrast, looked cool in her long silk robe.

The Hodman, dressed in last winter's fashion, was red-faced; Otorin of Lissen was composed; but only the Elector, in a loose linen tunic, sans ruff, was moving easily. His joints were at their best in this weather. Malum's own ruff was chafing his neck as he wended his way through them with a cooled goblet of fruit juice for his master.

After five minutes of general conversation, with old acquaintances chatting about their visits home, the Commission drifted to the table. The glass had been taken out of the windows and bees flew back and forth, attracted by the scents of the herbs strewn over the floor. The buzz of continuing conversation rose, generating a feeling of relaxation and goodwill. A positive omen, Malum thought.

The Elector broke the mood by rapping on the table. He didn't make a very loud noise, but it was enough to bring silence. They're all on edge, Malum thought, no matter how relaxed they appear.

"Madam Oligarch, my lords," Phalastra said into the bee-humming quiet, "I trust that you have all had pleasant times. Now, alas, we must return to the task at hand. It is my hope that today we shall finally vote on the proposal presented at the beginning of the summer without additions, subtractions, or amendments." The reedy voice faded away.

"I shall take your silence for acceptance," he continued after a brief pause. "Before we vote, I should like to welcome the Lord Darius of Gwyndryth, an old friend of mine and as much a hero in Umbria as he is here." He inclined his head in Darius' direction and the Holdmaster returned the gesture. "He speaks today for Queen Naxania of Paladine. Having said that, let us to the vote."

Malum rose and distributed copies of the map to each of the representatives.

"We shall be voting," Estragoth resumed, "on the acceptance of the partition as represented on the map before you, as I have said, without revisions. I shall start at the end of the table and work my way around. Hodman, how say you?"

"Songuard says no." The Hodman was mopping himself with a large kerchief, but his voice was deep and firm.

The voting continued, and when the tally was done, Umbria was the sole supporter of the proposal. Estragoth masked his disappointment well. There was no hint of it in his voice as he said, "Let the record show that the partition as presented has been rejected by a majority of the states. Does anyone wish to propose an amendment?" He looked around the table. The only indication of his anger at the result, at the betrayal he felt from those who had listened to him and spoken him fair, only to vote against him when the count was called, was a vein throbbing in his temple.

"An it please you, Lord President." There was no hint of triumph in Olivderval's voice. The tone was level and unemotional.

"The chair recognizes the representative from Isphardel." Phalastra matched her formality.

"Isphardel proposes that the territories marked out

on the map be accepted as drawn, with these conditions:

"One, roadways be built through the valleys of Gorodontiou and Saradonda and continue through the newly created Songean lands to the borders of New Isphardel.

"Two, gateways be constructed through the Upper Causeway to permit passage of both roads.

"Three, Isphardis and their goods, both personal and mercantile, shall pass freely at all times and shall not be subject to customs duties, tolls or taxes of any kind unless levied by the government of Isphardel.

"Four, the roads and gateways shall be maintained and kept in good repair by the Isphardi government.

"Five, all disputes arising from the use of these roads shall be decided by an international tribunal.

"Six, the freedom of passage shall be guaranteed by the international community and will be maintained, if necessary, by force of arms." She paused and looked around.

Jarrod raised his hand. "The Discipline is to be accorded territory, the exact size and location of which is still to be decided."

"Yes indeed," Olivderval acknowledged. She leaned forward and tapped a pile of papers in front of her. "I have copies of the proposals here, which I shall pass around." She gave a few to Otorin of Lissen, who sat to her right, and others to Borr Sarad on her left. "I should be obliged if you would all add the paragraph regarding the Discipline." She turned in her chair and looked back to the scribes' table. "I have some for you gentlemen," she said.

Malum got up and retrieved them. He could not bring himself to look at the Oligarch and mumbled his thanks. The rest of the Commission was reading the document, but no one, he noted, looked particularly surprised. They all knew that this was coming, he thought, everyone but us.

Phalastra of Estragoth looked up from his reading. "Is there any discussion of the proposal?" he inquired.

The Hodman spoke up. "Isphardel will build and pay for the roads, no?"

"That is correct," the Oligarch replied. "We shall, of course, welcome your help when it comes to manpower. It will be a long and costly job and I would think that a large number of your people will benefit as a result."

The Hodman grunted and nodded his head. "There is nothing here about Fort Bandor," he said.

"Since it does not concern the Outland, we felt that that was a matter for the Empire and yourselves to work out and hence not the business of this Commission. I have, however, made the position of my government on the subject quite clear."

She looked around the table for other questions to answer. Surely, Malum thought, Estragoth will raise some objection. None came. The sly bitch has got them all, he concluded and felt a touch of disappointment that his master had no counter.

"Further discussion?" the Elector asked. "No? Well then, let us put it to the vote. All those in favor of the partition of the Outland as shown on the map, with the addition of the provisos introduced by the Oligarch, raise your hands."

Hands went up all around the table.

"So be it then," Phalastra said.

"One moment, my Lord President," Olivderval interjected. "You haven't cast a vote and it would look much better to the world if the Commission was seen to be unanimous."

"No doubt it would, Madam, but the Empire of Umbria is abstaining," the Elector said dryly. "Now, if there is no further business, I thank you all for your patience and hard work over the years. My last action as President of this Commission is to call for a vote of dissolution." He was entirely gracious.

"Before you do that," Otorin interposed, "I should like to propose a vote of thanks to the Elector of Estragoth for the exemplary way in which he has handled these meetings. He has been an inspiration to us all."

There was a chorus of "Hear, hear" and then everybody applauded. The scribes joined in and there were tears in Malum's eyes as his master nodded his thanks with a tight little smile on his face.

Estragoth held up his hand. "I thank you all. It has been an honor to serve with you. And, on that note, I declare the Commission for the Outland dissolved." He pushed his chair back and stood.

chapter 15

Malum took his time returning to the suit of apartments in which the Umbrian delegation had lived for so many years. He wanted time to think and he was in no rush to confront the Elector. He looked around the quadrangles as he walked through them. There was a slightly hazy quality to the light engendered by the still air and the smoke from cooking fires inside and outside the walls. It left a pleasant tang in the nostrils.

He realized that he was going to miss the place. He had spent more time at Stronta in recent years than in either Angorn or Quern. In fact he had only spent a fortnight in Quern in the past two years and had found it depressingly provincial. Still, if old Estragoth retired, he would be dependent on its revenues unless he could find another place at Court. With the failure of the mission here at Stronta, that now looked a lot less likely. He climbed the stairs to the Elector's apartment feeling decidedly down in the mouth.

Phalastra of Estragoth, to Malum's surprise, was sitting quietly in his oversized, overstuffed chair, sipping at a glass of wine.

"Come in, young man," he said in this thin, creaking voice. "Join me in a glass."

Malum put his papers and his writing utensils down on the sideboard and did as he was bidden.

"I think we can congratulate ourselves," the Elector

said as Malum came over to his chair. He raised his glass. Malum, startled, followed suit.

"You are pleased with the outcome, sir?" he asked, surprise evident.

"Well, it wasn't the total triumph that the Emperor demanded," the old man conceded. "In fact, I shall probably have some difficulty convincing His Imperial Majesty of the wisdom of my point of view. The truth is that we achieved the territorial advantages that we sought." He looked up at Malum. "Get yourself a chair, young man, and sit you down."

"Yes," he continued after Malum had complied, "I think that we can be proud of our effort."

"But the Isphardis got their right of passage through Songuard," Malum objected gently.

"Yes, they did and just think what problems that's going to cause them," Estragoth said with satisfaction. "Add to that the fact that their lands are divided, their supply lines impossibly long, and our eventual annexation of their new territory will be simple."

"But they will have international support and guarantees."

"Bah." Estragoth was dismissive. "It is easy for the Kingdoms to pay lip service to that sort of thing, but can you really see them committing troops to the defense of the Isphardis?" His voice was rich in disdain. "No, no, they'll let that bunch of peddlers fend for themselves. As for the Isphardis, they are incapable of forming an army for themselves. They're afraid to fight. They may be able to pay the Songeans to fight for them, but the Songeans have no military tradition either."

"The Isphardis have a great many ships," Malum pointed out. "They could attack our south coast." He was thinking of Quern.

"Wouldn't do them any good," Estragoth returned

with satisfaction. "Ships are only good for landing soldiers and they have no soldiers. It might be different if they had the secret of the cannon, but that is ours." He smiled briefly. "Besides, they will be too preoccupied in building roads through Songuard to have much time for anything else. With a little bit of encouragement, some of the clans may prove less than helpful to them." The smile flickered again. "There is a long tradition of brigandage in the mountains."

"So you planned it this way all along," Malum said.

"Not entirely. The basic disposition of the various territories, yes, but for the rest I had considerable assistance from Olivderval. I helped it along, of course. Little things mostly; subtle touches. Like giving that armclock to the Mage." There was a small, dry chuckle. "Magicians can't abide machines."

What a wily old bird Phalastra is, Malum thought. He wanted the Isphardis to have their roads all along. At a deeper level there was resentment that the old man had not trusted him enough to confide in him. Nevertheless, the future suddenly seemed a good deal brighter. A place in the Imperial Household no longer seemed so unlikely.

"Well?" Greylock demanded.

"Olivderval did her work well," Jarrod replied.

Greylock put his book aside and took off his spectacles. He looked up at Jarrod and smiled slowly. "Going to be mysterious, are you? Going to make an old man wait. Very well; you've earned the right. Come and sit down and tell me in your own time."

"I'm sorry, sir," Jarrod said, taking the armchair opposite the Mage. "I didn't mean to be dramatic. I just feel drained and a little bit let down somehow. It was over so fast. It was all cut and dried and 'Commission dissolved.' There should have been more to it after fifteen years of maneuvering and impassioned speeches."

"Life has a habit of not living up to our expectations," Greylock commented softly. "But suppose you tell me what did happen."

Jarrod shrugged. "Estragoth reintroduced the Umbrian partition without any alterations, exactly as Ragnor said he would, and it was voted down. Then Olivderval introduced the compromise that she had discussed with us and it passed easily. The Elector was the only one who didn't vote for it. He abstained."

"Didn't put up a fight, try delaying tactics?"

"Nothing. I expected him to call for an adjournment and then follow up with a final attempt to twist arms, but he just opened things up for discussion and moved to a vote. He was quite gracious about it. He was entirely cordial with us, even the Oligarch, after the meeting. I just don't understand."

"Phalastra of Estragoth is a gentleman of the old school," Greylock said. "Grace in defeat is to be expected. Still, if the Empire is looking for an excuse to attack its neighbors, as the Archmage seems to think, the abstention makes some sense. Estragoth has put the Empire on record as being against the settlement without seeming to be unreasonable or obstructionist."

"Or as acquiescing without appearing to back down," Jarrod added.

"Either way," Greylock acknowledged. "It won't make a bit of difference if it comes to war."

Jarrod weighed his words before speaking. "I hesitate to say this, sir. I know that both you and the Archmage have the feeling that another war is in the cards, but I don't think that people of my generation feel that way. We feel that the world is tired of war, even the Umbrians."

"Well, I can only hope that you're right," Greylock

said without enthusiasm. "Mind you, Varodias might be counting on just such a reaction."

"How so?" Jarrod asked.

"The Umbrian-Isphardi border is a long way away, even further for Talisman and Arundel. Ostensibly, we have no vital interests to protect there. If the Empire has designs on Isphardi wealth or Songean resources, it may well be counting on a lack of will in the west to come to their aid."

"Let's hope it never comes to that," Jarrod said as cheerfully as he could.

"Selah to that. However, Ragnor thinks as I do and he has an uncanny way of being right when it comes to Umbria."

Jarrod smiled politely. Two old men trapped in the past, he thought, unable to understand that the world has changed.

"Be that as it may," Greylock said, "d'you think that the Oligarchs will live up to their end of our bargain?"

"I took the precaution of putting the agreement in writing and getting Olivderval's signature on it," Jarrod said with a touch of pride.

"Did you indeed. Well done. They'll pay Tithe in return for Weatherwarding. Excellent. It means that we'll have to emphasize it at the Collegium. We'll need a lot more Weatherwards in the future. Eventually we shall have to stretch the net to cover almost all of the Outland." He looked across at Jarrod and smiled. "It looks as if we shall have to encourage members of the Discipline to have children. We're going to need them." He stopped and thought for a moment.

"Speaking of the Outland, I presume that your Concordat includes Isphardel's new territory and that will mean that Songuard will be getting its weather controlled for free. Perhaps we should negotiate a treaty with them as well. We shall need Weatherwards in the mountains come what may." The smile reappeared and he stretched languidly. "Most of this won't be my problem anyway. We're looking twenty years into the future and I'll be dead by then."

"I wouldn't count on that," Jarrod said loyally. "Ragnor's at least twenty years older than you are."

"True, lad, but Ragnor's either Errathuel come back or a freak of nature. Either way, I doubt he'll be with us much longer."

"He seemed fine to me," Jarrod objected.

"He's very frail," Greylock said gently, "and the Season of the Moons is not too far off. He's never had much tolerance for the cold."

Jarrod wasn't comfortable with the turn the conversation had taken. "What do you suppose will happen next?" he asked.

"On the international front? Very little. There will be a proclamation of the Commission's decision. The adventurous and the desperate will move into the Outland and stake claims." He hesitated. "That reminds me," he said, "when are we going to resume the clearing of the Giants' Causeway?"

"As soon as Nastrus gets back. He's decided to take a holiday. I've got a bunglebird ready to send to Dean Handrom the moment that he reappears. With luck we'll get to our eastern border before he disappears again for the rutting season. After that, it's anybody's guess."

"You'd better ask him to recruit some of his kin while he's there," Greylock observed. "The broadsheets paid gratifying attention to our exploit at Celador, but if the effort peters out, opinion may turn against us."

"We could probably manage without the unicorn if we could persuade our Magicians to venture into the Outland. We don't have to move the stuff all that far. I imagine the new settlers would be grateful for some building material and Nastrus isn't very good at send-ing things to locations that he doesn't know first-hand." He felt a strong twinge of guilt at hiding his intentions from Greylock, and he made a mental note to pick a new site when Nastrus came back. There must be more than enough stone for the new building by now.

"Well, now that you're up to Talisman, you'll prob-ably get some help from the Chief Warlock."

"From Sumner?" Jarrod feigned mild surprise. "Isn't that rather out of character?"

Greylock gave a phlegmy little chuckle. "On the con-trary. It would be an opportunity to make himself bet-ter known, give him a chance to profit from the work that we've already done." He looked at Jarrod side-ways, eyes glittering. "Let us not forget that Sumner wants to be the next Archmage."

"That's not possible," Jarrod said flatly.

"I for one hope not, but he's a very ambitious man."

"He's never performed a significant piece of Magic," Jarrod objected.

"You're forgetting the defeat of the Outlanders in Arundel," Greylock said mildly. "He claims credit for that."

"That was just a jumped-up piece of Weatherward-ing," Jarrod said dismissively. "He wouldn't have pulled it off without Ragnor's tactics."

"You're being uncharitable," Greylock said with a smile. "The fact remains that he sees himself as the sav-ior of Arundel and he blames Ragnor for what he per-ceives as a lack of recognition. It would be a mistake to underestimate him."

Jarrod sighed. "I always thought that life would be simple once we had defeated the Outlanders, but it cer-tainly hasn't turned out that way."

"The irony is that it was the Outlanders who held

us all together, gave us a sense of common purpose. I've a nasty feeling that future generations will look back on these past fifteen years as the golden age of Strand."

"Perish the thought," Jarrod said. "No, I'm looking forward to the era of the Archmage Greylock."

The old Mage smiled. "Egregious flattery," he rejoined. "I still have to get the votes."

chapter 16

Greylock's conversation, with its talk about Ragnor's death, stayed with Jarrod and worried him. If the Archmage died, or even if he decided to abdicate his office in favor of Greylock, Jarrod's life was bound to change. No Archmage, to his knowledge, had ever stepped aside or been deposed, but Ragnor had manifestly accomplished everything that could be expected of an Archmage. He had invoked the Cloak of Protection to render Celador invisible when the Outlanders threatened and he had, in the popular mind at least, discovered and performed the Great Spell. If he wanted to lay down the burden, no one would gainsay him.

Jarrod's mind ran on. If Greylock became Archmage, and, despite the old boy's reservations, there really could be no question that he would, then he might well succeed him as Mage of Paladine. That was farther than Jarrod had ever thought to go when he was growing up and it would be enormously satisfying, but it would also mean that he would be tied to the Outpost and to Stronta—at least for the first two years.

He got up from his chair, went to the window and looked out. Greylock had also brought Nastrus to mind. Where was he? Jarrod wondered as he contemplated the townsfolk's grazing kina. It was ironic that Pellia, for whom he had had the greatest affection, had only been back to Strand twice, while Nastrus, who had, more often than not, been a thorn in the foot, was the one who stayed. He had come to count on the unicorn's presence, but he had no right to do so. The truth was that he needed the unicorn to turn his dream into a reality, and he now realized that if he didn't seize the opportunity soon, he might never get the chance.

He left the window and wandered over to the shelves that lined one of the walls. His mind continued to make calculations as he ran his eye over the handwritten books in their wooden covers and the carefully arranged ranks of scrolls in search of a text on building. There was nothing remotely useful. He had told Greylock that he would send a bunglebird off to Handrom the moment that Nastrus reappeared. He came to a decision. Even if he did send the message promptly, it would take a sennight for the Dean to assemble a cadre of Magicians and a fortnight more for them to travel to the point on the Causeway where work had stopped. That would give him three sennights, with Nastrus' help, to get his own work done, or at least to make a considerable start.

The decision made, he went to his desk and drew a sheet of paper toward him. He dipped a quill in the inkwell and began to make notes. There was a great deal of work to be done and most of it would have to be done in secrecy. There was sure to be enough stone available by now, but what he had in mind would require more than that. Worse still, he had no expertise in the area. He would need wood and roofing material and neither were available in the Outland. Before he did anything he would need advice. There was a Master Mason that he had met at the palace after Hall. If the man was still at Stronta, he might be able to glean some of the things he needed to know. On reflection, he thought, it would be best if Nastrus stayed away a while longer.

The following morning Jarrod went in search of Moresby Yarrow. His memory had retrieved the name as well as some information that the mason had volunteered. The man had been brought to Stronta by a midcountry baron made prosperous by the boom in the wool trade and desirous of constructing a new house to reflect his new status. Yarrow had complained that the baron had kept him cooling his heels while he had enjoyed the opening of the boar-hunting season. Had the potential commission not been a big one, Yarrow had said, he would have been on his way home days ago. Jarrod hurried to the Chamberlain' office, hoping that he would not be too late.

It took the best part of the morning to track the man, and Yarrow, when found hunched over a pint of porter in one of the better taverns outside the walls, matched Jarrod's memory of him in every respect save for his clothes. He was broad-shouldered and barrel-chested, with an outdoorsman's weathered face. He was bald and made up for it by being bearded. His hands were large with callused pads and his clothes, on this day, were good, but plain. If he was impressed by being sought out by a Mage, he didn't show it.

Jarrod's offer of another pint was accepted, and served by the landlord himself. Mine host was nervously ingratiating and clearly hoped that his new patron would leave as soon as possible. After a few minutes of aimless pleasantries, Yarrow looked at Jarrod and said, "I am flattered by your company, Excellence, but I rather doubt that this is one of your usual haunts. In fact the goggling of this riffraff"—he indicated the rest of the room with a toss of his head—"rather proves it. I imagine that you want something from me."

"Information," Jarrod agreed. "You seem to me to be the kind of man who would respect a confidence."

"Depends what it is," Yarrow returned. "I'll have no truck with politics."

"No politics, I promise you. I'd like to ask your advice about how one goes about building a modern castle."

"A castle?" Yarrow gave him a doubtful look. "Well, I'd suggest you do one of two things. Apprentice yourself to a good master or hire someone who knows what they're doing."

"Sound advice, but I'm afraid I can't do either of those," Jarrod said evenly, "but I'd be happy to pay you for your information."

"I see, pick my brains and then give the commission to someone else. It won't work, you know. Use inferior people and you'll get a botched job. Oh, it may look all right when it's first up, but as soon as you move in the problems will start."

"That isn't the way of it. The site I have in mind is extremely remote and there's no way of getting a crew there."

"Then it can't be done," Yarrow said flatly, and took a long pull at his porter. He wiped his mouth with the back of his hand.

"You're forgetting the Magic," Jarrod replied with a faint smile.

"Ah. So I did." He gave a faint shrug. "If you can do it all with Magic, what would you need me for?"

"I can't just look at a picture and reproduce it," Jarrod explained. "Well, that's not quite true," he amended. "I could produce an illusion solid enough for you to have to open the door to get inside, but it would disappear the moment I stopped concentrating."

"This begins to sound interesting," Yarrow said, draining his tankard, "but it's poor advice I give on an empty stomach."

Jarrod looked around and caught the innkeeper's eye. The man came over, bowing and rubbing his hands.

"Master Yarrow and I would like some food." Seeing the renewed nervousness in the man's face, he said, "Perhaps you have a private room where we could conduct our conversation."

"Oh indeed, Your Grace, if you and your guest would be kind enough to accompany me I can assure you of complete privacy. Perhaps some wine with your repast? My wife does a very nice capon and there are those who swear that her syllabub is the best in Stronta." He was backing and bowing and motioning them to follow him all the while that he was talking.

"Does this happen to you all the time?" Yarrow asked as they followed.

"I very rarely frequent taverns," Jarrod answered.

The innkeeper ushered them into a small, comfortable room on the second floor, bowed yet again and disappeared.

"Now, Excellence," Yarrow said as they settled in, "perhaps you could tell me a little more about this project."

"In the strictest confidence."

"Oh aye. This comes under the heading of a professional secret and I didn't get to be a Master Mason by having a loose tongue." He smiled for the first time. "Besides, it isn't healthy to cross a Mage, especially one who is prepared to buy me a meal. I am about to be in your debt."

"Very well then," Jarrod said, and launched into an explanation.

Moresby Yarrow ate stolidly while he listened. Serving girls came and went with platters and wine. The food was simple but well cooked and the wine was good enough to make Jarrod check his coin purse to see how much money he had brought with him. When the meal and the dissertation were over, Yarrow pushed his chair back so that he could stretch his legs and belched contentedly.

"A pretty tale, Excellence," he said, "and an even prettier problem. It intrigues me. The first people to push to the edge of the Alien Plain, the gods know how many years from now, come across a splendid, well-fortified castle where no such buildings should be." He leaned back and patted his belly. "I like it. What I like even more is the challenge of imagining something practical that will seem absolutely modern, oh, say a hundred years from now. Yes indeed, that's a commission worth taking."

"So you'll tell me what I have to know to build it?" Jarrod said with barely concealed relief.

"I have no objection to that," Yarrow said with a self-satisfied smile. "The only trouble is that I don't know precisely what will be needed. Besides, we're going about this with our feet over our heads. We need to talk to a designer of castles first. Once he has drawn his plans, I can build them."

Jarrod gave the mason a jaundiced look. "I really don't have the time to go around looking for experts. I need to know how many beams I need, how long they should be, how thick, what the best material for a roof is, how many chimneys I'll need. Surely you can tell me about those kinds of things."

"Not without plans I can't. Anyway, it won't take too long to find the man we need. He lives three streets from here. He's retired now, mostly because no one's building castles these days. His grandfather was the man who designed Stronta, the only star fort on Strand. There hasn't been a more advanced design since. The talent skipped a generation; Chatham's father played the country gentleman and ran through the fortune his father had made. Chatham has his grandfather's gift, but he's never really had the chance to exercise it. There wasn't much building in the last years of the war and since then the styles have changed. Loves turrets with conical rooves, does Chatham."

"Is Chatham his first or his last name?"

"First. Chatham Greygor is the full version. Why don't you pay up and we'll go and see him."

A quarter of an hour later Jarrod found himself climbing the none too salubrious stairs of a three-story house in the "old quarter," as the town within the walls was now called. The houses on the street were separated from one another, and the grimy windows of the stairwell showed a small plot of land in back. This had obviously been a prosperous neighborhood in times gone by.

Greygor himself was tall and thin. His beard and the fringe of hair that survived were grey. A pair of spectacles without sidepieces clung precariously to the end of a long nose. His clothes were out of fashion by at least a decade and none too clean. They also appeared to have been made for a bigger man.

"Come in gentlemen," he said. "Pick a chair and push a moggy off it. I'd offer you refreshments, but I haven't had a chance to go to the market today and I won't have strong drink in the house. It ruined my father, you see," he said by way of explanation. He was clearly flustered by their arrival.

"Don't fret, Chatham," Yarrow said. "The Mage and I have just eaten."

"Mage is it?" Greygor asked.

"Aye, Mage Courtak."

"Courtak? Oh, the unicorn man. Yes, I've heard of you. An honor, Excellence." He gestured to a large armchair occupied by a large feline.

Jarrod went over and dislodged the fat tabby before

taking his seat. The cat promptly leaped back up, turned round a couple of times and curled up, purring.

"Robes make irresistible laps, I'm afraid," Greygor said diffidently, "especially dark ones."

"Don't worry," Jarrod reassured him, stroking the rumbling creature, "I'm fond of animals."

"That's all right then," the architect said, tipping an orange-and-white out of another chair. "People are funny about cats. Don't seem to realize how affectionate they are. Too affectionate sometimes. That's why my drawing table is on a slant. All I have to do is unroll a piece of paper and they all want to sit on it."

"That's all very interesting, Chatham, but we didn't come here to talk about cats," Yarrow cut in.

"No, no, of course not." He paused, looking bewildered. "It's always good to see you, Moresby, but why have you and the Mage come?"

"The Mage has a commission that's right down your alley, but there are complications. I think I'd better let him explain."

So Jarrod outlined his plans again, more surely and swiftly this time. When he had finished, there was a long, long silence, broken, finally, by a drawn-out sigh from Greygor.

"It will be expensive," he said cautiously.

Jarrod was relieved that he hadn't said that it was impossible. "How much?" he asked.

"Well, you won't have to pay the workmen's wages, food and lodging, but we're talking about a very substantial structure and, even without the stone, there are a lot of materials to be bought. You are also asking for some design innovations."

"How much?" Jarrod pressed.

Greygor looked over at his friend. "About five hundred thousand crowns, wouldn't you think, Moresby?"

"Sounds about right to me," Yarrow concurred.

"One thing's obvious to me, though. We'll have to be there when he builds it."

"Out of the question," Jarrod said.

"Only way you'll get it built," Yarrow replied matter-of-factly. "You're no expert on site selection, there are always surprises along the way and you want something that will look up-to-date a century hence. We'll have to experiment."

Greygor nodded his agreement.

"If I could get you out there, and it's a very big if, entailing a trip through the void on a unicorn that could easily kill you, you would have to rough it in a wilderness without food or shelter. Why would you want to do that?"

"I can't answer for Moresby, but for me, buildings are my children," Chatham explained. "They are what I leave behind to keep my memory alive, the mark that says that I was here and did something worthwhile in my time." He smiled ruefully. "I'm a good maker of plattes, better than most I think, but I hate to compromise, to settle for the second-rate and, as a result, there aren't a lot of my children around, most of them are modest and some I took on because I needed to eat. I'm ashamed of some of those. Now you offer me a chance to do something major, something designed to last for centuries, and you ask why I'd be willing to take risks?"

"And you?" Jarrod asked of Yarrow.

"I'm bored of working for men like this puffed-up little baron with the manners of a swineherd. No, I take that back. I've know some civil swineherds. I like the challenge of this project. Being able to do something no one's ever done in a place that no one's ever done it. And I don't mind going to the grave with no one knowing that I've done it." He stopped. "One thing, though," he said, pointing a finger at Jarrod. "I want my name large and clear on that castle."

Jarrod smiled. "Done," he said. "If the two of you are prepared to take the risks and I can't do it without you, I don't see that I have much of an option. The final decision, however, belongs to the unicorn. He may not agree to take you; indeed, he may not want to have anything to do with the project. Unicorns look on buildings as prisons."

"I see," Greygor said doubtfully. "You have to ask the unicorn."

Jarrod caught the sideways glance he gave to Yarrow. "Don't worry," he said. "I'm not mad. The unicorn and I can communicate." He smiled briefly. "I'm afraid that I'm the victim of my own self-importance. I assumed that everybody knew that."

"I had heard something like it," Yarrow admitted, "but I thought it was just an embellishment by the ballad makers. Well, I suppose you'd better go and ask him."

"I'm afraid I can't do that. He's not at Stronta and I don't know when exactly he'll be back. I think we'll have to proceed on the assumption that he'll agree and try to have everything ready by the time he shows up. I'll be happy to pay you for the work you do," he added quickly, "even if we don't get to build the place this year." He saw the look of disappointment on Greygor's face and of skepticism on Yarrow's. "What's the first step?" he asked.

Yarrow stretched. "You and Chatham will have to work on the plans and I'll scout about for sources of wood and materials. Folks will assume that I'm making inquiries for Baron Hyde."

"Good," Jarrod said. He turned to Greygor. "When can we start?"

The man thought a moment. "I'll make some preliminary sketches from what you've told me and you can come back tomorrow afternoon. Or I could come to you."

"I don't think that would be wise. The Outpost is as full of gossip as a bathhouse. I'd as soon come here if that won't cause trouble with your neighbors."

Greygor smiled. "Oh, they already think I'm mad. It might even improve my credit with the local shopkeepers."

"I'll bring some money for you both," Jarrod promised, "but remember, no word of this to anyone."

The next sennight slipped by amid discussion of the merits of a ground floor hall against those of one built over a vaulted undercroft, the placement of the solar, whether it would be possible to design a privy tower so that there would be running water throughout, where the servants should sleep, how many fireplaces and where they should be located, if the kitchen should be built apart. Jarrod had expected Greygor to produce pictures of the main structure, but, instead, there was a steady stream of floor plans.

Yarrow reported back every couple of days to collect updated estimates on the number of beams needed, on what kind of wood was best for the new roof construction that Greygor envisioned and to collect money from Jarrod. Getting hold of that much ready coin was something of a problem, not because there was any lack of it, but because the rents from Jarrod's estates and the monies from the pensions he collected from the various governments were kept in the Outpost's strongboxes. After his first foray he decided to take Tokamo into his confidence and thereafter things went smoothly. The question of where to store the materials all that good coin was purchasing was not so easily solved.

Jarrod insisted that the building materials be stored beyond the Upper Causeway so that Nastrus, when he reappeared, would be able to transfer them directly to the mountains. To Yarrow's objection that it would take twenty men round the clock to guard them if they were left in the open, Jarrod promised to set a warding spell that would keep people out.

"Oh, and I suppose that after all this secrecy about your participation, you're just going to ride out there and perform Magic?" Yarrow retorted.

"Nonsense, Moresby," Greygor said. "The Mage will simply make himself invisible and ride out there with us. No one will be any the wiser."

"I can't do that," Jarrod said sadly.

"I thought all Magicians could make themselves invisible," Greygor said.

"Oh, we can. It's just that we're enjoined not to do it for personal reasons; the possibilities for abuse are too great. I'm sure lots of my colleagues honor that in the breach from time to time, but I am a Mage and I'm supposed to set an example."

They were sitting comfortably in Greygor's main room with a small coal fire burning in the grate and the rose reflections of the sunset sky tinting the old carpet and restoring its color. The light softened the outlines of the ubiquitous cats and added to the feeling of camaraderie.

"Got any bright ideas, Excellence?" Yarrow asked.

"First of all, if we're going to spend time together in the mountains, you're both going to have to stop calling me Excellence and the Mage. My name's Jarrod. And yes, I think I have an idea. It's going to take some practice, but I could shape-change. I'd have to revert to my normal self to set the warding in place, but if I stood right under the Upper Causeway I should be invisible from above."

Both the others looked uneasy. It was one thing to get accustomed to the presence of a Mage, quite another when he started talking about changing into something else.

"Have you, ah, have you selected your, um, alternative form?" Greygor asked.

Jarrod smiled, in part to calm their nervousness. "Well, I shall have to practice somewhere quiet and private and I shall need a model." He looked from one to the other. "Don't worry," he said. "It won't be either of you." He stretched his legs out and steepled his fingers. "Since I will have to take back my own body to perform the spell of protection, I can't simply take over some creature and leave my own body. I shall have to transform myself into that animal. The last time I did it I was a boy and I'm told that I made a very strange-looking sheep." He paused for a laugh that did not come. "I thought," he resumed hurriedly, "that I might try to become a cat." He gestured around the room. "There are any number of examples here and you, Chatham, can monitor me and tell me how successful I am."

"This isn't dangerous, is it?" Greygor inquired.

"Not for you."

"I wish you luck, Jarrod," Yarrow said, "and I'd love to stick around and see you try it, but I have to get back and change for Hall. I don't want my boar-hunting baron to think that I'm ungrateful for his continuing financial support." He got up and stretched.

"I should be going too," Jarrod agreed. "I'll be back tomorrow morning and I'll do some preparatory work then," he said to Greygor.

"I'll try to have some sketches of the curtain wall and towers ready," the older man said. He pushed a cat off his lap and stood up for the leavetaking. Yarrow paused with his hand on the doorknob. "You're a Mage," he said. "You can do anything you want. Why all this hocus-pocus?"

"Because," Jarrod said slowly, "while the Discipline

has been granted territory in the Outland, its location hasn't been decided upon. As you probably know, I was the Discipline's representative on the Commission. Now, if you were one of the Queen's spies . . ." He let the phrase die.

"Oh, so that's the way of it," Yarrow said, and slumped out.

Early the following day, Jarrod made his way to Greygor's lodgings with a tingle of anticipation. Although what he was hoping to do was not considered serious Magic, he felt, nonetheless, as if he was embarking on an adventure. The previous evening he had gone over the notes he had made as a boy. He had disliked the anatomy sessions that were an integral part of shape-changing, but he was glad now that Greylock had been so meticulous in his tutelage. The drawings of the musculature and skeleton of that long-dead cat were clear and precise.

Greygor opened the door at his knock and then bustled about preparing chai.

"Do you want me to go out for a walk?" he asked.

"Not unless you want to," Jarrod said. "In fact it would be rather a help to have someone to judge how successful my efforts are." He accepted a mug of chai and added, "You'll have to be absolutely quiet."

"I'll just sit in a corner and watch," Greygor promised. "D'you mind telling me what will happen?"

"Not much of anything to begin with. I shall just try to get into the mind of one of your cats first. I know what the body of a cat looks like, but I don't know what it feels like."

"You won't hurt the cat, will you?" Greygor asked anxiously.

"Not at all. If I do it right the cat won't even know I'm there."

"Oh well then, I suppose it's all right," Greygor said,

sounding not altogether convinced. He took his chai over to a miraculously cat-free chair by the wall.

Jarrod drank his fill and put his mug aside. He looked over the group of cats. Two were grooming each other, one was stalking a fly, three were intently watching something through the window and the rest were snoozing. He picked a large white stretched bonelessly in a patch of sunshine. He adjusted his own posture until he was comfortable and then shut his eyes and collected himself. He blocked out his awareness of the room and concentrated on the image of the cat. He reached out gently with his mind, seeking that other intelligence. He sensed a veiled consciousness, somnolent on the surface, alert below. He probed further and knew that the cat was aware of him. He felt an ear twitch. He slid further in.

The cat's eyes flicked open and Jarrod saw a segment of the room from the floor up. The cat shook its head. Huge chairs loomed. The ceiling was a long way off. Distance, however, occasioned no loss of detail. Everything was sharp and clear. Inside the cat there was wariness balanced by intense curiosity; a concentrated stillness that could explode into motion in an instant. The cat rolled from its side to its belly, hind legs prepared to spring into escape if that was needed. The head moved from one side to the other, scanning the other members of the extended family to see if they had noticed anything amiss. No visual evidence of that. The cat sniffed the air and Jarrod knew the pack smell made up of a dozen different strands. Chatham's odor was part of the familiar. His own, he realized, was less so, but the cat detected no sharpness of fear or anger coming from his body.

The head turned and looked over the shoulder just to make sure. Jarrod saw himself as a vast expanse of blue, tapering upward. No sign of a threat, but one never knew with strange humans. The cat was on its feet in one lithe move. It stretched, claws digging into the carpet. It sauntered across the room and lept up onto an unoccupied bench. Good vantage point, back protected. Whatever this disturbance within it was, there seemed no reason to display aggression. The eyes roamed over the room just to be sure. When in doubt, wash. Grooming commenced.

Jarrod withdrew and slowly opened his eyes. His sight, he noted, was not as sharp and his sense of smell seemed severely limited. He sat up.

"Interesting animals," he commented.

"Beautiful, mysterious and independent," Greygor replied.

"The surface is cool and collected, but it's completely feral underneath."

"Miniature warcats," Greygor said complacently.

"Fortunately I don't have to become one, just look like one."

Jarrod stood up and undid his rope belt; then he started to pull his robe off over his head.

"What are you doing now?" Greygor asked.

"Taking off my clothes," Jarrod said, his voice muffled by the cloth.

He folded the robe and put it carefully on the carpet. He unlaced his sandals and took them off. "No self-respecting cat would wear clothes," he said. "Besides, I'm going to have to make myself very much smaller and I'd get swamped." He undid his breachclout, folded it and put it on top of the robe.

"I hadn't thought of that," Greygor said, averting his eyes. "One thing. Perhaps you ought to try this in the other room."

"Oh, right, in case someone comes to visit."

"There is that, but I was thinking more of the cats.

They might not take kindly to a strange cat in their midst."

"A good point. I don't have the pack scent that says I'm harmless. You do, by the way."

"All the more reason," Greygor said, and opened the inner door.

The room was small and mostly taken up by the bed. The bed, like the furniture in the main room, attested to the family's past affluence, first by its size and then by its appearance. The wood was dark and lustrous. At some point in its history it had been carefully polished by a servant or a conscientious housewife. The posts were delicately carved, but the silk of the canopy was dim and, in places, tattered. Jarrod edged past Greygor and stood on a small rug. Greygor went and sat cross-legged on the bed. Jarrod rotated his head to ease his neck and shook his arms, hands hanging limp. He began to breathe deeply and rhythmically, clearing his mind of everything except the task ahead. His eyelids drooped and his chin sank.

Greygor found that he was holding his breath and forced himself to breathe normally. Life was passing strange, he thought. All those years of scrimping and make-work when nothing interesting happened from one month to the next and now his debts were paid and he was in his bedchamber staring at a naked Mage who was trying to turn himself into a cat. At that instant the Mage's outline wavered and Greygor blinked a couple of times to clear his eyes. The outline was sharp again, but it seemed to Greygor that the Mage was shorter than before. The blurring occurred again and this time he was sure. Courtak was shrinking.

After about half of an hour had passed, Jarrod was the size of a six-year-old boy and his skin was sheened with sweat. This was harder than he had expected, and he hadn't even begun on the transmogrification. He dropped onto all fours and began to concentrate on the bones and muscles of his arms. He brought the fore part of the cat to mind and started with his fingers.

The movement startled Greygor and, for a moment, he thought that the Mage had fainted. Then he noticed that the fingers of the hand nearest him were retracting while the hand itself arched and became clubby. The proportions of the arms changed so that the miniature Mage was canting forward. There was a pause when nothing seemed to be happening and then, with increasing swiftness, the legs began to change. From the coccyx a protrusion grew into a thin, ratlike tail. Hip and shoulder joints modulated. Greygor stared transfixed and slightly nauseated as the nose shrank and the jaw became rounded. The ears elongated up into points. There on the carpet was a pink, oversized cat, hairless except for a incongruous cap of tight, brown curls.

That too began to change. The curls straightened out, the hair became shorter and flatter and finer. Hair began to sprout over the rest of the body and the spindly tail bushed out. In a matter of what seemed like minutes a very large, dark brown cat appeared. There was another pause and Greygor could see that the animal's breathing was labored. The chest rippled and became more barrel-like, the hips slimmer. The breathing slowed. Gradually, like snow settling on a ploughed field, the brown fur turned white. There was another blurring of outline, and when the cat became solid again it was half its size. It was still big for a cat, but Greygor had seen cats of that size before.

The round head turned and Greygor saw the bright pink of the inside of the ears and of the nose. Vivid blue eyes regarded him quizzically. There was something not quite right, he thought, as the cat sat back on its haunches and curled its tail around them. Then it struck him.

"Whiskers," he said, and his voice came out hoarsely. "You need whiskers."

The cat's eyes closed and thin white filaments began to grow out of both sides of the button nose.

"Long enough," Greygor said. "They're supposed to be exactly the width of the broadest part of your body. That's how you know if you can get through a given space."

The cat's eyes opened and the pupils were no longer round, though the irises remained a startling blue. The transformation was complete. It stretched, first one way then the other, testing its new muscles. Then it walked quietly around the room, taking everything in. It circled back to the bed, looked up at Greygor, collected itself and sprang. It landed lightly on the bed and sat down with a look of palpable satisfaction. It lifted a paw to its mouth and nonchalantly began to groom itself.

Greygor laughed delightedly and applauded.

chapter 17

Jarrod's impersonation was declared an unqualified success, but the cost was higher than he had expected. His return to his own form left him weak, and all his joints ached. His ride back to the Outpost was slow and painful. He was fortunate in that no bullyboys lurked in his path: he would have been easy pickings. He spent the next two days in bed, and the aches and pains took a good sennight before they entirely disappeared. One thing was obvious to him: good as the disguise was, he could not afford to assume it too often.

Accordingly, he sent word to Moresby Yarrow to collect and hold the materials that he was acquiring and to assemble the means to transport them beyond the Upper Causeway all at one time. He did not know what he would face when it came to building his monument, but he knew that he could not afford to get there and find that his body could not handle the power needed.

On the appointed day, Jarrod rode into the town in the predawn dark and tethered his horse outside Greygor's house. Half an hour later, the architect came down and strapped on a saddlebag. He disappeared into the house again and when he reappeared he was carrying a large, white cat. He spoke soothingly to the horse and then draped the cat carefully across the spot where the neck emerged from the shoulders.

"Now you just stay limp while I get into the saddle,"

he said. "You'll be quite safe as long as the horse stays still."

Jarrod-the-cat wasn't convinced. He could smell the horse's nervousness. If the animal turned skittish, he had no way of hanging on except by digging in his claws and that, he knew, was a prescription for disaster. He felt and heard Greygor clamber into place. The horse, mercifully, held its stance. It was a good thing, Jarrod thought, that the yard was only half a mile away.

Greygor's hand stroked his back. "I'm afraid you'll have to stay where you are," the architect said. "There isn't as much room back here as I thought there would be."

Jarrod braced himself as the uncomfortable and undignified ride began. The one good thing was that, with Gregor keeping the reins short there wasn't much likelihood that the horse would drop its head and dump him onto the cobbled street. He prayed that they would not break into a trot. The swaying of the cobblestones beneath him was bad enough. He shut his eyes and resigned himself.

It might have been only half a mile, but the trip seemed to take half a lifetime. The yard, when they finally reached it, was a lamplit bustle. It would have been very large to the full-sized Jarrod, but to Jarrod-the-cat it was vast and dangerous. It was filled with stamping draft horses harnessed to long wagons filled with timber. Other wagons were weighed down with sackcloth-covered shapes. Roof slates or bricks, Jarrod surmised as he was lifted off the horse and set down upon the ground.

The view was terrifying. It was one thing looking up at Greygor's furniture, but quite another to face this prospect. The furniture, at least, stayed still. Flaring torches threw unreliable, shifting patches of light. Large men with big, hard boots lumbered around cursing and spitting. Horses moved restlessly, wheels creaked ominously. The combined noise was appalling. Orders were shouted, iron-shod hooves rang, bits jingled and, in the distance, there was the hideous barking of a dog. There was only one sensible thing to do. He turned, reared up on his hind legs, and reached for Greygor's knee with his front paws.

"Oh, we want to be carried do we," the architect said with a grin. "What a lazy great beast you are."

Jarrod found the tone of voice offensive. He was not accustomed to being talked to like a recalcitrant child, but he was grateful when the man picked him up and tucked him under his arm.

Greygor led the horse across the yard toward a wagon loaded with kegs. Jarrod, eyesight uncommonly keen, saw that Yarrow was sitting up on the box beside the driver.

"The best of the morning to you, Moresby," Greygor called out as they got close.

"And to you, friend Chatham, and to Your Excellence," Yarrow replied, and ducked his head to Jarrod with an ironic smirk.

"Take the cat, would you," Greygor said. "It's bloody heavy."

Yarrow complied and Jarrod found himself plumped down on the seat.

"What have you got in the back?" Greygor asked, jerking his head in that direction.

"Ale. The men'll get it after they've unloaded the wagons. You'd be surprised how much faster it goes when they know it's waiting for them when they've finished."

"Well, you won't need me for that," the architect returned. "I'll hitch the horse to the back and then I'll go on home. The walk will do me good. Besides, I've work to do. Seeing all this material gathered together gives me a feeling of urgency."

"Aye, it does tend to bring an air of reality to all those pieces of paper, doesn't it? Off with you then; we'll be off in a minute ourselves."

Jarrod enjoyed the trip out beyond the Causeways. The familiar terrain, known since boyhood, seemed oddly different. Movement, even tiny movement, caught his eye, though the early light was poor. He found that he was probing his surroundings with his nose and his ears. The breeze from the south brought wood smoke, the smell of oatcakes cooking, the complex stench of middens, the powerful scent of man and of kina and, closer, the sweat of horses. In the background was the freshness of dew on the grass. His ability to separate out the various scents and sounds amazed him, as did his awareness of where they all came from.

This new body pleased him. He enjoyed the perversity of being able to check on what was going on behind his back without having to move his torso. What he did not enjoy, however, was the feeling that the Place of Power engendered. It made his fur feel prickly. The guarding menhirs and the two towering steles, one white, one black, raised the hackles on his back. His tail lashed to and fro. Even when the structure was lost behind them in the dust kicked up by their procession, he could feel them.

The next landmark that came into sight was the Stronta Gate, whose defense had caused so much hardship and such loss of life all those years ago. Its shadow lay over Greylock still. The great doors had been repaired, but these days they stood open. There were guards still, however, though in this modern age they passed their time by making passage of the gate a slow and frustrating thing. It was not until all the paperwork had been read by three of them and a keg of ale had

changed hands that they were allowed to continue on
their way.

Through the first set of doors, down the wide, high
tunnel with the iron-tipped bottom of the portcullis
protruding from the ceiling like fangs, out again between the metal-sheathed northern doors and into the
light. Ahead of them lay the Alien Plain, the grass
scythed short for a good league. It was empty now, but
later in the day gentlemen and prosperous merchants
would come out to ride and to show off their horseflesh.

Once beyond the remnants of the older causeway, the
cart turned left and headed westward, followed by the
procession of wagons. Jarrod watched the wall go by
for a while and then curled up and napped lightly until
the cart came to a halt. He stretched and peered across
a broad area that had been cleared of stones. Yarrow
stood up and waved the convoy into the position that
he wanted. Then the business of unloading began.

Moresby Yarrow moved continually from wagon to
wagon, directing, ordering, jesting and, on more than
one occasion, lending a heavily muscled shoulder to the
stacking of a rough-planed beam of robur. His bald
pate gleamed in the sun and his voice rose above the
crashing and creaking and the curses. Jarrod, watching
from the wagon seat and luxuriating in the feel of sun
on his fur, reckoned that he had been exceedingly fortunate in his choice of mason-cum-foreman. Had he believed in such things, he would have said that it was
destiny, or, that the god in charge of building was beneficent.

It was obvious that it would take several hours to get
everything unloaded and the workmen back on the road
home and equally obvious that there was nothing for
him to do. He decided that he might as well explore.
The feline part of his nature expected it. Since he might
never be a cat again, it seemed a pity to waste the ex-

perience. He smiled to himself. Greylock had taught him well. One side of him condemned this ruse as frivolous, but if he used the opportunity constructively, he would silence the nagger in his mind.

He looked down over the side of the cart. The ground seemed farther away than he had expected. Furthermore, jumping down from a height was not something that he had practiced. It was time to banish his human doubts and let his feline instincts take over. He gathered his haunches under him and selected a spot. His body gave an involuntary wiggle just before he launched out.

He landed easily, legs bending to absorb the shock. He shook himself approvingly and walked away from the noise and the work with his tail standing proudly up in the air. The daymoon was up and his twin shadows slid along the ground in front of him. The sun had climbed halfway up the sky and the light was getting stronger. He contracted his pupils to cut down on the growing glare and padded on contentedly, head moving from side to side. Walking on four legs, he thought, was a much smoother, easier way of doing it. He broke into a trot and then put on a sudden spurt of extra speed. It was exhilarating. He was amazed at how rapid the acceleration had been. Even Nastrus couldn't move from a trot to a gallop that fast.

His run had brought him to the edge of a tumble of old blocks of stone, the edges rounded now by centuries of rain and wind. He was panting, mouth open, tongue protruding slightly, and his heart was beating fast. This body was good for the swift dash, but not for a sustained sprint. Better, he thought, to take a rest. He selected a rock with a flat surface and bounded up onto it without conscious calculation. From there he moved daintily from one stone to another, heading for one that was about a foot higher than its neighbors. When he was within a couple of feet of it, his hind legs coiled beneath him. The muscles bunched and released, propelling him into the air. He landed precisely, turned around twice and curled up, tail around his nose.

He drowsed, consciousness rising from time to time to take stock of his surroundings, his ears moving to monitor the area. His nose twitched. There was something interesting upwind. The ears turned. Minute scratchings. Food, said the nose. The eyes slitted open. Somewhere ahead, down in the jumble of weathered stone slabs, there was prey. Jarrod rolled to his stomach, front paws ahead, hind legs beneath his body. All his senses strained. His tail twitched in anticipation. He got up with deceptive slowness, arching his neck and unsheathing his claws. His eyes scanned the terrain and his nose quested into the breeze. Nothing to be seen, but there must be hundreds of passageways between the rocks. He would have to hope that the creature came out onto the surface—or could be forced out.

He would hunt it. There was no question about that. Vole, his nose supplied, two of them. The cold fever of the chase was already coursing through his veins, energizing everything. He felt much the way he did before he performed Magic. Everything had a special clarity. He jumped down from his vantage point and crouched, head thrust forward, tail lashing. He knew the direction and had a good idea of the probable distance. He darted forward, over and around, and then stopped. He took a few, careful paces more and stopped again, head up, ears forward, every fiber alert. Over there, just behind that protruding block.

His mind charted the best course of approach, using what cover there was. He was downwind, but there was no sense in taking the risk of being seen. He moved forward, almost prancingly, shoulders hunched, head low, and then darted into a patch of shadow. The voles had moved to their left, closer to the corner of the block.

The scent of them was strong. His tongue flicked out across his lips. He moved forward at a rapid trot, stepping lightly; no sound, no vibrations. He reached the lee side of a chunk of stone and slunk into the shadow.

Immobile now, watching, waiting. Patience holding all his instincts in check. If they are on the surface, they will come around that corner; if they are below, they could pop up anywhere. The tail twitched. Too many possibilities. Watch, wait, infinitely patient. He crouched there, single-minded, focusing on the terrain, interpreting the information that his nose and ears were bringing him, prepared to move in an instant. The human part of him marveled at the level of concentration and reveled in the feeling of being completely alive.

There was a blur at the corner of his vision and all his senses switched to it. A small brown head with round, shiny, black eyes and a quiver of whiskers. Mature, male vole, fast on its feet, very sharp teeth. The identification was instantaneous. Slowly, and with great caution, the little creature emerged. It sat up on its hind legs and its head moved quickly back and forth as it gauged the dangers and the possibilities for food. Not yet, Jarrod thought. Absolutely still. Satisfied, the vole dropped to all fours and pattered forward, looking for seeds, or lizards.

Jarrod exploded from his hiding place, feet moving effortlessly, back legs thrusting. The vole had begun to turn to flee. Too slow. The intervening distance evaporated and Jarrod struck it hard at the base of the skull and whirled around in time to see it tumble across the cracked stone. Mine! he shouted soundlessly, glee and triumph mingling. Mine!

The animal was dazed and struggling to get to its feet. Jarrod pounced lightly to stop it getting up. Mine! He batted at it with is left paw. The vole battled its way up and took a couple of wavering step. Jarrod waited for a moment and then caught it in a single bound, teeth nipping precisely into the loose skin of the neck. He tossed it into the air. Mine! Mine! Mine! Joy flooded through him.

The vole was up again and Jarrod pounced once more, coming down beside it, and then bucked into the air, legs straight, back arched, bouncing slightly on the landing. The vole was frozen. Jarrod crouched and watched his prey intently. Not dead, not trying to escape either, just stunned or shocked. In a little while it would try again. More fun. Perhaps, he thought, I'll kill it the next time. There's another one around here somewhere.

The casual thought jolted Jarrod's human side. He had been swept away and submerged by his feline instincts, but the time had come to reassert himself. He had done all too good a job in this shape-changing. Food, said the cat half stubbornly. By need of hunger and right of capture, by the law that governs the wild. Jarrod fought back and made himself sit up. The vole, startled out of its inactivity, or sensing a chance for freedom, made a dash for a crevice in the rock. Reflex took over and the cat pounced, but Jarrod, fighting with equal stubbornness, forced it to land short of the little animal, which scurried into safety. Jarrod prowled angrily about, tail lashing, furious with himself and relieved all at one and the same time.

Cats are not ones to dwell on the past, and the pacing became boring. The levels of excitement and energy had ebbed. It was time, he decided, to return to the others. He paused to spray the rock to mark the place as his. The sun was directly overhead now and the footing was becoming uncomfortably hot. Time to find some shade and wait for the work to be finished. Besides, there would be less temptation to hunt where there were men and horses milling around. To say nothing of the fact that any prospective prey would have been frightened off long since. He wasn't at all sure that he would be able to refrain from killing the next time. Not if he was truly hungry.

The site, when he saw it again, had been transformed into a place of giant stacks. He hoped that when he was restored to human form they would look less daunting. The carts and wagons were gone, but he could hear men talking over to the west. He walked around the clustered kegs of nails, the stacks of crisscrossed wooden beams and the squat towers of sacking. No harder to transport, he supposed, than the masses of stone that Nastrus had already dealt with, but formidable nevertheless.

He made his way to the outer edge of the compound and, when the humans were in sight, he sprawled in the shadow of a rectangle of tie beams and settled down for a nap. It took a while, Jarrod-the-cat had no exact notion of how long a while, for the men to finish drinking, climb aboard their wagons and drive off, leaving dust hanging in the air. Moresby Yarrow stood by the remaining cart with Jarrod's horse still tethered to the back and watched the convoy disappear. Then he turned and shaded his eyes with his hand.

"Eminence!" he bellowed. "Courtak!"

Jarrod sauntered out into the sunlight.

"Oh, there you are."

Jarrod could tell that the man was embarrassed to be talking to a cat who was also a Mage. He could smell it.

"Well, they're gone," Yarrow continued unnecessarily, "so, if you want to make your change, go ahead."

Jarrod sat back on his haunches and cleaned his whiskers for the last time. He felt a strange reluctance to abandon this body that was so much more supple than his own, so much quicker in reaction. Still, duty required. He tamped down his cat reactions and centered himself. He became oblivious of his surroundings, half-regretful of the need, and then he began the task of transformation.

Moresby watched, fascinated and repelled, as the large, sleek white cat lost its fur. Its naked limbs elongated and the joints seemed to slip into new positions. It stood up on its hind legs and began to grow. The shoulders broadened and became square, the ears shrank and lost their peaks, the nose lost its snubbed look and the skin took on a more normal shade. The changes took time, but eventually a tall, youngish man stood before him, hairless except for eyebrows. Hair began to sprout under the arms, at the crotch and on the chest, dusted along arms and legs and finally covered the scalp.

"Welcome back, Excellence," Yarrow said. "That was quite a demonstration." He turned away and fetched Jarrod's clothes from the saddlebag.

"Thank you, Moresby," Jarrod said, relieved that his voice sounded normal. "If there's any of that ale left, I'd appreciate some. I'm parched. If there's any food around, I'd appreciate that too. These transformations use up a lot of energy and I'm feeling a bit wobbly."

"At once, Excellence."

Yarrow was still nervous, though Jarrod could no longer smell it on him. Understandable, really; most laics were uncomfortable around Magicians. On the other hand, Jarrod reflected as he waited for the ale, Greygor had taken the transformation in his stride. Perhaps, living in the capital, he had become inured to the sight of Magicians.

Clothes felt a little strange to Jarrod but the food and the ale tasted wonderful. Better, he thought with a shudder, than raw vole. He wiped his mouth and took the tankard back to the cart before returning to the

stacks of material. They did, indeed, look smaller than-
they had previously, but there were still an awful lot of
them. He counted his steps while his eyes calculated the
volume of space that he would have to encompass. Another part of his mind was turning over the applicable
spells.

The simpler the better, he decided. He glanced up at
the Causeway to make sure he was not observed before
walking out toward the plain to survey the whole area.
He looked it over, committing it to memory, and then
he closed his eyes. He took a number of deep breaths
which, in his present, depleted state, made him feel light-
headed. He ignored it and summoned up the neatly
arranged stacks. A slight change in the refractive properties of the surfaces should be sufficient. He reached
out with his mind and made the adjustments, moving
from wood to cloth and on to the metal bands around
the kegs. He drew another long breath and opened his
eyes. There was a hazy shimmer in front of him. He
could still make out the lines of the individual piles, but
his eyes kept sliding away.

He nodded to himself in satisfaction. It was enough
to make any casual pilferer think twice, but not enough,
perhaps, to deter a determined thief. He turned and began to pace the bounds, laying down a basic warding
spell, much as he had when he had accompanied the
royal party back to Stronta after that fateful conclave
at Celador. He completed the semicircle and sighed.
What an innocent he had been then. He looked up and
saw Yarrow watching him.

"Would you mind walking forward as if you were
going to inspect the lumber?" he called.

Yarrow waved to show that he had understood and
started off, arms swinging. Fifteen feet from the edge of
the shimmering he stopped sharply and swore. He
nursed his left hand.

"What did you feel?" Jarrod asked as he approached.

"Something stung my hand," the mason said sullenly. "My fingers are all numb."

"Good. That's what is supposed to happen. Don't worry about your hand. The numbness will wear off very quickly. It's a spell we use to protect campsites. It's designed to keep out wild animals."

"And I'm sure it works very well," Yarrow said, moving his fingers gingerly. "How long will it last?"

"About a sennight, unless there are thunderstorms."

"And how long before you move the stuff?"

"That depends on the unicorn," Jarrod said.

"Oh aye, the unicorn. I'd managed to forget about the unicorn." He looked at Jarrod rather wistfully and said, "I suppose there's going to be a lot more of this kind of thing when we get to the other side."

Jarrod put his arm around the man's shoulders, partly to reassure him, but mostly because he was feeling weak again. "I'm afraid so," he said.

chapter 18

a good night's sleep restored Jarrod's vigor, and his spirits were further lifted by the news that Nastrus was back in the stables. He hurried down after breakfast and, as he strode through the archway, he felt the special pleasure that contact between their two minds brought. He realized anew how much he had missed that peculiar communion.

'And it's good to see you too,' Nastrus said as Jarrod came into the stall.

Jarrod walked over and put his arms around the unicorn's neck and then scratched him behind the ears. *'Did you have a good holiday?'* he asked.

'I went back to the Island to be with my own kind for a while, see how my offspring are doing. It was good to be back, but even there I couldn't get away from you humans.'

'How so?'

'The other you was in the territory,' Nastrus said laconically.

It made sense, Jarrod thought. The Guardian's creation had been given his memories and the unicorns were a very prominent part of them.

'How is he?'

'Physically, he appears to be healthy and he said that the Guardian treats him well.'

'You communicated?'

'Oh indeed.' Irritation and amused tolerance mingled

in the thought. *'He wanted to know everything that had happened since you left and all about Marianna, though there was precious little that I could tell him about her.'*

'The poor man must be feeling lonely,' Jarrod thought back, trying to suppress his own feelings on the subject of Marianna.

"Yes and no,' Nastrus replied. *'The Guardian has provided him with another Marianna, but it seems that she does not equal the original in his mind.'*

'Ah.' Jarrod didn't know what to think.

'Yes, he wanted me to bring him back to Strand with me.'

Sudden panic welled up in Jarrod, much to the unicorn's amusement. *'You didn't, did you?'* His anxiety was plain to see.

'Don't worry. The Guardian has imposed a ban.'

'A good thing too,' Jarrod said, relieved. *'It would create terrible complications here.'*

'Especially now that you have tupped her,' Nastrus said slyly.

Jarrod gave him a warning look. *'I suppose he still looks like me?'* he asked for want of anything better to say.

'Outwardly absolutely, but I can tell you apart. You think the same way, but the patterns are different.'

'Well, I'm glad you had a good time. I just hope that you are rested, because we have an important job ahead of us,' Jarrod said, changing the subject. *'I really need your help with this one.'*

'Yes, I know,' Nastrus returned smugly. *'Your thoughts are full of it.'*

'D'you think that you can do it?'

'I can't say. It's never been done before, has it?'

'No, it hasn't, and it is a massive undertaking,' Jarrod admitted.

Nastrus produced the equivalent of a sigh. *'You'd bet-*

ter let me deeper into your mind,' he said. *'It'll be quicker that way.'*

Jarrod closed his eyes in acquiescence and felt the thrust and the uncomfortable sense of fullness as Nastrus went through his memories. It was a relief when the unicorn withdrew.

'Can you do it?' he asked, half fearful that the answer would be no.

'If I had enough time,' Nastrus replied, *'but it's you humans that are the problem. There isn't enough fodder for you in those mountains. Now, if you were sensibly constructed and could eat grass, there would be no problem, but as it is . . .'* He let the thought die out.

Jarrod's shoulders sagged and he went and sat on the edge of the water trough. All that effort for nothing. All the designs, all that planning, all those materials, all wasted.

Nastrus moved over to him and nudged his shoulders with his muzzle. *'I may be the only unicorn on Strand,'* he said, *'but I'm not the only unicorn. I have colts, well, most of them are full-grown, who just browse their way around the territory waiting for the next rut. The part of me that loves to explore and try new things just doesn't seem to have transmitted itself to them. It would do them good to get off the Island. It's time that they contributed something to the Memory.'*

Jarrod looked up, hope flaring.

'First thing we have to do,' Nastrus continued, *'is to get that pile of stuff that you've accumulated to the proper place, with food at the bottom of the mountain and at the place where you intend to build. No animal flesh, mind. I suppose I shall have to transport the three of you, but then I'll go and fetch my idle foals and we can get to work.'*

'You really think they'll come?' Jarrod asked hesitantly.

'Just you leave that to me,' Nastrus said. *'I'm a very successful sire'*—there was no way the pride behind that statement could be ignored—*'and I've got a considerable number of offspring to choose from.'*

'I'm enormously grateful,' Jarrod said.

'I know you are, and you have every right to be,' Nastrus replied, leavening the statement with a trace of humor. He turned and ambled back to the hay rack and began to munch.

The transfer began before dawn the following morning so that there would be no onlookers. Jarrod rode Nastrus out through the Causeway at the Stronta Gate, surprising the guard, but provoking no challenge. Once the light from the lifted lantern disclosed a Mage and a unicorn, they were hastily waved through. Rank, Jarrod thought, has its advantages.

They took a wide, circling approach, and the gallop through the numinous dark left Jarrod exhilarated and anxious to Make the Day. Once the rite was over, Jarrod suspended the warding and then concentrated on his memory of the terrain revealed in his dream. The fear that he had felt that night had left a clear imprint of the surroundings, but it had, after all, been a dream. Better, he thought, to check it out than risk losing all the carefully acquired, not to mention expensive, material stacked behind them. It was one thing to use it as a destination for stone, but quite another when it came to human beings.

'I'm prepared to risk it if you are,' Nastrus answered him before he had posed the question.

Jarrod remounted and the unicorn turned to face the Alien Plain. Jarrod concentrated fiercely on the remembered area at the base of the foothills before the grey of Interim extinguished all thought.

'Come on, wake up, wake up, wake up. We've work to do.'

Nastrus' insistent sending roused Jarrod. He sat up slowly and looked around. The foothills and the peaks above them were as he had hoped they would be, that was clear to him even in the weak light and early-morning haze. It had been something more than a mere dream then. He felt a sense of relief. He had thought as much but, as one not given to visions, he had not been certain. He peered up the mountain slopes expecting to see a spectral outline of the castle, a castle far more solid since his work with Greygor on the plans, but there was nothing.

'If you're finished eating, I'm ready to go back,' he thought out at Nastrus.

'Just be patient,' the unicorn responded. *'There won't be anything decent to crop on the other end and there's a great deal of stuff to be moved.'*

'Well, while you're doing that, I'm going up to see if there really is a proper place to build,' Jarrod said belatedly.

'It will be quicker if I take you. Just give me a little while longer,' Nastrus replied, blunt teeth ripping up the grass.

It took them an hour to find the place. It would have taken Jarrod more than a day. When they came upon it, it was obvious that this must be the place, though there was no overt indication. They explored thoroughly and found a cave that led through the cliffs at the back into a broad valley with a lake in the center. The water was sweet and they both drank thirstily. Satisfied, they returned to the Causeway and began transferring the material and supplies. That took them two more days, and though Jarrod only used his mind, he felt, when he crawled into bed at night, as if he had used every muscle in his body. When it was over, he took two days off to do nothing but eat and sleep, much to the consternation of his Duty Boy. On the sixth day, he rode into town in search of his partners.

"Well, gentlemen," he said after finding a cat-free chair and accepting a mug of chai, "the task is finally upon us. I've already sent the material over, together with food, tools, cooking pots and whatever basic necessities I could think of." He smiled. "I was relieved to find that most of the stone from the Giants' Causeway that Nastrus had sent in that direction did, in fact, land close enough to be used. We rearranged it as best we could. Now it's your turn. You have a day to pack, one saddlebag each, and be sure to wear as much warm clothing as you can for the trip through Interim."

"I can't say as I like the idea of this voyage through nothing," Yarrow grumbled.

"Oh, come on, Moresby," Greygor said brightly, "where's your sense of adventure?"

"In the pit of my stomach," Yarrow retorted. "I deal in solid things, stone, wood and metal. It's you architects that live in a fantasy world. A thousand leagues in the time it takes to hiccup may be nothing to you, but to me it's plain unnatural."

"I shall accompany each of you," Jarrod cut in soothingly. "You shall come to no harm, I promise. You'll be weak for a while afterward and you'll be extremely hungry, but that's all. We've firewood and food and water on the other side and there are plenty of blankets."

"Easy for you to say, you're a Magician." Yarrow was unmollified.

"If an old man like me can do it, a strapping great lad like you should have no problem," Greygor said teasingly.

"Well you haven't done it yet, have you?" Yarrow objected. He looked across at Jarrod and caught the expression on the Mage's face. "Don't fret," he said dourly, "I'll not back out, but I have my doubts and I'm not afraid to admit it."

"I think that's the best way to approach things," Jarrod said diplomatically. "I really am counting on the two of you. Without you, the project cannot happen, so you can rest assured that I shall make certain that you come to no harm." He got to his feet and returned his mug to the table.

"Now," he said, "we'll meet outside the Outpost walls just after dawn tomorrow. I'll have a groom with me who will take your horses back to the stables. They'll be well taken care of until you return. Any questions? No? All right then, until tomorrow. Oh, and get a good night's sleep."

In the event, all went smoothly. He took the Master Mason through first and then went back for Chatham Greygor. He himself was chilled after the trips, but not unduly weakened. His tolerance of Interim was evidently growing. He made a fire and put on a pot of soup. Then he waited for the two men to regain consciousness.

They were cold and groggy when they woke and they both complained about their weakness and their hunger. The soup and some of the bread that Jarrod had taken from the Outpost's kitchen after Making the Day did much to restore them. The peace and beauty of their surroundings had an equally beneficial effect and, by midafternoon, they had walked slowly up the hillside to gain a better view. Nastrus stayed down on the plain gorging himself on the long, lush grass.

Jarrod was up before dawn, as usual. He walked to the top of the first hill and Made the Day with a calm mind and a high heart, happy to be establishing the age-old ritual in this new, unspoiled place. He was planting continuity and bringing the Discipline and all it stood for to its future home. When the rite was finished, he rose, feeling profoundly satisfied, and made his way back down to where the others still slept. He brought the fire back to life and put on a pot of water for chai.

After a breakfast of bread and honeycomb, the little party loaded packs and set out on the climb. Nastrus was nowhere to be seen, but no one made any mention of it. The day was clear and the breeze was cool, bringing a scent of grass from the east. That in itself was unusual. In controlled regions the wind almost always came from the south. Here, of course, they were well beyond the range of the Weatherwards. Jarrod was glad that he had thought to leave the makings of a shelter up above.

The mountain rose in a series of folds, the dips between liberally supplied with ponds and lakelets. The first slope was gentle and Greygor chatted happily as they walked. The successive gradients were steeper, though. The pace slowed and the talking stopped. They paused at midday and again two hours later. Greygor's face was bright red and the stolid Yarrow was mopping his forehead. Jarrod's longer legs were an advantage when going uphill and he had to continually rein himself in, but, seeing his companions' distress, he called an early halt.

They spent the second night beside a long finger of water with the crest of the hill they had just climbed affording some protection from the wind, which was now coming straight across the plain. It was good that it did for there was no wood for a fire. The hills were dotted with saplings, but there was nothing suitable for burning. They ate cold provisions, drank sweet water from the pond and slept early.

The morning climb was the steepest yet and, from the climbers' vantage point, there was nowhere up ahead that was remotely suitable for a castle. Indeed, beyond this long, steep rise, all that could be seen was a daunting expanse of cliff. Jarrod knew what lay up there, but he wanted them to discover the place for themselves, to come upon it unexpectedly as he had. There were clouds today, though there did not seem to be a threat of rain, and the wind was at their backs. They seemed to climb faster than they had the day before, and Jarrod surmised that the lingering effects of Interim had been banished. By midmorning the going had become so steep that they were using their hands to pull themselves up. Jarrod called a halt at the mouth of a gully that cut into an almost sheer face. He broke out the water sack.

"You sure you know where you're going?" Yarrow asked after he had taken a drink and passed the flask on.

"We're almost there, trust me," Jarrod said as he tried to find a comfortable place to sit. "This last part will be a bit of a scramble, but it will be worth it, I promise you."

Moresby Yarrow gave him a skeptical look, but held his tongue.

"Oh, I certainly hope so," Greygor said, unslinging his pack and rubbing the small of his back. "I, for one, will be glad when this climbing is over. I'm not as young as I used to be and, today, I'm getting older by the hour. These boots feel as if they have lead soles.'

"You've done wonderfully well, both of you," Jarrod said. "I suggest we rest for a few minutes and then tackle the gully. It goes up diagonally and it isn't as steep as the bit we've just climbed. Be a little careful where you put your feet though: there's some loose scree that can be treacherous and this is no time to twist an ankle."

They sat for a while watching the shadows of the clouds chase across the rippling sea of grass, and then Jarrod got to his feet. The other two rose reluctantly and shouldered their packs.

"I'll go first," Greygor said. "That way I can go at

my own speed and, if I fall, I'll have something soft to land on." His feeble attempt at humor was lost on Yarrow, but Jarrod was grateful to him for making the effort.

The architect turned and disappeared into the cut, and Yarrow, with a look over his shoulder, followed. Jarrod brought up the rear. One of the advantages that Greygor hadn't mentioned was that, as the first man up, he didn't have to dodge the bouncing pebbles that were dislodged. The light in the gully was dim and the walls intensified the sounds of labored breathing and Yarrow's occasional curse when a stone found its mark.

"By all the gods!" Greygor's voice was sudden and shrill with surprise.

Jarrod stopped and peered up around Yarrow. He feared the worst, but Greygor had reached the top. His head and shoulders were clear and his elbows were on level ground.

"What's the matter?" Yarrow called, fear evident in his voice.

"Oh, nothing, nothing. Quite to the contrary. Just come on up." Greygor was clearly excited and Jarrod was pleased that the place he had chosen or that had been chosen for him, had had the effect that he had hoped for.

Greygor's feet scrabbled for purchase, sending dirt cascading down, and then he thrust himself up and out of sight. He was back an instant later, leaning forward and offering Yarrow a helping hand. Jarrod pressed on up the final few yards and hauled himself out of the cleft. He looked up from his hands and knees and saw the backs of his companions as they contemplated the grassy plateau that had been hidden from sight. That he had expected. What he had not expected to see was a group of seven unicorns grazing peacefully.

Nastrus tossed his head and whinnied in greeting before trotting over. His mind radiated satisfaction. Yarrow and Greygor stood as if rooted. Jarrod stood up and dusted himself off. He was aware of the mental presence of the other unicorns, knew that they were making up for the deprivations caused by the long trip through Interim, but the only thoughts that were clear came from Nastrus.

'They have no practice in communicating with humans,' he said in Jarrod's mind, 'but we can try it if you like.'

'They're too busy eating,' Jarrod said, 'but I'm delighted to see them. I must say that this is something of a surprise.'

'It was meant to be.' Nastrus was complacent.

'I felt no trace of you while I was coming up the gully.'

'I knew you were there and I kept my thoughts very still.'

'They're a very handsome bunch,' Jarrod said. 'Are they all yours?'

'They are some of mine.'

'Well please tell them that my friends and I welcome them to Strand and are extremely pleased to see them. In the meantime, I think I'd better see to my human companions. This seems to have been a bit of a shock for them.'

The two men turned as Jarrod came up to them.

"They're quite magnificent," Greygor said, shaking his head slightly in wonderment.

"Aye, that they are," Yarrow agreed, his distrust of unicorns seemingly aside. "Is this where they come from?"

"No, no it's not. Nastrus brought them here. They're all descendants of his."

"And Nastrus would be this one closest to us," Greygor said. He smiled apologetically. "It's difficult to tell. They all look alike to me."

Nastrus, reading the statement in Jarrod's mind,

snorted. *'They're nothing alike. Only two of them come from the same dam and one of them is white and the other cream. Quite different.'*

'Make allowance for the fact that they're humans,' Jarrod said.

Nastrus harrumphed and trotted back to his brood and Jarrod turned his attention back to the other two. "So, what do you think of my site?" he asked.

They looked around, taking note of their surroundings for the first time. What they saw was a broad and uneven hemisphere of grass, dotted with yellow flowers. The cliff loomed tall at the back and tapered down as it approached the edge of the plateau. The area enclosed was about half a mile deep and three quarters of a mile wide.

"Plenty of room for a castle," Greygor said.

"Doesn't seem to be a water supply," from Yarrow.

"No need for a curtain wall and, besides, it would block off that extraordinary view." Greygor.

"Machicolations wouldn't be a bad idea if we could anchor them, but how are they going to feed people? You can't lug everything up from the plain." That last from Yarrow.

Jarrod's head was going back and forth from one to the other. It's like talking with the unicorns, he thought, everything comes at once. He held up a finger. "That's my next surprise," he said. "There's a cave at the bottom of that cliff." He pointed toward the back wall. "You can't see it now because the unicorns are in the way. It opens into a big cavern and there's a passage out of there that gives onto a fairly substantial valley that runs east-west. The main mountain rises directly from the other side. There's a big lake—that could be stocked with fish someday—and there's enough land for fields and grazing. We can have a look later, but now I'd rather like to get something to eat." He pointed again. "The supplies are over there, up against that low part of the cliff."

It took a sennight to get organized. The outlines of the central building and its two forward-slanting wings were drawn in the earth, slabs of stone were selected and moved by the unicorns from the plain to the plateau. Procedures were discussed, first between the humans, then between Jarrod and Nastrus and lastly between Nastrus and the other unicorns. Finally the day to start the actual building came.

Jarrod breakfasted on an infusion of simples that he had brought with him. They would ease the strain of the constant lifting he would do. They made him feel confident and clearheaded. The rows of stone across the front of the plateau were made up of blocks of roughly equal size. Once the blocks were lifted, each unicorn knew exactly where to deposit them, or at least that was the theory. Now they would see how well it worked in practice.

Jarrod took up his position behind the first block of stone. The younger unicorns were ranged behind him, their father off to one side. Greygor and Yarrow stood in the doorway of the lean-to that served as their sleeping place. The architect kept unrolling his plans, peering at them and letting them roll up again. The Magician closed his eyes and girded his concentration. The potion made it easy. He opened his eyes and the first block lifted into the air. It flew to its appointed place and settled gently between the lines. The second rose and, almost immediately, settled beside the first. Jarrod moved on down the line and, as he did so, the first unicorn peeled off, trotted behind his kin and joined the far end of the line. They kept it up for four hours, long enough for the first course to be laid, with gaps for the doorways and circular protrusions for the towers at each corner and either side of what would be the central door. The only thing the unicorns had trouble with were the footings for the towers, and that was soon corrected.

As soon as the unicorns went off to graze, the two builders hurried to inspect the work. Jarrod walked slowly back to the hut and drank a dipper of water. He wasn't tired, but he was hungry and thirsty and he wanted to sit down for a while. The two men came back to where he sat.

"Very neatly done," Yarrow commented. "The blocks are snugly butted."

"It looked very strange," Greygor added, "all those great big chunks of stone floating around, but I must say that they're all right between the lines." He turned to his companion. "How long, d'you reckon, Moresby, it would take you to get an outline of this size laid?"

"With a good crew, and everything going right, about four days. Mind you, that'd include the mortar."

"And you did it in four hours, Jarrod. Quite remarkable."

"Let's remember, Chatham, that I had some very effective help," Jarrod said with a smile.

"Aye, that's the pity about all this," Yarrow remarked. "Here I am, Master Mason for an important project, one of the largest buildings in the last hundred years, and I've got a crew that no one would believe if I told them, and the building itself won't be seen for another hundred years, like as not."

"We'll leave an inscription, cut so deep that it'll be clear reading in five hundred years. 'Chatham Greygor, Architect: Moresby Yarrow, Master Mason. They made this place with the help of unicorns,'" Jarrod said with a laugh. "But in the meantime, Chatham, would you put a small pot of water in the embers? I'm going to make myself another potion."

The work resumed in about an hour and it went faster than before. By evening there were three tiers of stone. The next day added another three and they could have started on the seventh row, but Jarrod called an early halt. Greygor came over, worry in the lines of his face.

"Are you all right?" he asked.

"Oh, yes. It's just that I'm going to perform a ritual tonight. Tomorrow I intend to perform some magic."

"I see." Greygor's mouth twitched into a crooked little smile. "I confess that I thought that the whole thing was going to be done in an instant. You'd study my plans, stand out there with your arms raised, say a spell in a voice that rolled like thunder, and presto"— he waved his hands—"a castle."

"Wouldn't that be nice," Jarrod said. "Unfortunately it doesn't work that way. Magic has a strict set of laws and, contrary to popular opinion, there's a limit to what it can do—at least all at the same time. No, tomorrow I'm going to try to solve Moresby's mortar problem. It'll be tricky and it will need a lot of control." He shrugged his shoulders. "I can get power from the unicorns, but the control has to come from me."

"Is there anything that Moresby and I can do?"

"Not a thing. It's a rite of purification and I've done it dozens of times."

"Pity," Greygor said succinctly. "There doesn't seem to be anything we can do these days."

"Just you wait. Who d'you think is going to fit the joists when we get to them? And lay the floors, and of course there's the hammer-beam ceiling to the Great Hall."

Greygor threw up his hands. "Enough. I'd better start taking some of those potions."

That evening, as he had done so many times before, Jarrod laid out the lines of a double pentacle, prepared the three beakers, and spent the night, naked, entranced, in the middle of the inner pentacle. When he emerged from his suspended state in the velvet dark, the lines of the pentacle were still glowing, their light turned into rainbows by the prisms of dewdrops. Jarrod extinguished the faery glitter with his mind and made his way back to the remnants of the fire to retrieve the third beaker. The liquid was still warm and it dispelled the chill in his bones. He felt strong, vibrant and cleansed.

When he returned to the shelter after Making the Day, he found the other two men up, despite the fact that first light had yet to bloom. The fire, made from some of the beams that had been damaged in transit, blazed merrily.

"Morning, Jarrod," Yarrow said. He eyed the Magician's robe that Jarrod had donned for the first time since leaving Stronta and added, "Or should it be 'Morning, Mage'?"

The Magician smiled. " 'Jarrod' will be fine." He took a mug of chai from Greygor and sipped it appreciatively. The other two stood and watched him. "You want to know what I'm going to do, don't you?" They nodded. "Well, we're up to the level of the first set of windows, arrow slits really since the ground floor is to be used for storage and workshops and stables and ought to be easily defensible, so I thought it was time to see if I could fuse the stone so that the walls will be weathertight. I shall need to be looking down on the whole thing so that everything comes out as level as possible. So, when the light is good enough, I'm going to climb along the top of the cliffs until I find a decent vantage point. The unicorns have been told to stay well back and the same applies to you. I can't afford to have anything distracting going on down here."

"You can rely on us," Greygor said.

At the seventh hour, Jarrod shucked his sandals,

hitched his gown up, secured it with the rope that served him as a belt and climbed up the short face of the cliff at the point nearest the edge of the plateau. From there he made his way on all fours along the crest, working his way backward and upward. The sun was to his right, and that made it difficult to see what lay to the east. Below him, to his left, Nastrus kept pace and provided him with a running, and occasionally ribald, commentary on how he looked from below. Finally Jarrod reached a spot where a portion of the cliff face had split away, leaving a broad ledge. He scrambled down to it and turned to face the enclosed region beneath him.

He felt strong and secure. The final potion was swirling pleasantly through him, buoying him up. He looked down and saw that portions of the foundations were in shadow. It would make no difference; the outlines were clear enough. Seen from above it was obvious that it was going to be an impressive building. He would need to project himself over the center to be sure that the work was uniform, but that should be no problem. He would not need Nastrus' support for that part, but some extra power would be helpful.

'I'm here whenever you need me,' the unicorn reassured him. *'The colts are over by the lip watching, but they won't get involved—they don't know how.'* Nastrus was proud of the ability that experience had brought him and pleased that he had a talent that the younger generation lacked. It brought a smile to Jarrod's lips.

He banished Nastrus from his mind and stepped to the front of the ledge. With the potion fortifying him, he felt none of the twinges of vertigo that occasionally bedeviled him and stared down at the outline with equanimity, imprinting it on his mind. He began to breathe deeply in and out. He began the chant for the accession of power, and his hands rose automatically as the energy rose within him. By the time his arms were stretched to the sky, he was floating above the infant structure.

Pressure, pressure to generate heat, to make stone run, to fill the crevices. He gathered his strength and, holding the whole in his mind, pressed down. The stone resisted. He increased the gravity of his persona, spreading himself out to cover the whole area. He summoned more power and pressed himself down. The rock yielded fractionally, compressing in on itself, beginning to flake at the edges. Jarrod summoned the heart of fire, the white heat of the banked ember, and applied it delicately along the running length of walls. The stone began to glow, rock began to run.

Gently, Jarrod thought to himself, gently. He eased the pressure and felt, rather than saw, the stone slow and solidify. He willed himself lower so that he could see more clearly. There was a sheen to the surfaces, almost a slick polish, and the outer sides appeared to be one smooth surface. It had worked. It had been easy. His choice of spell had been right and, as far as he could judge, the overall height of the walls was only down by an inch or so. The exertion hadn't tired him, far from it. It had been quick and easy and he had all this energy stored in him. It would be a criminal shame to waste it. The plans that Greygor had drawn and that he had pored over for so long came into his mind. He had told the architect that Magic didn't work that way, but, given the circumstances, he could surely use his power for more than this.

Nastrus intruded into his concentration. *'I see what you intend and we will help you if you decide to proceed. If you can hold the plan in mind and lift the stone on the plain, we will place it for you.'*

'Done,' Jarrod replied without hesitation.

What followed terrified and amazed Greygor and Yarrow, crouched against the cliff beside the shelter.

First, three of the unicorns disappeared, and then blocks
of stone began to fly through the air. That was not a
new sight, as such, and they had become inured to the
presence of unicorns, but what overwhelmed them was
the sheer volume of the performance. A second thickness was added to the outer walls, with openings for
fireplaces and spaces for chimneys. Piers appeared in
double rows and, as they watched, developed branching
vaults, the stone tendrils growing as if they were trained
along wires. Bricks filled in the angles. Interior walls
appeared, and then the upward march of the outer walls
resumed. The burgeoning towers developed interior
channels for the disposal of human waste exactly as the
plans had laid them out. Just when the multiple activi-
ties threatened to daze them into numb acceptance,
there would be a pause when the entire expanse seemed
to shudder and grow a shiny skin.

For Jarrod it was like being the master of a supernal
juggling act. He held Greygor's plans, with all the little
side panels filled with detail, in his mind and made sure
that Nastrus understood them. Another part of his
memory recalled the disposition of materials on the
plain and lofted them as needed so that the younger
unicorns could send them up the mountain. Nastrus
would direct them to their proper place and Jarrod
would then fuse them. The activity was multifarious and
nonstop and Jarrod gloried in it. He held the power
thrumming through him in exquisite check.

The work became simpler when the ground floor was
complete. There could be no more interior building until the beams were in place and the subfloor laid. Jarrod,
drunk with the opportunity to perform in a major way
after so long a hiatus, used the opportunity to embellish
the corbels, create hoodmolds over the windows in the
wings and stone tracery in the those of the Great Hall.
He grew cocky and added an oriel to the solar where

there had been none in the plans, tapped into a chimney and added a fireplace and fused blocks of stone together to create a curving staircase from the undercroft, through the east end of the Hall, and on up to the solar. When he was finished, the battlements were crenellated and brick chimney stacks, modeled after those at Celador, sprouted. Others would have to await the completion of the roof.

The volley of materials slowed to a halt. There was no more that could be done at this stage. Jarrod was disappointed; the energy was still strong in his body, he felt no fatigue. Putting his memory, his mind and his will to work, he lifted the rest of the material from the plain and floated it up to the plateau with no assistance from the unicorns.

'Most impressive,' Nastrus said sardonically when the last piece was grounded. *'It's time for you to climb down now. You may not be tired, but the rest of us are.'*

Jarrod returned reluctantly to his body. He allowed the energy to drain out of him and felt his arms float down to his sides. The compensatory euphoria rushed in to take its place, but, for once, it didn't provide the ultimate pleasure. He had enjoyed functioning at that high level, felt hugely alive and useful. He opened his eyes and blinked at the setting sun. Had it really been that long? He looked down at the shell of the castle and smiled. It would be nice, he thought, to sit here for a while and survey his handiwork. He had gone beyond what he had thought was possible, caught by the frenzy of creation.

'You couldn't have done any of this without us,' Nastrus reminded him. *'Why don't you climb down while you still have the strength. You probably look like a prune with mold on the top.'*

'That's what I love about you,' Jarrod thought back lazily, *'you're always so supportive, so positive.'*

By the time Jarrod reached the ground, he was unsteady, and, from the reaction of the two men, Nastrus had been close to the mark. He was glad that there was no looking glass at the camp. He had no memory of being put to bed, nor of the storm that raged for the next three days. From then on he took little part in the completion of the work. He would lift the heavy beams so that the unicorns could move them. On occasion he held them aloft while they were fitted into the slots that Yarrow had chiseled into the walls, but he was capable of little else. There was a minimum of conversation around the fire at night because the other two were as tired as he.

Nevertheless, the work progressed. The details seemed endless, but, at the end of the fourth sennight, even Yarrow was convinced that there was no more that they could do. Jarrod used magic once more. He carved an inscription in the stone over the main door dedicating the building to Greylock and giving credit to the architect, the mason and the unicorns as he had promised Yarrow that he would. They bade good-bye to the younger unicorns and, accompanied by Nastrus, made their way back down to the Alien Plain. It took them a day and a half. It took a fraction of that time to return to Stronta.

chapter 19

Varodias was striding up and down the Presence
Chamber, high heels clacking on the polished wood. He
was dressed all in black, save for an oversized ruff at
the throat and a short fall of lace that covered the join
between sleeve and glove. On a perch beside the throne
a falcon moved uneasily from foot to foot, responding
to its master's mood. Malum stood two paces behind
the Elector of Estragoth and watched his sovereign
crossing through the pools of light thrown by the leaded
windows close to the roof of "the hunting room," as it
was popularly called. It was the first time that he had
been in it, and he found it quite extraordinary. It was
painted to look like a forest glade complete with
branches overhead and leaves upon the floor. As remarkable, perhaps, was the fact that, apart from the
Emperor, the Elector and he were the only people in
the room. The Emperor stopped and pivoted.

"It is an affront to our national honor, Estragoth.
We are diminished in the eyes of the world." The high
voice was agitated.

"I think not, Your Imperial Majesty," Phalastra replied calmly. "The record will show united resolve on
the part of the Commission to do what was best for
Strand. It was for that reason that I abstained on your
behalf."

"And are we not a laughingstock in the Courts of

Arundel and Paladine?" The Emperor's voice was back under control, his face a mask with small, slitted eyes.

"No, Sire." Phalastra paused ever so briefly. "Let me amend that. The courtier rabble undoubtedly gossips, but the rulers and their councillors are perfectly well aware that Isphardel has been handed a long and costly setback. No one likes the economic power of the Isphardis and while they will not say so publicly, your cousins of Paladine and Arundel are delighted to see that power diminished. The division of the Isphardi territories was Your Imperial Majesty's prime objective. That objective has been achieved."

"They have, however, extracted sureties from Talisman and from the Magical Kingdoms." Varodias walked back to this throne and seated himself. The falcon, reassured, ruffled its feathers and settled down.

Phalastra permitted himself a brief, brittle laugh. "International guarantees," he said sardonically. "They could scarcely do otherwise when one considers the trade concessions that were offered to them, but neither of the Royal ladies would send troops to Songuard."

"Naxania of Paladine sent troops to Fort Bandor," Varodias observed.

"True, Sire, but that was against the Outlanders and to avenge the massacre of Your Imperial Majesty's garrison. I cannot see her sending men against a brother monarch in defense of clansmen or Oligarchs."

"There is that," the Emperor conceded. His gloved hand went out and stroked the bird's poll. "We suppose that the important thing is that our plan of colonization can begin. We have already instructed our Rotifer Corps to survey our lands and to pick the best sites for settlements." His voice had warmed. "There will be no entry fee for those of our soldiers long since promised land, but there will be obligations and a new oath of fealty.

Estates will be awarded." Varodias produced a small, satisfied smile. "They will not be cheap."

"Your Imperial Majesty has borne the entire cost of the development of the rotifer and the research on the captured battle wagons," the Elector said diplomatically.

"Indeed we have," the Emperor agreed complacently, and then the mood turned as he added, "Fifteen years and precious little to show for it. They were a strange breed, those Outlanders."

He might make better progress, Malum thought, if he allowed some of the other scientists near them.

Varodias settled back into the throne and the fingers of the left hand began to dance on the arm. The Elector knew the sign. Varodias was wearying of the audience.

"We commend you, my Lord Elector," the Emperor said, "and you too, my Lord of Quern. It seems that you have performed your long and arduous tasks well after all."

Both men bowed.

"We suppose, my old friend," he said to Estragoth, "that we shall have to find some new employment to keep you from mischief." The accompanying smile, for once, was genuinely warm.

"Your Imperial Majesty is most kind," Phalastra replied, "but it I may be permitted to crave your indulgence?"

The Emperor's eyebrows rose, but he nodded.

"I have served your illustrious father and yourself for better than five decades and this old flesh grows weary. I have spent long years away from home of late and I would as lief spend what years are left to me in Estragoth."

Varodias sat up sharply, his eyes wide. "You intend to abandon us?" His tone was incredulous.

"Ah, my liege lord, I would not have you see it so. I

am an old man and my late embassy has taken me from your side. There are younger men who have counseled you in my absence and it is time for me to make way for them." He smiled gently, sweetly. "Have no fear, Sire," he said as if to a boy, "I shall be your devoted servant and loyal vassal as long as there is breath in my body."

Malum listened, his heart suddenly beating faster. It was not unexpected, but the Elector had given him no hint.

"We shall have to think on this, old friend," Varodias said quietly. " 'Tis true that you have served our house long and well, but we were not expecting this and we are loath to part with you."

"I shall serve you unto death, if that is your will," Phalastra said simply, "but if you would reward me, let me go."

"We shall think on it. You must give us time," Varodias replied.

"Should you accede to my request, Sire," Phalastra said, "I would commend Malum of Quern to your attention. He has served me well. He is loyal, discreet, he has a good mind and I have trained him."

"We shall think on these things. We shall think on them," Varodias said with a touch of irritation. The falcon studiously groomed its wing feathers. "Leave us now. We need to be alone." The fingers flicked out in dismissal.

Both men bowed and retreated, backward, from the presence.

Once they were outside and the doors were closed, Phalastra nodded to the guards and started off down the corridor with Malum trailing him. When they were out of hearing, he stopped and let Malum catch up. "I'm sorry, lad," he said in the Common Mode, "That must have come as something of a shock. Truth to tell,

I had not intended to bring it up today, but, over the years, I have developed an instinct when it comes to the Emperor's moods. When he allowed himself to be convinced of the success of our mission, I seized the opportunity. Let us go back to my apartments and discuss things."

They ensconced themselves in the Elector's withdrawing room. The servants came and went and Malum sipped his wine silently, trying to put his thoughts in order. He had been counting on a spell here at Angorn in the Elector's service to give him a better sense of where the next generation of power truly lay. An appointment directly to the royal household would, of course be ideal, but what was he to do if Varodias did not act on the Elector's suggestion? Fond as he was of the old man, he wasn't prepared to go into retirement with him.

"I have spent so many years in these chambers that they feel as much home to me as my own castle," Phalastra said, breaking the silence. "My older boy will probably want to redecorate them. It shouldn't worry me because I doubt that I shall ever see them again, but it does somehow."

"Are you sure that the Emperor will let you go, my lord? He has depended on you for most of his life and it didn't seem to me that he relished the prospect of losing you."

Phalastra smiled. "Varodias hates change, somewhat strange in a man who prides himself on being a scientist, but true nevertheless. No, he doesn't like the idea, but he is an intensely pragmatic man. There will be no emotion involved in the decision despite the years we have spent together. If he refuses me, it will be because I am one of the very few, man or woman, that he trusts. His Majesty does not confide in men, but he trusts me.

"What I did today was to remind him that it is past

time that he found someone to replace me. Neither of my sons has a head for politics and most of the capable men at Court would as soon replace him as serve him. Fear is the only thing that keeps them in their place. That is why I recommended you. If he takes you on, remember this: it is not rank that counts, but influence. A man of modest title with the position of His Imperial Majesty's secretary excites little envy, but that man has the Emperor's ear and determines who gets to see him and when."

"But there is no such position," Malum interjected.

"I took great care that there should not be," Phalastra said, "but that is where I should like to see you. Varodias is an exceedingly volatile man. He needs a steady hand behind him, someone with the knowledge of the broader canvas and the skill to manage things from the shadows."

"You flatter me, sir, but I fear that I am as ambitious as the next man," Malum said with a flash of honesty. "What makes you think that I would serve the Emperor so selflessly?" The last was delivered jokingly, but he was serious.

Phalastra gave him a long, level look and drank some wine before answering.

"Because you are his son," he said.

Malum had been about to take a drink himself, but his hand stopped in midair. He stared at the Elector. His mother had said something of the sort in the days before she died, but the wasting fever that took her had first stolen her wits and Malum had dismissed the notion as delirium. He couldn't remember now exactly what she had said.

He lowered the goblet carefully to the small table at his elbow. He felt surprisingly calm now that the first shock was over. The Elector was not the kind of man to make that sort of bitter jest. There would be turmoil later, that he knew, but for the moment he was back in his habitual role of the observer. The difference was that he was a key player in this scene.

"Did you say what I thought you said?" he asked evenly.

"I did."

"Does the Emperor know?"

"You would not be alive if he did," Phalastra said tersely.

"I should be grateful, my lord, if you could explain," Malum said gravely. His hands, he was glad to note, weren't trembling, so he picked up his goblet again and took a drink.

"Your mother was my ward. She was a very beautiful girl and though she did not have much in the way of a dowry, I managed to make an advantageous match for her. Her husband was Master of the Imperial Hounds; the position is normally a sinecure, a well-paid token of the Emperor's favor, but he took the job seriously. After the wedding, your mother was given a place at Court as one of the Empress's ladies-in-waiting. She caught the Emperor's eye and did not know how to refuse him. Her husband was sent off to the outlying Electorates in search of new bloodstock for the kennels so she was all the more vulnerable. When she became pregnant, she came to me for advice."

He paused and sipped, watching the young man. The boy seemed to be taking the news with remarkable aplomb. There was color in his cheeks, but no other sign of emotion. He was simply waiting with a look of polite interest. The boy should go far. He had taken him on when he first came to Court out of an old-fashioned sense of obligation, but he had chosen well.

Malum had, in fact, retreated behind one of his masks to think. He had always supposed that the Elector had taken him into the household because he was a hunting companion of his son, Coppin. The real reason was now clear. A pang of fierce pride struck him. Imperial blood flowed in his veins. The young noblemen at Court had made fun of him for his clothes, his lack of height and the modesty of his title, behind his back to be sure, but he had known. He could ignore the smirks now, the whispers behind the hand, knowing that he was the Emperor's son. . . . He became aware of the Elector's eyes upon him and he produced his smile.

"What was your advice, my lord?" he inquired.

"I told her that if she valued her life, and that of her child, she should say nothing of it to Varodias; that there must never be a hint of scandal attached to the Imperial name. The problem was that her husband had been away from Angorn for three months and was not expected back from some time. Anyone who could count would know that the child was not his and, more to the point, the Emperor would know that he was the father. He has executed two of his legitimate sons because cliques were beginning to form around them, so . . ." He let the phrase die. This time Malum did not prompt him.

"The normal solution would have been for her to retreat to her husband's estate to have the baby," Phalastra resumed, "but in this case that was not possible. Her mother-in-law had never approved of the marriage, thought that her precious son could have done better for himself." His lips tightened in remembrance. "Old Lady Belgaroth was a formidable woman was well as being an exceedingly unpleasant one. Had your mother taken refuge at Castle Belgaroth, she would undoubtedly have died in the birthing."

"I always assumed that Quern was our ancestral home," Malum remarked.

"No, it was one of my estates. It reverted to me on

the death of one of my vassals. It was far from Angorn and the cane harvest made it self-supporting."

"But didn't my father, I mean my mother's husband, object?"

"Ah, well, the poor man met with an unfortunate accident. It would have been quite improper for your mother, as a newly widowed woman, to stay at Court."

"And I don't suppose that you had anything to do with the 'accident'?" Malum said.

"That is an entirely scurrilous suggestion," Phalastra replied without heat.

"I apologize, my lord," Malum said, equally bland. "And did the Emperor make no attempt to contact her thereafter?"

"He did as a matter of fact, somewhat to my surprise," Phalastra said, knowing that the young man would prefer the lie, "but your mother, doubtless to protect you, or at any rate preoccupied with your birth, declined to return to Court. The Emperor, of course, found another favorite."

Phalastra sat back. "So now you know," he said. "I felt a responsibility to your mother and I have felt a responsibility for you. I feel that I have discharged them both. I would not have told you, save that I feel that I owe you the truth and because I know you to be wise enough in the ways of the Imperial Court to understand that you can never claim your birthright. If Varodias has never been a father to you, that is not his fault. Nevertheless, you owe him blood loyalty. He does not need to know why you serve him so well; indeed, if you value your life, he must never know. You do understand that, do you not?"

"Yes, my lord, I understand," Malum said, and he did.

Phalastra nodded. "Good. I am glad that the secret is out. I have carried it a very long time. Now I think I shall get me some rest. Do you get up a report on our meeting with His Imperial Majesty. We can go over it"—he glanced at the clock on the mantel—"at the seventeenth hour."

"Until then, my lord," Malum said, rising.

When he was back in his own room, the Emperor's bastard spent a long time in front of the looking glass trying to find hints of Varodias in his face.

chapter 20

Two months had gone by since the Commission for the Outland had been dissolved. The heat of summer had diminished and while the middens stank less, the biting flies were everywhere. Perhaps it was the cooler nights, or even the unwanted attention of the flies, but there was a feeling that the land was coming to life again after the torpor of summer. Jarrod was certainly active. He had taken the opportunity to resume work on his history, but he did not neglect his body. He rose, as always, before dawn, rode for an hour, after Making the Day, on a three-year-old roan he had bought himself as a namingday present and then went in for breakfast. The roan was spirited and possessed of a mercifully comfortable gait, but he could not match the pleasure that Jarrod derived from riding Nastrus. The unicorn, however, had returned to his job of clearing the Giants' Causeway. Jarrod missed him, but not enough to go with him.

After breakfast Jarrod spent four hours on research, broke for lunch and then worked for two hours on his manuscript. He closed the energetic part of his day with an hour of sword practice. He was still rusty after all the years of neglect and his stamina was not what it had been when the Guardian's servitor had put him through his paces, but he was improving. He trained with Robarth Strongsword's old Master-at-Arms. Ranulph was delighted to have a pupil. The new generation of noblemen had abandoned the short fighting sword in favor of a longer and more graceful blade. "All stick and no cut," as Ranulph said derisively. Jarrod preferred to build on the strengths he already possessed.

He bathed after sword practice and dined, most nights, in the Outpost's Hall with the other Magicians. Once a month, however, he made a point of dining at the palace. He had no administrative duties for the moment, but he knew that, at some point, he would succeed Greylock as Mage of Paladine and then he would need the goodwill of the nobles and Court functionaries that he was cultivating. He usually spent an hour after Hall with Greylock and then retired to bed. Once every couple of weeks he spent an evening with Greygor. Yarrow had snagged the baron's commission and gone south. It was, in many ways, a perfect life.

He was working contentedly on a crisp morning with an early fire crackling in the grate when the Duty Boy rapped on the door. Jarrod looked up, annoyed at being disturbed.

"The Lady Marianna of Gwyndryth," the boy said, and stood aside.

Jarrod rose from his desk as Marianna swept in. She was dressed for Court and her color was high. Jarrod was never sure before she spoke whether the condition was the result of the ride over or because she was angry.

"Marianna, my dear, what a pleasant surprise," he said, advancing across the room, hands out. "Your hands are freezing," he said after clasping them. "Come over to the fire and warm yourself." He looked at the boy. "A couple of tankards of mulled cider, if you please."

He turned and ushered Marianna to the fireplace. He had, for the most part, managed to put the events of Celador out of his mind. The memory of her body returned to him in the drifting moments before sleep, but, since he had heard nothing from her, the possibility of a child had been banished. Now it was back. He glanced at her waist and saw no change.

"You're looking very well," he said.

"I've just come from my father," Marianna said without preamble. "He's inclined to horsewhip you."

"Charming," Jarrod said, drawing back slightly. "I take it that you are pregnant."

"You take it correctly."

"That's good news then," Jarrod said with decidedly mixed feelings.

Marianna looked up at him with a ghost of a smile. "I hope you mean that. I really do."

"Well it's what you wanted."

"Yes it is, and, as you know, I intended to raise this child unencumbered. Daddy, unfortunately, is being obstinately old-fashioned. He insisted on knowing who the father was and I couldn't sidetrack him."

Jarrod had his doubts about that, but said nothing.

"I'm afraid he's insisting that we get married," she added.

"I see."

Marianna reacted to something in his voice. "I didn't intend for this to happen, you do realize that."

He looked into her eyes. "You haven't heard me object, have you?"

She caught her top lip between her teeth and her eyes filled. At that point the Duty Boy returned with the cider. Jarrod took the tankards from him, thanked him and, by the time he had withdrawn, they were both composed.

"I don't know about you," Marianna said, "but I don't want a big wedding."

Jarrod took a long pull at his cider. "You must forgive me," he said, "but this has come on rather suddenly. D'you think we could sit down?"

Marianna laughed as she dropped into the chair. "That's the sort of thing the woman's supposed to say."

"It's true nevertheless. You've been through this before; I haven't."

"Poor Jarrod. You don't have to go through with this if you don't want to. It was never part of our bargain."

"I know. The trouble is that your father isn't the only old-fashioned one. Our agreement never did sit comfortably with me, but you're a difficult woman to say no to."

"I'm rather relieved to hear that under the circumstances," she said lightly. "So what kind of wedding would you like? After all, it will be your first."

"I think I should like Greylock to marry us and I've never been one for ceremonies."

"Perhaps we could have it before I go back to Gwyndryth," she suggested.

"What, no honeymoon?" Jarrod exclaimed, making it sound like a joke.

"I have to get back as soon as I can," Marianna said reasonably. "The harvest is coming in and there will be the accounts to do. Besides, in my condition we can't . . . I mean we just can't."

"How romantic," Jarrod said sarcastically. "What you're telling me is that this is just a marriage of convenience."

"Please, Jarrod dear, don't be difficult," Marianna said. "I've had a trying morning. I explained to you at Celador that I don't want a husband in the conventional sense and you have no intention of giving up your life here and retiring to Gwyndryth. I've already told you that you are the only man on Strand that I wanted to father my child and I've proved it. As far as

the rest is concerned, we'll just have to work it out as
we go along. You will, of course, be welcome at Gwyndryth whenever you want to come, but if you prefer to
stay here, I shall quite understand."

Jarrod sighed. "You never did do things the way
other girls did," he said. "I don't know why I should
expect you to start now."

"Does that mean that you'll go through with it?"

"I suppose so. I don't relish the prospect of being
horsewhipped by your father."

She smiled at him and reached out her free hand.
"Thank you," she said. "I'm sorry that it had to happen
this way, but I want you to know that I'm grateful.
Now I suppose we ought to decide about the wedding."

"Does your father have any preferences?" Jarrod
asked. He had no wish to start off this odd alliance by
alienating the Holdmaster.

"Daddy wants me married as fast as possible. This
baby is not to be born early, that's his dictum." She
gave a snort that wasn't quite laughter. "I'm not quite
sure how I'm supposed to pull that off, but I'll have to
work something out." She looked across at him. "You
don't know how lucky you are not to have a parent to
deal with." She shook her head slowly. "The bloody
man simply will not admit that I am an adult. I mean,
I've been running Gwyndryth for how many years now?
And he still treats me as if I was fourteen."

"We're getting off the point," Jarrod said mildly.
"The thing is that he has no objection to a quick, quiet
wedding."

"The sooner the better," she agreed.

"Perhaps we can have the ceremony upstairs in Greylock's rooms and we can spend the wedding night here."
He grinned suddenly. "I'll finally have a chance to wear
the outfit the Guardian gave me."

Her smile lit her face. "What a good idea. I'll get Daddy to send a cloudsteed to Gwyndryth for mine."

"A cloudsteed?"

"I don't see why not. He is the general, after all, and he owes me that much."

"D'you ever think of those days?" he asked.

"Every time that Amarine or her offspring visit."

"When was the last time she came?"

"It must be three years." There was a wistful note in her voice. "I miss her."

From then on they reminisced comfortably. Like an old married couple, Jarrod thought ironically, though the idea rather pleased him.

In the event, the only decisions that they made that afternoon that survived were their choice of clothes and of Greylock. Queen Naxania saw the marriage as an opportunity to add luster to her waning popularity and decreed that the wedding be held in the abandoned Maternite chapel that her brother had built. Marianna protested to her father, but got nowhere. Jarrod complained to Greylock and found that the Mage considered the marriage of the discoverers of the unicorns a boon for the Discipline. He went so far as to issue orders for the return of Nastrus from the Causeway. Marianna fumed and Jarrod commiserated, but they were effectively trapped by their reputations.

Darius seemed to be the only person who was genuinely happy. Even the Queen appeared to have her reservations. They were together in the royal withdrawing room going over the details of the guest list for the reception when she turned to him and said, "I will not have Abercorn here."

"It never occurred to me to invite him."

"You realize that Courtak will inherit the Dukedom."

"I know it's a possibility," Darius replied easily, "but

there's no reason why Paramin shouldn't marry again and father a child." He smiled at her. "After all, he's my age, give or take a year."

"Not likely. He's been a broken man since the rebellion failed and I am told that his health is parlous. He has been consumed by the black humors and his chest is weak." There was a note of satisfaction in her voice.

Darius raised an eyebrow. "You seem very well informed."

"His Wisewoman is in my pay," she returned shortly. "I have taken a leaf from your friend Lissen's book."

"I see," Darius said, reflecting on how much she had changed since they had first met. She was becoming hard and suspicious. No, he corrected himself, she had always been suspicious, but the soft side that she had always shown him was seldom in evidence of late. Once in a while after they had made love, but that didn't happen very often these days. He had learned to accept that, as he had learned to turn a blind eye to her occasional affairs with younger men. She had always been discreet and she had always returned to him. For his part, the gods help him, he still cared for her. They had been lovers for sixteen years and they shared a lot of memories. He felt a wash of affection for this proud, stubborn and undoubtedly beautiful woman.

"You know what that means," she said, breaking into his thoughts.

He looked up, blinking slowly.

"It means that your daughter will be Duchess of Abercorn and a grandson of yours will inherit in his turn."

"Yes, I suppose it does. I hadn't really given it any thought." He got up and went over to the table for a sweetcake. "Does that bother you?" he asked around a mouthful.

She snorted. "Courtak's first allegiance is to the Discipline and I am perfectly well aware that your daughter does not like me. Not exactly the combination I could wish for in one of my principal fiefs."

"You take altogether too bleak a view of things," he said gently. "Jarrod has always been loyal to the Crown and Marianna is too attached to Gwyndryth to meddle in Paladinian politics. Besides, think of the romance of it." He walked over, stood behind her chair and began to massage her shoulders. "The discoverers of the unicorns, companions in peril when they were young, finally falling in love and getting married. It's what the common people have wanted for years."

"Oh yes, it's very popular." Her shoulders were relaxing, but she didn't sound soothed.

"You know," he said lightly, fingers stroking, "this alliance between the two countries could provide the perfect setting for a further cementing of relations." He paused and then took the plunge. "Why don't the two of us get married?"

Naxania almost sprang from the chair. She whirled to face him.

"Are you mad?" she said, dark eyes snapping.

Darius drew himself up. "No, I am not. I have served both you and this country loyally and well for a good number of years. I have loved you even longer. Your people are used to seeing me by your side. I have asked you to marry me before, but there was always some 'reason of state' for you to hide behind. I am an old-fashioned man, my love, and I'm tired of backstairs skulking. This is the perfect opportunity to announce our betrothal."

Naxania had herself under control again. She smiled at him, reached out and patted his hand as it rested on the back of the chair.

"You are a dear man," she said, "and you know that I am very fond of you, but you can be singularly obtuse when it comes to statecraft." Her voice was soft and level. "It is precisely because your daughter is likely to become Duchess of Abercorn that I cannot marry you. It would concentrate too much power in the hands of one family—and an Arunic family at that."

She stood looking at him expectantly, but he made no reply.

"You do understand, don't you?" she asked.

Darius' lips tightened and he nodded slowly. "Yes, I understand. I understand that it is time for me to leave Stronta, time to go back to Gwyndryth. I should have done it a long time ago."

"Come now, Darius dear," Naxania said, advancing around the chair and taking his arms. She looked up at him. "There's no need for that. We have been very happy and we will continue to be happy. I need you. The country needs you."

He smiled ruefully. "It is time that you found yourself a younger man to run your army and a 'suitable' man to sire an heir. I shall tender my formal resignation after the wedding and I will stay until I can hand the Royal Forces over properly to my successor."

He disengaged his arm gently and left her. He did not look back and she made no move to stop him. Men are such children, she thought. It never crossed her mind that he meant exactly what he said.

Jarrod woke in darkness on the nuptial day. That was normal, as was the urge to Make the Day. What was decidedly strange was the fibrillations of nervousness that he felt. Marriage. Something that he had thought about idly from time to time, but never pursued. Marriage to Marianna; something that he had fantasized about when he was young. That was the result of the hot humors of his salad days. Now it was thrust upon him and he wasn't certain that he really wanted it. She was, in many ways, his best friend and their mutual past provided an undeniable bond, but he wasn't at all sure that he really loved her. What if he met a woman he fell head over heels for? He would be locked in. Darius would never permit a second divorce.

He got out of bed reluctantly. It was too late to back out now. He had given his word. It struck him suddenly that he had never actually proposed or asked her father for her hand. Be that as it may, he would have to go through with this for the sake of the child, his child. There were worse reasons for getting married. He was going to be a father and that was more important than the circumstances of the wedding. Of course Joscelyn was his son in all but conception, but he'd never been a father to the boy. It would be different with this baby. Having talked himself into a semblance of confidence, he got dressed and prepared himself for the ritual. It was not the marriage itself that was making him nervous, he concluded, only that the marriage ceremony had mushroomed beyond his control.

At breakfast, he took the ribald jesting of his fellow Magicians in good part, but he didn't linger and reached his rooms with a feeling of relief. He walked into the bedchamber and saw that the Duty Boy had laid out his clothes. It had been a long time since he had seen them, but they looked none the worse for their sojourn under lock and key. The dark pink of the brocade was as vivid as it had been on the Island at the Center. The triangle of rubies and garnets that gave definition to the waist gleamed, the diamond buttons sparkled.

The Duty Boy brought chai and watched while Jarrod shaved himself. His hand wasn't entirely steady, but he managed to avoid cutting himself. He bathed in a copper tub that the boy had filled. The water was lukewarm, but the lad was so eager and so excited that he didn't have the heart to complain. Then came the robing. First the linen breechclout, followed by the silk hose and the shirt with the dark red lace spilling from the sleeve ends. Next the slim-legged trousers with the bottoms anchored by pebble-sized rubies. The burgundy-colored lace jabot was tied around his neck, and all that was left to don was the jacket.

He had some trepidations about the jacket. The waistband of the trousers was uncomfortably tight and he remembered the jacket's fit as being snug sixteen years ago. He bent his knees tentatively. If the seat was going to split, better now than later. The trousers held and he straightened thankfully. Why hadn't he thought to try the clothes on before this? The boy was holding the jacket out. Jarrod slouched backward and the Duty Boy went up on tiptoe. Jarrod slid his hands into the sleeve holes and pushed and wriggled until his shoulders were firmly encased. The boy came round to the front. The first button was a minor struggle, but the others proved easier. Finally he stood before the looking glass, a vision of stiff magnificence, girded in as if for war.

There was a group of Magicians waiting for him at the bottom of the stairs. Two carried mandolins and he was serenaded all the way to the stables with what they considered appropriate songs. Nastrus stood waiting for them, mane brushed, coat burnished, silver hooves shining. He whickered a welcome and the singing stopped. Jarrod walked across to the mounting block and Nastrus positioned himself.

'I'm going to do this very slowly,' Jarrod thought. 'These trousers are a mite snug and I'm not about to go through my wedding with my backside on view.'

'Humans!' Nastrus returned, his mind filled with slightly malicious humor.

'None of that. We'll ride over at a smooth canter.'

Jarrod tried to sound forceful, but the unicorn's underlying enjoyment of the situation was infectious. He suddenly felt as if the whole occasion might turn out to be fun after all.

'*Mind you,*' Nastrus said as Jarrod climbed gingerly into the saddle, '*I do not understand the reasons behind this ceremony. It is the duty of a strong male to take as many females as possible.*'

'*We see things somewhat differently,*' Jarrod replied. '*For us it is the affirmation of the love between two people and, later, for the protection of the children.*'

'*Raising colts is dams' work,*' Nastrus said dismissively, '*and I can see in your mind that you are uncertain about this love. You have already rutted, why all this extra fuss?*'

'*This is not the time,*' Jarrod thought back with what severity he could muster, '*to try to explain the differences between human and unicorn. Let's just get on with it, shall we?*'

They rode out of the stables to the cheers of the assembled Magicians, and Jarrod smiled and waved to his friends and colleagues. They were all there except Greylock, Tokamo and Agar Thorden, who had spent the previous night at the palace. He felt their approbation as a palpable force. These men were, in a very real sense, his family and he was glad that he had thought to pay for a feast for them that night. If things had worked out as originally planned, they and not the Court would have been the wedding guests.

As they cleared the Outpost's fortified gate, he decided to ride to Stronta through the Great Maze. They were supposed to make their entrance into the capital through Westgate, but this seemed more fitting. Nastrus obediently swung off the road and onto the path that led to the ancient enigma.

'*I've never been through this Maze of yours,*' Nastrus remarked. '*Are you sure that it will let me through?*'

'Certain. I took Marianna through and her only Talent was being able to talk to your mother.'

Nastrus moved easily into the required canter. 'If it's all the same to you,' he remarked, 'I'll walk when we get to it.'

'Nothing will happen to you; trust me,' Jarrod responded.

He proved correct. The Great Maze embraced them. He had half expected the experience to be different when viewed through Nastrus' eyes, much as it had been when they had ridden through the forest created by illusion, but the glitteringly insubstantial gold and silver fronds that parted at their approach looked the same to both of them. There was no trace of discomfort in the unicorn's mind, just a happy sense of wonder and an almost smug pleasure that he was recording yet another first for his kind. Emerging into the ordinary daylight with the ever-open North Door ahead was an anticlimax for them both.

Stronta was mercifully quiet and Jarrod rode unheralded across the broad quadrangle behind the gate and into Royal Court. A crowd had gathered in front of the palace to watch the arrival of the notables in their finery. Jarrod guessed that the rest of the population was spread between Westgate and Royal Court. He hadn't thought of that when he had decided to cross the Great Maze and knew a twinge of regret for depriving the townsfolk of a sight of the unicorn.

He saw Tokamo, Agar Thorden and the Royal Chamberlain waiting at the top of the stairs leading to the Great Hall, but neither they nor the crowd were looking in his direction. He smiled and Nastrus pulled up. Jarrod dismounted with care and then, with the unicorn following, made his way through the startled throng, and up the stairs. There he was greeted by the little delegation and led into the Great Hall with the cheers of the crowd ringing in his ears. In later years the legend would say that both he and the unicorn were invisible until they appeared at the doors of the Hall.

Nastrus was unsaddled and led away by young Lazla, now a middle-aged man. Jarrod was escorted to a withdrawing room where he was given a goblet of fortified wine. The Chamberlain explained that Her Majesty would enter the chapel in twenty minutes, at which time he would return for them. He ran over the duties of Tokamo as ring bearer and where Jarrod would stand, as if they had never rehearsed the moves. Jarrod listened politely, knowing from experience that the Chamberlain was unstoppable in the performance of his duty.

When the man had finished and gone away, Tokamo grinned at his old friend.

"That's quite an outfit," he said admiringly. "I suppose all those jewels are real?"

"I'm afraid so."

"I remember your talking about this"—he waved his hand up and down, indicating the clothes—"when you were recovering from the Great Spell, but I never really visualized the size of those stones."

"Wait till you see what Marianna's wearing," Jarrod said quickly, uncomfortable with the conversation.

Tokamo picked up on his tone of voice immediately. "Well," he said brightly, "are you feeling nervous?"

"I was when I got up," Jarrod admitted, "but Nastrus is having such a good time with this whole thing that I stopped worrying. Everyone else is taking care of all the details, so what do I have to be nervous about?"

Tokamo cocked an eyebrow, thinking that a marriage was more than just a ceremony, but he held his tongue.

"And speaking of all the details," Jarrod continued, "you do have the ring, don't you?"

Tokamo's face froze. "Of course I do," he said, fishing in his left sleeve pocket. The eyebrows came down into a solid line and he switched to the right sleeve. The mouth puckered and the eyes widened as he went back to the left and then frantically to the right sleeve again. When he raised his head, his face was a mask of bewildered contrition.

"Oh Tok," Jarrod said in exasperation. "You couldn't . . ." He was stopped by Tomako's grin. "Not funny, Tokamo," he said angrily. "Not funny!"

"Easy, easy," Tokamo said, unabashed. "Drink your wine and relax. This is the happiest day of your life, remember?"

Jarrod managed a tight smile. "Have I ever told you that you have a perverse sense of humor?"

"Frequently," Tokamo said happily as the Chamberlain swept back into the room.

The chapel was of modest proportions as public spaces in the palace went, but it was the size of a servant's hall in a prosperous manor. The walls seemed to be made of stained glass, not unlike the Cathedral of the Mother in Belengar. The morning sun streamed in through the east windows and added a layer of extra color to the bright costumes of the guests. It dappled Nastrus' hide as he stood to the left of the marble table that had served as an altar. It made the runestitching on Greylock's gown glimmer.

Jarrod and Tokamo paced up the central aisle toward the Mage, and Jarrod's spirits were lifted anew by the intense enjoyment emanating from the unicorn. All was right with the world once more. They paused at the front row of seats and bowed to Naxania, and then Tokamo moved to the right and Jarrod advanced to stand before the Mage. They smiled rather awkwardly at one another while a hum of conversation rose in the chapel as the guests waited for the next development. The time seemed to stretch interminably and Jarrod was itching to see who had put in an appearance. Darius, as the only parent, had done most of the inviting and that meant that the Queen had had a considerable say in the selection.

'Oh, go on,' Nastrus prompted. 'None of these humans will think the worse of you. Besides, most of them are too busy watching me to notice.'

'Only because there's nothing more interesting going on,' Jarrod retorted, but he took the advice and turned slowly to look down the chapel.

To his left, Queen Naxania sat in a high-backed chair on the aisle. Beyond her were two empty seats, one for Darius and one for Tokamo. Joscelyn sat at the far end wearing the brown gown of an Apprentice. Jarrod smiled at him, but the boy's attention was elsewhere. I wonder what he thinks about his mother getting married again? Jarrod thought belatedly. Has Marianna talked to him about it? Probably not. He would have to make an effort to make the boy feel that his place in his mother's affections wasn't being usurped. If Joscelyn were older or younger, it would be easier, but he was at the awkward cusp of youth where emotions were in turmoil. Still, Joscelyn was an obligation that he would assume with the marriage. His eyes slid away.

To Jarrod's right, the aisle seat was occupied by Agar Thorden, and next to him sat Lord Otorin of Lissen. The rest of the row was occupied by members of the Royal Council. Behind them ranged the Court. Conspicuous in their colorful clothes were the Marquis of Bethel and Soldan of Erdamin. There were some men in black with white ruffs, but the majority seemed to have abandoned the fashion, though none with the flair of the two young noblemen. Compared to most of them, his own clothes seemed restrained. The thought pleased him, bolstered, of course, by the knowledge that his right trouser cuff contained more wealth than most of them could muster, the Marquis included. The women, he noticed, seemed to be favoring small hats on high-piled hair this year.

The rising buzz of talk and Jarrod's observations were terminated abruptly by a fanfare of trumpets. The empty doorway was suddenly filled. Darius of Gwyndryth stood there, tall, lean and imposing with his white hair and trim white beard. He was dressed in the full uniform of a General of the Paladinian Royal Forces, gold braid at his shoulders, a scarlet sash across his chest and an Umbrian order on a broad ribbon around his neck. All the guests had turned in their seats, even Naxania, and, impressive as Darius was, all eyes were on Marianna.

She was worth the study. The dark red hair was swept back past her ears and curved down to touch her bare shoulders. Pearls crossed her brow and circled to keep her hair in place. Sapphire and emerald earrings dangled and were repeated in the necklace that ended in a square-cut sapphire. The same combination of gems, two rows deep, curled around her forearms. The dress had tiny sleeves and swooped low over the bosom. The waist was nipped in and girdled by a rope of pearls. The skirt belled out to the floor. The material was dark and though the windows patched it with colors, it contained rippling hues of its own.

They paused on the threshold as if giving the crowd time to ogle them and then moved forward as the players in the gallery struck up a stately march.

They paced up the aisle to the altar, where Darius handed his daughter on to Jarrod. Both men bowed and Darius retired to his seat beside Naxania. The couple exchanged a smile before turning and facing forward.

Jarrod and Marianna stood side by side before Greylock as the Mage's deep voice rolled out over the assembly in the simple words of the marriage rite. They promised to love and support each other all the days of their lives. Tokamo advanced and the rings of troth were exchanged. Then the compact was sealed with the nuptial kiss. In no time at all, or so it seemed to Jarrod, they were walking back down the aisle, hand in hand, with the musicians playing a lilting air.

The wedding feast, held in the Great Hall, passed in a welter of noise, heat and extravagant dishes. Then the tables were cleared and pushed to the sides and the dancing began. The wine continued to flow and the noise increased still more. The bridal couple danced twice, once with each other and once when Jarrod led out the Queen and Darius partnered his daughter. Thereafter they endured the good wishes of the guests. After about an hour, Marianna looked at her husband and said through the fixed smile that she had acquired, "If we don't get out of here, I'm going to scream."

"I doubt if anyone would hear you, but I agree."

He took her hand and led the way through the jostling throng. No one seemed to notice, much less try to stop them. The noise of the revelry pursued them down the corridor, but once they had turned the second corner, it died mercifully away.

"They're going to be angry when they look around to escort us to the bridal bed and find us gone," Jarrod said.

"They'll bloody well have to lump it," she replied. "It's a barbaric custom. I've been through it once and I've no intention of doing so again."

"They'll come banging on my, er, our door and create a rumpus. They'll all be drunk and they may well break it down."

Marianna groaned. "You're right, of course." She stopped and tugged him to a halt. "Tell you what," she said decisively, "I'm going to my room to change. You do the same and meet me at the stables. Father keeps a mare for me to ride and if Nastrus isn't there, you can borrow one of Daddy's hunters."

"We're going to the Outpost?" Jarrod asked.

"Well, we've agreed that we can't stay in your room here." A hint of her old grin appeared. "We couldn't get married there the way we wanted to, but I don't see why we shouldn't spend our wedding night there, do you?"

"I married a very intelligent woman," Jarrod said. He leaned down and kissed her on the forehead. "I'll see you at the stables in half an hour."

So Jarrod spent his wedding night in his own bed, a bed that had never had a woman between its sheets before. Marianna had gone to sleep almost immediately, but the headache he had acquired at the feast kept Jarrod awake awhile, curled protectively and contentedly around his wife. He smiled at the word. He was aware that he did not love her as he had loved her when he was a boy, but, he decided, he did love her. He knew, too, that she had never been in love with him. She was fond of him, of that he was certain, and they had been good together in bed. She would come to love him. He hugged her gently and drifted off to sleep.

chapter 21

"**W**e are informed that you demanded an audience, Revered Mother." The Emperor's voice, manipulating the cadences of the Formal Mode into sarcasm, emphasized the "demanded."

The Mother Supreme compressed her lips. She had taken a risk in forcing this meeting, but Varodias had given her no other option. She had been petitioning for an audience for a fortnight and his refusal to see her was both a personal slight and an insult to the Church. That could not be tolerated. She felt the anger rise in her again and pushed it away. She could not afford to be emotional with this man.

"Access to Your Majesty's presence is one of the traditional privileges of my office," she said quietly. "I do no more than claim what tradition has sanctified."

Varodias turned to stroke the feathers of the gyrfalcon that sat on the perch to his right. Let her stand and wait, he thought. She may have coerced my Chamberlain but she will not coerce me.

"We have been much preoccupied of late," he said lazily, his attention still on the raptor. "The times are unsettled. There are a great many things that demand our attention."

"Oh, I am aware of that," Arnulpha replied. "I did not return to Angorn in search of frivolity." She kept her voice pleasant. "It is precisely the troubled times that I wish to discuss."

Varodias turned his head back slowly. "Indeed?"

She put on her professional smile. "It was my impression that the last time we spoke we had reached an agreement." Her knees and her ankles hurt. The Emperor had yet to descend from the throne as custom required and did not appear to be ready to offer her a chair. Blast the conceited little man, she thought, but she was not about to give him satisfaction.

"An agreement?" Varodias was enjoying himself and he let it show.

"As I recall, I agreed to dismiss the Church's retainers and you agreed that Imperial troops would be deployed to protect Church property. I was to encourage our priestesses to preach support for the Imperium and you were going to open the Alien Plain to settlement, with a provision for the establishment of new churches in the conquered lands. I have kept my part of the bargain, but you have not kept yours."

It was a simple declaration, devoid of overt animosity, but she radiated the authority that accretes to a person who has been obeyed for twenty years.

The Emperor watched her with distaste. He was aware of her aura of power, but it could not daunt him. Irritate him, yes; intimidate him, no. She had presumed to treat him as an equal at their last meeting and it was fitting that she suffer for it. Besides, the unpopularity of the Church was proving to be a useful diversion for the lower orders and it did not seem to be hurting his own popularity.

"You do us wrong, Lady," he said. "Our troops have indeed been deployed and new maps of the Outland are even now being drawn. Old soldiers are drawing lots for land. Our contributions to the Church have been paid in timely fashion. In short, we cannot see the justice in your complaint."

She gave him a long, level stare. It was obvious that

deference was getting her nowhere and she decided to change her tactics. "Oh spare me," she said contemptuously. She looked around and spotted a chair by the wall.

"Since you have not thought to provide a chair for me, I suppose I shall have to get one for myself." Her tone was that of a mother addressing a son on a breach of manners.

She stumped off, got the chair and brought it back. She gathered her skirts and settled herself. "Now, let us start with the troops," she said.

Varodias' lips were drawn down, his gloved hands gripped the arms of the throne. Bad signs, but her blood was up. Let him do his worst, she thought. No Emperor was a match for the Great Mother.

"It is true that Imperial troops have been deployed around the country, but they have studiously avoided any action. This abominable hermit person travels freely and is inciting people against us once more. Novitiates have been attacked and postulants have been violated, Church estates have been raided and the kina driven off, property has been vandalized and congregations put to flight. Your men have stood by and done nothing. What say you to that?"

Varodias forced himself to relax. "We say that it is unfortunate that the Church of the Mother is losing its appeal for our peoples. Your priestesses are seen as rich and slothful and the Church has the reputation of being a harsh landlord. On the other hand, the nobility, without the rowel of war upon its flanks, seem to have become more materialistic and disputatious. The common people tend to ape their betters."

"I did not ask you for a lecture on the moral climate of the realm," Arnulpha said coldly. "I asked you why your men have stood by and done nothing."

Varodias sat very still. The gyrfalcon tossed its head

and let out a screech. The Emperor was very angry. How dare this pudding of a woman talk to him in that tone of voice. He would not, however, afford her the satisfaction of seeing that she had provoked him. His face remained bland.

"We understand that a troop of the Imperial Guard turned back a mob at Hallenberg and they have responded elsewhere according to reports." He kept his voice matter-of-fact.

"Hallenberg was the sole occasion that they arrived on time," she responded tartly.

"We can assure you that the commanders have their orders," the Emperor said enigmatically. He permitted himself a wintry smile.

"And what of this Simlan the Hermit?" The Mother Supreme asked, changing her tack slightly. "Why is he still at large?"

"He has some powerful friends, as you pointed out when last we conversed. He appears suddenly, mostly in towns, preaches and then vanishes again. That requires organization and money."

"The Electors of Ondor and Flaxenholme," she said flatly.

"So it appears," Varodias said smoothly, though he was surprised at the accuracy of her information.

"And have you asked yourself why they are spending time and money on this man?"

"They are approaching middle years and they are bored," he responded. "They led their men in battle when they were young; now they are reduced to making mischief."

Arnulpha let the jejune characterization pass, though it annoyed her. "They do it because they aim for the throne. The Church is but a stalking horse, practice for a bigger game. I suggested that before and I am certain of it now."

The Emperor froze and the raptor stirred uneasily. The Mother Supreme knew that she had penetrated his armor.

"And how know you this?" he asked quietly.

She paused before answering, wondering if he had his scribe hidden behind the throne. "Men come to us for the rite of confession." She paused again before adding, "A rite that Your Imperial Majesty has avoided for many years."

And as we now see, with good reason, Varodias thought, but he gave a short bark of laughter. "We lead an exemplary life," he said.

"Be that as it may. I suggest this hermit be eliminated for both our sakes."

"And create a martyr, Revered Mother? We think not. You may be an expert in the politics of the hereafter, but when it comes to the here and now . . ." His right hand fanned out and he let the words die away.

"Very well," Arnulpha said, "let us discuss the here and now. Your Imperial Majesty is no doubt aware of my feelings on the subject of the Discipline."

"We are aware that the Church considers the practice of Magic to be a contravention of its teachings."

"Magic is the antithesis of everything the Empire believes in," the Mother Supreme said bluntly. "The Church has always endorsed science and the progress that comes with it. The Discipline clings to the past and promotes superstition."

"This is an old argument, Serenity," Varodias said with a trace of impatience.

"Indeed," Arnulpha agreed with a sly smile, "but I wonder at Your Imperial Majesty's lack of concern when the Discipline conspires with the Isphardis to bring Magic to your very borders."

Varodias looked at her for a long moment. "Would you care to elucidate?" he asked as casually as he could.

The Mother Supreme's eyebrows rose and the half-smile returned. "Surely Your Imperial Majesty is aware of the secret Concordat between the Discipline and the Oligarchs to bring the practice of Magic to Isphardel?"

"Naturally," Varodias lied. "We are somewhat surprised that the knowledge has reached you. Another confession we suppose."

"Not this time," Arnulpha said enigmatically. "I am sure, however, that you feel as I do that this cannot be allowed to come to fruition and for that you will need our help."

"It would seem so," the Emperor allowed.

"Can the Church count on some protection in the here and now?" Arnulpha asked pleasantly.

"We shall iterate our orders to our commanders," Varodias replied flatly.

The Mother Supreme looked up skeptically, eyes narrowed. She relaxed and sat back as if she had changed her mind. "Now, about the endowment of the Church on the Alien Plain," she began.

Varodias raised a hand to cut her off. "One thing at a time, Reverend Lady. We have many matters to contend with and our time is limited. We regret, but this audience is at an end." He turned to the gyrfalcon and began to pet it.

Arnulpha took a deep breath and got to her feet. She would get no more from him at this point. She knew him well enough for that. She would not, however, retire in defeat.

"Have a care, Majesty," she said. "If your troops fail in their duty, I shall not hesitate to excommunicate you." She turned on her heel and clumped out.

Varodias glared at the broad back as if retreated and then, when the doors were closed behind her, "Scribe!"

"Yes, Majesty." The man scuttled out from behind the throne and bowed deeply.

"Destroy your record of this meeting. Leave us and do you tell the guard to summon the Lord Malum of Quern."

"As Your Imperial Majesty commands."

The scribe bowed again, sidled away to retrieve his papers and then backed from the Imperial presence to the door.

Varodias sat and waited, staring at the vacant chair, the fingers of his right hand drumming on the arm of the throne. She had threatened him. The insufferable woman had dared to threaten him. His mind fumed, contemplating revenge. She was damnably well informed. The business about the Discipline was bad enough, but the challenge to the throne was crucial. If her information was right, however, and it mirrored his own, he had larger problems than an overweening priestess. If two of the Electors were plotting against him, there would be others. This operation was too subtle for the likes of Ondor and Flaxenholme.

Grandmere of Rotherbach? Possible. He had not been to Court in over a year and he had no kin at Angorn. Baramin of Augspern? Too old to be an effective plotter. He cursed quietly under his breath. Where was Estragoth when he needed him? He should never have allowed him to go home. A thought struck him. The younger son had never returned to Court. He shook his head. No, not Estragoth. Nevertheless a pointed invitation for his son to resume his post would not be amiss.

There was a rapping at the door and Varodias came out of his reverie. The doors opened and the guard announced Lord Quern. He watched as the little man, dressed all in black, save for a small ruff, advanced across the floor, limping very slightly. Quern came to a stop beside the chair that the Mother Supreme had abandoned and bowed.

"You sent for me, Imperial Majesty?"

"We have just received confirmation from an impeccable source that the Electors of Ondor and Flaxenholme are indeed plotting against the throne," the Emperor said in a deceptively placid voice. "Since you have charge of our intelligence, it pains us that we have come by our confirmation from an outside source."

It was intended to shock, but Varodias saw no sign that the young man was disconcerted. A cool customer, he thought, not for the first time. Estragoth had chosen well.

"As Your Imperial Majesty knows, I was aware that the two Electors are supporting the man known as Simlan the Hermit, but that is in a crusade against the Mother Church. The Church has extensive estates in both Electorates and it is reasonable to suppose that they intend to annex them when the opportunity arises."

"And did it not occur to you that an attack on one pillar of the establishment can easily be redirected against another? Once the populace has been induced to riot, rebellion can follow. Or had that possibility escaped you?"

"No, Sire, it had not." Malum's insides were troubled, but he kept his voice steady. It was obvious that the Emperor was in a bad mood, and he would have to tread warily. "In fact I have agents in the field who are directing the popular animus against the Electoral Houses." He forced a brief smile. "I thought that the people were most easily aroused against the authorities that were closest to home, those whose actions most directly affected them. Those that have treated their folk well have nothing to fear. The rest will have less time for plotting."

"Indeed?" Varodias sat back and his shoulders relaxed. The falcon, sensing the change in its master's mood, ruffled its feathers and began to preen. "We trust that those Electors who are loyal to us will not be discommoded."

"The public beast is relatively easy to arouse and to turn, but difficult to direct with accuracy," Malum said with more certainty than he felt. "Those lords who have been good to their people and are perceived as being just should be relatively safe. Those who have oppressed will be at risk, no matter how loyal they are to Your Imperial Majesty." He shrugged. "Of course," he added, "if the conflagration becomes general, madness sets in and nobody is safe. There are, at present, no signs of discontent in Your Majesty's own Electorate and the capital is quiet."

Varodias smiled, the long, thin face warming briefly. "We are happy to hear that," he said. The face darkened again. "Nevertheless, the fact remains that treason is afoot and we wish to know the particulars. Ondor and Flaxenholme are too light of mind and will to carry it off successfully. There are others involved. We would know their names. With this we charge you."

"As Your Imperial Majesty commands." Malum bowed his head, knowing that he had been lucky. It was obvious that the Emperor's source was the Mother Supreme; the question was, how accurate was her information?

"It has occurred to us that both these Electors have kin at Court. It might be well if they were moved from their quarters to a place where they could be more closely watched. What think you?"

"I would advise against it, for the moment, Sire," Malum replied. "While it might dissuade one or the other from further action, it would signal our knowledge of the plot and that would undoubtedly make the others more cautious and hence harder to detect."

"A good point." Varodias nodded in approval. "We concur." He paused and looked at Malum. The boy had said nothing to him about a secret agreement between the Isphardis and the Discipline. He may not have known about it or may have decided to keep the knowledge to himself. Neither prospect sat well. Should he reveal his newly acquired information? No, he decided. Better to hold it in reserve. The right hand came up, forefinger raised. "We should hope that your spies are more efficacious in other areas," he continued, voice neutral and thus, to Malum, infinitely threatening.

Feeling like a novice, even after all these years with Estragoth, Malum dropped his gaze as the Emperor turned and made little mewling sounds to the bird. Proximity to the throne, he thought, was intoxicating, but it was also unnerving. Estragoth, secure in himself and older than the Emperor, had been immune, but Malum had been living on the edge for some months now and it was playing havoc with his digestion.

"The Elector of Estragoth had a number of excellent sources, Sire," he said cautiously, "but they do not have the contacts with the younger generation and there are those who, quite naturally, do not trust me in the same way that they trusted my Lord of Estragoth. I have some of my own men in place now, but it takes time."

Varodias turned his attention back from the hawk. "It would be well, given the changing circumstances"—his left hand described a vague circle in the air—"if we had intelligence of Isphardel. In my predecessor's day, traders sufficed, but we think it wise now to know what the Oligarchs are planning. It is our opinion that they intend to make Isphardel into a major power and, since we share a border, it behooves us to know what is in the minds of their Council." Here is his chance, he thought. If he knows he will tell me now.

Malum smiled to himself, but allowed no trace of triumph to show. "I have made a start in that direction, Sire," he said. "Unfortunately the Isphardis are a venal lot so it is an expensive undertaking. The good in that is that their venality makes them relatively easy to suborn. I have an informant placed high in the household of one of the Oligarchs."

"A good beginning," the Emperor allowed, "and you shall have money as you need it. What says this man?"

"That the Council is taken up with the logistics of road building," Malum replied, not bothering to inform his sovereign that his informant was a woman.

A peal of disconcerting laughter rang out, startling both the hawk and Malum. The Emperor's gloved hands beat together like a child's. "And think of the cost," he crowed. "If a couple of setbacks occurred, it could end up bankrupting them." He has failed, he thought behind the facade of mirth. He needs another test.

"Your Majesty is most wise," Malum said, making a mental note.

The Emperor allowed his good humor to subside. The long, mobile face became stern once more.

"There is a commission that we would have you perform for us," he said. "The Mother Supreme is, as you know, here at Angorn. She is an old woman and unhealthily obese. We should not care to have the Church in the throes of change if there are severe problems in the realm. It is our opinion that the lady's time has come. Better now than at a more inappropriate date. It would be fitting if she ate something that disagreed with her, or mayhap choked on her food. It must appear an entirely natural death. Do we make ourselves clear?"

"Absolutely, Sire."

"You may go then."

Malum bowed once more and retreated. Varodias turned to the gyrfalcon. He hummed to himself as he stroked the fierce head. An interesting session. What was obvious was that the Mother Supreme had an excellent network of spies and that meant that there would be some in the Imperial household. He would root them out. Their deaths would be slow and painful. He smiled at the thought.

chapter 22

The Oligarchs of Isphardel were gathered to discuss policy. It was as discreet a meeting as could be arranged, given the fact that Belengar was a place where no secret was safe and that it was impossible to disguise the fact that every Oligarch was out of the city at the same time. There was no regulation that forbade it, it was just that it went against mercantile self-interest and that was enough to provoke comment.

That the Oligarchs should seek relief from the heat and odors of the city during the Season of the Moons was not unexpected. It was the rainy season and the coastal regions were always the hardest hit. Dark clouds rolled in off the Inland Sea and disgorged torrents of rain on a daily basis. Ships rode high in the harbor and the culverts that ran down the streets overflowed. There was a rumor that the Magicians of the western realms were going to control the weather, but there were few who believed that they could harness the daily downpours. Even if they did manage to drive the clouds north so that the rains fell on Songuard, it would only mean that the Illuskhardin would burst its banks and drown the city. Kadif, kadaf, as the locals said. If not one thing, then the other.

The roads leading north were all paved, but the wise and wealthy always added extra horses to their teams at this time of year when business called them away, or when their families escaped Belengar's pervasive damp for the drier uplands. The absence of their families notwithstanding, only an outbreak of plague could drive all of the Oligarchs out of the city.

The meeting was being held at a summer villa on the shores of Lake Grad, though "villa" was an ingenuous word for the sprawling, honey-colored, stone mansion set in five acres of gardens and surrounded by a further three hundred acres of carefully maintained parkland. Clouds moved slowly overhead, but every now and then shafts of sunlight speared down between them and danced on the leaden surface of the lake.

Inside the house the fires were lit, even though the rest of the world would consider the temperature balmy. In the main withdrawing room, the furniture had been moved back to make space for a broad table. There was food and drink on smaller tables, but there were no servants. There were eight people in the room, all of them Oligarchs.

Isphardis tended toward olive skins and brown eyes and these heads of the old mercantile houses ran true to type. The general population tended to be dark-haired, and most of those about the central table had been dark-haired when young. Only one, Torrant Larridan, was black-haired now, and everyone knew that he dyed it. There were five men beside Torrant; Calliost of the Grandons, Marwin of the Pintarels, Asphar of House Urcel, Rully of the Narboresa and Festin Manyas, son of the former ambassador to Arundel and host to this gathering. All were dressed finely in the samites and light velvets considered proper to the season.

The two women were a contrast in styles. Olivderval, eldest of the Maricii, still wore summer silks in vivid hues and her jewelry outshone anything that the men wore. Leonida, widow of the Oligarch Dromahl, was tall and slim where Olivderval was short and stocky. She wore the deep purple of her widowhood, the combs

that held her upswept white hair in place were of ame-
thyst and a long braid of gold hung unpendanted
around her neck. The only ring she wore was a broad,
plain wedding band. She looked frail and simple in that
company, but she had taken over the family businesses
on her husband's death some fifteen years before and
had doubled the profits within three years. No one at
the table had bested her in a deal, though all, save
Olivderval, had tried.

"And now to our business," Festin Manyas said from
his chair at the head of the table. "I should like to call
upon friend Olivderval of the Maricii to bring us up to
date on the latest intelligence from abroad." He was a
spare, fussy man, slightly younger than the others, and
would not have been chairman had they not been in his
house.

"Thank you, Festin, and may I compliment you on
your admirable hospitality." She smiled down the table
at him among murmurs of assent. "As you know," she
proceeded briskly, "the first installment of money has
been paid to the Discipline according to the terms of
our secret compact. There is a working group of the
Weatherwards on Harbor Island examining conditions
in the skies and I am told reliably that special emphasis
is being placed on that aspect of the training of the
Apprentice Magicians at the Collegium. Needless to say,
they will have to produce a great many new Weatherwards in the years to come. I have no doubt, however,
that they will be able to improve our conditions considerably, even, let us hope, in the rainy season. I think
that it is worth our while to be patient.

"Our relations with the Magical Kingdoms and with
Talisman continue to be good, although the unrest in
Paladine this past summer produced a slight downturn
in flax and the cereal trade. Wool and leather, however,
were unaffected. Indeed the number of fleeces increased.

From all reports, Queen Naxania is firmly in control again, though she is not markedly popular. In short, there is no reason to suppose that next year's profits should not be up to, or beyond, last year's. The same holds true for both Arundel and Talisman. So much for the good news."

Olivderval paused and drank some water. She glanced at her colleagues and was pleased to see that no one was taking notes.

"Conditions in the Empire," she resumed, "are far from smooth. The general unrest is continuing. The preachings of Simlan the Hermit have affected the manufacturing towns and the production, particularly of cloth and metalware, is down substantially. That, combined with an indifferent harvest in most Electorates, has led to an increase in imports, notably of grain, and a decrease in exports. It is my judgment that, within a year, Umbria will become a debtor nation."

There was a brief silence, broken by Marwin, whose increasing weight and wispy hair gave him the look of an oversized baby.

"If Varodias spent less money on his army, he might be able to pay his bills."

"Scant chance of that while there's rebellion abroad," the Oligarch Larridan replied.

"I would think that it is too early to label it rebellion, but the question is, are we going to extend him credit?" The observation and question were couched in Leonida's cultivated tones.

How does a reed that thin produce such a rich sound? Olivderval wondered. She waited for someone to answer. When none did, "I think we must," she said. "We do not want to give him an excuse to turn on us, not yet."

"Not yet?" The query came from Calliost.

Olivderval smiled across the table at him. He was tall,

still slim in robes that disguised his paunch, and his thick, grey hair made him look younger than he was. Olivderval and he had had an affair when both were young. It had petered out gracefully and she was still fond of him.

"It will come, my dear Calliost, it will come," she said regretfully. "Nobody loves a creditor, as we are all well aware, but Varodias has deeper troubles and is beginning to look abroad for a diversion, something to take the people's mind off their domestic problems. We are the obvious target."

"When you say that the Emperor is already beginning to look at us with envy, are you just being logical or do you have some proof?" The question came from Torrant.

"Oh, I have proof," Olivderval said pleasantly. "Now that the Elector of Estragoth has retired to his estates, his place has been taken by his former secretary, one Malum of Quern, with one difference. Young Malum is also Varodias' spymaster. Young Quern, whose acquaintance I made at Stronta, has sought, quite successfully I am happy to say, to suborn my tiring woman—and I am sure that he has other sources in Belengar."

"And why are you happy to say that your tiring woman has been enlisted as an Umbrian spy?" Festin asked.

"Because she is a loyal soul," Olivderval replied sweetly, "and she came straight to me." She shrugged and raised her hands. "I, of course, told her exactly what I wanted Lord Malum to hear. I shall continue to do so."

"And have you taken steps to acquire reliable information from Umbria?" Leonida inquired.

Olivderval smiled. "Naturally. We all have our own network of traders and I question mine closely, but, in addition, I have found some Umbrians who are more than willing to supply information for ready cash." She flashed a look around the table. "Umbrians are easy to snare," she said contemptuously. "They're too greedy to look ahead and, once committed to treason, too afraid of betrayal to back out."

"And wh at did you tell your maid to tell the Umbrians?" Marwin asked.

"That the Council was too bogged down in the details of building roads through Songuard to think about much of anything else."

"Well, that's the truth," Rully of the Narboresa put in sardonically. "That's what we're here for, isn't it?"

Olivderval looked at Leonida and then at Calliost, hoping that one of them would take the initiative. Both knew her thinking on the matter, but they both avoided her eyes. She took a breath.

"Only partly," she said. "That is why we have taken such precautions about this meeting and why no word of what is decided here can seep out, even to members of your families." She stopped and pushed her chair back as quietly as she could. She levered her bulk up and walked softly to the doors. She opened them quickly and stepped out into the passageway. At the end of the corridor, two of Festin Manyas' servants were deep in conversation. There was no one else in sight. She turned an reentered the withdrawing room.

"I apologize for the melodrama," she said lightly, "but, from now on, one cannot be too careful. The future of the State depends on it."

She felt as well as heard the skeptical silence and retook her place with deliberation. She sensed the antagonism of the men. They had yielded to her hard work and experience long ago and treated her as an equal, but they still did not like it when she took it upon herself to formulate policy for them. Too bad, she thought;

if we waited for them we'd be a province of the Empire. She smiled up and down the table, inviting them to see the humor in her fears, despising herself for the gesture as she performed it.

"My caution may seem overdone to some of you, but the reality is that we must prepare ourselves for war with the Empire."

"Oh come now, Olivderval," Torrant expostulated. "Your imagination has taken control of your usually admirable practicality. The Empire has no need to expand. It has vast new territories that it can't possibly populate and they have absolutely no reason to fear us."

"You are being logical, Torrant," Leonida said dryly, "and also obtuse. We have already heard about the unrest in the Empire and we now know that Varodias considers us important enough"—there was a wealth of sarcasm in the "important"—"to spy on members of this Council. I recommend, gentlemen, that you look to your households. If this Quern person has seen fit to spend gold on the servants, you may wager that he has made similar efforts elsewhere." The level brown eyes scanned the faces around the table. "It would, of course, be far more productive to have one of us in his employ." She let the statement linger accusingly in the air.

"Fear is not Varodias' prod," Olivderval resumed, "or at least not direct fear of us; fear of his own people maybe. Envy is the spur. We do not grow, we do not spin, we do not manufacture, but we prosper. Success inspires resentment and it fosters greed."

"Beautifully said, dear lady." Asphar of Urcel's genteel voice dropped languidly into the debate. "Now, you know that I admire you beyond measure, but I also know you passing well. For you to have risen to such poetic heights means that you are about to propose something deucedly expensive." He smiled across the table at her and sprawled back carelessly in his chair.

And I know you, Olivderval thought, a dandy with a mind of honed steel and a grudge-bearing ability that the gods would envy. She replicated his smile, though with difficulty. When they were both children—he was fourteen, she twelve—he had beaten her dog because, when they had both called it, the dog had gone to her and not to him. She had been a mere girl then with an older brother to fight her battles for her, but he had died and she was Oligarch now.

"Oh aye," she said pleasantly, proud of her control, "it will cost, but less I think than would the wholesale disruption of world trade, or having our houses fired and Isphardis put to the sword." Her voice was light, to the extent that it natural depth allowed. It was not he way she had intended to approach the subject, but she was reacting to Asphar. Damn the man! Why did she have to spend her life reacting to him?

"And what is your suggestion?" Marwin asked cautiously.

Olivderval took in a breath and made herself relax. "We shall have to arm and train a militia." She held up a hand as babble broke forth.

"I know, I know," she said. "We have never resorted to arms, but times have changed."

"Changed?" came the clotted voice of Calliost. "We have avoided arms in times of war, what possible reason could we have to resort to them in times of peace?"

"Thank you, Calliost," Olivderval said slowly. "To begin with, we shall have to have a force to protect our roadbuilders in Songuard. Their government is new and relatively powerless and, to compound the problem, what sway they hold is in the north whereas we shall begin our operations in the south. I put it you that the sight of all that activity will prove too much for the southern clans. We shall need armed men to protect our workers, our mules and our equipment."

She sat back and surveyed them again. "Of course," she added, "that would be the legitimate cover. No one could object to that. I gained promises from the western countries that they would protect us if need be, but we cannot expect them to do that if we are unwilling to protect ourselves. As I said, that would be the ostensible reason for a militia, but the real danger comes from Umbria and we shall have to build an effective army to counter that."

"And while we are at it," Rully chimed in unexpectedly, "we ought to consider arming our merchant fleet. All the Umbrian fortifications face north."

Olivderval flashed him a look of gratitude. "Our excuse could be an increase in piracy, preferably from the shores of the Magical Kingdoms," she said approvingly.

"I don't know about this," Manyas said nervously. "This is a major undertaking, an expensive undertaking, and there is no profit in it."

"Think of it as insurance against ruin," Leonida said crisply. "Any estimates of the costs, Olivderval?"

The Oligarch referred to the papers in front of her. "A start-up cost of three hundred thousand ecrus for the training and equipping of a force of fifty thousand men."

"Fifty thousand men! That's insane." The agitated objection came from Festin Manyas.

"And that does not include monies for the development of cannon," Olivderval pressed on relentlessly. "We have acquired, by the way, the secret of the manufacture of cannon and I do not doubt that Isphardi ingenuity can improve upon the original."

Hubbub ensued.

chapter 23

Jarrod was relaxing in his main room and was feeling satisfied. Nastrus had just returned to Stronta and had reported that the Giants' Causeway had been cleared away as far as the Songean border, a prodigious amount of work for both Magicians and cloudsteeds. The unicorn had been tired and proud and he had certainly earned the right to feel that way. There was no more work to be done on the project, for this year at any rate. The weather would begin to close in by the end of the month, the more so in Songuard where it was uncontrolled. Indeed, there were reports of fresh snow on the mountain peaks. Nastrus would be returning to the Island at the Center soon for his annual visit and Jarrod knew that he would have to come up with a convincing reason to tempt him back. It was important that the Empire see the benefit of the enterprise, that the Discipline be seen to be helpful to them.

He stretched his slippered feet toward the fire and was contemplating a nap when there was a rapping at the door. He swiveled and saw the Duty Boy's head. He gestured and the boy slipped into the room.

"Sorry to disturb you, Excellence, but there's a bunglebird message that just came in."

Jarrod beckoned and the boy came over quickly and handed him a tiny roll of paper. Jarrod smoothed it out and leaned it into the light so that he could decipher the writing. "Child expected in a sennight. Come if you've a mind to." It was unsigned. His heart gave a little lurch and his brain began to calculate. It would have taken the bird at least four days to fly here from Gwyndryth. That meant that it was due any day. The baby could already have been born. A trip through Interim was the only way to get there in anything like time.

"Any return message, sir?" the boy asked.

"Oh, er, no. It wouldn't do any good. I'd be obliged, though, if you would pack me some clean linen, hose, a couple of robes and my washing things. Use the saddlebags. Fetch me my shoes first. I've got to see the Mage."

Five minutes later he was being ushered into Greylock's bedchamber. The Mage was sitting at his desk working at some papers.

"Sit yourself by the fire, Jarrod, I'll be with you directly," he said without looking up. "There's some mulled ale in the hearth, help yourself."

Jarrod sat and watched the fire, warming his hands on the mug and taking small sips. He was excited and the hot liquid seemed to steady him. He heard sand being sprinkled on paper and sat up. Moments later the old Mage joined him, ladled out some ale and sat down opposite.

"What can I do for you?" he asked.

"I just got a message from Marianna," Jarrod replied. "The baby's due and I would like to be there." He smiled sheepishly. "It's my first, and possibly my last, child."

Greylock's lips tightened; not the reaction that Jarrod had expected. "Deuced awkward," he said.

Jarrod waited.

Greylock sighed and then looked up at his protégé. "The fact is," he said, "I'm planning to go to Celador."

"I realize that you would rather we weren't both away

at the same time, but Thorden and Tokamo are quite capable of keeping things running. They've done it before." Jarrod recognized the defensive note in his voice. Surely Greylock couldn't deny him this?

"Yes I know," Greylock said on cue, "but the reason I'm going to Celador is that the Archmage is ill."

"I hadn't heard," Jarrod said soberly.

"Nobody's heard. He sent me a private message, oblique as usual, but I have a feeling that he wants to settle the succession."

"But there's no question of that, surely? Everybody knows that you are going to be the next Archmage," Jarrod objected.

"Nevertheless, it's always wiser to be at the scene," Greylock said darkly.

"Is it that bad?"

"I certainly hope not, but there's no getting away from the fact that, for a Magician who has accomplished as much as he has, survival into one's eighties is close to a miracle."

"And you would rather that I was here," Jarrod concluded.

"No, I should prefer you be in Celador in case someone calls for a quick meeting of the High Council in an attempt to ram their own candidacy through. The only trouble is that if we both turned up unexpectedly it would undoubtedly start rumors and might even precipitate action. The Outpost, however, is a lot closer to Celador than Gwyndryth and days could make all the difference."

"I plan to go through Interim, if I can persuade Nastrus," Jarrod said, relieved.

"I must be getting old," Greylock said with a shake of his head. "I keep forgetting. Are there bunglebirds at Celador that home to Gwyndryth?"

"There ought to be, but it might be a good idea to take one from here. There are four in the cote."

"In that case," Greylock said with a smile, "you'd better get going. The baby isn't going to wait for you, you know."

"Thank you, sir. Just send a message if you need me and I'll be there within hours. Oh, and please give my best to the Archmage," Jarrod added, getting to his feet.

Succession of a sort was on Malum's mind as well. He had thought long and hard about the Emperor's commission. He had had a momentary qualm, but it hadn't been enough to keep him awake at night or even intrude upon his dreams. The Emperor had ordered it and he was the Emperor's sworn man; besides, it was a job and could be considered solely on that plane. Lastly, it was an interesting problem. The death must appear to be a natural one—not too difficult with a woman as fat as the Mother Supreme—but there should be a certain elegance to it. It should also be quick, final and neat. Not a job that he could entrust to anyone else.

His mind made up, he went into the Imperial Forest for a solitary ride. Nothing unusual in that; he had done the same thing often enough before. He returned with a selection of mushrooms that he hoped were poisonous. Once back in his room, he cut them up and boiled them over the fire in a pannikin. He reduced the liquid to concentrate it and then drew some off. He set a gobbet of raw meat in it and left it to steep overnight. The next morning he made his way to the twisting streets of the old town, picked his way along the muddy path beneath the overhanging buildings until he found a stray cur in an empty lane and fed it the meat. The dog died in silence and with gratifying rapidity.

Well pleased, Malum returned to the palace and ordered a tray of marchpane from the kitchens. The

Mother Supreme was known to have a sweet tooth and the strong almond scent would disguise the odor of the mushroom juice. He set the marchpane to soak and then went out again to purchase a wooden box inlaid with nacre. That done, he cut the sweetmeat into squares and assembled them into a suitable-looking offering. Then he dispatched a page to ask for an audience with Arnulpha.

The Mother Supreme sat in a wide, padded chair. Behind her sat three lesser priestesses quietly doing embroidery. She was not wearing the cloth-of-gold gown that he associated with her, but rather a voluminous robe of dark blue silk with darker patches beneath the armholes. Matching slippers peeped out beneath the hem. She had, Malum noted, surprisingly small feet for a woman of her size.

He advanced across the room, the box clamped firmly against his side, and made his court bow.

"Be welcome, my lord. We are pleased to see you." The formal mode rolled out in a low, pleasant voice. She smiled up at him and the small eyes well nigh disappeared.

Malum masked the distaste of the congenitally thin for the overweight. "I am grateful that Your Serenity consented to see me," he replied.

Arnulpha watched the dark little man with an interest tinged with wariness. He was somewhat of a mystery at Court. He seldom appeared at Imperial functions, but he was said to have the Emperor's ear.

"Had you not requested an audience, my Lord of Quern, we should have sought you out."

Malum's look of surprise was only partly feigned.

"Oh come, sirrah," Arnulpha's said, warm amusement surfacing, "you have established yourself in our Emperor's confidence in a remarkably short time. That makes you a man of importance. We are not in Angorn that often. Surely you would expect that we would wish to take advantage of the opportunity to make your acquaintance?"

She arrogates the use of the royal we to herself, Malum thought. I wonder if she dares do it in front of Varodias. Was there also a touch of the flattened vowels of the south in her speech? She cozens, he thought. She is mid-Umbrian born and a daughter of the nobility. She plays with me. And the Emperor was right; she was damnably well informed. He produced a self-deprecating smile.

"You do me too much honor, madam. Any influence that I have is owed not to my talents, but to the good offices of my former master, the Elector of Estragoth. I think that His Imperial Majesty talks to me on occasion because I remind him of his old friend. I fear that he does not listen to me," he said with apparent frankness, "on those rare occasions when he asks me for an opinion. In truth it seems to me that His Imperial Majesty has been ill advised of late, though not by me, in his dealings with the Mother Church."

"Say you so?" The Mother Supreme's eyebrows were raised. Whatever it was that she had been expecting from him, that was not it. "Mayhap we should make ourselves more comfortable." She gestured toward the hearth, where a low table and three chairs were set. She heaved her bulk up, waved a dismissal of the three priestesses and led the way.

Malum heard the breathlessness that the effort caused and smiled inwardly. If all went well, he would not have this chance again. He should get what information he could before offering his gift.

"I have always considered," he said as he waited for the Mother Supreme to lower herself into a chair, "that the Church is one of the binding forces that unites the Empire. Tradition, of course, is the other great mortar in the structure—village tradition, hereditary lords bound by liege oaths—but tradition is more easily sundered than the people's belief in the Great Mother."

He placed the box on the floor beside his chair as he sat and saw Arnulpha's eyes flicker over it. "It seems to me," he continued, "and I would ask that this does not leave this chamber . . ." He paused until she nodded her head. "That His Imperial Majesty embarks upon a course of folly when he opposes the Church." He sat back and looked at her anxiously.

She leaned forward and rang a small china bell. "We cannot say that we disagree with you, my lord," she said. "Indeed, we could wish that your counsel had more weight with the Emperor." She glanced sideways at him and smiled briefly. "Have no fear," she added, "we know Varodias passing well. He is not a man subject to overt pressure. Subtlety and persistence are needed." She broke off as a novice entered and then ordered chai and honey cakes without consulting Malum. She waited until the girl had withdrawn.

"You are an ambitious man, my lord, and nothing comes for nothing. What is that you would want from us?"

"From Your Serenity, nothing," Malum replied smoothly. "My former master's great influence with the Emperor was founded in his love of the Empire. He sought her good, not his own gain. I would follow in his footsteps. As I told you, ma'am, I am convinced that harmony between Church and Emperor is essential for the health of the Empire."

The Mother Supreme was about to reply when the novice returned with a tray. She arranged the crockery and the cakes and then poured the chai. When she had withdrawn once more, Arnulpha said, "We have warned His Imperial Majesty that the Church cannot tolerate further attacks on her people and her property. If there is anything that you can do to see that the Imperial Guards act upon the assurances given us, you would be doing the Emperor a service and you would not find us ungrateful."

Malum nodded and reached down for the box. He stood and held it out. "A small token, Serenity. I thought that honey and almonds bound together formed a symbol of what I hope can be the relationship between yourself and His Imperial Majesty."

"Prettily put," Arnulpha said, opening the box. Her face lit up. "Marchpane," she exclaimed. "A favorite of ours." She reached into the box and then stopped. "Will you join us, my lord?" she asked.

Malum had prepared for this eventuality. The two rows closest to the side with the clasp were untainted. He produced his smile. "Willingly." He leaned forward and took one, biting into it without hesitation. The Mother Supreme sipped her chai and watched him swallow. Then she helped herself.

Malum drank some chai and then helped himself to one of the honey cakes. He watched the Mother Supreme out of the corner of his eye.

"Good," she said. "The almond taste is a little strong, but not unpleasant. We thank you." She took another.

"I am glad they meet with your approval," he said politely.

The Mother Supreme licked her fingers and drank some more of her chai. "If the Emperor will agree," she began, and then stopped suddenly. Her eyes widened and she clutched her belly. Her mouth opened and a choking sound emerged.

"Is something the matter, Serenity?" Malum asked disingenuously.

Arnulpha's hand groped out, reaching for the bell. Malum rose swiftly and moved it out of the way. Realization dawned in the Mother Supreme's eyes, but was quickly extinguished by a spasm of pain. Her heavy body twisted in the chair and her mouth tried to form words. Her hands grasped the arms of the chair as she tried to stand, but a convulsion threw her back. The mouth began to work again, then the body arched, belly thrusting upward, and collapsed. Her heels drummed briefly on the floor and then the head lolled forward, spreading out her chins.

Malum looked down at her for a beat and then pressed his fingers into the flesh of her wrist, searching for a pulse. There was none. He unbuttoned the top of his doublet, scooped up the remaining pieces of poisoned marchpane and dropped them down it. He did the buttons up again and patted himself lightly to make sure the pieces didn't show. He rearranged the rest of the marchpane so that it looked as if a lot had been eaten. As a final touch he broke off a piece of one of the cakes, opened the Mother Supreme's mouth and stuffed it inside. He dropped the other piece on the floor as if it had fallen from her hand. He stepped back and surveyed his handiwork before ringing the little bell violently. He shouted for help.

When the Mother Supreme's attendants came rushing in, they found Lord Malum of Quern pounding their mistress on the back.

"Water, get water!" he shouted at the flustered priestesses. "She's choking." He found that he was enjoying himself. He would not say a word about this to the Emperor, he decided. Not unless he asks directly, he amended. Word of the Mother Supreme's death would get out almost immediately. If he made no demands, the Emperor would be certain of his loyalty. Let others have the titles; he would control the policy.

He abandoned his efforts and set the Mother Supreme upright. He propped her body against the chair back. The jaw hung slackly. He looked at the two women, who were hovering futilely.

"I think one of you should get the Emperor's Wisewoman, unless Her Serenity travels with one of her own," he said.

Gwyndryth was basking in sunlight when Jarrod and Nastrus came out of Interim. The meadow that the unicorn used as a reference point had been brought under cultivation and they emerged while women were gleaning the stubble, causing consternation. By the time that Jarrod had recovered from the effects of the trip, the women were clustered around the unicorn, rubbing its coat for luck. When they had first come to Gwyndryth, Jarrod reflected, they had had to sneak the unicorns in by the back postern and hide them in the cellars. Now Nastrus was a symbol of good fortune. Since no one was paying the slightest attention to him, Jarrod took the opportunity to remove the extra clothing he had donned for protection against the cold of Interim. No sooner done than he was recognized.

"It's the new lord," one of the women cried, pointing. The others fell back and ducked their heads in acknowledgment.

'There's a fine thing,' Nastrus grumbled. *'You're the one commanding respect and all you did was rut with Marianna.'*

Jarrod ignored him. "Give you goodday, ladies," he said. "I have come for the birthing. Is the Lady Marianna delivered yet?"

"Not yet, Lord," the observant one said with the thick burr that characterized the speech of the region, "leastwise the bell 'asn't rang and they allus ring the bell for a birthing."

"I'd be best on my way then," he said, and they moved farther back to give him room.

He nudged Nastrus into a trot and waved to the women. They were cantering by the time they reached the road. Even though his thoughts were on the Hold, he noticed that the trees were beginning to turn and that they weren't as colorful as those up north. The lichened walls of the Hold came into view and he saw that the gates were open. No one challenged them as they rode in, but both he and Nastrus were greeted at the stables as old friends. Jarrod's new status did not seem to affect the ostlers and the grooms.

He took his saddlebags and slung them over his shoulder, bade Nastrus good-bye and made his way to the house. As he approached the steps, he was greeted by a middle-aged man he did not know. The man, obviously a gentleman by his dress and his bearing, was accompanied by a young squire.

"May the best of the day be before you, my lord." The man bowed deeply. "I am Kerris of Aylwyth, Seneschal of Gwyndryth."

He must have had a lookout posted to get here this fast, Jarrod thought. "And may your night be tranquil," he returned politely. He unslung his saddlebags and the squire quickly retrieved them. "May I ask what happened to Sir Ombras?"

"Lord Obray retired to his estate two months ago," the Seneschal replied. "His eyesight's failing and his hearing is none too good."

"I am sorry to hear that. He was a good man and he served the family well. I must make a point of riding over to pay my respects while I am here."

"I am sure that it will be much appreciated, Sir Jarrod," Aylwyth replied smoothly. "In the meantime, your quarters have been made ready against your coming."

"I am obliged to you." He moved forward. "How is the Lady, er, how is my wife?"

Sir Kerris looked at Jarrod speculatively and then seemed to come to a decision. "Quite impossible, my lord," he said straight-faced.

Jarrod's eyes opened wide and then he threw back his head and laughed. "By the gods, you are a gambling man, sir. However, the Lady Marianna that I know can express herself, ah, somewhat forcefully."

Sir Kerris smiled. "She resents being confined," he said companionably, "and it must indeed be a great trial for someone as active as my lady. Wisewoman Jaffney thought it best because the Lady Marianna is"—he glanced up at Jarrod—"not overly young to be with child." The lips twitched upward slightly. "The Lady Marianna did not take kindly to the suggestion."

"I can imagine," Jarrod said sympathetically. "In fact I'm surprised that she agreed to it."

"Well we have Mrs. Merieth to thank for that. She's the only one who can give my lady orders."

"Merry? I'm surprised that she's still alive."

"She's alive all right and sprightly with it," Aylwyn said as they climbed the steps. "Her husband died a good ten years ago. She's been at a loose end since Master Joscelyn went off into your care. She is really looking forward to this baby and she is not about to let Lady Marianna take any unnecessary chances." He stood aside to let Jarrod go through the door first.

"I forget my manners, my lord," he said. "You must be tired and hungry after your journey." He snapped his fingers.

"Hungry more than anything else," Jarrod admitted. He was, in fact, ravenous.

The squire with the saddlebags appeared.

"Take those up to my lord's suite and put water on for a bath." The Seneschal turned to Jarrod and gestured to the staircase. "Permit me to escort you to your quarters," he said formally. "I trust that they will be to your liking. If there is anything lacking, or anything that you want changed, you have but to tell me."

"I'm sure it will be perfectly satisfactory," Jarrod said soothingly letting the man lead the way.

"That I think I can promise," Sir Kerris replied, "but this is, after all, your home and your rooms should suit you to a T."

My home, Jarrod thought as he mounted the stairs. I suppose he's right. No, this will always be Marianna's home. The Outpost is mine.

At the doorway to the apartments he was handed over to a short, swarthy man with a neatly kept mass of black hair. He was ushered in with an extravagant Court bow of unexpected grace. Jarrod turned and thanked Sir Kerris and asked, diffidently, if some food could be sent up as soon as possible.

"At once, my lord," the Seneschal said, and departed.

I like the man, Jarrod thought. No "Is there anything in particular you feel like eating?"

"I bid you welcome, Lord. I hite Semmurel and have the honor of being your personal bodyservant." The man's Common was impeccable, but the accent of the Southern Marches gave it flavor.

"Greetings, Semmurel," Jarrod returned, looking around at the dark paneling and tiny windows of the anteroom. Gwyndryth was one of the oldest Holdings in Arundel and had, to all appearances, never been modernized. It had seemed picturesque to him the last time that he had stayed here, but he had become accustomed to light and fresh air. There would be suggestions that he'd be making to Sir Kerris after all.

Jarrod looked down at his new servant. Bright, black, button eyes looked back, curious and alert. "You don't have to use the Formal Mode," he said, "unless there is company that would require it." He gave a quick, impersonal smile. "I'll warn you now that my Arunic, while not perfect, is good, especially when it comes to swear words. I had an excellent tutor."

Semmurel grinned. "I shall be mindful of that, my lord. May I show you the rest of the rooms?"

"By all means." Jarrod followed him through the inner door.

The bedchamber was large and well appointed. The windows were larger here, the traditional inside shutters folded back against the walls. It wasn't gloomy, the walls were whitewashed, but Jarrod still found it cheerless. The bed was large and canopied. There were two clothespresses and a wardrobe, all three heavily carved, a fireplace with a cauldron hanging over the flames, two armchairs with rush seats, a table against one wall and half a dozen side chairs around the others. There was a well-worn carpet by the bed, but apart from that the planks were bare.

"Through yonder door there is a writing cabinet with the garderobe off it. It's big enough for the jakes and a decent tub." He produced an ingratiating little smile. "Luckily for my not too stalwart back, the fireplace is big enough to heat the water in. Lucky for you too, my lord; your baths will be hotter."

"Are there quills and ink?" Jarrod asked.

"There are, and there are a number of pieces of parchment."

"Good. I shall also need shelves for books, but that is not an immediate concern."

"Very good, my lord. I shall make a note of it." Semmurel gestured to the wardrobe. "That is your wardrobe and there are some of the outfits that the Lady Marianna bade me make for you." He made a self-deprecating little movement. "I am by way of doubling as a tailor," he said.

He coughed, as if embarrassed. "Her Ladyship made

it very clear to me that . . ." His voice petered out. "That is to say that Her Ladyship would prefer it if you did not wear Magician's robes while in residence." He took half a pace back as if anticipating an outburst.

Jarrod watched him for a couple of beats. "In that case, let us see what my wife considers suitable attire." He was far from certain that he would like her taste in men's clothes.

"As you say, Lord," Semmurel said quickly. "And, if it would not be too much trouble, I should appreciate it if Your Lordship would try on a couple of things. Just until the food comes," he hastened to add. He essayed a smile. "Her Ladyship was quite precise about the sizes, but memories can sometimes play tricks."

"Quite so."

Jarrod began to unbutton his jacket. He hadn't known what to expect at Gwyndryth, but it definitely wasn't this.

An hour later, wearing pale blue with dark gray piping, bathed, shaved and scented, he was shown into Marianna's bedchamber on the top floor. It had a big window that opened onto the roof and the midday sun shone in brightly. The Lady of the Holding was propped up in the grand, carved bed, wearing a pale green nightrobe, with a matching ribbon securing the pulled-back hair. There was an open account book on the counterpane beside her. She did not look up and he had a moment to study her. The first thing that registered was that she was plump, a mild shock in one who has always been thin. The second was the enormous bulge beneath the covers. She glanced in his direction and her face lit up. She is truly beautiful, Jarrod thought as he smiled at her.

"Jarrod! They didn't tell me that you'd arrived. When did you get here?"

"Just over an hour ago," he said, advancing to the bedside. "Long enough to have a bath and a meal and don this finery." He extended his arms and rotated to display the clothes. "What do you think?"

"You look very handsome and everything seems to fit properly," she said. "I was afraid that the sleeves and the trousers would be too short."

"No, they're fine, though I shall have to watch what I eat. My new man gives me to understand that robes are unwelcome here."

"Well, as my husband, you are required to show an amount of state. The tenants expect it. It's important for our standing in the region and people are very sensitive to that. In a great many cases, their self-esteem is attached to us. Besides, most people tend to be afraid of Magicians and especially of Mages."

"It's a shame, then, that I can't do anything about my height," he said with more asperity than he had intended.

"Now don't be difficult, Jarrod dear," she said with unwonted calmness. "You have to realize that, at Gwyndryth, you have to play the part of my husband. What you do at Stronta, or at Celador for that matter, is entirely your affair, but here we have customs and traditions that go back for centuries. What matters here is the peace and productivity of the demesne and of my father's tenants. There are certain obligations that come with your position. You will have to preside at Hall tonight for instance, and we shall have to have a feast for the vassals and tenants in your honor."

She looked up at him and smiled. "I can't promise that we won't have to give a feast to celebrate," she patted her stomach with both hands, "the arrival of this one."

Jarrod sat down on the edge of the bed and reached out a tentative hand.

"Go ahead," she said. "It won't bite."

He placed his hand gently on the swelling covers. All he could feel was the curving counterpane with its welts of embroidery.

"How are you doing?" he asked.

"Oh, I feel bloated and uncomfortable," she said as if ticking off her blessings. "My back hurts, I feel as if I need to go to the garderobe every ten minutes and my feet and ankles are swollen." She favored him with a mincing smile more usually seen on the faces of Court ladies making light conversation.

"Most of all, and most oddly of all, I have the distinct feeling that this is not my body. It does what it wants and I have no control of it. It is as if I were outside myself observing this other person. At other times it is as if I were trapped in someone else's body."

"Is there anything that I can do?" he asked.

She laughed. "Not unless you have a spell to speed delivery and make it painless." Her eyes widened suddenly and she caught her breath.

She grabbed Jarrod's hand and pulled it back to her belly. He felt the baby's kick clear through the covers. He looked at Marianna, his own eyes round.

"Oh gods," he said. "It's alive."

"It's a very active little person," she replied in a tone of amused resignation.

"When . . . ?" he began.

"Soon," Marianna said. "Pray to the gods that it be soon."

"And the Wisewoman's good, is she?"

"Bloody woman treats me like a fragile child," Marianna said with a flash of her old belligerence. "She's even got Merry convinced. Bland food, no wine, no mandragora—you'd think I'd never had a baby before."

"I'm sure they know best," Jarrod began soothingly and then changed his tack when he caught the look on her face. "Well, I'll undertake to put on a brave show at Hall if you promise to behave yourself."

She made a face. "I don't have much of a choice do I?" she said with a trace of bitterness. "The unspeakable Jaffney won't let me do anything. Every time one of my factors visits, it takes a battle royal to get him admitted. The harvest is in and all the shipping arrangements have to be made. We had a bumper crop this year and the Isphardis are paying a decent price for a change." She tapped the account book. "If I can arrange for quick delivery before the other Holdings get themselves organized, this will be the most profitable year I've ever had. I should be down at Seaport. Instead of which, I'm cooped up in this room."

"Can't Sir Kerris help?" Jarrod inquired mildly. "He seems to be a competent man."

"Oh, he'll make a good enough Seneschal. He's well liked and he's honest. But he knows nothing about commerce. In fact he would be highly offended if I suggest that he get involved. My factors are good, but they need watching. If you don't keep a sharp eye on them, they'll rob you blind."

Jarrod noticed that her explanation of her business difficulties had restored some of her good humor. "The Oligarch Olivderval thinks highly of your trade venture," he remarked, "and coming from her, that's quite a compliment."

Marianna smiled. "It doesn't stop her from driving a hard bargain," she said. "The men are far easier to deal with."

I'll just wager they are, Jarrod thought. "Well, I'm

pleased to see that you are looking so well and I'm glad
that I got here in time. And don't worry, I shan't let
you down with the tenants." He leaned over and kissed
her on the forehead and then made his escape while she
was still in a good mood.

The Lord Chancellor hesitated before entering the
Privy Chamber. He had been announced and the Queen
had to have his report, but he knew that she would be
distressed by the news and, given the wrong royal mood,
such distress could result in the removal of his head. The
trouble was that Her Majesty had been in a series of
terrible moods ever since the wedding. He drew a deep
breath and plucked up the front of his robe. Whatever
the outcome, he would make a suitable entrance. He
cleared the sill and let the garment go as he advanced
into the presence. The skirt of his robe swept the floor
and gathered sweet herbs as he crossed the room. The
Queen, dressed this day in an eye-disorienting combination of plum and puce, sat waiting upon the throne
while her ladies-in-waiting chatted quietly. He came to a
halt and bowed deeply.

"My Lord of Brynhaven, we are pleased to see you,"
Naxania said, though she looked far from pleased.

He cleared his throat before speaking. "I am here to
report to Your Majesty upon a development in your
realm." He was nervous and he sounded stilted. Naxania had a very poor record of dealing graciously with
bearers of bad tidings.

"And what is it that our Lord Chancellor has to tell
us?" Naxania inquired.

"The Duke of Abercorn is dead, ma'am."

He stood and waited for the tongue-lashing.

"It is not unexpected," the Queen said mildly.

"Mage Courtak is his successor of record," the Chancellor added.

"We know that. We do not like it, but we know that."
There was no mistaking that tone of voice. She looked
at him and Brynhaven felt a shiver of fear between his
shoulder blades. "What to you intend to do about it?"
she asked sharply.

"Do about it, Majesty? I do not understand. There is
nothing I can do about it. There is no other direct heir."

"Then find one."

"I am sorry, Your Majesty, but there is no other direct successor, and, much as I would like to please you,
ma'am, with Jarrod Courtak, the discoverer of the unicorns, living, there is nothing that can be done."

"Are you telling me, Chancellor," she said with terrible quiet, "that if it is our royal will that this Courtak
be destroyed, or, more simply, deprived of his inheritance, that you would not obey us?"

Lord Brynhaven's chin descended to his chest and he
swallowed. He did not think of himself as a brave man,
but in this he knew that he would have to oppose her.
He lifted his head.

"If Your Majesty permits, I would suggest that Jarrod Courtak is beyond reach at this point, short of as-
sassination. If you attack him, the people will rise on
his behalf. As a Mage, he oppresses no one; as a land-
owner, on the other hand, he will rouse his share of
opponents. Therein may lie Your Majesty's advantage."

"There is no advantage to the throne in that man's
assumption of the Dukedom of Abercorn. It puts entirely too much power in the hands of the Discipline.
Besides, he has too much money as it is." She sounded
peevish.

This was obviously not the time to remind the Queen
that she herself was a Magician. "Your Majesty can
impose a very stiff inheritance tax," Brynhaven suggested.

"Indeed we can." The Queen smiled a small, unpleasant smile. "And who knows, our young Mage will yet be tempted into politics." The smile broadened. "Once that happens, a charge of treason is a relatively simple thing and then we can confiscate the lands." She nodded two or three times before fixing him with a glittering eye. "See that the estate is assessed at the absolute maximum," she said. "You may go."

Lord Brynhaven backed from the presence profoundly grateful that he had survived the ordeal. Life at Court had become as unsettled and unsettling as it was said to be at Angorn.

The news of the birth came just as the welcoming feast was reaching its climax. The oohs and aahs that greeted the appearance of the elaborate desserts were silenced by the abrupt cacophony of a bell. Jarrod glanced inquiringly at Lady Aylwyth and then the meaning struck him. He pushed his chair back and jumped to his feet as the cheering broke out. He raced from the dais without a word to his dinner companions and took the stairs two at a time. He pulled up in front of Marianna's antechamber and did his best to get his breathing under control.

He walked quietly through the empty outer room and entered the bedchamber without knocking. Marianna was lying in the bed with the covers pulled up to her chin. Her eyes were closed, her face was white except for the black half-circles under her eyes, and her hair was dark with sweat. The coverlet was almost flat. Mrs. Merieth was sitting on the far side of the bed and the Wisewoman was standing on the near side. She turned and he saw a bundle in a white blanket in her arms. She smiled broadly at him and dropped a little curtsy.

"You have a bonny daughter, my lord," she said, and held out her arms.

He walked over, feeling suddenly unsteady, and looked down at the small, creased, red face. Fine brown hair was plastered to the skull. The eyes, like her mother's, were closed.

"Is she . . . ?"

"Indeed she is. Perfect in every limb. She screamed the place down until she was washed and then the little beauty went straight to sleep."

"It'll be nice to have a girl to tend again," Merry put in.

"And my wife?" Jarrod asked.

"Sleeping too. She'll be braw when she wakes and better still when she's fed the bairn." Merry nodded at her own wisdom and knowledge.

"Did she have . . . ? Was it difficult?"

Merry smiled, revealing missing teeth. "Och, she wailed and cursed like a dying soldier, but it was no harder than her first. She always was one for the dramatics."

Jarrod found himself grinning inanely at the women. He was a father. That miniature ancient in the Wisewoman's arms was his daughter. He reached out an enormous forefinger and smoothed the slick, silk hair, marveling at the tiny perfection of ear and mouth. He felt the rising euphoria that he associated with Magic making. He blinked and found that his eyes were full of tears, blurring his sight of her. He looked mutely from one woman to the other and swallowed convulsively. He brushed the tears away and caught his lower lip between his teeth. He walked softly to the bed, stooped and kissed the sleeping Marianna.

He straightened up, beamed at the two women, blinked hard again, and then made his way carefully to the door. He turned.

"Regrettably, I have guests below. Thank you, ladies," he said. "If I am not here when the Lady Marianna wakes, tell her that I love her."

He bowed to each in turn and let himself out. His whoop of joy rang clearly through the doors and the two women smiled at one another knowingly.

"Mayhap she's made a good choice this time, m'dear," Mrs. Merieth said.

chapter 24

Jarrod spent the next two days in a state of intoxication that had little to do with alcohol, although he was required to drink more than a few toasts. In an effort to break free from the castle's attentions, he rode out to visit Sir Ombras. The old man was glad to see him—inactivity obviously weighed on him—but Jarrod found himself feeling sad at the way that old age had treated the Seneschal and oddly resentful of the way that the feeling intruded on his happiness. Nothing, however, could cloud his mood for long. He relished the banquet that was held to celebrate his daughter's arrival. Flushed with wine, he went so far as to kidnap the baby from a protesting Merry and parade her around the Hall as if she were a special dish, which, from his point of view, she was. Merieth followed behind them muttering imprecations and cautions, but making no overt moves to restrain him.

He visited Marianna every day, but she was doing her fair share of sleeping. Occasionally he was allowed to peek in on her and saw that she was resting in what seemed like peace. He worried, nevertheless, and voiced his concerns to Wisewoman Jaffney. She seemed so pale and lifeless, in contrast to the lusty yelling and redness of his daughter. While his daughter had assumed, uninvited and of a sudden, an enormous place in his heart, he still worried about his wife.

Quite normal, he was assured. The Lady Marianna

was considered old, from a childbearing point of view. Jarrod smiled to himself at the idea of what Marianna would have responded to that had she been awake. His wife, he was told, had led an active life and her muscles were those of a much younger woman, but she needed rest; labor was never easy; he must have patience. The final phrase, dismissive, was "You'll be sent for when Her Ladyship feels up to it." And with that, he had to be content.

Jarrod retired to his rooms feeling useless, his former elation quite dispelled. He took off the clothes that he had donned with such care and went and sat on the bed, chin in hands. He was used to being in control of things—other people did his bidding, usually without his having to ask—but Marianna remained an unreachable enigma. His eyes sought the window and he was reminded again of how small it was. He was circumscribed here, the lord, the "new" lord, but scarcely head of the household. Both Marianna and Darius preceded him and always would. He was a foreigner here, an outsider. He had titles, yes, and land, but they meant nothing in these parts. The baby was his only claim to consideration.

It was in this melancholy condition that Semmurel found him.

"My lord, my lord, a message, a message from Stronta."

Jarrod looked up. "Calmly, calmly. Now, what does it say?"

"I don't know, sir," the valet said, brimming with righteousness. "This one was written and it was not my place to read it."

"Quite right, Semmurel." Jarrod held out his hand and a small, tightly rolled squip of paper was placed in it. "The magnifying glass if you please."

Jarrod smoothed out the message and moved the glass back and forth until the words came clear.

"Your uncle Abercorn is dead. You have inherited title and estates. Congratulations. Tokamo."

He read it twice and the valet, watching closely, decided that the news was bad. Such stillness did not bode well.

The truth was that Jarrod was having difficulty comprehending. He had denied his family for so long, blocked off the hurt that their denial of him had caused, that he could not react now. They were all gone and he had never known a one of them, not even his parents. Action of some sort was required, that he knew. He would have to swear fealty to Naxania at some point and, knowing the Queen, there were bound to be complications. He sighed, confirming Semmurel's suspicions. He had never wanted this, he had avoided any and all involvements, but now events had caught up with him. He sat up and, with difficulty, ripped the little message into smaller shreds. Semmurel hovered expectantly, but Jarrod didn't feel like confiding.

"I thank you," he said. "You may go."

He waited until the doors were closed and then went and got his blue Magician's gown out of the press. In this at least he could be his own man. He made his way up to the bunglebird cote and sent the keeper off on an errand before coaching a none-too-cooperative bird in a message for Tokamo. He took it up to the launching platform and released it. He stood and watched it circle before it lurched off in a northeasterly direction.

He was distracted at Hall that night and less than the perfect host. He was aware of it and hoped that the others put his mood down to the strains of becoming a first-time father rather than displeasure with their company. He was also aware that that would be taken as a sign of weakness. Noblemen were supposed to take such things in their stride and he was now, beyond all doubt, a nobleman.

That night he tossed and turned before he slept and, when he did, he dreamed. He was back at the castle that he had helped to build, but it was different. There was glass in the windows, for one thing, and there were signs that the place was occupied, though he could see no people. The peculiar dread that he had felt in the first dream was with him again, but this time he knew the reason for it. The invisible occupants of the castle were threatened, though by what, or by whom, he did not know.

He turned and looked out over the plain. Nothing but waving grass to be seen, but that gave him no comfort. When he turned back, he saw that there was someone standing on the battlements above the main door. He could not make out the features, but the figure's scarlet robe blazed in the sunshine. He struggled forward, trying to see who it was, but his feet were mired. If he could get free, he could help; he knew it. He fought, but his progress was infinitely slow and the man's face grew no clearer. The menace was building and he was going to be too late. He tried to shout a warning, but no sound came. He tried again, hurling himself forward, and the effort brought him awake, tangled in the sheet, teeth clamped on the bolster.

Jarrod rose and washed and Made the Day, as was his wont. For once the ritual did not have its restorative power and, after a hasty breakfast, he headed down to the stables. A ride with Nastrus would undoubtedly clear away the lingering cobwebs.

'*A cloud in the sunny skies of your disposition,*' the unicorn commented as Jarrod saddled him. '*I suppose the wonderful feelings had to wear off eventually, but I had hoped that they would keep going a while longer. Your happiness is quite irresistible, even if it is occasioned by something as mundane as siring a foal. I admit, though, that it has generated a strong urge in me to return home and join in the rut.'*

'*Stay a little while longer,*' Jarrod thought back as he guided Nastrus through the busy courtyard and out through the gate. '*I shall need your support if anything happens to Marianna.*'

'*Typically human,*' Nastrus rejoined as he broke into a canter. '*If you spent more time enjoying the moment and less time bothering about things that you can't control, you'd be a lot better off.*'

'*I know you're right,*' Jarrod said, leaning forward to adjust to the change in gait, '*but I have a lot on my mind. There's Marianna and now this business of having very large new estates to take care of and, on top it all off, I had a very peculiar dream last night. About the castle we built.*'

'*Show me,*' Nastrus responded laconically.

Jarrod transmitted the memory and waited for Nastrus to comment. Nothing came.

'*Well, what do you think?*' he asked.

'*It makes no sense,*' Nastrus said dismissively.

'*Nor did the first one,*' Jarrod thought back with rather more heat than he had intended, '*but I saw conical turrets in that one and it turned out that Chatham Greygor had a fondness for them. I didn't seek him out. I didn't say anything about the place that I had dreamed about, but he reproduced it. How do you explain that?*'

'*I don't,*' Nastrus replied. '*It could be happenstance, it could be destiny. How should a unicorn know? Besides, how do you know that this latest night vision has anything to do with you? You didn't know the person on the walls. If there is any truth in it, and I'm not saying that there is, what makes you think that you will be involved, human vanity apart? If I recall correctly, there was much talk between you humans when we were building the place about how it would be many of your generations before humans came there again. As I said, if you spent less time getting into a lather about things you can't control, you'd be a lot happier.'*

'Fat lot of help you are,' Jarrod said grumpily.

'Ah well, maybe one of these days you'll listen to me,' Nastrus said complacently. *'In the meantime, I'd like to get in a decent gallop.'*

As Nastrus accelerated smoothly, Jarrod began to meld into the flow and control of the powerful muscles as they ate up the ground. The unicorn's pleasure at the speed and movement became his own and his worries seemed insignificant. He breathed in deeply. There was a tang and crispness to the air and the wind of their passage felt cleansing. His spirits rose. Nastrus was right. The countryside was lovely, the weather was sparkling, his duties at Gwyndryth far from arduous, his daughter was healthy and sure to be beautiful. He was indeed the most fortunate of men.

'Of course I'm right,' Nastrus thought condescendingly and accelerated before Jarrod could reply.

Marianna's summons came the following day. Jarrod made Semmurel show him five outfits before he settled on one. Then he changed his mind. He shaved himself, though he had done it when he first got up, and he spent a long time brushing his hair. Semmurel watched him with a knowing smile and helped him to dress. Jarrod felt absurdly nervous and the feeling lasted through the corridors and into Marianna's room.

She was still in bed, propped up against the pillows, but there was color in her cheeks and her hair was neatly dressed. He walked over and kissed her on the cheek.

"How are you feeling, my dear?" he asked.

"Almost human," she replied.

"I was beginning to worry," he said, sitting down on the edge of the bed.

She took his hand and pressed it gently. "You're very sweet, but I shall be fine. We Gwyndrths are a tough lot. I shall be up and about again in a day or so." She let go of his hand.

"You take all the time you need," Jarrod said quickly. "You don't want to overdo it too soon."

One eyebrow went up. "Have you been studying to be a Wisewoman?" she asked with a touch of her old mischief.

"How's our girl?" he asked, changing the subject.

"Sleeping for now. She'll be hungry soon." Marianna shook her head as if in disbelief. "She's always hungry."

"That's a good sign, isn't it?"

"I suppose so."

"Is she big for a girl baby?"

"Is she going to grow up to be Talented, that's what you man, isn't it?"

"Well, it's a natural question," Jarrod replied defensively.

Marianna's hands plucked at the coverlet and she watched them as if they belonged to someone else. Then she lifted them in the equivalent of a shrug and looked up at him. "There's no way to tell. They don't start growing tall until they're six or seven. At least that's the way it was with Joscelyn."

"You'd rather she wasn't Talented, wouldn't you?"

"Frankly, yes." She was blunt. "I've already got one child who's going to be a Magician, I'd prefer that this one stayed home. Besides, it would make things harder for her. I doubt that young female Magicians are much courted, or have an easy time finding playmates."

Jarrod nodded, not knowing what to say. "It's a shame that Joscelyn couldn't be here for the birth," he ventured.

"I know," she said. "I thought about it, but, given

his record, plus the fact that he came to the wedding, I didn't think that Dean Handrom would take kindly to the suggestion."

"I'm sure you're right," Jarrod concurred.

"But what I wanted to see you about was the baby," Marianna added.

"Her being a Magician?" Jarrod asked. "We can't do anything about that. She'll either turn out to be Talented, or she won't."

"No, silly, not that. About calling her 'the baby,' 'the child,' 'the girl.' It's time that she had a name. Do you have any preferences?" She glanced up at him. "There's no need to look so surprised," she said.

"I'm surprised at myself. The fact is that I really haven't given it thought." He smiled sheepishly. "The fact is that I had sort of assumed that it would be a boy."

"Are you disappointed?"

"Not in the least," Jarrod said with conviction. "I loved her the moment I saw her." He noticed her smile and misinterpreted it. "How about you?" he asked. "I know you wanted another son to continue the line."

The smile widened. "We'll just have to make sure that Josceyln marries and has children. Still, that's in the future. What we have to decide on now is a name. If it had been a boy, I wanted to call it after my father, but I don't have any strong preferences about a girl's name."

"That reminds me," he said, "I rather expected that your father would be here by now."

"He's on his way. It takes a little longer without a unicorn."

"We could call her Daria," Jarrod suggested. "It's got an nice sound to it."

Marianna's eyes lit. "Daddy would love it," she said, and then paused. "There's only one problem."

"And that is?"

"Well, he was bound to spoil her, but this will put the cap on it. I'm going to have my work cut out undoing the damage that you two will do."

"I'm perfectly capable of being an evenhanded father," Jarrod objected.

"Rubbish," Marianna said succinctly and good-naturedly. "Little girls are born with the ability to wrap their fathers around their little fingers."

"Ha! Seeing the way Joscelyn's turned out, it can be argued that boys can do the same with their mothers," he said teasingly.

"Unfair; low blow," she protested.

"Maybe the next one will be a boy and then I'll come into my own," Jarrod said.

The eyebrow went up again. "The next one?" She snorted and pressed herself back into the pillows. "The man's way of controlling an intelligent woman; keep her pregnant." There was a tinge of acid in the voice. "Well, husband mine, the equation is a little different for women. A night of pleasure, if we're lucky, nine months of discomfort and hours of agony. You'll forgive me if I don't look on the process with quite your enthusiasm."

"Daria, Duchess of Abercorn; it's got a nice ring to it, don't you think?" Jarrod asked.

"What are you talking about?" she asked back.

Jarrod grinned. "Well, she'll have to wait awhile, of course, and there can't be a brother. I haven't had a chance to tell you, but my uncle died and I've inherited the title. You are now the Duchess of Abercorn."

"Am I indeed." She smiled up at him. "Very grand. Do we have a nice coat of arms?"

"I'm not really sure," Jarrod admitted. "I think it's got stags and sheaves of corn."

"Oh Jarrod, you are impossible," she said. Her eyes narrowed in speculation. "We'll have to go down and show ourselves as soon as I'm fit to travel. A grand tour of all the properties. I can use my old gowns there, people won't have seen them, and get a new set for here. In the meantime we shall have to appoint a really good seneschal. If we don't, your rights will be eroded."

She sat up, eyes sparkling. "It would be best if it was a Paladinian. Country folk don't take kindly to being ordered about by foreigners. Do you know anyone suitable?"

This is the most animated she's been since I got here, Jarrod thought.

"As a matter of fact I've asked Tokamo to go down and take inventory for me," he said.

"Oh yes, he was our ring bearer. Are you sure you can trust him?"

"We've been friends since we were boys," Jarrod returned. "Besides, he's wonderful with figures and the appearance of a Magician at Oxeter ought to engender respect, if not outright fear." He gave her a sly smile. "People seem to have difficulty lying to a Magician."

"Clever man," she said, and pulled him down for a kiss. "Oh I am glad that I married you." She let him go and vertical frown lines appeared in her forehead. "D'you suppose that my father knew that you were going to inherit when he insisted that I marry you?"

"Knowing your father, I shouldn't be at all surprised. I was probably the only person in the Kingdom who wasn't expecting it."

She looked at him for a beat as if about to criticize. Instead she said, "Ooh, Naxania is going to hate this." There was glee in her voice.

"Well I'm glad that the title makes you happy," he said, turning his head. There was no mistaking the tone of voice.

"Jarrod?" She reached forward. "Jarrod, there's something bothering you. I can tell. I've known you too long. If there's something that's bothering you, you have to tell me. After all, isn't that what marriage is about?" She widened her eyes and leaned back into the pillows, inviting his confidence.

He sat silent for a while, encouraged, but embarrassed. His hands wanted to twist together, but he stopped them. His lips, unsupervised, pursed and moved from side to side.

"This is very difficult," he said, head moving awkwardly like a schoolboy's. He took a breath and then looked at her directly. "Look," he said. "I know that this wasn't part of your master plan, but," he paused, "but," he hesitated again, "I love the baby very much," he concluded in a rush, "and I love you very much as well," he ended in a mumble.

"I'm enormously fond of you too, dear," she said, reaching forward and patting his hand. "But you have to understand that we made this arrangement precisely because we both had individual lives to lead." She shook her head and then looked at him. "Jarrod, my very dear," she said slowly. "I went into this because I wanted a child, not a husband, I made that perfectly plain. You accepted those terms. The marriage wasn't my idea, though I'm enormously grateful that you consented to it. I am, as I said, hugely fond of you, but I will not countenance you, or any man, walking in here and taking over Gwyndryth." The eyes narrowed. "Gwyndryth is mine. My father has titular control, but no other man will until I am dead." She stopped and looked at him, half defiant, half sad.

Jarrod held her gaze. His eyes were steady, but the inside of him was bubbling. He reached out and captured her hands. He smiled at her and the smile grew. It disconcerted her. He knew it and it pleased him.

"You silly, little goose," he said, and then the smile broke into a grin. "I could care less about Gwyndryth.

It's yours to have and to hold and to run any way you please. All I care about is you and our daughter." He sat back and the grin faded. "I won't interfere," he said seriously, "but I expect to see you and I expect to see our daughter on a regular basis."

She smiled, and the smile was warm, and she squeezed his hands before she let them go. "I'm a very lucky woman," she said. She looked back up at him. "You know, I really do love you." She sounded surprised. The eyes narrowed. "However, you'll oblige me by not letting it go to you head," she added with her old spirit. "Now, go and see your daughter."

He bent down and kissed her on the cheek before taking his leave.

Mrs. Merieth was standing in the anteroom with the baby cradled in her arms. Jarrod went straight over to her and bent over the bundle. "We're going to call you Daria," he crooned.

"Daria is it then?" Merry said. "The Master will be pleased with that."

"Marianna said he'd spoil her rotten," Jarrod said, straightening up.

"So he will," Mrs. Merieth replied comfortably. "That's what grandparents are for."

Jarrod gazed down at the sleeping child and felt the tenderness well up. The face had lost the angry red of birth and was soft and still and pink. There would be so many more changes in the weeks and months ahead and, he realized with a pang, he would not be there to see them. He reached out a tentative finger and stroked her cheek. And what sort of mother would Marianna be? She was not the type to stay in the nursery. She had a Holding to run and a business besides. And, in truth, it was Gwyndryth that was her first love, would always be.

"I wish," he said to Mrs. Merieth, "that I didn't have to leave her and go back to Stronta."

"You're a sweet man, my lord," Merry said, rocking the baby gently, "but there's no place for a man in a nursery. Raising bairns is woman's work."

"I know, but you'll have to admit that the Lady Marianna isn't exactly the domestic type."

Merry cackled. "Gods love you, I'm the one that'll tend to that. I raised the young mistress and you'll have to admit that she hasn't turned out badly. There's no need to fash yourself, Little Daria will be just fine."

Jarrod was not at all certain that he wanted his daughter to grow up to be exactly like her mother, but there was no way he could say that to Mrs. Merieth. Tradition was too strong to allow him to make too many demands. There was no cult of the Great Mother in Arundel, but there might as well have been.

"There are no better hands that she could be in, Mrs. Merieth," he said diplomatically.

"You take care of the mistress and I'll take care of the young 'un," she said with a knowing grin.

Jarrod nodded and smiled. I must arrange some way of seeing more of my daughter, he thought as he walked out, though he had no idea of how he could arrange it.

There were no guests at Hall that night and, perhaps as a consequence, Jarrod drank too much. He did not make a spectacle of himself, managed to talk civilly to both Sir Kerris and his wife about matters pertaining to the Holding, but he was aware as he negotiated the stairs to his chambers that he was a mite unsteady. Semmurel was waiting to help him undress and to put his clothes away, but if he noticed that anything was amiss, he was wise enough not to let it show. Jarrod washed with care and bade the man good night as the bed curtains were pulled. He did not remember going to sleep.

When he woke to Make the Day, his mouth was dry and his head hurt. Cold water alleviated the symptoms and the ritual banished the pain. He was contemplating going back to bed, but Semmurel was waiting for him when he reached the room. He looked excited and he was holding a piece of paper in his hand.

"A message, sir; from the capital, sir; by bunglebird." He waved the paper. "I took the liberty of transcribing it," he added, his previous rectitude apparently forgotten.

"Let me have some chai first, Semmurel, then you can read me the message," Jarrod said and went and sat on the bed.

Semmurel complied and waited patiently as Jarrod sipped the hot liquid. When his master was finished, Semmurel cleared his throat and read, "Ragnor dead. Return Celador immediately." He looked at Jarrod. "It is from Greylock. At least that is what I think the bird said."

Jarrod felt a sudden emptiness that had nothing to do with the previous night's indulgence. "Why didn't you tell me that right away?" he said tiredly, and then waved his hand to cut off the answer that he knew would come. He felt tears prick at his eyelids.

"Get out one of my Magician's robes, Semmurel," he said gruffly. "Then go and ask Sir Kerris to attend me here immediately. Word of this must be taken to the Holdmaster. After that, present my respects to the Lady Marianna and tell her that I must see her within the hour."

"Immediately, my lord. And shall I be accompanying you?"

"I'm afraid not. I shall be leaving alone and I shall

travel by unicorn. There's no possible way that you could keep up."

"Very well, sir. I'll pack some things for you. And, sir, I'm very sorry to have been the bearer of such bad tidings."

"The worst of all possible tidings," Jarrod said sadly. "He was a great man, but he was also my friend."

chapter 25

Jarrod had spoken from his heart, but he had also expressed the feelings of a great many people on Strand. Ragnor had been Archmage for as long as most could remember. There had been no other Archmage, with the possible exception of Errathuel, seen by so many in the flesh. His long tenure, coupled with the final defeat of the Outlanders, had fueled rumors that he was the legend returned. It was a rumor that the old man had never denied. He had told Jarrod, on their triumphal tour around Strand, that such speculation enhanced the image of the Discipline, but, close as Jarrod was to him at that point, he wasn't certain if the Archmage was being serious or simply disingenuous.

The news of the death raced across the land. It took a fortnight to reach Angorn and a sennight more to penetrate as far south as Quern. Even in the Empire, where magic was viewed with suspicion at the best of times, there was a sense of personal loss. This was one death that struck a universal chord. Peasants in Umbria, tradesmen in Isphardel, herdsmen in Songuard, all felt his passing as keenly as the Magicians at the Outpost.

In was in Arundel, however, that the outpourings of grief were most intense. Ragnor's time as Regent was recalled with nostalgia in town, hamlet and holding. Contributions to the Discipline flooded in. Flowers and offerings were left at the bases of the many statues that had been erected at the time of the victory over the Everlasting Foe. Ragnor would have enjoyed it all immensely. The Court was in deep mourning and the crowds that thronged into the capital were subdued, though there was an undercurrent of excitement. Every crowned head and notable on Strand was expected to attend.

Jarrod and Marianna materialized in the post-harvest stubble of the field beyond the walls. Jarrod had expected to make the trip on his own, but Marianna had been adamant. She had been up yelling for her tiring woman before Jarrod was out of the room. Nastrus pulled grumblingly at the brown stalks and Jarrod slipped off his back to lighten the load. He took off his cloak and slung it over the back of the saddle. As they approached the city they saw that the walls were draped with black cloth. There were no flags flying. The guards at the gate wore purple sashes. In the courts there were groups of people talking quietly. They stopped and stared at the unicorn as it passed, but there was none of the wild welcome that Nastrus was used to. When the little party reached the stables, things were quiet; no noblemen taking their horses out to hunt, no Royal Messengers preparing to gallop to the ends of the kingdom. A groom came out, exchanged a few civil words and led Nastrus to his accustomed byre.

"I'd better get to Magicians' Court and see how Greylock's doing," Jarrod said as they stood with the saddlebags at their feet.

"Oh no you don't," Marianna countered. "First we go to the Chamberlain and get ourselves assigned a decent apartment. You may be a Mage, but you are also here as my husband. I imagine that we are among the first ones here, of those of any account, I mean, and that's fortunate. This place will be aswarm in a sennight and I want to make sure that we are comfortable and in quarters that reflect our joint status." She looked up at him and the eyes were sharp and undeniable.

"Yes, dear," he said meekly.

"Good. Now get one of these lads to carry our bags and be sure that you tip him properly."

She lifted her skirts and set off across the cobbles. Jarrod secured the services of a stable hand and hurried to catch up with her. When they reached the palace steps, he proffered his arm and she took it with a smile.

"If we have any problems with the Chamberlain, leave the talking to me," Marianna said. "I know more about the accommodations than you do and I've dealt with the man before." Jarrod nodded his acceptance.

The Chamberlain proved amiable to the point of obsequiousness and, to Jarrod's surprise, Marianna accepted the man's first suggestion. Pages were sent for and they were escorted to a rather grand set of rooms with a cabinet and a private privy. The Chamberlain had, with the merest hint of reluctance, agreed to assign a maid and a manservant to them, and Marianna had sweetly agreed to interview suitable candidates that afternoon. Jarrod had the distinct impression that the Chamberlain had not intended that there be any choice, but Marianna was not an easy woman to deny, especially when she was being charming. Apart from polite hellos and equally polite good-byes, Jarrod had said nothing.

"Rather fancy," he said after the last page had left in search of the wine that Marianna had ordered. "Anteroom, a separate sitting chamber, the lot."

"Yes, I know," Marianna said with a mysterious little smile. "I've been entertained here before." The smile broadened. "You see, my dear, the combination of the Discipline and the old aristocracy is hard to top."

"And you didn't even have to haggle."

"I didn't need to," she replied lightly. "This occasion

is going to be managed by the Discipline, even though it is a state funeral. The Queen is a member of the High Council of Magic. My husband is a Mage." She cocked her head to one side. "Now what choice did the poor man have? He is perfectly well aware that I know my way around the palace and that most of the best suites haven't been assigned as yet." She laughed mischievously. "There was no need to tell him that you are the Duke of Abercorn."

"I think we should keep it that way, don't you, dear?" Jarrod said quickly.

She gave him a look. "It guarantees us a seat at the High Table, at least until the royals get here."

"Well I'm glad to be of use."

She caught the irony in his voice. "Marriage to me hasn't exactly hurt your chances of being the next Archmage," she rejoined.

"Don't be absurd," Jarrod said sharply. "Greylock's going to be the next Archmage. He's the obvious choice and he's Ragnor's acknowledged successor."

"I wouldn't be too sure of that," she said, sitting herself in an armchair. "Ragnor is dead, but politics never die. By marrying me you have access to the Arundelian vote. Since you are a Paladinian, and a very powerful one now, Naxania should have no problem endorsing you if Greylock's candidacy runs into opposition. Better you than the Chief Warlock, wouldn't you say? And it would effectively remove you from Paladine." Her eyebrows rose and her eyes opened wide.

"You are incorrigible," Jarrod said, folding himself down onto a divan. "But you can spare yourself the machinations. I would never allow my name to be put forward against Greylock."

"Of course you wouldn't," she said complacently, "but Greylock's an old man and there's always the next election to think about."

Jarrod shook his head and smiled at her. "And I think it's time for me to go and pay my respects to the next Archmage." He pushed himself back up to his feet.

"By all means," Marianna said. "I'm going to move some of this furniture around, make the place a little more comfortable since we're going to be here for a while. Then I shall have a bath. D'you think you'll be taking your midday meal here?"

"I really can't say. That'll depend on Greylock. And I don't think that you should be moving furniture so soon after the baby."

"Very well. Oh, by the way, do you have access to funds here? I only had room to pack one gown and there's no guarantee that it survived the trip. I found a dressmaker in the town on my last trip who's both skilled and reasonable." She glanced up at him.

"Oh, don't look like that, Jarrod," she said with a touch of impatience. "Gwyndryth has a long-established reputation to uphold and state occasions are never cheap. Think how much it would have cost us to travel here by coach. If we had, I could have brought a suitable wardrobe; as it is, I'll have to be inventive for a sennight with what I've got. I tell you plainly, my dear, that I have no intention of embarrassing my father, who, need I remind you, will be here before too long. Besides, I'm a little fatter than I used to be."

"I'm sorry," Jarrod said. "I'm just not used to such concerns. Yes, I can draw money. Just let my know how much you need."

She smiled at him meltingly and his heart seemed to turn over.

"I'm glad you understand, my sweet. It's not just my vanity. If we don't make a good showing at Court, the word will get around that the Holding is in trouble. We are not without our greedy neighbors. My father's reputation as a soldier has kept them respectful, but he hasn't been back to Gwyndryth for a long time. So long as we appear prosperous, Aberwyn and Dynsdale assume that, though I am a mere woman"—there was asperity in the voice—"I can command sufficient loyalty from our vassals, or, if push came to shove, could afford to hire a sufficient number of mercenaries to repulse them and possibly annex their land." She smiled wryly. "I doubt if you have ever had the occasion to price a mercenary, but I can assure you that a handful of gowns cost a great deal less."

"I hadn't realized," he said.

"No reason why you should," she said lightly and got to her feet. "Oh, and speaking of dress, do you intend to stay in your blue robe, or does the Discipline have something special for funerals?"

"The Mages of the various countries will wear their regalia," he replied, "but I have none. I suppose I could borrow one of Ragnor's robes. He always used to twit me about being underdressed for grand occasions." He broke off and put a hand up to his mouth as his eyes suddenly filled.

Marianna put a hand on his arm. "Wear what you like," she said softly. "With your reputation, you can wear anything that pleases you."

He put a hand over hers and pressed it gently. "I really must go and see Greylock," he said.

"Very well, but tomorrow you must come with me to pay our respects to Arabella. Promise?"

"I promise."

She went up on tiptoe and kissed him on the cheek.

"Do you think you can ever come to love me?" he asked.

"I've already told you that I love you," she said briskly. "If you're talking about sex, it takes time after a baby, Jarrod. You must be patient with me."

He held her at arm's length and then enfolded her in a silent hug.

Greylock was ensconced in spacious rooms on the ground floor of Magician's Court. The windows, as did all the windows in the Court, looked out on the Archmage's Tower, swathed now in a winding of black cloth. The Mage was in a high-backed chair by the fire and, when Jarrod was shown in, the square face broke into a smile.

"I'm glad you're here," he said. "I wasn't sure when you were going to arrive."

Jarrod went over and touched palms. "If it hadn't been for Nastrus, we would have taken a great deal longer. As it is, we got here soon enough to get lodging that Marianna finds suitable to her station."

"Ah yes, you're a married man now, and a father?"

Jarrod grinned. "Yes indeed. A bonny little girl named Daria for her grandfather."

"Congratulations."

"Thank you, sir. I'd be honored it you would stand for her on my side at the naming ceremony."

"I should be delighted. In return I have a favor to ask of your wife."

"Name it."

"I should appreciate it if she would walk beside the unicorn in the procession. People associate the unicorns with Ragnor and she was one of the discoverers."

"I'm sure that she would be more than willing, but"—Jarrod hesitated—"I think she would prefer it if the request came directly from you."

"No problem with that," Greylock said easily. "I'll dictate something this afternoon." He settled back in the chair and Jarrod knew that the small talk was over.

"Now, there's to be a meeting of the High Council tomorrow morning. Ragnor named me his successor before he died. Arabella and Handrom were there when he did it, but the meeting is traditional. It takes a majority to confirm me."

"It will be a formality," Jarrod said confidently. "Confirmation by acclaim."

Greylock sniffed. "Not necessarily. The Chief Warlock was on the scene before I was and he has been quietly campaigning to overturn the decision—or so my sources tell me. Sommas Handrom will vote for whoever he thinks will do the most for the Collegium. I can expect support from Naxania, but Sumner is, after all, an Arundelian. So you see, it's not so simple."

"What possible reason could there be for setting aside Ragnor's express wishes?" Jarrod protested.

"Sumner claims that I am too old to perform strong Magic, should that be required. Says that the Discipline has been run by a figurehead for fifteen years and that it is time for more than a caretaker. There is, of course, some merit to that." Greylock spoke dryly.

"You can perform Magic if you want to, you know you can. You proved it at the demonstration on the Causeway."

"Not, it would seem, to the Chief Warlock's satisfaction."

"He wasn't even there," Jarrod said. "Besides, it doesn't matter what he thinks. He doesn't have the votes. If the worst came to the worst, the Council would split down the middle and Ragnor's wishes would prevail."

"That might be true if Naxania were here," Greylock said wearily. "Unfortunately our beloved Queen has seen fit to delay her departure."

"Ah, no doubt she sees herself casting the deciding vote and extracting a price for it." Jarrod looked at his mentor speculatively. "May I have your permission to get a chair?" he asked.

"Yes of course. I'm sorry." The smile was wan and perfunctory. "This business is making me forget my manners."

Jarrod got a chair and installed himself opposite Greylock. "Well," he said, "it seems that we'll have to adopt Ragnor's methods."

"Such as?" Greylock's voice was wary.

"I spent a lot of time with him over the years and he would have seen two major ways to deal with this; intimidation or old-fashioned horse-trading."

"I don't approve of intimidation," Greylock said primly.

"Then we trade."

"But I haven't got anything to negotiate with," Greylock complained.

"You would if you were Archmage."

"Yes, but . . ."

Jarrod held up a hand. "Hear me out. Sumner has two major weaknesses. He's ambitious and he's a snob. He detests Talisman, we know that. He thinks that the country is beneath him and, what's worse, Talisman knows it. So, wouldn't it be a mercy for both parties if he moved from there?" Jarrod rocked in the chair, eyes narrowed, and then a thin smile crept up. "Ragnor was Mage of Arundel as well as Archmage," he said, "but there's ample precedent for the two posts being held by different people. If you offered Sumner Arundel, not only would it get him out of Talisman, but he would be close at hand where you could keep an eye on him."

"What makes you think he would take it? He's aiming for Archmage," Greylock said dubiously.

"That's where the snobbery comes in. The man's always lusted after a secular title. He wants to be part of the aristocracy. So, if we could persuade Arabella to grant him a Holding, on the condition that he became Mage of Arundel, I think he'd agree."

"You've grown up to be a devious young man, Jarrod Courtak," Greylock said, but there was an approving note in his voice. "D'you think that Arabella could be persuaded?"

"Ragnor was a father and more to her. I think she would want to see his last wish fulfilled."

"You may be right. So who becomes Chief Warlock, you?"

"Oh, I don't think so. Dean Handrom would do very well, don't you think? Besides, with you here and me in Fortress Talisman, who would keep Naxania under control?"

"Quite right. So, you become Mage of Paladine, which is a perfectly natural progression, and the appointment of the new Dean of the Collegium would be in my hands."

"Precisely. Confirmation by acclaim."

"Very neat," Greylock conceded.

"It's probably a good thing that Naxania isn't here. I'm sure that she would make a strong bid for the Mageship. I wouldn't put it past her to throw her lot in with Sumner if he promised it to her."

Greylock's eyes met Jarrod's. They were troubled. "I wouldn't like to think so after all these years, but you might well be right." He shook his head sadly. "It's at times like this that I feel my age. I have no stomach for these kinds of plottings."

"Why don't you leave it all to me, sir? It's best that you stay above the fray anyway."

"Think you can do it?"

"I can certainly try. My wife intends to ask for an audience with Arabella. We'll just try to move it up to this afternoon. If I can convince the Queen, the rest will fall into place."

Greylock thought for a bit, rubbing his forehead with his thumb as if he had a headache. He looked up after a while. "Very well," he said.

When Jarrod returned to their rooms, he found Marianna pacing and agitated.

"What's the matter?" he asked, doffing his cloak.

Marianna came to a halt and turned to face him. "It's Joscelyn," she said. "He's missing."

"What do you mean, missing?"

"I went to the Collegium while you were with Greylock. I wanted to pay my respects to the Dean and find out how Joscelyn was doing. Handrom said I was the one who should be telling him. He never came back after the wedding and Handrom assumed he was at home. Whatever are we going to do, Jarrod?" Her eyes were wide and her hands were twisting together.

Jarrod went over and enfolded her in a hug. "I'll send a bunglebird to Stronta and have the Outpost organize a search. I think you should send one to Gwyndryth and have them do the same, just in case he's in the area. I'd go looking myself, but we can't leave until after the funeral and besides, I don't know where to look. Now, you must stay calm. He's a big boy and he knows how to look after himself."

"He's only fifteen," she reminded him.

"We weren't much older when we went looking for the unicorns, and we survived."

"What would make him do such a thing?" she demanded.

"At that age, who knows? Perhaps he was unhappy at the idea of your getting married again. There's no point playing guessing games. Let's go and send off the bunglebirds and then we have to get ready for our audience with the Queen. Greylock has requested that it be moved up to this afternoon. Now get your cloak and we'll go over to the cote."

The rest of the day passed quickly. The audience went well, and Marianna, pleased by their reception, seemed to put her worries behind her. They dined separately that night, Marianna in the Great Hall and Jarrod at the Collegium. By the time he got back, she was already asleep. He climbed in beside her, but he found it difficult to relax. The residual excitement of the high-level dealings was compounded by Marianna's nearness and worries about the boy. Sleep claimed him eventually and, in the morning, he was doubly rewarded, first by a sleepy but affectionate wife and later by the unanimous confirmation of Greylock as the next Archmage of Strand.

chapter 26

queen Naxania regarded her image in the looking glass with disfavor. The spots in the polished tin exacerbated her disgruntled mood. Arabella should have seen to it that she was better housed. Her suite had the same number of rooms as the one given to Varodias, she had checked on that, but the Emperor's quarters had been newly refurbished whereas the area assigned to her was, to put it mildly, dingy. She turned her head and peered sideways, catching a glimpse of her tiring woman, who was fussing at her robe with a small sponge. She concentrated on her own image. There was an undeniable softening of the jawline and, despite the candlelight and the unreliability of the spotted tin, definite crease marks around her eye.

She snatched up her hairbrush and began to pull it through her long black hair. No grey yet, thank the gods. Her pale skin, fine eyes and her hair gave her allure. She was still beautiful, but she had looked better. It had been a bad year all around, she concluded. First the rebellion, then turning forty and now Darius. Had he deserted her because she was getting older? He, who should have minded her aging least of all? Men, she thought sourly, were all alike. All they were interested in was young flesh, the new conquest. Darius, to his credit, had proposed marriage, but he must have known that it was impossible. Typically male, making it seem as if the woman were at fault.

"Please hold still, ma'am," the tiring woman said in professionally meek voice. "I cannot get these wrinkles out if you keep moving around."

"A perdition on your wrinkles!" Naxania screamed, swinging around. "Out! Out of my sight. Out, out, out!"

The tiring woman's eyes grew satisfyingly round and she began to back from the presence. Naxania flung the hairbrush at her to hasten her progress. She watched the door close and felt better. She lifted the hem of the purple robe so that it would clear the herbs strewn across the floor and went and retrieved the brush. She squared her shoulders. Every important male on Strand was at Celador. She had her throne and she still had her looks. Perhaps she could cull a proper husband at this funeral. She returned to the looking glass and resumed her brushing.

Her late arrival at the Arundelian capital had backfired. Instead of her controlling the election, events had passed her by. They had not even the grace to wait for her. She slanted her head in the other direction. Greylock, as Archmage, was no bad thing for Paladine's prestige, but Courtak as Mage of Paladine as well as Duke of Abercorn was a potential disaster for the Crown. If she was barred from the Mageship because she sat on the throne, should not a Mage be barred from being a major vassal? It was unfair. If she had been a man, they would have waited and listened to her arguments. She shook her head and her hair swung, gleaming in the candlelight. She scowled at her reflection. Charming, she told the glowering eyes, remember that you have to be charming. She tired out a smile and even she knew that it lacked warmth.

I am a Queen, she told her image. I do not have to make an acceptable face for any man. The House of Strongsword is second to none on Strand. She patted a stray strand of hair into place and then pinched her

cheeks to bring color to them. Not bad, she thought.
You look closer to thirty than forty. She rang the small
hand bell for her attendants and prepared to descend
into the subdued festivities that preceded dinner.

She swept down the stairs toward the servants' hall
that, because of the number of guests, was now the royal
withdrawing room. Two ladies-in-waiting and three
pages hurried to keep up with her. The hall was a sea
of dark blues, blacks and purples, but, as the Chamberlain announced her, the crowd parted to allow her
through. The women curtsied and the men bowed as
she made her way to the relatively quiet enclave of royalty at the head of the room. She kissed Arabella on
both cheeks, acknowledged her husband's bow, touched
palms with the Emperor Varodias and gave the Thane
of Talisman a bob of the head. Greylock greeted her
warmly and Sumner, whom she still thought of as Chief
Warlock of Talisman, was effusive. Her smile to Courtak and his Arundelian wife was cool. She turned as the
Prince Consort approached.

Saxton, she thought, was a comely man and he had
shown a considerable knowledge of Paladine. She
brightened under his attention and found herself discussing agricultural policy with unwonted verve. She
was sorry when he passed her on to the Thane, whose
conversation was all of his family. She took the opportunity to regale herself with a drink from a passing tray.
Wearying of the Thane, she excused herself, went in
search of another glass and found herself face-to-face
with Varodias.

"Well met again, cousin," she said. "We do not see
your wife among us. We trust that she is not indisposed?"

The Emperor, in contrast to the rest of the guests,
was dressed in dark grey. The piping on the jacket and

trousers was black as was the lace at throat and wrists. He wore black gloves.

"Our thanks for your concern," he returned. "The truth is that the Empress Zhane no longer travels." He produced a small, apologetic smile. "She has the dropsy. She had a great regard for the late Archmage and would have come if she could have. Her Wisewomen would not countenance it." His hands rose in a helpless gesture.

"Ah yes," Naxania said, "we may be monarchs, but it is the Wisewomen who are the true tyrants. Be sure to convey my deep regard for her and my wishes for a speedy recovery."

"You are most gracious, Lady." He paused and looked quickly around the area before looking back at her. "We are not the only one unaccompanied," he said. "It is a shame that a woman as lovely as you has yet to find the joys of matrimony." He bowed slightly and moved on, leaving Naxania fuming.

How dare he, she thought. Marriage, as he very well knew, was a dynastic matter and it was for her, as ruler, to decide who and when she should marry. She regarded the company as she tamed her rising temper. Greylock, wearing the chain of the Archmages, was deep in conversation with Sumner. As she watched, they were joined by Courtak and the Gwyndryth girl. She had put on weight and was wearing a vulgar amount of jewelry. Hard to believe that she was Darius' daughter.

Arabella and Prince Saxton were chatting with Varodias, and Naxania caught sight of a dapper, slim man hovering at the Emperor's shoulder. Quern. What was his first name? No matter, he was unimportant, indeed he had no right to be at this end of the hall. Attendants should know their place. Her eyes narrowed. Varodias was, if anything, an even greater stickler for the conventions than she was. If Quern was so closely in attendance, he must have considerable standing with the Emperor. When she had last seen him, he had been Phalastra of Estragoth's secretary. Evidently a man worth watching. She advanced on the group.

"We were just speaking of the difference that dear Ragnor's death will make," Arabella said. "People tend to forget that he ruled Arundel when I was a girl. I relied on his advice right up to the end."

"He was certainly a force for unity," Naxania replied.

"Let us hope," Varodias interposed, "that his spirit will continue to watch over us." He turned to Naxania. "You are to be congratulated, by the way, for your prompt suppression of the rebellion."

She smiled, thinking that it was less than polite of the Emperor to bring the subject up. "It had no popular support," she said, "and the traitors' heads now adorn our battlements. We hear that things are not so settled in your own realm," she added maliciously.

Varodias rubbed his gloved hands together briefly. The smile he produced matched hers for lack of warmth. "We are fortunate that our subjects love us. There have been some local disturbances aimed at one or two landowners, but we have been spared the kinds of uprisings that you have suffered. You were fortunate," he added, "to have had the services of the Lord Observer." He deliberately used the title by which Darius had been known when in Umbria.

He turned his head as Malum materialized again and whispered something. The corners of the Emperor's thin lips twitched upward. That disagreeable little man, Naxania thought, is telling him about Darius' defection.

"We understand," she said, resuming the conversation, "that a good deal of the animosity was aimed at your Church. An unfortunate time, perhaps, to have lost your Mother Supreme." She was gratified at the way that both pairs of eyes fastened on her.

"A great loss," Varodias agreed noncommittally. "Arnulpha, however, was one of those women who are better at telling other people how to run their lives than in ordering their own. We can but hope that our newly elected Mother Supreme shows more self-discipline."

"And how very considerate of her," Arabella cut in quickly, "to come all this way for Ragnor's funeral, especially when she must have so much to do in her new position. We find it most heartening. Relations between the Church of the Mother and the Discipline have not always been of the best. Should you see her before we do, please convey our gratitude."

"Indeed, yes," Naxania murmured. "It is gratifying that, even in death, the Archmage can provide unity."

Varodias smiled frostily and turned away as the little group broke up. Naxania looked down the hall and spotted Darius talking with his daughter. She was tempted to go over and join them. What she missed most, she realized suddenly, was the opportunity to talk with him. He was a comfortable lover, but that aspect was relatively easy to replace. The truth was that she had no one else she trusted as well, who would not take advantage, who was unfailingly, sometimes annoyingly, fair and entirely discreet. She hesitated for a tiny moment before deciding against it. To approach him would be a sign of weakness.

As Naxania turned away, Marianna left her father and went in search of her husband. Her place was swiftly taken by Malum of Quern. He had heard of the General's return to his estates and was curious.

"Good evening, General," he said in Common, remembering that Darius preferred not to use the Formal Mode.

"Plain Holdmaster now, friend Quern," Darius returned pleasantly. "I am once more a gentleman of leisure."

"I must confess that I was surprised that Queen Naxania allowed you to leave. A military leader of your skill and experience is hard to replace."

"Paladine is peaceful now. The Queen has no opponents worthy of the name."

"Ah, but the State is never secure," Malum observed. "Ambition sleeps, but it never dies."

"Maybe not in Umbria," Darius replied, "but that is because you have retained your martial ways. Your Elector-Scientists' idea of progress is to fabricate ever more dangerous weapons. You pillage the ground for coal to drive you engines. You subjugate your people and force them to work in manufactures. If you truly want a peaceful and contented country, you will have to change."

Malum smiled sardonically. "Become more like the Magical Kingdoms, no doubt?"

Darius shrugged gently.

"Quaint, rural," Malum continued. "trapped in tradition like insects in amber; dependent for power on unreliable Magicians. That is not exactly an inspiring vision for the future, Lord Holdmaster."

"Well, maybe I am a romantic, or perhaps just an old fossil, but I like our ways. Oaths of fealty are respected, the weather is beneficent, village Magicians work for the common good, the air is sweet and the people, by and large, contented. Not a bad prescription to my way of thinking. I have spent my life as a warrior, but I am happy to lay down my sword and tend my fields. Let us pray that our visions of the future never clash."

"Selah to that, my lord," Malum said politely.

Naxania was casting about for someone to talk to

when the Oligarch Olivderval materialized at her elbow in a rustle of silk.

"Give you good evening, Oligarch," she said.

"Your Majesty's obedient servant," Olivderval replied. She made an attempt at a curtsy. "Your Majesty must forgive an old woman of considerable bulk," she said with a friendly grin at her own failings, "but I cannot sink as far in the curtsy as once I could."

Naxania permitted herself to be disarmed. "It is forgiven," she said. "And what may we do for you?"

"Majesty," Olivderval said in mock umbrage. "How could you assume that I had a request?" Her deep-chested laugh both underlined and undermined her point, and it set the Queen to laughing.

"You are a wicked woman," Naxania said, "and you always have business on your mind. We are gathered for a sad occasion, but we doubt not that you will profit from the occasion."

"Ragnor always enjoyed a good laugh and while he would have loved the pomp, I do not think he would have wanted long faces," Olivderval replied bluntly. "Your Majesty was looking sad and distracted and I but sought to lighten your mood." She looked up at the Queen and her eyes twinkled. "However," she added, "the late Archmage was a practical man and I am sure he would not have objected if I . . ." She saw the look on Naxania's face and put a hand out in denial. "Nay, nay, Majesty, I seek no boon. I would simply remind you of the treaty obligations that now obtain between Isphardel and Paladine." Her tone was soothing.

Naxania was instantly wary. "To what end, Oligarch?" she inquired.

"Paladine is signatory to an agreement to defend Isphardel while she is building roads through Songuard."

She looked at the Queen and saw a sallow and dissatisfied woman. She almost pitied her—almost.

Naxania pursed her lips. "Technically true," she said with a sketch of a smile.

"Oh, more than a technicality, royal lady," Olivderval replied, "oath-bound." She reached out patted the Queen's arm and saw her freeze. She withdrew her hand quickly.

"As we recall," Naxania said coldly, "we are a guarantor of the freedom of passage rather than a defender of Isphardel."

"One leads inexorably to the other, Majesty, but I doubt if we shall ever reach that pass."

Naxania drew back slightly. "Are you absolutely sure of that?" she asked with as much lightness as she could muster.

The Oligarch shrugged. "Absolutes are for gods and, in Isphardel, there are many gods."

Naxania looked directly into Olivderval's eyes. It was a tactic that had cowed a number of young men of rank. "Tell me," she said, gaze locked, "does Isphardel intend to seek our intervention?"

"Only if absolutely necessary," Olivderval said cheerfully. "If the Umbrians behave, it won't be necessary. The fact remains, though, that if aught should go awry, Paladine is pledged to respond."

"We shall abide by our treaty obligations, Oligarch. Have you any reason to doubt that?"

"None whatsoever, Majesty," Olivderval demurred. "It does my heart good to hear your Majesty affirm your country's commitment." She performed her half-curtsy again and backed slowly away, aware that she had attracted attention. She faded in among the other guests, well pleased with her work.

Naxania was puzzled at the woman's behavior, but her speculation was cut short by the soft chiming of gongs announcing dinner. The guests began to file out and make their way to the Great Hall. Royalty remained aloof, drinking a final glass of chilled fruit juice, designed to sharpen the appetite. Arabella left first with the Emperor. Prince Saxton offered Naxania his arm.

"We can either go in looking like gloom personified," he said as they wended their way through the corridors, "or I can tell you ribald stories until we reach the Hall." He had abandoned the Formal Mode.

She flashed him a grateful smile. "There is only one problem with that," she replied, following his lead. "When a jest gets past my guard, I tend to lose control. I doubt that it would be too seemly if you had to carry me to my chair."

"Then this certainly is no time for me to embark upon my repertoire."

"Perhaps at a more auspicious occasion," she said. He had treated her like a woman and a friend rather than an honored guest and she appreciated it.

They arrived at the Great Hall in companionable silence and he escorted her to her chair. Her brief burst of goodwill evaporated when she saw that her dinner companions were Varodias, seated to Arabella's left, and the Thane of Talisman. It was to be expected, but she was disappointed nevertheless. Think of it as diplomatic opportunity, she told herself.

She smiled at the Thane, partly because she knew that she would be talking to him during the first course and partly because she was still annoyed at Varodias. She took advantage of the lull that preceded the serving to cajole herself into a more social mood. At home, she reflected, she would not need to speak if she did not feel like it. The Court would take its cue from her. Here, alas, set between Emperor and Thane, the manners drummed into her by her mother obtained. To the left for the first course and to the right for the second. A bowl of soup was slipped in front of her and she turned, dutifully, to the Thane.

In the event, the Thane proved easy. He had a catalogue of problems that he wanted to talk about. She listened, attentively at first, to a lamentation on the declining number of cloudsteeds, a discourse on a murrain that had cut sharply into the wool trade and the difficulties of collecting taxes from the independent-minded farmers of Talisman. All Naxania needed to do was nod and make sympathetic noises between spoonfuls of broth. When the bowls were withdrawn, she was almost sorry to take her leave.

"We have the pleasure of your company once more, cousin," Varodias said.

Naxania smiled and nodded, noting as she did so that the Emperor looked even shorter sitting down.

"Since we have this unusual chance to speak face-to-face, and more or less privately," she said, "are there matters of state that we might usefully discuss?"

"Matters of state are best decided between those whose divine right it is to rule," Varodias agreed.

"We have no quarrel with that," Naxania concurred, though she felt that divine right had little to do with fitness to rule.

"Let us say, therefore," Varodias continued, "that it grieved us to see you in colloquy with the Isphardi Oligarch. They are an untrustworthy people with no sense of national honor."

Naxania bridled internally at the criticism, but she kept her face still. "We have trading relations with Isphardel and, of late, treaty obligations," she said reasonably. "Common sense, and common good manners, would dictate a certain level of social intercourse between us. Besides, the Oligarch Olivderval was at

Stronta for the meetings of the Commission for the Outland."

"The Isphardis are leeches," the Emperor declared flatly, "battening on the labors of honest men and sucking the profit from their enterprises."

Naxania shrugged and picked up her fork. "They have the expertise and they control the sea-lanes. We do our best to foster a merchant fleet, but Isphardel lies between the Empire and ourselves. Our captains must, perforce, put in at Isphardi ports and the levies imposed make direct trade between us unprofitable."

"All the more reason, think you not, to eschew any notion of aiding them with arms?" It was less a question than a statement.

"Your ambassador was head of the Commission that drew up the treaty," Naxania reminded him tartly. "If nations renege on their sworn obligations, chaos results."

"You speak as a woman," Varodias said dismissively, "ever clinging to the rules laid down by others. You cannot, in all seriousness, consider sending troops into Songuard. The distances are too great, and Paladine lacks the resources." He paused to cut his meat.

"We would remind you, cousin,"—there was a bite to the word—"that it was we who recaptured Bandor and not you."

Varodias chewed and swallowed before replying. "A matter of luck," he said, "and with a general who is no longer yours to command."

"The success of our armed forces does not depend on the Holdmaster of Gwyndryth," she retorted hotly. She speared a wedge of vegetable and bit into it.

"Oh, come now," Varodias said smoothly, appearing to enjoy himself, "you cannot pretend to have an army to match ours. You have no rotifers, you have no battle wagons, you have no cannon. You rely on an antiquated cavalry and ill-equipped infantrymen. You cannot think that your forces can equal Umbria's."

"Not only are they a match, sirrah, but you underestimate the power of Magic. Combine the two and Umbria is a penitential dog." She spoke with controlled anger.

Varodias smiled imperturbably. "Brave words, my dear, but foolish. We know full well that Magic is impotent in the face of science and frankly, sweet cousin, your forces may be sufficient to put down the occasional rebel but, given the amount of money that you have spent on training and arming them in the past ten years, they can hardly be considered a threat to a professional army."

Naxania considered a moment before replying. Tact and diplomacy warred with her pride in the Discipline and in her own forces. In the end, it was her distaste for Varodias and his condescending assumption of supremacy that won out.

"Should the Isphardis," she said measuredly, "require our support, you may rest assured that we will supply the troops. Should the need arise, we shall use our influence with the Discipline. Were we you, my lord, we should hesitate to provoke such a response." She finished with a formal little smile and felt much better for having spoken her piece.

"Have a care, lady," Varodias said frostily. "Hasty threats are oft repented at leisure and paid for in blood." He turned away from her as the pages swarmed in to retrieve the plates.

Naxania realized that she had eaten practically nothing and that, she thought, was the fault of the Emperor. He had been right about one thing, though: she had spent too little on the army. Very well then, she would rectify that when she got home. Darius had been the one who had held her back, but Darius was gone. It would mean raising taxes and the people would complain, but then the people always complained. Varodias had challenged her and she meant to be equal to the challenge. She would show the puffed-up little man what a Queen could do.

chapter 27

The Celador that Marianna and Jarrod surveyed from the privileged vantage point of their apartments was reassuringly unchanged. The recent influx of guests meant that there were lines outside the bathing places, but the capital did not show the strains that had manifested themselves when it had been threatened with siege. There were no campfires in the courts, no lines of washing strung, no broken windows. This time it was the aristocracy that was the invading force. Servants seemed continually ascurry, and a forest of splendid tents grew up beyond the walls.

As the numbers swelled, it became apparent to those in charge of administration that an event of unanticipated magnitude was taking place. The palace staff had known from the beginning that everyone of note on Strand had been invited, but they had not reckoned that so many would attend. Lesser folk were accommodated in the town, but that was no more than a stopgap measure. The truly great, as usual, swanned above the turmoil; the rest battled and settled as best they could.

Routines were abandoned from time to time to watch the arrival of royalty. The Emperor of Umbria had arrived on the Upper Causeway at the head of a caravan of steam chariots. The display was impressive, but there were persistent rumors that they had been pulled by horses for the majority of the trip. Queen Naxania's entry through the East Gate in a coach painted deep purple and drawn by six black horses with ebon plumes nodding over their heads was obviously designed to cause comment, and it did. The image was quickly supplanted by the Oligarchs of Isphardel, who came in a group and a welter of somber samite. They had taken up residence in great silken tents outside the south wall. Their relative modesty caused even greater comment, much to the chagrin of the Queen of Paladine.

Pages in the royal household, farmed out among the visitors, gathered of an evening to discuss their experiences. Those detailed to attend Varodias and his entourage had the best stories, tales of mechanical clocks and pet raptors. The Songeans had bizarre requests for food. Those who served Naxania told of bursts of bad temper. All were awed by a sense of occasion and the awareness that, difficult or not, this opportunity would never come their way again.

The Collegium, normally an oasis of order, came in for its share of disruption. The Archmage's embalmed body lay in state on the dais in the Students' Hall, and people great and small filed through, day after day, to pay their respects. Indeed, since there were no tourneys or balls, it was one of the few distractions available. For the aristocracy, there was much visiting back and forth, and manuevering for seats at dinner in the Great Hall became an art. The Chamberlain, who had to juggle conflicting protocols and deal with touchy personalities, was transformed into an irritable tyrant.

He was not the only one burdened with administrative duties or the intricacies of national pride. The Collegium had the job of working out the funeral arrangements. The placement of the chief notables in the procession to the Burning Ground and where they could be seated once they were there took a full sennight, and even then not everyone was satisfied. The final order of march decreed that the bier, borne by six

Magicians, would be followed by Marianna of Gwyndryth and the unicorn. Immediately behind them would
come the "virtuous youths and maidens," one for each
year of Ragnor's life, dressed in long white tunics. Ragnor, in his final days, had insisted that he was ninety
years old, but most of those who knew him thought he
had rounded up the figure. Nevertheless, it made for an
even division of the young people and was allowed to
stand.

Behind them would be the Mages, Greylock, Sumner
and Courtak and the new Chief Warlock of Talisman.
Both Arabella and Naxania had opted to take their positions among the heads of state and would walk just
behind the leaders of the Discipline. The rest of the
details were left to the hapless Chamberlain. One thing
was clear to those who labored late at the Collegium:
this was an event of supreme importance for the Discipline. The whole of Strand would be represented, in one
way or another. Even the Mother Supreme would attend. Ragnor had served them in death as he had in
life. This was his final triumph.

Jarrod woke early on the morning of the funeral. He
slipped quietly out of bed so as not to wake Marianna
and went to wash and dress. He donned his usual blue
gown. He would change later into something that Ragnor would have approved of, indeed something that the
Archmage had furnished. Part of the old man's will had
left all of his robes to Jarrod. Sooner or later, Jarrod
thought with fond humor, the old rascal always got his
own way.

Almost every Magician on Strand was gathered on
the grounds of the Collegium that morning for the
Making of the Day. The Weatherwards had had to stay
at their posts, but those who were able to travel had
done so. It was the first time in living memory that so
many had come together for this essentially private rite,

and it was an occasion that none of the participants would forget. The feeling of communal energy, of a combined merging, was thrilling.

Part of that charge clung to Jarrod as he made his way back toward the palace, and he decided to visit Nastrus before returning. No one challenged him as he walked through the stables to the unicorn's stall.

'*My but you're in a good mood, considering what's going to happen today,*' the unicorn commented.

'True. Part of it is because I've had time to get used to the fact that Ragnor's dead, but most of it is due to the Making of the Day. It was quite extraordinary.'

'*I would love to go for a gallop with you while you're in this mood.*'

'So would I,' Jarrod replied, 'but it wouldn't be considered seemly and I have to get back to Marianna.'

'*Marianna, Marianna, it's always Marianna,*' Nastrus complained. '*You never spend any time with me anymore.*'

'Now, you know that isn't true,' Jarrod said. 'I spend as much time with you as I can. It's just that I'm a married man now and I have responsibilities.'

'*Sires do as they please.*'

Jarrod ignored the remark. '*They'll be along to groom you in a while. You and Marianna will be the first ones, right behind the coffin. It's a considerable honor.*'

'*I liked him,*' Nastrus said thoughtfully. '*He used to bring us treats and take us out for exercise. There was a great deal of affection in him.*'

Jarrod smiled both mentally and physically. '*He loved you all. He loved to watch you, and going riding with you was a huge thrill for him. He always felt that you and your family were the key to our victory.*'

'*An unusually intelligent human,*' the unicorn concurred. '*Will you be keeping watch over the candles again?*'

'*No Candles of Remembrance this time,*' Jarrod replied. '*Ragnor didn't even want a tree. He just wanted his ashes buried at the foot of the Archmage's Tower. He said that there were enough statues to keep his memory alive longer than anyone wanted, but they are going to plant a tree in the Collegium grounds anyway.*'

'*I'm glad that I can share in this,*' Nastrus said. '*However, once this is over, I shall return to the Island at the Center.*'

'*Of course. I'm grateful that you have stayed this long.*' Jarrod paused. '*I hope you will continue to visit us. I shall miss you terribly.*'

'*You are a married man now, with responsibilities,*' Nastrus reminded him, none too kindly. '*I make no promises. I have already devoted a great deal of time to this world.*'

'*And we are grateful,*' Jarrod said. '*Know that you and your offspring will always be honored.*' His sending was courtly and formal.

Nastrus responded in kind. '*As you are part of the Memory forever, Jarrod-almost-unicorn.*'

They were both aware of the other's subtext and Jarrod moved forward and put his arms around Nastrus' neck and hugged him.

'*I can rely on you to behave, can't I?*' he said, with an attempt to return to his old style.

'*As much as you ever could,*' Nastrus returned good-naturedly.

'*If not for me, for Ragnor,*' Jarrod said.

He patted the glossy flank and turned to leave. The unicorn's benign amusement stayed in his mind as he crossed the stableyard.

When he got back to the apartments, he found that Marianna was already in the long black gown that she had had made. It was long-sleeved, had a high neck and was absolutely plain. The maid was moving around her putting up her hair and pinning in it place.

"There's chai and some sweet rolls in the bedchamber," she said. "You had better eat now. There's no knowing when we'll see food again."

"That dress is very becoming," Jarrod said, "but it's making you dramatic. There are banquets after the funeral both here and at the Collegium. We shall be welcome at either."

"Well, eat your breakfast anyway. You'll need your strength."

"Yes dear," Jarrod said, and went through to the bedchamber.

The procession from Magician's Court to the Burning Ground outside the walls was an impressive sight. The black-draped coffin, the gleaming unicorn, horn, hooves, mane and tail shining in the sunlight, accompanied by the woman in black, the young men and women in a double file of white, the Mages in their rune-threaded gowns and then the rulers and the nobility in their splendid mourning clothes, all were part of the pageantry of death.

Arabella of Arundel was escorted by Varodias of Umbria; Naxania of Paladine was accompanied by Brem Argolan, the current Thane of Talisman. They were followed by the Oligarchs of Isphardel, Olivderval among them, her bulk supported on an ebony cane. Next came Hodman Forodan of the Territi with the newly elected Mother Supreme at his side. There was a gap and then came Saxton Horbinger, Arundel's Prince Consort. He was followed by the cream of the aristocracy, divided into national groups. Darius of Gwyndryth and Otorin of Lissen walked with their fellow Holdmasters; the Umbrian delegation included Malum of Quern, the Margrave of Oxenburg and all the Electors save Phalastra of Estragoth, who was absent for reasons of health. The chief families of Paladine were well represented, though their ranks had been thinned by the rebellion. After that came well-connected men and women too numerous for anyone save the Chamberlain to list.

All along the route through Celador, on either side of the gates, up on the battlements, lining the roadway leading to the Burning Ground, the common people stood in silence as the great ones of the world passed by. Some had traveled as much as fifty leagues to bid farewell to the Archmage and to witness the spectacle. There were a surprising number of children, surprising until one realized that a long chapter in the history of Strand was closing. Folk wanted their children to have the link to them that Ragnor had provided between themselves and their own parents. They wanted the children to remember the Archmage, if only in death.

Jarrod, pacing slowly along among his colleagues, could feel the sadness radiating from Nastrus and knew that the unicorn was reflecting the mood of the crowd. Ragnor, he thought, would have considered it no more than his due. The Discipline was giving the people an extraordinarily impressive show. The old man would also have approved of Jarrod's choice of robe. It was black, which suited the occasion, with a band of stars in silver thread and diamonds which ran from the right shoulder, across the body, to the hem. The ring of the Keepers, functional now that the Place of Power was back, was on his right hand and, for the first time, the diamond tiara of the Mages of Paladine was on his head. It was hard to believe that he would never hear the rheumy chuckle of approbation again.

As the bier passed under the East Gate, there was a commotion. The crowd on the right-hand side parted to allow a young man in a travel-stained cloak to lead a unicorn through. He fell into step beside Marianna and Nastrus.

"Josceyln?" Marianna's voice was a mixture of relief and exasperation. "What is the world are you doing and where have you been? Your clothes are a disgrace."

"I've just come through Interim with Astarus, Mother, and I haven't had time to change my clothes," the youngster replied levelly. "I only heard about Ragnor's death yesterday. We wanted to pay our respects."

"But where have you been all this time? You frightened us half to death," Marianna said, trying to keep her face composed for the crowd.

"I went to the Anvil of the Gods to look for a unicorn," Joscelyn said, "and I found Astarus." He tried to sound noncommittal, but there was no mistaking the pride in his voice.

"I'll want to talk to you when this is over, young man," Marianna said dangerously. "In the meantime, straighten your cloak and keep your head up and your shoulders back."

Jarrod could not see what was happening ahead, but he was alerted by the rapid burst of thoughts from Nastrus. It was too fast for him to follow and obviously not aimed at him, but he knew that the unicorn was asking questions.

'What's happening?' he thought out. *'Is anything wrong?'*

Nastrus finished his conversation before he answered. *'One of my offspring has arrived with Marianna's son. They have joined the parade.'*

'Is the boy all right?'

'He appears to have survived Interim intact,' the unicorn returned dryly.

'Interim?' Jarrod was startled. *'How did he learn to do that?'*

'It appears that the ability to talk to unicorns runs in

certain human families.' Nastrus was not sounding pleased.

The idea that Joscelyn had found a unicorn that he could talk to and had mastered Interim troubled Jarrod. The boy was an exceptionally strong, raw Talent with a wild streak that was natural for his age, but could prove dangerous if he did not outgrow it. Now he had established contact with a unicorn. That could spell trouble unless this new unicorn exercised a restraining influence. He would have to ask Nastrus about that, but this was not the time. Perhaps he should try to talk to the newcomer when the funeral was over. He would certainly have to have a few words with the new Dean of the Collegium.

The cortege turned off the road and in to the broad meadow where the pyre waited. The draped coffin was carried up the ramp and placed upon the squat pyramid of logs. Marianna and Nastrus, with Joscelyn and the new unicorn in tow, positioned themselves on the south side as the white-clad youths peeled away. Jarrod and the Chief Warlock took the east and Sumner the west, leaving Greylock alone at the north end. Once he was in position, Jarrod got his first glimpse of the unicorn. It was certainly a noble-looking creature, despite its rough coat and tangled mane. It was impossible to tell its age, but it looked fully mature and stood as tall at the shoulder as Nastrus. The two were conversing and Jarrod could tell that the older unicorn was angry.

Arabella and Varodias passed near Jarrod and snagged his attention. He saw that the Queen was weeping. There was no show in her grief; she uttered no sound and her bearing was regal. The face was an immobile mask, but tears trickled slowly down. The sight banished all other thoughts. Jarrod's eyes stung and there was a sudden lump in his throat. It was as much in sympathy for the Queen as it was for the memory of

Ragnor. Jarrod had lost a friend, but Arabella had lost her second father, a man that she had loved all of her life.

The last of the procession was in now and the meadow was filled. Pale faces stood out against the dark clothing. The feeling of sadness was palpable to Jarrod and so was a certain sense of anticipation. Out of the corner of his eye he saw Greylock step back, turn, and face the royal enclosure.

"It is my sad and solemn duty to say farewell to my old friend and colleague, Ragnor." The deep voice rolled out, carrying easily. The crowd was silent and still and Jarrod knew that Greylock was using the Voice to compel attention.

"He was a remarkable man. He served as Mage of Arundel, Regent of Arundel, and Archmage of Strand. He was adept at administration, whether of the Discipline or of a Kingdom. He was astute in diplomacy, wise in counsel and a warm and loving friend. To all this must be added that he was a powerful and inventive Magician who performed feats never before attempted. He succeeded at everything to which he turned his hand.

"That, perhaps, was his most remarkable quality, his willingness to reach for new solutions. After what, for any other man, would have been a long and distinguished career, he did not hesitate to launch the quest for the unicorns and, at an age when a Magician hesitates to test his powers because of the toll that spellcasting takes, he summoned the Cloak of Invisibility to protect his beloved Celador. Not content with that, he then, with the assistance of the Mage Courtak, performed the Great Spell that rid our world of the Outlanders."

True, all true, Jarrod thought, but he's going to be fixed in people's memories as infallible and unvaryingly heroic. The real Ragnor was also vain, irascible, impulsive, manipulative and filled with sly humor. Despite that, Jarrod realized, the man would exist henceforth as an object of veneration and awe. The faults and qualities that made him lovable and exasperating by turn, that made a Queen weep for him, would be burned away with his body. All that would remain would be the immutable approximation of the man—like the statues of him on a hundred village greens. Someday, he resolved, *I shall write his history and restore his humanity.*

". . . will go down in history as the greatest Archmage since Errathuel."

Jarrod realized that the eulogy was coming to an end and that he had missed the bulk of it. He sneaked a look at the crowd and saw that they were rapt. The years of practice seemed to have given him an immunity from the effects of the Voice, but, for the rest of the people within earshot, it was a compulsion they could not break and would not forget. Small wonder that so few were given knowledge of it.

"And so we bid farewell to the man who was the heart, the conscience and the salvation of Strand," Greylock concluded.

The new Archmage turned and faced the pyre once more, the tiara of his office blazing in the sun. Jarrod braced himself for what was to come and was aware, simultaneously, that Nastrus was also prepared. With one accord the assembled Mages concentrated and, as they did so, flames began to lick around the bottom of the logs. The unicorn added his strength and the pyre ignited with a roar, causing the others to retreat from the sudden rush of heat. Small wisps of smoke curled towards the sky and the air above the coffin danced.

In a matter of minutes, the fire fell in with a spitting, crackling flash. Sparks flew in every direction and the flames leaped in one final, incandescent burst before the conflagration subsided into a mound of fiercely glowing reds and oranges. Of the coffin, there was no trace. The skin on Jarrod's hands and face felt seared and dry, but he was not about to retreat any further. The colors became muted as he watched. Flakes of ash spiraled upward in the wavering air. The fire sighed and settled in upon itself. The edges began to turn grey.

Good-bye, Archmage, Jarrod thought, and heard it echoed by Nastrus. The unicorn was also thinking of the moment when they had translated his brother, Beldun, back to the Island at the Center. It was fitting somehow. Both were rare creatures and both would live on in his memory. There was no sadness now in Nastrus' mind, but, in spite of that, Jarrod felt a pang. An age had ended as surely as it had on the night that the Outlanders were destroyed. Nothing will ever be quite the same again, he thought.

As the funeral pyre died, the assembly stirred, released from its thrall. At that moment, Joscelyn stepped forward and led his unicorn round the glowing remnants to face the royal enclosure. No one else moved. Jarrod's mind flashed out to Nastrus in query, but he received no answer.

"Thus says Astarus the unicorn to his Imperial Majesty, Varodias of Umbria," Joscelyn pronounced in a clear, carrying baritone.

His voice has finally broken, Jarrod thought inconsequentially, and then concentrated on what the boy was saying.

"I have traveled in your land and seen what you do to the earth and the waters and the skies. You permit desecration and for this you will be held to account. It is no business of mine what you do to the humans under your sway, but the unicorns will not remain idle if you continue to despoil the land.

"My brethren and I have decided to dwell at the far side of what you humans call the Alien Plain. There is space and grazing enough for all and there is no reason why we cannot coexist in peace, but I have observed your doings, Emperor of Umbria, and I have seen into your heart. Keep within your proper bounds and all will be well between us. If you do not, you will rue the day." Joscelyn paused, as if listening, and then his head came up. "Thus speaks Astarus the unicorn," he declared.

There was a frozen, shocked silence and then the boy turned and sprang lightly onto the unicorn's back. He bent forward and twined his hands into the mane. Both of them disappeared. One moment there, the next gone.

The crowd stirred, as if released anew, and a buzz of conversation rose. Varodias, who had, at first, gone deathly pale and then had progressively reddened with anger, turned to Arabella.

"What is the meaning of this?" he demanded, voice squeaking with passion. "And who was that young upstart? Is this some conspiracy by the Magical Kingdoms to publicly demean the Empire?"

"We can assure you, cousin," Arabella said shakily, "that we have no knowledge of this. We are as amazed and affronted as you. You may rest assured that we shall inquire into these circumstances forthwith and will deal severely with the miscreant. We shall not tolerate this insult to an honored guest." She drew a deep breath. "In the meantime, we suggest that we return to the palace. The boy is gone. There is nothing that we can do here."

She beckoned to a page. "Do you go immediately to the Lady Marianna and the Mage Courtak and command them to attend us in the private withdrawing room." She turned to Varodias and said, "If anyone knows about unicorns it will be those two."

She held out her hand to the Emperor and, head high,

moved out of the royal enclosure and back onto the road to Celador.

'Talk to me,' Jarrod pleaded as the procession re-formed.

'I am deeply ashamed,' Nastrus replied slowly as Marianna and he walked away from the Burning Ground. *'I do not remember who his dam was, but there must be bad bloodlines there. Perhaps I am getting old. I do not understand this new generation.'*

'Yes, yes, yes,' Jarrod thought back with barely suppressed annoyance, *'but what was all that about my brethren and I living on the Alien Plain?'*

There was a sigh in Nastrus' mind. *'You remember the colts that I brought to help you build your castle? Well, they went back and talked to their kin about the uncounted leagues of virgin grass here on Strand. You have seen our portion of the Island at the Center. It is cramped and every year our numbers grow. This Astarus, it seems, has a position of leadership among the younger unicorns and he convinced the others that they should move to Strand. It appears that this new breeding is more aggressive that we were. They talk of defending territory.'* His tone turned sarcastic. *'Some of them may have looked into the Memory, but they have not seen the destruction of the cloudsteeds at first hand. This world has dangers that they cannot comprehend.'*

'How many are coming? Where will they go? Where did Astarus and Joscelyn go?' The questions crowded forth.

'I don't know,' Nastrus admitted. *'Astarus is arrogant. He would not submit to my authority. He told me very little.'* The thought turned bitter. *'He considers me a spent force, an aging sire no longer capable of keeping other males away from my dams. His opinion of humans is none too high either. I fear that you will have trouble with him. As to where they have gone, I suppose to the*

castle. Where else on the Plain would he have a homing point?'

They completed the journey back to Celador in troubled silence, each caught up in his thoughts, each gloomy for reasons that had nothing to do with Ragnor's funeral.

Jarrod and Marianna regained their rooms quickly and set about changing their clothes. They exchanged what information they had, knowing that as the discoverer of the unicorns and as Joscelyn's parents, they were doubly responsible.

"Why didn't you tell me about this castle before?" Marianna asked.

"Because it was none of your business," Jarrod said shortly. "There are only a handful of people who know. It was a Discipline project, but even Greylock doesn't know about it. Ragnor knew, of course, but he's dead."

"Then we certainly shan't tell Arabella," Marianna said, unabashed. "Honest ignorance is what we have to project. My son appeared suddenly and joined the cortege saying that they wanted to pay homage to Ragnor. Josceyln is obviously under the influence of this strange unicorn. We didn't know that they were coming and we don't know where they went." She looked at him. "Well, it's the truth," she said.

Jarrod made no reply and she went took him by the arms and shook him slightly. "Listen to me. Gwyndryth could lose all influence at Court because of this. If Varodias insists, we are going to be made scapegoats even though we have done nothing wrong. They can't do much to you, you're a Mage, but they can cripple Gwyndryth. Our only hope is to be bewildered, but helpful. If we are seen as part of a possible solution, we may be spared. Just follow my lead."

Jarrod disengaged her hands gently and looked down

at her. "No, my dear," he said firmly. "This is more important than Gwyndryth. The unicorn was essentially correct in many of the things that he said about Varodias, but that is beside the point. What we have to do is to make sure that this does not get blown up into an international incident. Unicorns come within the Discipline's purview and this is our problem. Joscelyn may be your, er, our son, but he is an Apprentice Magician. You will follow my lead in this. Is that quite clear?"

Marianna looked up into his eyes and whatever she saw there quenched the spark of rebellion in her own. "Very well," she said with a little shake of the head. "But if you put Gwyndryth in jeopardy, you shall answer to me," she added before turning away to complete her preparations for the audience.

They were ushered into the withdrawing room by a gentleman-of-the-bedchamber who smirked at them as they passed. Bad news travels quickly, Jarrod thought. Arabella was ensconced in an ornate chair, looking grim. Another, unoccupied, stood close by.

"I am so sorry, Your Majesty," Marianna said, unbidden, as she rose from a deep curtsy, "that this should have occurred on this day of all days."

Arabella waved her into silence.

"We need hardly tell you," she said, "that the Emperor is exceeding angry. He has been attacked and insulted in front of a gathering of every personage of note on Strand. We have asked you here because you know more about unicorns than anyone else and, some way or another, we must get to the bottom of this." She looked at Jarrod. "You can converse with the unicorn Nastrus, can you not?"

"Yes, ma'am, and I have done so. He has told me that a number of younger unicorns have decided to come to Strand. It seems that they are running out of space and grazing in their current home."

"And what of the challenge to the Emperor?" Arabella asked.

"Nastrus was at a loss to explain. This other unicorn refused to acknowledge his authority and would tell him nothing."

"And what of the young man? Did your unicorn know him?"

Marianna looked at Jarrod and he nodded. She faced the Queen again. "He is my son, Majesty," she said quietly. "Unbeknownst to us he ran away after our wedding and went in search of a unicorn. Today was the first time that I save seen him since Stronta."

"I see," Arabella said. She looked back to Jarrod. "Did you send him on a quest?" she asked.

"No, ma'am. It may be that our marriage triggered thoughts of emulation in his mind. He is at an impressionable age."

"What can you tell us," Arabella began, but was interrupted by the opening of the doors.

"His Imperial Majesty, the Emperor Varodias," the usher announced.

Arabella rose and Jarrod and Marianna turned. The one bowed, the other genuflected to the floor. They held their positions as the Emperor stalked across the room, the heels of his boots clacking on the floorboards. He nodded to Arabella and took his seat. He regarded Jarrod and Marianna with undisguised hostility as they rose to face him.

"So," he said, his high, light voice cold, "the authorities on unicorns. Tell us, is it possible that the boy was speaking for the animal, or was he put up to it by those who wish the Empire ill?"

"It is possible, Your Imperial Majesty, for humans to understand the thoughts of unicorns. It is, as far as we know, extremely rare and the ability to converse with one unicorn does not mean that we can talk to others.

The Lady Marianna can understand a mother unicorn, but I cannot reach her. I, on the other hand, can speak, as it were, with the offspring, but the Lady Marianna cannot. Neither of us has ever encountered this particular unicorn before."

The Emperor sniffed disdainfully. "In your expert"—there was a sneer in the word "expert"—"opinion, was this urchin giving a true report of this creature's thoughts?"

"I think that it is almost certain. If the boy could not communicate with the unicorn, he would not have been able to go into Interim with it and thus disappear from the Burning Ground."

"And what of the threat to our person?"

"Unicorns are as different from one another as are humans," Jarrod said seriously, "but the unicorns that we have encountered thus far have been Strandkind's friends. One even gave up his life to enable us to destroy the Outlanders. They could undoubtedly be dangerous if roused—those horns are no mere decorations—but only in the way that a cornered boar is dangerous. They have no magical powers as such, though they can harness certain energies to transfer themselves from place to place."

"Then why, pray, would this creature confront us?"

"I cannot answer that, Your Imperial Majesty. I can only surmise that it was overcome by the grandeur of the occasion—unicorns are sensitive to atmosphere—and felt some need for vainglorious expression. I do not think that it need be taken seriously."

"Do you not, i' faith?" Varodias' voice was mocking and his hands made an airy little gesture. "We shall have to wait and see about that. In the meantime, where did this precious pair disappear to?"

"I cannot say for sure, sire," Jarrod replied. "I can

only assume that they are somewhere out on the Alien Plain."

The Emperor's eyes narrowed and he pursed his lips, weighing alternatives known only to him. "We suggest that you find them," he said finally. "Unicorns are creatures of the Discipline and if anything untoward comes of this, we shall hold the Discipline responsible."

He rose from his chair. "Cousin, we are sure that you will make the apprehension of this miscreant your chiefest priority. When he is apprehended, we shall expect that a public example be made of him." He bowed curtly to Arabella and walked out.

Marianna was white-faced as she rose from her curtsy and she turned a beseeching face to the Queen.

"And can you find them?" Arabella asked Jarrod once the doors had closed again.

Jarrod sighed. "I doubt it, Majesty. Nastrus is returning to the Island at the Center. I cannot prevent him. We could send out cloudsteeds, but I expect that the unicorns are beyond their range. Our best hope is that Joscelyn will return. There is ample fodder for unicorns out there, but precious little for humans."

Marianna's hand flew to her mouth and Arabella looked at her with compassion. Then she fixed Jarrod with a skeptical eye. "We do not know what this is all about, though we doubt that there was a plot to embarrass the Emperor. Nevertheless, we want answers. We cannot countenance anything that could damage the amity that currently exists between Arundel and Umbria." She looked from one to the other. "Perhaps, under the circumstances, it would be better if you dined at the Collegium." She shook her head. "This is most unfortunate." She paused and her face became stern. "We expect to be kept informed of any progress you make."

"As Your Majesty commands," Jarrod said, and bowed.

They withdrew, knowing that they had been reprieved, but not exonerated. Marianna was silent and Jarrod, his mind filled with questions, was grateful for that. When he had been listening to Greylock earlier in the day, he had felt a sense of renewal, had felt that the Discipline had regained the respect and affection of the people and would grow and prosper. Now everything was clouded again. What was worse was that his newfound family and his unicorns appeared to be central to the problem. He felt old before his time.

Jarrod was right to think that the world had changed, though his presumption that the causes devolved onto his own shoulders was hubristic. There would indeed be change, as there must always be change. The peace that the unicorns had helped to achieve had begun to unravel years before. This would be the last peaceful gathering of these great folk, though no one at Celador that day realized it. Soon, unconscionably soon, there would, once again, be talk of war. The Age of Ragnor, as Jarrod was to call it in his monumental history of Strand, was over.

As Jarrod and Marianna made their way toward the Collegium, Strand's two moons shone down on them. This was their season; the time when both, obeying the laws set down for them by the gods in a time so far gone by that the mind of man could not comprehend it, appeared together in the night sky. The men and women whose lives they lighted took the phenomenon for granted. It had always been thus and it would always be. It never occurred to them that their fates and frailties, though less predictable, would fulfill cycles of their own. The philosophers among them would have found both hope and despair in that. Had Strandkind been cursed with foresight on that tranquil, cloudless evening, there would have been many who would have despaired. Some would have prayed to the Mother, some to the spirits of the land and some that there might still be unicorns.

It was a matter of indifference to the circling moons. Wars would come and go, nations wax and wane, but they would ride the heavens with a certainty that the merely mortal could not match. Somewhere in the fathomless darkness beyond them, in his quarters on the Island at the Center, the Guardian doffed his viewing helmet and vowed that he would never watch again. The moons of Strand were unaware of that. They were concerned with themselves, the sun and the planet beneath them. Nothing else was important.